ALONE IN THE DARK

"You shouldn't be out here by yourself, Mrs. Butler."

"But I'm not," she countered. "You're here." And was he ever. So close Abby could smell the distinctly masculine scent he used. So close she could put out her hand and lay it upon his sleeve, feel the coiled muscles in his arm beneath the fabric of his frock coat. So close she could place her lips upon his cheek, if she dared.

God, what fanciful notions had burrowed into her brain, twisting it into knots of sensually driven thoughts? Thoughts dark and deep, unfolding with a heat that flooded her body.

Dangerous.

That word aptly described him. Dangerous to her senses, to her sense of well being. Dangerous to her carefully constructed web of lies.

"You should go back inside, where it's safe."

Safe.

Was she?

Would she ever be completely safe?

LUCK OF THE DRAW

GAIL LINK

LEISURE BOOKS   NEW YORK CITY

A LEISURE BOOK®

March 2006

Published by

Dorchester Publishing Co., Inc.
200 Madison Avenue
New York, NY 10016

ISBN 0-8439-5663-1

The name "Leisure Books" and the stylized "L" with design are trademarks of Dorchester Publishing Co., Inc.

Printed in the United States of America.

Visit us on the web at www.dorchesterpub.com.

*This book is lovingly dedicated
to two very special people:*

*To the memory of my dad, Fred Link,
whose love of reading he passed along to his daughter.
I miss you every day, Daddy!*

*To my mom, Frances—
for all your love and support.*

ACKNOWLEDGMENTS

To all my friends for hanging in there and encouraging me to keep at it, even when things weren't *happening*. Your good thoughts meant the world to me when I needed it.

To some special friends who cared—the two "Susans," Marti, Barbara P., Lori H., Betsy, Pat, Kate H., Flora S., Joan B. Your constant e-mails, letters, and conversation were a warm blanket of comfort in the dark hours and beyond.

To the wonderful ladies of the TREASURED HEARTS!

To Eric McCormack for his talent—your sexy Southern gentleman was an inspiration.

To the "old-timers": Kath, Joan and Marci.

For Alicia Condon—for being there in the beginning, and now for the rebirth. Thanks for your faith in my work.

And to one special friend—my "big" sister of the heart, Linda Cutler Smith. Thanks for being there whenever I needed you. For all the fun of long lunches and finding treasures in the resale shops. For the long hours of conversation that ran the gamut from politics to entertainment. For always being in my corner. Your friendship has added immensely to my life.

LUCK
OF THE DRAW

Prologue
Into the Fire

"You're joking, right?"

The man paused in the act of pulling on his knee-high black leather boots, casting an arch glance over his shoulder at the feminine speaker. When he answered her query, his voice was a low, soft rumble of sound, his accent flavored with the slow drawl of the South. "Darlin', you know that I never joke about money."

"But it's crazy, Beau. Leaving San Francisco for a backwater in the middle of nowhere." A visible shudder went through the woman's body, a body that still reveled in the afterglow of the man's expertise in pleasuring a woman. "No," she stated with a pout, "I won't hear of it."

He rose from the rumpled bed and turned, facing the older woman. "You've got nothing to say about it, Carla. It is, as they say, a done deal," he said with a dazzling smile that took the sting from his words.

Her dark eyes narrowed on his bare chest, his lean torso a well-balanced mix of flesh and muscle. "I could make you stay," she replied in a husky voice. "One word from me and some of my more powerful friends would see to it that you remained here indefinitely."

"You could, darlin'," the man acknowledged, "but you won't." He reached to take his pleated white shirt from where it rested on the tiny brocaded chair, slipping into it with ease. He then pulled on a gray silk vest, checking his appearance in the wide mirror hanging over the woman's dresser as he fastened the buttons.

"How can you be so sure?" Carla watched as her lover knotted a darker gray silk cravat about his throat, artfully letting the ivory sheet slip to her waist as she scooted herself higher against the pile of down-filled pillows. Her eyes remained fixed on him as he picked up her tortoise-shell comb and arranged his thick, damp, dark hair into a semblance of order.

He turned, quickly reading the invitation in her pose, amused at her obvious ploy to lure him back to her bed. "Because I know you, *cherie*," he responded. "You're a lot of things, *ma belle*, but mean-spirited isn't one of them." Carla was, he knew, a hardheaded businesswoman, owner of the most exclusive sporting house in San Francisco. It catered to clients who could afford the best and were willing to pay for it. When he left the city, he'd miss it, and her. Especially her. They had an understanding, an easy relationship; neither was looking for the happily-ever-after trap of love and marriage. They enjoyed one another in the most basic way possible, the only way either cared to.

A sigh caught in Carla's throat and she expelled it slowly. "You're one absolutely handsome son of a bitch, Beau McMasters."

He laughed, a deep, rich sound that filled the room. "My, my. You do know how to flatter a man, darlin'."

Carla tossed back the rest of the sheet, giving Beau an unobstructed view of her charms, all of them. "Are you sure I can't change your mind?"

His response was another low chuckle. "Sorry." He

2

picked up his gun rig from where it lay curled like a sleeping serpent on the chair, and buckled the well-worn leather holster about his slim hips. Out of habit, he removed his Remington pistol, checked it carefully, and slid it back into its sheath. All that remained was his frock coat and hat.

"Promise me that you won't leave town without saying good-bye."

Beau crossed the short space that separated them and leaned down, kissing Carla quickly on her still swollen mouth, tasting himself there. "I won't."

As he made his way to the door, he felt the thump of an object hit him square in the back. One large pillow landed at his booted feet. Giving her an arch look, he bent and tossed it back in her direction.

"Damn you, Beau," she said with a dimpled grin, hugging the object to her chest, inhaling the faint traces of him on the linen as he closed the door.

He exited the multistoried brick mansion by the front door, although there was a discreet "gentleman's entrance" in the back. A cynical smile tugged at his lips at the thought of some of San Francisco's finest blue bloods, or those who pretended to be, sneaking through the gardens and up the stairs into the waiting arms of the classiest whores in the city. They were men with something to lose.

He, however, had nothing to lose—the war had seen to that.

Beau paused, reaching into his coat pocket for his sterling silver cigar case, which had belonged to his grandfather. He traced the engraved design of a falcon in a dive, claws extended, ready to seize what it wanted. Opening it, he withdrew a slim cheroot. He then snapped it shut and replaced it, removing a small match safe from his vest pocket, and lit the cigar. Inhaling deeply, he released a thin spiral of smoke into the crisp morning air. Like the fierce hunting bird, he was going to grasp the chance that he'd been given.

Walking slowly down the hill toward his hotel, Beau filled his eyes and ears with the sights and sounds of the city. He had been here for almost a year, expanding his fortune slowly and steadily at the gaming tables. Then, two days ago, an opportunity too good to pass up had come along. An all-night high-stakes poker game had come down to himself and another player. A final hand of cards would determine the winner, as each had bet heavily, driving up the stakes. The other man, a visitor to San Francisco, had wagered every dollar he had, including various deeds to property in the town he lived in.

Beau had been reluctant to accept pieces of paper for what could be worthless land, until another man, a local banker, who'd dropped out of the game but stayed to watch the outcome, verified the value of the older man's holdings.

With that, Beau changed his mind and allowed the deeds to cover the man's final bet.

In the end, it was Beau's luck that held out. His three queens beat the man's two pair.

The luck of the draw had changed his fate, opened up a new world. He was a man of property and influence for the first time in his life, albeit in a place called Heaven's Grace, far from the cosmopolitan delights of San Francisco.

"The devil's own luck," his opponent had declared as he signed over the deeds.

Beau preferred to think of it as the "McMasters touch."

There was already a nip in the air in Denver, even though it was only mid-August.

Glad that she'd dressed warmly, the young woman who emerged from the brick townhouse hurried down the busy street toward the nearby mercantile shop. The goods she'd ordered had finally come in and she was anxious to pick them up. It was an extravagant indulgence, ordering fabric and patterns from one of the fanciest dressmakers in New York, but after so many months of scrimping and saving, of looking over her shoulder, of wearing drab and dull colors so as not to stand out in a crowd, she wanted a reminder of her former life. Something beautiful and gay.

"Good day to you, Mrs. Butler," the shopkeeper said with a welcoming smile when she entered his establishment. "We've got the material all set aside for you." The short, balding man reached under the counter and promptly produced three neatly wrapped bundles. "I would have been happy to send Seth over to the boarding house. No need for you to come here yourself."

"I couldn't wait, Mr. Pedersen." She opened her reticule and took out several bank notes, handing them over to the shopkeeper. "Thank you for going to all the trouble."

"It weren't no trouble, Mrs. Butler. Happy to oblige." He handed her a hastily scribbled receipt for the merchandise. "Anything else I can do for you, you just let me know."

With a smile on her face, her packages in her arms, Abigail Butler exited the shop. Her jaunty walk and golden-red hair drew admiring glances from passersby, especially men, but she didn't pay any attention; she was intent on reaching her next destination, the post office. She'd ordered several volumes from a bookstore back east to supplement what she used in her classes at the Fairfield Academy for Girls and she thought she would check to see if they'd arrived.

Entering the building, she took a place in line, thankful that there weren't many customers this afternoon. Looking around the room, her glance fell on the numerous posters hanging on one wall. Wanted posters were predominant, but one in particular caught her eye. It was the sketch of a young woman under bold letters that spelled out REWARD.

Cold shivers ran along her spine as she recognized the face. She tried not to panic, telling herself to stay calm.

No one else seemed to be paying attention to the bulletin board except her.

"Can I help you?"

Abby wet her lips as she stepped to the counter. "Yes. I want to see if any packages have come in for a Mrs. Butler."

The youthful clerk gave her an oily smile, trying his best to impress. "Got one in today. Wait a moment." He scurried to find the item and reappeared moments later. "Might heavy, ma'am. If you don't mind waitin', I'll be happy to lend you a hand."

"That won't be necessary," Abby stated, anxious to leave this place before anyone else noticed the resemblance between herself and the wanted woman. "Thank you for the kind offer, though. I can manage." She forced herself to give him a polite smile.

"Okay then," he said as he handed over the oilskin-wrapped parcel.

She placed it on top of the others and moved slowly toward where the notices hung. As casually as she could manage, Abby pretended to study several of the posters, surreptitiously checking to the right and the left to see if anyone was watching her. Placing herself in front of the one with the woman's face, she managed to remove it without attracting notice.

Less than twenty minutes later, she was safely back within the confines of her room at the boardinghouse, her heart beating rapidly. Dropping her packages on the iron bed, she smoothed out the wrinkled sheet of paper, turning up the oil lamp on the small bedside table to better read the notice.

Reward for information leading to the whereabouts of Miss Abigail Breckenridge of New York. Wire the Pinkerton Agency or Harold Breckenridge, Breckenridge Bank, New York.

A brief description of the woman was listed below the artist's rendering.

Abby's left hand clenched into a fist, crushing the picture. She bowed her head and momentarily closed her eyes. He wasn't going to give up until she was back where *he* thought she belonged, under *his* control, doing what *he* wanted her to do. No matter what it took; no matter whom he hurt. He'd never be satisfied until he broke her, until she capitulated to his will unconditionally.

But that day, she'd vowed to herself the night she left his house, would never come.

Abby looked around the room, filled with touches she'd added to make it her refuge, her sanctuary. She'd been happy the short time she'd been there, enjoyed the work she did, felt she'd made a difference in her pupils' lives. Now all that was going to change. She couldn't remain. Once again she was going to have to run, to try to stay ahead of his human bloodhounds.

She glanced at the packages on her bed. Material for dresses that would never get made; books for classes she wouldn't be able to teach. The volumes of poetry would be her parting gift to her students, something to remember her by, instead of something to share daily. Classes were to start next week; now they would do so without her. By then, she'd be gone.

But where to?

Later that evening, Abby found her answer.

By chance, one of the other boarders who'd been dining at her table had left his newspaper in the parlor. Curious, she glanced through it when something caught her eye. A heaven-sent opportunity too good to pass up.

The next morning she was up early as usual, but instead of having her breakfast first, she made her way to the telegraph office to send a wire. If all went well, she thought as she strolled back to the boardinghouse, she would be on her way to a new town—a new life—within days. Far from *his* reach. A part of the country where he'd never think to look for her.

Maybe then she could stop running. Settle down and really build a new life for herself. Have a real home. A real future. Put down roots that would last.

A wistful smiled curved her lips. Maybe even fall in love.

As Abby sipped her strong coffee and ate her plain boiled egg, she couldn't help deepening her smile at the sound of the town's name that could be the key to her new tomorrow.

Heaven's Grace.

PART I

RENEGADE HEARTS

Chapter One

He had the most beautiful eyes: the color of sun-kissed amber, a pale golden-brown ringed with a darker hue that fascinated her. They were set beneath thick sable brows and surrounded by long dark lashes.

Abby realized that she'd been staring at the stranger for far too long when he gave her a wry smile, acknowledging her interest.

He must think her rude, or perhaps forward, when in fact she was neither. It was just that in such a confined space as the stagecoach, it was impossible to totally ignore him, especially considering he was the only other passenger.

She turned her head, concentrating instead on the magnificent vista outside her window. Rolling hills, colorful wildflowers, majestic mountains, tall stands of trees that seemed to go on for miles. And the sky. Never-ending blue so bright it hurt.

So much space. A landscape of wonder, soon to be her new home. A world away from New York and her life there.

It was *his* destination as well.

She'd noticed him when she arrived at the stage depot this morning. He was standing outside the door, beneath the overhanging roof, smoking a thin cigar. He'd tipped his hat at her as she entered the building to pay for her ticket to Heaven's Grace.

There was something singular about him: he was a man who would stand out in any gathering. Probably his dress, she'd decided. Other men in the town were attired in dungarees or homespun faded cloth and chaps, a typical wardrobe. He, however, was dressed to perfection in black: wool trousers, frock coat, boots. The only variations in hue were the white of his pleated shirt and the burgundy of his silk vest.

An impressive dandy, even by New York standards. Abby had also detected a subtle masculine fragrance as she'd passed by. A splash of something expensive.

The only thing he appeared to have in common with the other men was the gun he wore. That had taken some getting used to when she first ventured west: men openly wearing weapons—and using them. Her initial shock had given way to acceptance. Abby even carried a gun now. A smart little pearl-handled derringer, hidden in her reticule. It was for protection, though she often wondered if the time ever came for her to use it, could she? Would she?

She doubted that *he* was a novice with a gun. Some instinct told her that the stranger knew how to use it and use it well, which made him dangerous.

Though he looked far from dangerous now, she thought, as she snuck another glance at him. What he most resembled was Milton's proud fallen angel, handsome in a way that compelled. A carefully trimmed dark beard hugged the contours of his jaw; a small mole rested on his right cheekbone; long sable waves of hair fell past his collar.

Beau was amused by the woman's attempt at studying

him. She was trying hard to be discreet, and failing miserably. He, however, had no compunction. He'd boldly sized her up when she'd approached the stage depot earlier that day. Her face was fresh and youthful. It lacked the beaten-down-by-life, older-than-my-years look he'd seen on far too many female faces in his life. There was an openness, a warmth, a vitality to hers, and it touched him in an odd way. A way he couldn't define.

He liked the cut of her velvet traveling dress: it flattered her well-shaped figure, drawing, he'd observed, many a masculine eye to her as she passed by. It was a deep, rich blue that complemented her creamy skin and red-gold hair, and although he judged it not to be brand new, it gave her a style and sophistication all her own.

He couldn't believe it when their driver had called out their destination—she was going to the same place. Too good to be true, he thought.

What was she doing way out here, a lady of her obvious breeding? Journeying to such an out-of-the-way town? Her accent placed her from back east; he'd recognized it as soon as she'd spoken to the driver. His father had had the same accent, a cultured Yankee inflection.

She opened a book. Beau studied the author and the title, printed in gold on the spine. *Leaves of Grass* by Whitman.

Beau's lips curved in appreciation. Quite a bold choice for a female.

Good. The lady had a mind of her own. He liked that in a woman.

"Rest stop," the driver called out as he pulled the team into the relay station and halted the coach. Jumping down from his perch, he opened the door. "We'll be taking a meal here and changing horses. Should be back on the road in about an hour. Be in Heaven's Grace well before nightfall."

Abby slid a leather bookmark into the book to mark her

place, even though she hadn't been concentrating on the poetry. It was just a way to force herself to focus on something other than her fellow passenger.

Beau alighted from the coach first, holding out his hand. "Miss?"

A shiver went through her upon hearing that single word. Abby gave him her gloved hand, then murmured a proper "Thank you" when he assisted her from the stage.

He inclined his head in a slight bow. "My pleasure to be of service, miss."

He was from the South. His soft, mellifluous drawl pinpointed his geographical origin.

Was he a refugee, like herself? Or perhaps an opportunist, seeking fortune's favor? Or the family black sheep, fleeing scandal?

Abby took the arm that Beau offered. He led her into the large interior of the station, where a tall, rail-thin man stood cooking over a stove.

"Make yourselves to home," the man said, indicating a long table. "I'll have your meal fixed real soon. There's fresh coffee and cream."

Beau held out the chair for Abby, then took the seat opposite her. "Would you care for some, miss?" he asked, picking up the battered blue granitewear pot.

"Please," she responded, removing her gloves.

It was then that Beau saw the wedding band on her left hand. *Married*. Where was her husband?

He poured the hot liquid into a cup sitting in front of her, filling another for himself. "Cream?"

"Oh, yes," was her quick reply.

He preferred his coffee black and strong, having grown up with the chicory-laced brew of his native New Orleans. Beau watched as she added a small spoonful of sugar to her cup. White and sweet. *Café au lait avec sucre*.

He hadn't realized that he'd spoken the words aloud until she answered *"Oui."*

That eased the tension between them somewhat. "Forgive me, I was merely thinking aloud."

"Force of habit that I responded in kind," she explained. "It seems as though my schoolgirl French lessons weren't wasted." Harold Breckenridge had seen to it that she'd had a French tutor to make sure she spoke the language with the ease of a native. One never knew, he said, when that could come in handy with business associates on the Continent.

"Perhaps I'd better introduce myself, ma'am," he said. "My name is Beau McMasters."

"And I'm Mrs. Abigail Butler." The half-lie slipped off her tongue with practiced ease.

They were interrupted by the cook, who slapped two chipped ironstone plates on the table before them. Each contained a thick slab of pan-fried beef and beans. A moment later a tin of cornbread appeared, along with a small crock of butter.

"Hope you're hungry," the man muttered.

Both Beau and Abby looked at the meal with skeptical eyes while the man waited.

Suddenly, both grinned and dug in. The cook returned to his stove.

While she cut up her steak, Abby reflected on Mr. McMasters's smile. He had white teeth that stood out against his dark beard, and a full lower lip. He'd also removed his hat, giving her an unrestricted look at his face, at the waves of dark brown hair, a lock of which curled upon his high, wide brow. He possessed a strong nose, straight and true. His skin had a slightly golden hue.

Mr. McMasters, she suspected, had the kind of visage that artists longed to paint. The kind of face that once seen, was never forgotten. A face a woman would forever find attractive.

Sweet heaven, what was wrong with her? It wasn't as if she'd never seen a handsome man before. New York society had plenty, and she'd met more in her travels. There was simply *something* about this man that she couldn't quite put her finger on, but the word charismatic came to mind.

"May I be so bold as to inquire why you're going to Heaven's Grace, Mrs. Butler?"

His question caught her off guard. "I'm the new school teacher."

His response was a raised brow and a softly murmured, "Indeed?"

Abby took a sip of her coffee. "Yes."

"And your husband, will he be joining you?"

She regretted the need for a lie, but she couldn't tell the truth. "I'm a widow, Mr. McMasters."

"Forgive me, ma'am. I didn't mean to bring up painful matters."

"I've learned to live with the loss." It was really quite easy, she thought, especially when one didn't have a husband to begin with. A pretend spouse that had no claim on her heart or mind was indeed easy to forget. A figment of her imagination trotted out for convenience's sake. A make-believe man she'd invented for the sole purpose of giving herself a new identity.

Abby doubted, however, that anyone married to Mr. McMasters could, or would, ever forget him so easily. He was far too vivid, too *alive*.

Beau observed as Mrs. Butler grew quiet. Thinking of her loss, he presumed. Had she loved the man? Mourned him? Did she mourn him still? Or had he been a mere expedience? A liability? A boorish clod who didn't appreciate the gift placed in his care? Was theirs a tragic love story, or a simple marriage of convenience?

Damn. What business was it of his? None, except that the widow piqued his curiosity. Intrigued him in some basic way.

"What about you, Mr. McMasters? Do you have business in Heaven's Grace?"

"Of a sort, ma'am." He refilled his ironstone mug. "I've recently come into some property there."

"It would appear that we're both new to this territory. Strangers come to start afresh."

"So it would seem, Mrs. Butler."

Abby lifted her mug and held it out towards him. "This calls for a toast, don't you think? To new beginnings."

It should have been champagne, he reckoned. A bottle, or two, of the finest vintage, served in an elegant setting, somewhere other than a line shack. He imagined velvet, silk, a large, comfortable bed, and candlelight. The subtle smell of perfume.

Lifting his mug, Beau clinked it against hers. "To new beginnings," he repeated, his eyes meeting and holding hers. They were blue, bluer than the deepest shade of the Pacific near Monterey. And just as deep as the ocean.

"Hate to rush you, folks, but I'll be ready to pull out in about ten minutes," the stage driver called out from the doorway. "Got me a schedule to keep."

Abby dropped her gaze, focused instead on quickly finishing up her meal. Her new life, she thought, was off to a good start. She'd made a friend, of sorts, in Mr. Mc-Masters, a most elegant man with manners and obvious breeding. But with a dangerous side. She couldn't ignore the gun he carried. He was not a man to be taken lightly, or simply at face value—that much was clear to her.

And then there was that voice. A voice that brought to mind magnolias and mint juleps, live oaks laced with Spanish moss. One of her father's clerks had been from Mississippi. He'd told her about his home, described it in detail so graphic that she could see it as it had been before the war.

But where the clerk's voice had been light and sunny, this man's was dark, more midnight than noon.

Damnation! She was doing it again. Letting her imagination run rampant, like a wild-spirited mustang. She had to remain practical and focused. Alert. And, above all, true to the role she was playing. Her life depended upon it.

"Sure I can't interest you folks in a piece of my rhubarb pie?" the cook asked, his grin revealing several broken teeth.

The driver poked his head back in. "Ike, they ain't got time for that. I'm fixin' to pull out now."

Beau was up and out of his seat, hat adjusted and waiting to escort Abby back to the coach.

As they walked through the door, he said, "Never could abide rhubarb."

This brought a smile to Abby's mouth as she responded with a light laugh, tilting her head back to look into his face. "Neither could I."

"Then we have that in common as well, Mrs. Butler," he drawled, helping her back into the stage.

She watched him getting in, liked the way his lean body moved with a certain grace. "It would appear so, sir."

"Perhaps, if you would do me the honor of having supper with me one night soon, we can discover if we share more than a dislike of rhubarb?"

She should say no. Refuse him outright. After all, he was still a stranger, albeit a handsome and charming one.

"I'd be happy to, Mr. McMasters," she heard herself answer.

He smiled. "You've made me very happy, Mrs. Butler." Very happy indeed, he thought. A most lovely and intelligent woman sharing a meal with him. Who knew where it could lead? Yes, she was the new schoolteacher, a position that demanded a certain code of behavior, but she was also a woman. A widow.

He wondered again how long her husband had been dead. Long enough for her to be beyond a proper period of mourning? Long enough to miss a man in her bed?

Time would tell. And he was in no particular hurry. Some things were best discovered slowly.

The town was smaller than both expected, and exactly what each was looking for.

A crowd had gathered outside the stage depot. A banner had been hung over the door, spelling out the community's welcome to the new schoolmarm.

"Looks like they're ready for you, Mrs. Butler."

Abby leaned out the window to see the assembled people waiting.

"Nervous?"

"A little," she confessed.

"Don't be. They need you, remember that. You hold the winning hand. Think of it like that. A word to the wise," he cautioned, leaning closer to her, "life's like a good card game—never let them know what you're holding. Always keep them guessing, especially if you're bluffing."

So, he was a gambler too. A man of chance who played the odds. Right now, so was she. Taking on a big gamble and hoping that it paid off. "I'll keep that in mind."

"I trust you will." He smiled and gave her a tip of his hat.

The coachman pulled the stage to a halt, and it was surrounded by a curious throng of men, women, and children. The door was opened by an elderly man who held out his hand to Abby.

She turned her head to say good-bye to her traveling companion and found herself alone. While she'd been watching the crowd, it seemed as though Mr. McMasters had slipped out the other side.

"Step back and give the lady room to breathe," the man instructed. "We don't want her getting so frightened that she jumps back on the stage and hightails it outta town, now do we?"

The crowd stepped back, almost as one.

"That's better," the man stated, removing his hat. "I take it you're Mrs. Butler?"

Abby nodded.

"Good. Then welcome to Heaven's Grace, Mrs. Butler. We're sure mighty proud to have you here. I'm Benjamin Cooper, mayor of the town. We're right happy that you've come and we wanted to show you a proper reception."

"Thank you," Abby responded, searching the faces of the people gathered. They looked nice enough. Some might have been farmers. Others shopkeepers. Working men and women. And the children. Fresh, eager faces of all ages and sizes. Some held bouquets of wildflowers in their hands.

"These are for you, ma'am," one boy said, extending his hand towards Abby.

She bent down so she was level with his face. "Why thank you most kindly. I love flowers." She took the proffered gift, brought them to her nose and sniffed. "Sweet."

Several other pairs of hands pushed through, handing her more bouquets. She grabbed as many as she could hold, then stood up. "Thank you all."

"I know that you must be plumb tired after your trip, Mrs. Butler, so we'd best be seeing you settled. Tomorrow there's a church supper in your honor." Mr. Cooper motioned a couple people to step forward. "This here's Carl and Gussie Travers. They run the hotel where you'll be staying. Figure that you might like to stay there a spell until you decide if you like the house we bought for you."

"A house?" That hadn't been mentioned in the advertisement, nor in the cable she'd received replying to hers, offering her the position. It was a delightful and welcome shock.

"Yes, ma'am. We wanted to surprise you."

"You've managed to rather effectively," she replied.

"Course it's nothing fancy. You're probably used to better, but it's all your own."

"I'm sure that it'll be wonderful."

An older, sallow-faced man moved to the foreground. "This is the Reverend Whitcomb."

Abby held out her hand. "Pleased to meet you, Reverend." It could have been a trick of the fading light, but his pale blue eyes looked cold and flat. His handshake was barely there, as if touching her might contaminate him.

"Ma'am," he muttered.

Abby contrasted his speaking voice with that of Mr. McMasters. What a world of difference. McMasters made it sound like an endearment; Whitcomb made it sound like a curse.

A man and a woman, with children clinging to them, stepped around the Reverend as he moved back. The woman's face was open and friendly, as was her tone. "I'm Mary James and this here's my husband, Efrem, Mrs. Butler." They shook hands. "These two here are my children, Robby and Susanna. They'll be among your pupils. We own a spread not far from town."

Mayor Cooper announced, "We'd best save the rest of the introductions for tomorrow night and give this lady a chance to rest."

Gussie, a big-boned woman who towered over her husband, and just about everyone else, spoke up. "Let's get her settled 'fore she passes out. Zeke," Gussie indicated the stage driver, "you give Carl her bags."

"I also have a trunk."

"Then send that over too, Zeke." Gussie placed her arm around Abby's shoulders. "Now come with me, dear." She steered Abby away from the throng. "I've got a room ready for you, plus a hot bath that won't take no time to fix. When you're done, I'll bring you up something to eat so's you can relax without a passel of eyes watching your every move."

Like bees to a honeypot, Beau thought as he watched from across the street in the shadows as Mrs. Butler was lead in the direction of the hotel. He exhaled a thin cloud of smoke, never taking his eyes from her until she was in the door. He wondered what she would say if she knew that tonight she was sleeping under his roof. Well, half his roof, actually. When he wired his money from the bank in San Francisco to the Wells Fargo branch here, he also inquired about further investments in the town itself. Discovering several opportunities at a reasonable price, he snatched them up.

Sounds came from the building behind him, the saloon. This place, he'd been told, already turned a tidy profit.

Beau tossed the remains of his cheroot into the street, turned and walked into the establishment, then stood just inside the creaky doors. The interior was dull: in need of a good cleaning. Dim lights masked the cheap furnishings. The stale smell of unwashed bodies and spilled liquor assailed his nose.

However, he saw potential. The potential of making a sizable profit, not just a tidy one. Revamped and renovated, it could be a veritable gold mine.

Beau made his way toward the bar through the hazy smoke from cigars and cheap lamp oil. "Whiskey," he stated, "and I prefer it in a *clean* glass, if you don't mind."

The bartender shrugged his beefy shoulders and reached for another shot glass under the bar. He held it up, checking to see if it met his customer's requirement, then placed it in front of the well-dressed man, pouring the liquor inside.

Beau took a taste and hastily swallowed before he could gag. "Is this the best that you have?"

A slovenly woman sidled up to him. "You be wanting something more than whiskey, mister? I can offer you a right good poke, the best in town."

Beau turned his head to the left, looking at the woman, who could have been anywhere from twenty-five to forty. Her hair was matted and greasy; her clothes were stained.

He could well imagine that she was diseased, too. "No, thank you."

The whore shrugged. "Suit yourself, honey. Don't know what you're missing though," she said as she sashayed her way over to another customer, someone less discretionary than Beau.

Ah, but I do, he thought.

She would have to go. Cheap wasn't the image he wanted in his place.

"I asked you for a whiskey," he repeated to the bartender. "Something better than this swill. Do you have it or not?"

"It'll cost you extra, mister."

Beau produced a silver coin from the pocket of his waistcoat, holding it up between his index and middle fingers. He waved it near the barkeep's face.

With a gap-toothed grin, the bartender provided a sealed bottle of Kentucky bourbon.

Beau recognized the label. "That's much better," he said, giving the man the coin. He poured what was left in his glass into a dusty one that had been left on the bar. Breaking the seal, he opened the bottle and tasted what was inside. Bourbon as smooth as silk. Beau poured himself another, then with the bottle, left the saloon and headed for the hotel, his head filled with the changes he was going to make, starting tomorrow.

Abby breathed a contented sigh. All-in-all, it had been quite a day.

Her luggage was piled against one wall, with one carpetbag open. Her fancy traveling dress was repacked in her trunk and her clothes for tomorrow were laid out.

A small fire was lit in the black iron potbellied stove, giving a measure of warmth to the rapidly cooling night. She glanced out the long window that led to the second-floor balcony. There were so many stars out. The sky was saturated with them, much like the wildflowers that carpeted the meadows surrounding the town.

Abby felt refreshed after her long bath. Now in her nightclothes, she was relaxed and happy. Content. Satisfied that she had made the right choice in coming here.

Her stomach growled delicately. Gussie, true to her word, had fixed Abby a supper tray. Padding barefoot across the pine floor, she helped herself to a still warm fried chicken leg. A glass of cold buttermilk had also been provided, along with fluffy biscuits and a slice of blueberry pie.

Slipping her index finger along the oozing edge of the pie, Abby scooped up a sample of the fruit, sucking the digit clean.

Absently the thought crossed her mind—she wondered if Mr. McMasters liked blueberries.

And where was he right now? He'd vanished so abruptly this afternoon, without a trace.

Why? Maybe the better question she should ask herself was why she cared at all. He was nothing to her. Just a man who'd been going to the same town, who happened to be sharing the same method of transport.

Yet try as she might, she couldn't ignore the disturbing feeling she had that he was much more than that.

Wishful thinking?

Or an acceptance of some soul-rooted belief?

Chapter Two

Abby was surprised to see Mr. McMasters sitting by himself at a table near a window in the hotel's dining room when she went down for breakfast the following morning. Every other table appeared filled to capacity.

"Good morning, Mrs. Butler," he said, rising, dabbing at his mouth with a linen napkin. "Won't you join me, if you have no other plans? I took the liberty of keeping a seat reserved for you since it seems quite busy this morning."

She quickly moistened her lips with her tongue. "Why thank you, Mr. McMasters, I'd like that." So he'd saved a spot for her at his table. Abby was flattered and just a little bit thrilled. He was by far the most elegant man in the room, a cynosure, she noted, of many eyes.

Beau held out the chair for her, aware of the delicate scent of roses clinging to her. "I trust that your first night in Heaven's Grace was a pleasant one?"

"Quite quiet, actually." She gave a covetous glance at his steak and eggs, her mouth watering.

"After all that fuss when you arrived, I wondered if you'd get any time to yourself."

"You saw that?"

"Indeed I did," he admitted, "as I was standing across the street."

"You were?"

He gave her a slight smile, his eyes locking on hers. "They seemed mighty glad to see you."

Soft color tinted Abby's cheeks pink. "I think they would have done the same for anyone."

"Still, it's nice to know that you're wanted."

Something in the way he said that last word made Abby mentally question if he'd ever been made to feel unwelcome anywhere. Perhaps it went deeper than that? Or was she reading too much into one simple word, one inflection? And, what would he think if he were to discover that she was in fact *wanted,* albeit in a different sense.

"Morning," Gussie said in a hearty voice, handing Abby a large cup brimming with hot coffee. "Did you sleep well?"

Abby gave the woman a smile as she added cream and sugar from the heavy ironstone set. "Yes, I did."

"Good. Know it can be hard on a body to get used to a new bed, but I put you in the most comfortable one we had."

"It was just fine."

"How about you, Mr. McMasters? You satisfied?"

Now there was a word that a man could take several ways, Beau thought as he glanced at his companion. He was certainly satisfied with how Abby Butler looked today. Her hair was arranged in a loose knot at the back of her neck. She wore a pristine white blouse that was tucked into a rust-colored wool skirt. A simple gold and topaz pin was fastened to the collar of her blouse.

"With my lodgings, eminently so." At his hostess's puzzled glance, Beau amended his comment. "Yes."

Abby suppressed a grin as Gussie beamed.

"Now, Mrs. Butler, what can I get you for breakfast? My

husband Carl does all the cooking 'round here and he's the best."

"I'll have the same as Mr. McMasters."

"How do you want your steak?"

"Medium." Abby gave her the rest of her order and asked, "Could I have some toast? That is if it's not too much trouble, while the rest is cooking?"

Gussie grinned. "Hungry?"

"Uh-huh."

"That's good to hear," she remarked. "Last schoolteacher we had here had the appetite of a finicky child. Always seemed afraid to eat, like she was gonna be thought of as less than a lady if she had a more than a few mouthfuls, 'specially if there was a man about." Gussie smiled, then said in a conspiratorial whisper, "As if a man don't want some meat on his woman's bones." She shot a pointed glance at Beau. "Ain't that right, Mr. McMasters?"

Two pairs of feminine eyes stared at him, awaiting his reply. "I couldn't agree with you more, Mrs. Travers."

Abby, far from being a skinny, bone-thin girl, was rather pleased to hear his words. Growing up, she'd been endlessly admonished to eat less because men didn't like their wives to have too healthy an appetite. It wasn't, her mother stressed, "ladylike to eat like a common laborer. Any real gentleman would find that off-putting and extremely vulgar. You're a Breckenridge, my dear, not some slovenly hired girl."

A ghost of a smile played over Abby's wide mouth. Obviously not all gentlemen espoused her mother's dictum. McMasters didn't think so. And he was a gentleman, no doubt in Abby's mind about that.

Abby directed a question to Gussie. "What happened to my predecessor?"

"Your what?"

Beau stepped in. "The last schoolmarm."

"Oh," Gussie nodded her head. "Died of a fever. She

27

weren't nothing but skin and bones when it happened. She upped and caught a chill, then took to her bed. Doc tried everything to get the fever down, but it weren't no use. Weather can be pretty mean around here, even in late spring. Hits a body hard if you ain't used to it.

"Lord, here I am just runnin' on when you've been wantin' your breakfast, Mrs. Butler. I'll be back with your toast." Gussie trotted off, leaving them alone.

"I like her. She seems a good soul," Abby commented, enjoying the strong flavor of the coffee as it hit her throat.

Beau arched an eyebrow. "Indubitably."

Abby couldn't help herself; she chuckled.

"I think you have your work cut out for you," he said, finishing his steak.

"I look forward to the challenge."

"Is that why you came here?" he asked, his sharp, focused glance and low, intimate tone shutting out the rest of the diners in the room. "For the *challenge?*"

Abby forestalled answering right away by taking another sip of her coffee. "It's one of the reasons, yes."

Her cool response told him that he wouldn't get any other reason. "Forgive me. I didn't mean to pry." Maybe, he thought, she needed to put some distance between herself and where she lived with her late husband. He could well understand saying good-bye to a place that held its share of painful memories. He'd done the very same when he'd left New Orleans all those years ago. He'd said farewell to the past and its buried secrets, moved on, as he'd had to do to survive.

"You weren't," Abby assured him. How she wished she could confide in him, in anyone. Tell her story and share the details. But it was a useless hope. If she let her guard down, it could be a colossal error. One she couldn't afford to make. No matter that he seemed an eager listener, she hadn't come this far to turn back now.

Gussie reappeared, two small china plates in her big

hands, piled high with slices of toast. "Didn't know if you wanted butter or not, so I brung both." She placed them in front of Abby. "Eat up," she instructed. "There's more where that comes from." Hands on hips, she asked, "You want some preserves? We got strawberry and peach."

"Strawberry," Abby replied, picking up a buttered slice.

"Be right back."

"She reminds me of my aunt Hettie," Abby said as Gussie went back towards the kitchen. "A born mother hen." The words had slipped off her tongue before she could think better of uttering them. Damn! Why had she let her guard down now when she'd been so careful for almost three years? And moments after she'd admonished herself that she couldn't trust anyone.

"I know what you mean," Beau remarked. "I had a great-aunt Gabby who was much the same. Always clucking about everyone else's chicks, as she had no children of her own. She adored my mother, and consequently, she transferred that love to me."

It had been *Tante* Gabby who had urged him to leave New Orleans after the war; he'd never forgotten the last conversation they'd had. "Go, *chèr*. Leave all the bitterness behind you and never look back. What's done cannot be undone. Do not waste your life trying to repair the past. It's gone and cannot be resurrected. *You* are what's important. And, one day, you will find your promised future, with all the happiness you need and deserve when you least expect it."

Beau hadn't put much store into his great-aunt's words until now. Maybe she did have the second sight that she'd always claimed. He wondered what she would make of the woman sharing his table.

"Do you ride, Mrs. Butler?"

"I used to." Abby hadn't many occasions to go riding anymore, not since leaving New York. And she sorely missed it, she realized. What had happened to her champion bay mare, Juliet? Was she still in the Breckenridge stables? She really loved that animal and it had hurt to leave her behind. But there was no one she could ask. No way she could ever find out the animal's fate without alerting the family of her whereabouts. So she was left with questions and no way to obtain answers.

"Then would you care to join me one afternoon?"

As much as Abby would have liked to promise him, she couldn't. "We shall have to see, Mr. McMasters. I should be very busy with school most afternoons."

Had he pushed too far too fast? "Then we'll speak of it later, when you can give me a definite answer. Consider it an open invitation, if you will."

"As you wish."

Gussie came back, bringing Abby's breakfast.

Beau rose, put on his ubiquitous black hat. "Ladies." He tipped his brim to both of them. "If you'll excuse me, I've got some business to attend to. I wish you each a most pleasant day."

Gussie took his seat, and along with Abby, watched him stride away. "Lordy, that there is one handsome fellow, with the manners to match. The single ladies hereabouts are gonna be after him like flies on dung. You mark my words, Mrs. Butler. If he aims to stay a spell here, someone's gonna have him branded, harnessed, and in front of a minister in no time. Be a darn shame to let someone like him get away."

"Or," Abby observed in a wry tone, "someone's going to try. Whether or not they succeed, now that's another matter entirely. I'd guess that Mr. McMasters is a man content with his status as a single gentleman."

Gussie snickered. "Every man's like that till a woman shows him the way. Didn't you find that out with your man?"

Abby picked up her cup and took a drink, then answered. "No, actually my husband was as eager to wed as I was."

Gussie rolled her eyes. "Oh Lord, I'm sorry. I just remembered Benjamin Cooper said you was a widow. How thoughtless of me to bring up things you might not want to think about."

"That's quite all right," Abby assured her. "I've had time to deal with his *death*." She was becoming bothered by the pretense, more so lately. She'd lied before, convincingly, with nary a qualm. It's what she *had* to do to survive, to live another day in freedom. So why did it seem so loathsome now? Gussie was such a sweet woman who meant no harm. It was Abby who should have begged her pardon, for lying.

However, she couldn't. She must keep up the role of widow, even if it was predicated upon one untruth after another. Lies heaped upon lies.

Gussie sighed. "Don't know what I'd do without Carl."

"How long have you been married?"

"Since I was sixteen and he was nineteen. That's thirty years." Gussie gave Abby a penetrating glance. "That's longer than you been around, isn't it?"

Abby nodded her head. "Yes. I'm twenty-three."

"Still young enough to love again, and you will, mark my words."

"I hope so." And Abby realized that she did. She wanted to experience what she'd read about in books, in poems, and seen in some instances. A love that didn't have to stop the world on its axis, as long as it was true. A love that nurtured and accepted, never controlled. Never constricted.

"Good. That's the way to think, my dear." Gussie rose. "I'd best be gettin' back to my work. You enjoy the rest of your meal."

* * *

Beau entered the Wells Fargo office. For such a small town, it was a big bank. There were two tellers helping customers, while another handled paperwork at a desk.

He walked up to the man and announced in a soft drawl, "I'm here to see Mr. Davis."

The bespectacled clerk looked up. "And what's your name?"

"Tell him Beau McMasters is here to see him."

The name obviously made an impression on the older man, as he scuttled to his feet. "Wait right here, sir, and I'll tell him you've arrived."

Beau's lips curved in a cynical twist. He'd discovered money always made a difference in service. Even in a small town like this, there were few exceptions. Happily, it appeared that Gussie Travers treated everyone the same, which boded well for their co-ownership of the hotel. When the time seemed right, he'd tell her and her husband that he'd bought up the outstanding note that the bank held on the property.

A bluff, hearty man opened the door to his office. "Come on in, Mr. McMasters. I've been expecting you." He waited until Beau walked in. "Please. Take a seat. I've got some papers for you to sign."

The banker took his chair behind the large mahogany desk. "Just as you asked, I kept this under wraps."

"Good. I'd like to handle all the other details in my own way." Beau glanced quickly over the papers, noting that everything he'd requested was taken care of and all his funds had been transferred. "All the deeds are in order?"

"Yes sir. Malcolm McFadden handled that."

Beau recalled the name from the banker's wires; Mc-Fadden was an attorney. "And I can take possession of the saloon and the ranch as soon as I wish?"

"Whenever you like."

"Excellent." He accepted the fountain pen that the

banker handed him, swiftly signing his name to the documents. "I want to see the ranch."

"Then how about right now?"

Beau rose to his feet, handing over the pen and the paperwork. "Let's go."

They got horses from the local livery, Beau making do with a rather tame mount, not the spirited horse he would have liked. He and the banker rode across the sagebrush covered hills, through stands of aspen and pine, across and through two creeks, for almost an hour before they came to the spread Beau had won.

Beau halted his horse on a hill overlooking the property. Snow-capped mountains, about half-a-days ride away, formed a natural backdrop. He could see a large ranch house made of stone and timber, a barn, and further away, a bunkhouse. About thirty head of cattle, a few Texas longhorns mixed in, grazed nearby. Inside a stone paddock were about ten horses and two foals.

"As per your instructions, Mr. McMasters, I sent word to the men that they now had a new boss, and that they should be expecting you to call. Obviously, they're anxious to meet you, to see what changes you're gonna make."

Beau responded, "If things run smoothly, I don't anticipate making any right now."

"If you don't mind my asking, do you know anything about ranching?"

"No," Beau admitted candidly, turning his head in the banker's direction. "But I learn quickly, especially if it's in my best interests to do so."

Mr. Davis chuckled. "It certainly will be."

Beau gazed back at the ranch, breathed deeply of the cool, crisp air. This was all *his*. His land. His to mold; his to change; his to command. The cornerstone of a new life. A fresh start.

"Ready to see the ranch house proper?"

For a response, Beau urged his mount forward.

In a matter of minutes, they were through the gates, met by several hands.

Davis made the introductions after they dismounted, and Beau made it a point to greet each man personally. He wanted to look each in the eye, garner a sense of the man, read if he would be loyal. They were *his* men now and he wanted that understood.

"This here is Pike, the foreman." Davis indicated a tall, lanky man, topping Beau by several inches. He had a thick gray mustache drooping over his top lip.

Just as Beau was sizing up his hands, the foreman was sizing up his new boss. Silence stretched for a few moments.

"Mr. Davis has told me that you're one of the best at what you do."

A stream of tobacco landed close to Beau's booted feet. "That's right." There was no brag in Pike's response, just a simple statement of fact.

Beau dropped his gaze to the brown spot in the grass, then his mouth quirked up in a smile. He respected a man who knew his own worth and wasn't afraid to stand up to anyone in defense of it. "Then I hope that you'll stay on." He offered the man his hand. "I'll need an experienced second, someone I can trust to do the job that needs to be done."

They shook hands and the rest of the men visibly relaxed.

"Are the horses in the paddock broken?"

Pike nodded.

"Then cut out the Paint," Beau instructed one of the men closest to him. "Throw a saddle on him and bring him here. I intend to use him as my personal mount."

Pike addressed the hand, jerking his head towards the paddock. "You heard Mr. McMasters. Do it!"

The bowlegged man did as he was told.

Beau spoke to Davis. "Let's go inside."

As the two men entered the ranch house, dust assailed them. Beau struck a match so he could see, then found an oil lamp and lit that. The interior was revealed, marked by cobwebs and dirt. The furnishings were minimal, and not of the best quality. A chill ran through the house, the stone fireplaces not having been used in several months.

Davis looked around. "The construction is sound, it just needs a cleaning."

It needed more than that, Beau thought as his booted feet echoed along the bare floors. What it needed was an immediate transformation. A sign that a man of substance and position lived there. He wanted it to be both a showcase and a home. Like the plantation his grandfather had owned, renowned for its hospitality.

Granted, this was a lot rougher and far less grandiose, but he didn't care. This house would be exactly what he needed it to be. He'd make sure of that. Damned sure.

Beau climbed the stairs and investigated the upper floor. There were several rooms; all looked unused except for one, the largest bedroom. It appeared half-empty because there was only a small single bed pushed against one wall, a couple of blankets tossed over it and a rough pine desk with a lamp nearby. Dust had settled over every corner and the windows were covered with grime.

He heard the sound of skittering paws across the floor. When he shone the lamp in the direction of the sound, a small, beady-eyed field mouse stared back at him before it disappeared.

"Mr. McMasters? You okay up there?"

Beau walked back to the landing, leaning over the wooden railing. "Just fine. I'll be down in a minute."

The previous owner of the house lacked vision, taste, and imagination, all of which Beau knew he had in abundance.

That settled, he rejoined the banker. "Until this place is the way I want it, I'll continue to live in the hotel." First things first, he decided. The renovation of the saloon would need all his attention for the present. Besides, it would take some time to get the furnishings he wanted for his home sent here. Things he had kept in storage until the need arose for their use. And time was something he had a lot of now. Time and money.

"I've seen enough for today."

When they went back out into the bright Montana sunlight, the horses were waiting for them, including the brown and white Paint Beau had requested, the livery saddle thrown on him.

The horse tossed its head and stamped one hoof.

"He was a tough one to break," Pike said as he handed Beau the reins. "Wild and stubborn. Still is when he's of a mind to be. But he's one of the fastest horses I've seen run."

"Then let's see what he's made of," Beau stated as he got into the saddle.

The animal bucked slightly, then accepted Beau's weight, responding smoothly to the rider's command. They rode off, galloping around the area, through the gate and over the hill, the hands, Pike, and Davis watching carefully.

Beau loved the feel of the spirited animal beneath him. He sensed the stallion's love of speed, and gave him his head. The Paint showed what he could do, tearing across the countryside, until Beau brought him under control with skillful handling, returning back to the ranch house.

"He'll do just fine," he said with a contented smile, patting the horse's neck. "Does he have a name?"

Pike grinned. "Not so you'd say. Mostly we call him sonofabitch, but I guess that's not what you'd be looking to name him."

"No," Beau agreed, smiling at the horse's moniker. "I think I can come up with something more *apropos.*"

"More *what?*" Pike asked.

"Fitting," Beau clarified. "I'll be back in a few days to go over some things with you."

"You're the boss," Pike said.

That I am, Beau thought as he and the banker rode back to town. *That I am*. And what a damned good feeling it was.

Abby was on her way out the door of the hotel with Gussie when they ran into Mayor Cooper.

"Good day, Mrs. Butler. I was just coming to fetch you. See if you wanted to go and see the schoolhouse and your new home."

"And that's where I was fixin' to take her," Gussie added.

"Then let me escort you both."

Abby fell into step between him and her landlady. "I still can't believe the town went to all this trouble for me."

"Well," Mr. Cooper explained, "getting someone of your experience who was willing to come here, the townspeople felt we owed it to you to show our gratitude. We love our town, but we do realize as remote as it is, we don't always have what other places can offer, places much more suited to ladies."

"How long has the town been without a teacher?"

Gussie answered. "Mabel Prentice died near six months ago."

"You've been without a teacher that long?"

"Yes ma'am," Cooper responded, tipping his hat to a woman coming out of the mercantile store.

"I can see I'll have my work cut out for me then."

They walked past the town's storefronts, along the street about half a mile. "Well, here it is," Mayor Cooper said, opening the door to a one-room brick schoolhouse.

Abby walked inside, noticing the neatly lined up desks and the chalkboard, which had a vocabulary lesson still written on it. She inspected the two wooden bookcases, glancing through the volumes on hand. Adequate to start, but she would need more eventually, given the range of the children she had seen so far. Volumes that would challenge her students, books that would open their eyes to new ideas, new worlds, and most importantly, *possibilities*.

Excitement raced through her veins at the notion of being able to lead the children where she wished. For the first time, the curriculum would be up to her. She was in control, charged with a powerful task. Education. The tool, she firmly believed, that made so many things equal. The key to many locks. Indeed, it had helped *her* escape. Without it, she would have been trapped, a prisoner of ignorance forever chained to a cruel jailer.

"If you're ready," Mr. Cooper said, exchanging a smug glance with Gussie, "we'd like to show you the house."

Abby nodded.

The residence was so close to the school that she wouldn't have to travel far, yet she would have privacy, of a sort, as it was set near a grove of trees. The building was small, a one-story fieldstone dwelling, more like a cottage. Inside there was one bedroom, a cozy kitchen, and a tiny parlor. White lace curtains hung on every window. Plain, well-crafted furniture filled the spaces: a square, solid pine dining table and chairs for the kitchen; a rocker and two horsehair chairs for the parlor; a pine bed and dresser for her bedroom. Two thick quilts were heaped upon the bed, as were several pillows. A vase on the dresser was filled with fresh flowers.

Abby walked through each room, marveling at the generosity of the town's citizens. A set of cast-iron cookware was on the stove; a shelf in the pantry was filled with jars of preserves. Another held a smoked ham, along with a crock of dried fruit.

The welcome she was receiving was beyond her expectations. Tears formed in Abby's eyes, threatening to spill down her cheeks.

"Do you like it?" Cooper asked.

Gussie rolled her eyes. "Of course she likes it! All you have to do is look at her. Maybe you'd better think about gettin' a new pair of spectacles, Benjamin."

Abby blinked back the moisture, then spoke from her heart. "I'm simply overwhelmed."

Mayor Cooper cleared his throat. "We just wanted to make you feel welcome, Mrs. Butler. To show you how important you are to this town."

Abby placed a hand on his arm. "Believe me, Mayor Cooper, you have."

"Then," he said with a wide smile, "I'm mighty pleased about that."

"Thank you," Abby said in a voice brimming with emotion. She turned to Gussie and impulsively hugged the older woman, "And please convey my thanks to everyone who had a hand in this."

"It's us who should thank you," Gussie stated, responding warmly to the younger woman's gesture. "I've lived here most of my life. Never had much in the way of schooling, leastwise the formal kind. But I do know if you want a town to grow, you gotta have a fittin' place for young'uns to learn."

"I promise I'll do my best to make you glad you hired me," Abby vowed.

"That's all we can ask," Gussie replied. "Now we'd best be gettin' you back. Remember, there's a supper tonight at the hotel for you. It's so you can meet more of the townspeople."

Giving a last look around her intimate kitchen, Abby felt a growing sense of belonging. A sense of community. Here she was accepted for who she was and what she could do. She had a purpose. She wasn't expected to be a pampered household ornament, with no clear function except to be decorative. To adorn the arm of a wealthy husband, smile dutifully and keep her place. To have the impeccable manners of a well brought up child in a woman's body. To live in the shadows of life and never question why it must be so.

Here, in this town, it seemed her place was what *she* wanted it to be.

Chapter Three

"Well, I'll be," Gussie declared in what was supposed to be a whisper, stopping in her tracks as she and Abby walked back to the hotel. Mayor Cooper had left them to go back to his mercantile establishment. They had tried to make it back to the hotel earlier, but several ladies had waylaid them, begging them to stop for tea and cake. It was at least an hour before they could actually break away.

Abby glanced towards the caked earth street to see what had caught Gussie's eye. She saw two riders and three horses moving in the direction of the livery stable. One of them was Beau McMasters. The other man she didn't know, nor at that moment, did she care.

McMasters sat his mount as though born in the saddle, completely at ease, very much in charge. The Paint he rode pranced, occasionally tossing its head, its long brown mane and tail flying like a banner in the wind.

"What a magnificent animal," Abby declared, admiration in her tone.

"Which one?" Gussie asked, giving a hearty laugh as she sliced Abby a sidelong glance.

Abby blushed at her new friend's earthy observation, though both man and beast *did* look extraordinary.

That was one of the things Abby discovered she liked best about people in the West—their ability for plain speaking, for expressing their honest opinions. Had the same comment been made in New York in the presence of her mother or one of her mother's friends, they would have thought the speaker coarse and vulgar, the observation unworthy of a lady's notice.

Abby, however, found Gussie refreshing. "Both," she responded.

"Ain't that the truth," Gussie said, grinning.

From the corner of his eye, Beau caught sight of the two women. "Excuse me," he said to the banker as he directed his horse closer to the wide wood plank sidewalk where Abby and Gussie stood, almost as if waiting for his approach. Wishful thinking perhaps, he fancied.

"Ladies," he said in a smooth drawl, tipping his hat.

"That there animal doesn't come from Stephen's livery, I'm guessin'," Gussie announced.

Beau's lips curved into a wide smile, enjoying again how lovely Abby Butler looked. Her eyes sparkled and her cheeks had a rosy glow. "You're right about that, Mrs. Travers," he stated, reluctantly removing his gaze from the younger woman's form and forcing his attention to the hotel's landlady. He stroked his hand along the Paint's neck, the horse responding with a low nicker. "I picked him out from my stock for my personal use."

Abby spoke up. "*Your* stock?"

"Yes, Mrs. Butler."

She liked the way he said "Mrs." It sounded like "Miz," low and soft, enticingly intimate.

"Are you a horse trader, Mr. McMasters?" Gussie asked, carefully watching the byplay going on between the two newcomers.

42

"No ma'am. I'm the owner of what used to be the Lawrence ranch."

"Barton Lawrence's place?"

"Yes, ma'am."

"Talk was that he lost it in a card game when he went to San Francisco to visit his sister."

"He did."

"So," Abby stated, a gentle smile on her face, "with a turn of the cards you won a brand-new life."

His answering smile was rife with amusement. "It would appear so."

Gussie gave him a sharp look. "Are you thinking on staying a spell then?"

"I certainly plan to, Mrs. Travers."

"My, my," was the older woman's reply, giving the repeated word extra emphasis.

Abby took a step forward. "May I?" she asked, holding out her hand, indicating she wanted to touch his horse.

"You can try," was Beau's reply. "It's up to him, as he's got quite a mind of his own."

Much like his owner, Abby decided. She reached out her bare hand and laid it upon the stallion's nose, keeping her gaze locked with that of the horse.

Beau watched as she stroked her fingers along the horse's white face, listened as she crooned softly to the animal, who responded with a puff of breath and a nod of his head.

In an instant, he imagined that hand on his face, her fingertips skimming along his skin in the sweetest of touches, stroking his bearded jaw.

He took a deep breath. "If you ladies will pardon me, I have some matters that need looking after, and I'd best tend to them now." He repeated his familiar gesture of tipping his hat before he rode off.

"That horse suits him," Abby remarked, her eyes on his back.

"Don't it just?" Gussie agreed.

To Abby's way of thinking, the animal was as much a dandy as its rider. Proud and capable of turning heads when it passed by. Mr. McMasters had chosen well—the horse supremely complemented him. No ordinary mount would have done for this man; he needed an animal that matched his own temperament and style.

A few minutes passed before Gussie said, "We'd best be gettin' on back."

Abby nodded her head, forcing her eyes away from the sight of Beau as he rode into the livery. She made her way to the hotel, listening as Gussie prattled on about the evening, her wide mouth kicked up into a smile. Beau McMasters was staying on in Heaven's Grace.

Destiny?

Coincidence?

Whichever, Abby suspected that she might have reason to be grateful to whatever had brought him.

Besides, she'd never had a male friend before.

And was that what he was? What she wanted him to be? She didn't know. Too soon to tell, though she hoped so.

But friends shared, confided. Truly talked. They offered advice and kept secrets. They *trusted*.

She couldn't. Not yet. Maybe not ever.

The late afternoon had taken a decidedly warmer turn. Abby left the balcony door open slightly to let in the air while she took a short nap. Curled up on the single bed in only her cotton chemise and single petticoat, her feet bare, her hair unbound, her arms curled about a fluffy pillow, she looked like a sleeping princess in a fairy tale to the man who stood outside looking in.

He knew it was rude, bordering on the worst of bad manners, a betrayal of his status as a gentleman, but he couldn't resist. Mesmerized beyond anything he'd felt before, Beau remained rooted to the spot. He'd doffed his coat and vest when he'd returned to his room, rolled back the sleeves of his white shirt and stepped outside to smoke a cigar and think. It was then that he saw that the door to Mrs. Butler's room was ajar.

He'd debated with himself the wisdom of walking the short distance and speaking to her while he finished his cheroot. Was he presumptuous to seek her out? Would she welcome his call? Or slam the door in his face?

The answers would have to wait.

The urge to wake her with a kiss, to slide his hands along that silky flesh, to slowly unbutton that thin piece of lace-edged cotton and cup the womanly curves beneath, was filtering through his body, heating his blood.

But Beau didn't act on his impulse. Instead, he leaned one hand on the door jamb, simply watching her sleep, like a child with his nose pressed against an invisible window, knowing there were treats to be had inside the sweets shop and understanding they weren't his to take. Another time. Another place. Maybe. But not here, and certainly not now.

Yes, all in good time, he thought. If there was one thing he'd learned in life, it was patience when the prize was worthwhile.

Abby woke with a start, the feeling that she was being watched in the forefront of her mind. Pushing aside the heavy curtain of her hair, she sat up, her gaze fixed upon the open door, expecting to see someone outside.

There was no one there.

The only thing that moved was the breeze, sending a cool shaft of air along her skin as she rose from the bed and went to stand in the doorway. It was gentle, like the touch of a hand skimming along her skin and clothes.

Still, the sensation of someone having been there was so real. It was as if she could feel him. And it was definitely a *him*. She had no idea how she knew that, but she did.

A shaft of warmth uncurled in her belly, slowly spreading upward as she closed her eyes and imagined a face for that spectral feeling. Hauntingly beautiful amber eyes that one could get lost in, and a sensual lower lip surrounded by a carefully trimmed dark beard.

Now she was being ridiculous, she chided herself. Letting her imagination get the best of her. As if Mr. McMasters had nothing better to do than spy on her as she slept. As if he'd even care. A man with his looks would have no trouble finding a woman to spend time with.

The sun was hanging low in the sky, and the air was suddenly cooler. Abby stepped back, her hand on the glass doorknob, ready to pull the door shut, when her attention was captured by the splendor of the landscape before her. Looming mountains and stretches of prairie were laid out as far as the eye could see. Overhead was a sky so wide and beautiful a shade of blue as to take her breath away. It was a spectacular view, made more so because it was unfettered by constrictions of any kind.

How quickly she was coming to love this place. To feel as if she belonged somewhere for the first time in her life; that maybe this was where she was meant to be.

She'd never felt that way about New York. Never felt anything but trapped by the circumstances of her birth and her name.

Abby reluctantly closed the door. She pulled on her dressing gown and checked the time on her pocket watch. Flicking open the case was an act she'd performed hundreds of times. Instead of her own hands, in her mind's eye she saw another pair of hands performing the same task. Masculine hands. Long, slender fingers that pulled the solid gold watch from a pocket in his vest.

Would Mr. McMasters be coming to tonight's dinner?

And, more importantly, would he be sitting at her table?

She certainly hoped so. Abby wanted him to share this

experience with her, much the same as Gussie would be doing.

A deep smile touched Abby's lips at the notion of befriending a gambler and a woman who ran a hotel. "Not our sort," her mother would have said with a condescending sniff in her voice. "Not our sort indeed, my dear. Such people have their place, but it's not with us."

And what would her mother make of her daughter now? Abby wondered. She'd never understood Abby's need to be independent, to think for herself, to make her own choices in life. God knew she had never comprehended Abby's aversion to marrying a man she didn't love. "Money. Position. That's what's important for us. Marriage to a powerful man can ensure that. Those other notions are silly," her mother had said on numerous occasions. "And worse than that, pathetic in a girl of your breeding. It's a foolish whim that you'll outgrow."

But Abby hadn't outgrown those ideas. Try as she might, she'd never been able to make her mother understand. The cold, loveless union of her parents wasn't something she wanted to repeat, or endure in her own marriage.

If I'd stayed. . . .

She would have ended up being sold in bondage as surely as any former slave on the auction block had been. Her life and future taken from her by a powerful man who saw her as only a means to an end. His legal property, his chattel, to dispose of as he saw fit. Without consultation or care for her feelings. All because she had been born a daughter instead of a son.

Thankfully she was beyond his reach here. Lost in the anonymity of a small, remote town. Secure for the time being. Free to enjoy her new life, her new circumstances.

And enjoy them she would tonight.

Yet first, checking her watch, she wanted a bath. Gussie had promised her that she would have one waiting for her about this time. A hot, relaxing soak in the tub was just what she needed.

Pinning her hair up into a loose knot, she gathered a change of underclothes and her toiletries, then peeked outside to make sure the corridor was empty.

Beau relaxed in the hot water, letting the warmth soak into his skin. He needed this; the ride to his ranch had been long and hard, much more strenuous than the simple pleasure rides he was used to. Yet it had been well worth the effort.

Anything worth having, he mused as he leaned back against the tub's rim, was worth the expenditure, be it time, money, or charm.

Abby Butler. Her name whispered inside his head.

He closed his eyes, conjuring up her image easier than his own. He recalled the look of unguarded appreciation on her expressive face when she saw his new horse. She deserved a mount equally as fine.

But would she accept such a personal gift from him if he offered it? Flowers. Chocolates. These were acceptable tokens of regard for a gentleman to give to a lady.

He'd seen what Stephens's livery had to offer. Perfectly satisfactory horses. Able mounts for just about anyone. A knowing smile tugged at the corners of Beau's mouth. Abby Butler wasn't ordinary. Either in looks, manner, or breeding. For her, a conventional, commonplace nag just wouldn't do. She ought to have the best. An animal with spirit and fire. One with grace and speed.

He had just the horse in mind.

But how to present it to her?

He'd worry about that later. Right now a much more pleasant thought crept into his mind. A dance with the lady.

When he'd entered the hotel after seeing to other aspects of his business, he'd noticed that the hotel's dining room arrangement had changed. Some tables had been pushed against one wall, forming a long buffet on which to place the mounds of food being set there. Chairs were set to the other side of the room, keeping the floor free. A space had been set aside for the musicians.

Not quite the formal settings that he'd been used to in New Orleans and San Francisco. In those cities, ballrooms oozed with elegance, dripped with sophistication, serving no other purpose except to be the stage for the best that money could buy. Formal attire was *de rigueur*, as were the rules that one was expected to adhere to. Rules and restrictions.

Beau doubted that the same criteria would be in effect here, which would be to his advantage.

A memory long buried resurfaced as he stroked the lathered washcloth across his skin. He'd been barely ten and had heard his parents discussing a ball that his grandfather was giving at his plantation outside of New Orleans. Even after all those years, Beau could still hear the sadness in his mother's voice as she reminded her husband that there were good reasons why she wouldn't be welcome at her father's house, and the anger in his father's tone as he cursed the father-in-law who'd caused his beloved wife a moment's distress.

Determined to have a look for himself, Beau had snuck out of his home, borrowed his father's horse, and rode to his grandfather's house. Fear of the night and the distance held no meaning for him. All he wanted to know was why his *grand-père* wanted nothing to do with them.

He'd left the horse tied to a moss-draped live oak, carefully making his way over the manicured lawn. Sounds of music floated in the air, wafting all around him. The closer he got to the enormous house, the louder it became, though not quite drowning out the voices inside, or the rapid beating of his heart.

Sneaking even nearer, Beau crept silently until he stood in the shadows, observing the animated crowd through the open French doors. Everyone seemed to be having a good time. Men and women drank, ate, danced, laughed. And there, standing among them, like a king with his subjects, was his grandfather. Beau recognized the snowy-haired gentleman; his mother had once pointed him out in the street in New Orleans, holding her son back when he would have spoken to the old man. *"Non, mon chèr,"* she'd whispered, "let it alone, for my sake and your own."

He'd obeyed her then, but couldn't now.

"What are you doing here, boy?" asked the tall, well-dressed black man who grabbed Beau's shoulder.

Beau turned, the older man's hand still in place. "I came to see Monsieur Rivage," he'd explained.

"What you want with him?"

"He's family."

The old man looked at the boy, his dark eyes sharp. He released his hold and inhaled deeply. "There be no doubtin' that," he'd stated. "Just you wait here. Don't move. Understand?"

Beau nodded.

He hadn't had to wait long. Barely a few minutes had passed before the elderly black man returned; this time he was accompanied by Jean-Marc Rivage.

Stamped on his grandfather's face was the same mole that Beau carried on his cheek; the old man had the same pale green eyes as his mother. The boy he'd been couldn't help smiling. Surely his *grand-père* wouldn't deny him any longer. He'd tell him that there had been some mistake. That he and his parents were welcome. Any time, starting right now.

The proud old Creole stood silent for a moment, looking down at the boy before he said, "Get rid of him, Judah. I never want to see his face again on my property. Is that clear?"

The black man nodded his gray head. "Yes, sir."

"Then do it." Jean-Marc Rivage turned on his elegantly booted heel and made to leave.

"Wait, *grand-père*," Beau protested as Judah led him away.

The old man spun around more quickly than expected, his words cold and cutting to the child. "Never call me that. You are nothing to me." He left and Beau hadn't been able to stop the tears that formed in his young eyes. Sheer willpower stopped them from falling as he was escorted away.

"Don't be comin' back here, boy," Judah warned. "Ain't nothin' here for you but sorrow."

Beau found his horse and made his way back to the city, where he found his parents waiting for him, frantic with worry for their missing son. It was the night he'd discovered the secret that his mother had kept hidden from him.

It was that secret that shaped his life and eventually uprooted him from his beloved city. The same secret that he would never deny, nor choose to reveal.

God, why am I thinking about that? Beau wondered. It had no place in his life now. And certainly not tonight. Tonight was for happier thoughts. For chances and betting against the odds.

He felt the shaft of cool air hit him as soon as the door was thrown open.

"I trust that you'll forgive me if I don't stand?" he drawled as the intruder was revealed.

Flushed from sleep, that virginal white silk wrapper tied around her slim waist, accentuating the flare of her hips, Abby Butler stood stock still in the doorway, blue eyes wide and round. She was definitely the kind of woman a man would want to wake up next to, Beau thought as he watched the color rush to her face. That sweet blush fascinated him. As a widow, the sight of a man in a bath shouldn't have evoked quite that sort of reaction.

Or, could it be that she'd never seen a naked man, not even her husband?

He slowly angled one leg so that it was covering the lower part of his body, hiding what the water clearly revealed for the sake of her modesty, a trait he found unexpectedly endearing.

"I'm sorry," Abby said in a small voice, her eyes still locked on the man in the tub. "I thought I'd arranged to have this time. . . ."

"Then it would appear that I've appropriated your bath, Mrs. Butler," Beau stated, gaze fixed on hers. "Pray forgive my bad manners in having done so. I assumed that it was mine since I'd put in a request with Clara for one when I came back to the hotel."

"Oh yes, Clara," Abby said, the words trailing off. Clara was a girl who helped out in the hotel, slow but goodhearted. "It would seem that we both asked for one, then."

A delightfully wicked thought entered his head, though Beau doubted that Mrs. Butler would be open to the suggestion that they share the surprisingly spacious tub. Someone must have had that idea in mind by the design of the bath. Maybe Gussie herself. Now that Beau could very well believe.

What was causing that smirk on his lips? Abby wondered, her feet still firmly planted on the wooden floor. What amusement did he find in this situation?

The only thing flooding her senses was embarrassment, and an unexpected tingle upon her skin, a warmth in her blood, at the sight of him. By all rights she should have covered, or at least lowered her eyes, and withdrawn quickly. Instead, she seemed unable to move, her gaze captured by his like a prize animal captured in a hunter's sights, unwilling to break the temporary bond between them.

For better or worse, and she suspected the latter, Abby stared at that long, lean body tucked into the space of the claw-footed tub. She was aware of the curl in his damp hair, the smile on his mouth, the knowing look in his eyes, the muscled chest, dusted with a dark smudge of hair across the upper reaches, and over his nipples. Fine dark hair also dusted his legs and arms. His was the type of body Italian and Greek masters sculpted from the finest marble, giving life to man-made gods. His skin had color, though, warm gold instead of cool white, giving him a patina all his own.

Would it feel warm if she reached out her hand and touched it?

Merciful heaven, but she was behaving foolishly. Like a wanton, without regard for his feelings or propriety. It didn't matter that she was supposed to be a widow. As soon as she opened the door she should have closed it immediately instead of standing there like a gawking child, or a woman in a sporting house, assessing a prospective customer.

What must he think of her? That she was loose? Or desperate for a man's attention? Enough to risk her good name? Her new position?

She forced herself to tear her eyes from his. "Please forgive my intrusion, Mr. McMasters." She had turned to go when his voice stopped her.

"We all make mistakes, Mrs. Butler, even honest ones." Her back was stiff and straight: a few stray tendrils of hair cascaded from her topknot. Beau could see a hint of her bare nape. What would it taste like?

"Mistakes?" she said, turning her head slightly, though not enough to see him.

"I'll see to it that more hot water is brought up for you, though it may take a while."

"Don't trouble yourself, Mr. McMasters. I'll make do with a wash in my room," she said, referring to the pitcher of tepid water that waited for her.

"I'm truly sorry, ma'am," he said in that low, intimate drawl.

53

Beau watched as she closed the door behind her. The cooling water couldn't lessen the impact her sudden and unexpected appearance had had on him. Blood coursed hotly through his body, pooling in his groin, tightening and lengthening his aroused flesh, reminding him of her feminine power. It had been mere weeks since he'd sampled a woman's charms. What about her? How long had it been since she'd been with a man? Was she aware that he'd seen the telltale hardening of her nipples through the thin layer of fabric? Had she known her tongue had snaked out and wetted her lips? Lips he wanted to feel against his own mouth. Against his skin, trailing softly against his chest. Had she known he longed to put his hands on her? To be free to explore? To touch where and how he would?

Beau doubted she did. Her eyes, despite her former married state, had been strangely innocent, and oddly humbling.

Abby shut the door to her room with a snap, locking it securely behind her, though she doubted that a mere lock would ever stop a man like Mr. McMasters from attaining any goal he really wanted.

She turned and stared at the wooden door as if she expected to hear it rip from its hinges at any moment.

Realizing that she was wasting time, Abby removed her robe and tossed it on the bed, poured a measure of the water from the china pitcher into the basin, splashed it about her face and neck to cool her heated skin. In doing so she was reminded of how the droplets of water had clung to his skin, glistening in the glow of the bathroom's wall sconces.

Good gracious, she was being overly dramatic, like some heroine from a grandiose melodrama. Her time would be better spent getting ready for this evening and in making a favorable impression on the people who had hired her.

Yet as she searched through her trunk to find just the right dress after she finished her impromptu wash, Abby couldn't help but acknowledge that the townsfolk weren't the only people she wanted to dazzle that night.

Chapter Four

She was nervous, and strangely excited.

Abby could hear the sounds of multiple voices coming from downstairs, indicating that a fair number of the townsfolk were gathered below. The ladies of the local church had organized this event, and according to Gussie, deemed it a chance to get their husbands dressed in their Sunday best for a second day of the week.

She stood before the full-length oval mirror, looking at her reflection from several angles, making sure she was satisfied with the results. The talented seamstress she'd hired in Denver had worked wonders in such a short time—as good, if not better, than any in New York. The color and cut of the two-piece outfit flattered her figure. She'd kept her hair simple, pulling half of it atop her head, anchored by plain combs; the rest hung in loose curls about her shoulders, thanks to Clara's skill with a hot curling iron.

Well, Abby thought, she couldn't dilly-dally up in her room any longer. Making a fashionably late entrance to a party was accepted, even expected in New York society.

Here, in Heaven's Grace, it was, she suspected, the height of bad manners.

Taking one last look, she turned to leave, then remembered she'd forgotten to add a touch of her favorite perfume. Picking up the small green glass bottle of scent, she lifted the stopper and dabbed it behind her ears, trailed it along her throat, and touched her wrists. There was very little left of the expensive blend, which she'd brought with her when she'd fled her home. It was an exclusive scent, named *La Belle Heure*, sold in only one store in New York.

But tonight, she decided, was a special occasion, which called for something far more special than lilac or rose water. It had nothing to do with a certain Southern gentleman who was sure to be at the party.

Of course not, Abby told herself. Whether or not Mr. Mc-Masters liked her perfume was of no consequence to her.

Perhaps, if she repeated that sentiment over and over again, like a litany, she might just believe it.

Beau stood, a glass of cold lemonade in one hand, chatting with Benjamin Cooper, who was extolling the virtues of his town in a nonstop monologue. He listened politely, nodding every now and then. He made do with the boring drink, wishing it were a glass of vintage champagne, or Kentucky bourbon. However, he'd discovered that spirits weren't a welcome addition to this affair, especially since the churchwomen were sponsoring it. Pity, he thought as he sipped the tartly sweet drink.

He flicked his glance toward the stairs. What was keeping her? Ever since their unexpected encounter in the hotel's private bathroom, reserved, he later found out, for special guests, he'd been anxious to see the new schoolmarm again.

Besides the obvious fact that he found her extremely attractive, there was something about the widow Butler that intrigued him. She was different from any female he'd known in recent years. The small amount of time he'd spent in her company had brought a fleeting glimpse of another life to mind, a bittersweet reminder of a gentler era, when life was sweet and meant to be savored, when time crept by slowly, its pace intertwined with the sultry, humid days and nights of Louisiana.

Funny thing was, even though he'd been born into that life, it really wasn't his. It never would be. At least not in New Orleans.

"Oh good, she's come down at last. Thought we was going to háve to send the cavalry up after her," the mayor joked as he turned in the direction of the honored guest.

Beau lifted his head, then inhaled sharply, his eyes captured by the woman on the stairs.

Handing the mayor his glass without a second thought, he crossed the space of the dining room and was first to greet her when she was halfway down. "Good evening, Mrs. Butler," he crooned seductively. Lifting her bare hand to his lips, he kissed it, breathing in the exquisite scent of her perfume.

Gardenia.

Subtle. Tempting. Memorable.

"May I compliment you on your choice of fragrance, Mrs. Butler?" he whispered. "On you it is perfection."

Abby wet her lips. His honeyed words, slowly intoned, and his intense eyes, caused a shiver of heat to flood her body, as did his warm mouth on her skin. She'd always worn gloves for formal occasions and had had a pair made to match this outfit. They'd been left upstairs, at the urging of Clara, who, upon seeing them, insisted that no lady hereabouts used them. Not wanting to appear as if she were putting on Eastern airs, she'd chosen to leave them behind. Now, with his lips on her flesh, she was glad she had, else she never would have experienced the tingling sensation jolting up her arm.

It was as if they were alone in the crowd, the only two people in the room who existed.

Gussie's voice broke the spell, returning Abby to the reality of the present. "Excuse me for interruptin', but we gotta make sure that this gal meets everyone. There'll be plenty of time later for you to socialize, Mr. McMasters."

"By all means, Mrs. Travers," Beau stated, stepping back so that Abby could finish her descent of the stairs. "I yield to you willingly." And with that he took Gussie's work-roughened hand and brought it to his lips in a perfunctory salute.

"My, how you do go on, sir," Gussie remarked with a light laugh. "I do believe that you could even insult a body and make them like it, listening to that silken tongue of yours. Are you Irish by any chance? I used to know a miner that was from Ireland, and Lordy, could that man talk to charm the hide off a buffalo."

"Some generations back, ma'am, on my father's side," Beau acknowledged.

Abby allowed her gaze to meet his, giving him a warm smile. "Charm is something I'd guess Mr. McMasters learned in the cradle, Gussie. What wasn't bred in the bone was taught as a matter of course. Am I right, sir?"

Beau returned her smile with a dazzling one of his own. "Far be it from me to argue with a lady, Mrs. Butler."

"Come now, Abby," Gussie instructed. "I want you to meet Ida Smith, who helped arrange this evening. You'll be teachin' her six little darlin's when school starts."

Beau watched as the two women moved away from him. Damn, Abby Butler was a rare beauty. From the crown of her reddish-gold hair so artfully styled, to the cut and color of her dress—a shade of turquoise that brought out the blue of her eyes—to the finely crafted black shoes that she wore. The only thing lacking was something to grace the low-cut neckline of the outfit. It needed a distinctive necklace, a stone to flatter that lovely throat. A bracelet, or two, to set off those wonderful hands. The pearl earbobs were nice, but he would have chosen a more dramatic set of earrings. Diamonds. Or maybe sapphires. Yes, most definitely sapphires. Blue fire. Cool to the eye; warm to the touch. Like he imagined her skin.

He kept a silent vigil from across the room as Gussie introduced her to one person after another and saw a pleasant smile curve her mouth. She handled this newfound position with grace and charm; she was not overly obstreperous, nor aloofly reserved. Abby Butler was genuinely warm.

Her husband had been a lucky man. If he hadn't thought so, then he was ten times the fool.

Somehow the thought of her wed to a fool was intolerable.

No matter how many faces she was introduced to, Abby found her eyes searching the room for a particular masculine face, a face she had no claim on, nor knew much about, except that it was, without a doubt, the most handsome here tonight. While the majority of the townsmen were dressed in what she knew was their Sunday finery, he was the essence of a proud peacock. His choice of a smoky-gray frock coat and trousers, with a silver brocade vest and matching neckcloth over a frilled shirt made him stand out. Tonight his familiar knee-high boots had a highly polished gleam, as did the silver spurs. The ever-present gun was still fastened around his slim hips. The only time, come to think of it, when she hadn't seen the gun was when he was in the bath.

Why couldn't she get that particular image out of her mind? Why had it persisted in haunting her while she dressed?

Because she was letting him become more important than he really was.

"Have you had a moment to yourself since you arrived

in Heaven's Grace?" asked Mary James, handing Abby a glass of lemonade.

"A few," she answered.

"Good. I imagine that all this can be mightily over-whelming. It should get easier once you're in your own place."

"I still can't get over how generous you've all been to me."

"People hereabouts are pretty nice," Mary responded, refilling her own glass from one of the cut-glass pitchers. "When you finally get settled in, I'd like you to come out to our spread and have dinner with us, if that's all right with you. We're not so far outta town."

"Are you near the former Lawrence ranch?"

"Near enough, I s'pose, give or take a few miles." Mary nodded at her husband as he helped their daughter fill up her plate from the vast selection of items on the table. "Yeah, I did hear that the ranch changed hands. We're a small operation compared to what Lawrence used to own, but we do—and of course I'm bragging here—have the best beef in the whole of Montana territory." Mary sipped her drink. "You do like beef, don't you?"

Abby thought of the thick, juicy cuts that she'd learned to love early on in her life, cooked to perfection with mushrooms and shallots by the Breckenridge chef. "Oh, yes," was her quick reply.

"Then we'll see to it that you have what you need. We supply the hotel, too."

"Did Mr. Lawrence have cattle?"

"Yes, but he mainly shipped his to markets back east. Guess the new owner will do the same, leastwise I hope so."

"Hmmm, I wonder," Abby said.

"Lawrence had a nice herd of horses, too. Used to sell quite a few to the army."

Abby thought of the pinto stallion Mr. McMasters had procured for himself. If that was an example of the stock that he had inherited as part of his land deal, then he was indeed fortunate. Maybe, if things worked out, and she was able to stay, she might buy a mount for herself. A proper saddle horse, but one that had some mettle.

"Wonder when the new owner is gonna show his self?" Mary asked.

"The new owner of the Lawrence place?"

Mary nodded.

"He already has."

"What?" Surprise registered on Mary's round face. "You know who owns the spread?"

It was Abby's turn to nod. "Beau McMasters."

"Who's he?"

"Do you see that man standing in the corner talking with Gussie's husband?"

Mary looked. "The one in the fancy clothes?"

"Uh-huh."

"I been wondering who he is. Figured it was just someone passing through."

"From what I've heard, he's here to stay."

"Well, ain't he pretty," Mary remarked in an amused voice. "I wonder how long he'll last?"

Till hell freezes over if there's something here he wants, Abby thought, not questioning how she knew, but accepting it as truth. Beau McMasters didn't look to be a man who backed down from a challenge, or she reckoned, remembering the lethal weapon he carried, from a fight.

Gussie joined them. "We're about to start the dancin', so if you'd like to choose a partner, Abby, we can begin this shindig. First dance is yours, considerin' you're the guest of honor. And," Gussie continued, looking into the assembled faces, "we got plenty of men here who would love to take a turn about the room with you."

Abby hesitated for only a moment before she left the two women talking and walked across the room. She stopped when she found her target. Before she could lose her nerve, she asked, "Would you care to dance, Mr. Mc-Masters?" surprising herself with her boldness.

He bowed slightly in acknowledgment of her offer, taking her hand in his. "I would be honored, Mrs. Butler."

A buzz of voices erupted as the couple moved to the space that had been cleared for dancing. She fit into his arms perfectly, her body moving with his as the assembled musicians began their version of a waltz tune.

She probably should have chosen someone else. That would have been the sensible choice, the safer choice. As Gussie said, the room was full of men who would have done just as well.

But Abby couldn't.

She wanted *him* to be the first.

"Thank you."

"For what?" he asked.

"For being willing to partner me."

"It's hardly an onerous task, Mrs. Butler," Beau responded, his charming smile for her alone. For the opportunity of touching her, holding her tonight, he would have crossed any distance, taken any risk.

"But you didn't know that when I asked you. For all you knew, I could have been a dismal failure, stepping on your toes."

"Impossible."

"How gallant of you," she declared, wishing that this one dance could last the rest of the evening. He moved as she had known he would, effortlessly, with grace and strength. Smooth and sweet as warm maple syrup on a cold winter morning.

Then, all too soon their dance was over.

"Now it is *my* turn to thank *you,* ma'am." Beau started to lift her hand once again to his mouth and then thought better of it. "Perhaps you'll favor me later with another."

"I'd be delighted, sir," she responded.

His eyes stared into hers with that intensity she'd come to regard as his alone. "Your servant, Mrs. Butler."

She watched as he passed through the crowd of men who came to surround her, all eager to have a dance with her. Abby chose the mayor as her second partner, as the band played a lively tune.

"Mrs. Travers, may I have the honor?" Beau inquired of Gussie when he reached her side. "That is," he directed his request to Gussie's husband, "if you have no objections."

"You sure can," she replied, taking his hand before Carl could form a response. While they whirled about the room in time to the music, Gussie couldn't help commenting, "You and Abby made a most handsome pair, Mr. McMasters."

"I dare say that Mrs. Butler would make any man look good, ma'am."

"That could well be," she said, "but the two of you together were most delightful."

Was the woman playing matchmaker? Beau wondered. If so, he hated to throw cold water on her scheme, but he wasn't in the market for a wife. Adroitly, he changed the subject. "I'll be staying at the hotel for a bit longer, if that presents no problem."

"Glad to have you. You're welcome for as long as you like."

Now was as good a time as any to tell her that he held the paper on the bank's former half of the hotel, but he let the opportunity slip by. That was business; this was social.

The music stopped and Gussie sighed. "That was fun." She turned to her husband when Beau returned her to him. "Come on, Carl. You're next."

"Okay, pumpkin," was Carl's response as he linked arms with his wife.

Beau smiled at the couple as they took their places on the increasingly crowded floor. It was then that he spotted a rather plain woman standing in the corner with a stern-looking man at her side. Her eyes had caught his momentarily before she hastily glanced away, her head bowed. In that space of time, Beau recognized the telltale signs of a broken soul. Tall, skinny, with a sallow color and lackluster hair, the woman was like too many he'd seen after the war. Defeated and alone, dragging through life as best they could. That made up his mind.

He crossed the space that separated them until he stood before her, introducing himself. "Would you care to dance, miss?"

Her head lifted and he saw a small spark of life in her dull blue eyes.

But, before she could reply, the man standing with her snapped an answer to Beau's request. "My daughter wants nothing to do with a good-for-nothin', dirty Reb son of a bitch, so clear off."

Beau's nostrils flared and his eyes hardened at the insult, his hand automatically reaching for his weapon, his fingers curled around the walnut grip of the Remington.

The girl looked mortified, shrinking against the wall, her protestation a mere croak of sound. "Father, please."

Beau uncoiled his hand, forcing it to his side as he coldly replied in a deadly voice, "Consider this your lucky night. Had this been elsewhere, I would have demanded satisfaction for your words. If, however, you are ever so stupid as to repeat them, then I will be forced to teach you some manners. Make no mistake about it."

The man glared at Beau, sweat popping out on his brow. "Do you understand?"

When the man didn't answer, Beau repeated his question.

The man nodded, then grabbed his daughter and pulled her roughly from the hall, to the murmured comments of those standing nearby.

"Don't put no stock in that man's words," Benjamin Cooper advised Beau.

"Who is he?"

"Hank Baser. Lost his only son in the war and hasn't been right since then."

"There were terrible losses on both sides," Beau said, thinking about his own family, his parents especially.

"Some people can't forgive and forget," the mayor stated. "It ain't in their nature."

That was something Beau could well understand, but it was not an excuse for the cruel look in Baser's eyes.

"He's had a lot of bad luck in his life, what with losing his wife and the farm, then his daughter being taken by Indians," Cooper explained. "Only got her back this past year."

Beau hated to think what the young woman had suffered. What a shame that she'd been brought back to a man as bitter as Baser obviously was. "We'll have no trouble as long as he stays out of my way."

"Fair enough," Cooper commented. "Now let's get back to the party, shall we?"

About an hour later, Abby decided to catch her breath and sit down for a while. She couldn't remember ever dancing as much as she had that night, or having as much fun. Here people danced because they enjoyed it, not merely because it was a social custom one must endure.

Yet of all the partners she'd had this evening, she longed for one man in particular to seek her out again, and so far, he hadn't. However, Mr. McMasters hadn't lacked for willing partners. Several times she'd seen him dancing, though never with the same woman twice.

She searched the room for him now, but to no avail. He'd disappeared, and some of the sparkle in the room had left with him.

Where was he?

Gussie took a chair next to her, a large glass of lemonade in her hand. "You've got to hear what happened."

When the younger woman didn't respond, Gussie tapped her on the shoulder. "Abby?"

"Excuse me, did you say something?" Abby had been so wrapped up in her thoughts about Mr. McMasters that she hadn't paid attention to anything else.

Gussie clucked her tongue. "I most certainly did, my dear girl. It's about Mr. McMasters."

"What about him?" Abby asked.

"Seems he was involved in a bit of a fracas earlier."

"Was he hurt?" Was that why he wasn't around any longer?

Gussie shook her head, sharply regarding her new friend's agonized look. She figured that it didn't take no genius to realize Abby Butler had a soft spot for the rakish gambler. It was plain for anyone to see in those blue eyes of hers. "No cause for worry."

Abby calmed her breathing, realizing that she'd revealed more of what she was feeling than she meant to. "What happened?"

"Seems Hank Baser made some remarks that Mr. McMasters found insulting. He almost called Hank out."

"But he didn't?" Abby couldn't disguise the concern in her voice.

"No," Gussie assured her. "Benjamin Cooper said that Mr. McMasters handled himself real well." Gussie took a hearty swallow of her drink. "Hank's got a way of lettin' his mouth run away with him. He's a damned fool if you ask me. One look at Mr. McMasters should have told him to forget tryin' to tangle with him. Anybody can see just by lookin' that Mr. McMasters is no greenhorn when it comes to his weapon."

"What did he say to get Mr. McMasters so upset?"

"Benjamin said that Hank made a snide remark about Mr. McMasters being from the South."

"The war's been over for fifteen years," Abby declared.

"Besides, I doubt that Mr. McMasters had anything to do with that—he must have been a boy at the time."

"Some people can't let go of the past, my dear," Gussie explained. "We lost a few good men from Heaven's Grace in the fighting."

"I'm sorry to hear that. But you don't hold a grudge, do you?"

"No point." The older woman shrugged her big shoulders. "Ain't gonna bring them back now, is it? 'Sides, they lost men on the other side too, didn't they? We gotta do, I figure, what Mr. Lincoln wanted us to do before he got killed, get on with rebuilding our country and forgive the past. If we can't do that, then we ain't gonna measure up to anything."

Abby impulsively hugged the other woman.

"Now what was that for?" Gussie asked, surprised.

"For being who you are," Abby replied, aware that if she didn't get up and out of here, she might well burst into tears, so strong was her reaction to Gussie's words. Here was a woman who had learned important life lessons, forgiveness and compassion. Would that her own mother had been as well schooled.

Abby rose. "I'll be back in a few minutes."

"Where you off to?"

"To get some fresh air. I'm feeling a bit lightheaded right now." It was a small lie, but a necessary one. A twinge of disgust pricked at Abby. How adept she was becoming with white lies. With any lies.

"Go on then," Gussie instructed. "There's a back door you can get to from the kitchen that leads outside."

"Thanks," Abby whispered, making her way toward the kitchen, repeating, "Excuse me" and "Pardon me" as she went.

Once outside, she took a deep breath, filling her lungs with the crisp night air. She stepped to the edge of the planked walk beneath the upstairs balcony and looked up.

Stars dotted the sky, like diamonds on a bed of dark blue velvet. Funny how close they seemed here in Montana. As if she could reach out her hands and grab a handful.

"Beautiful, aren't they?"

Abby started at the sound of the unexpected voice, then relaxed when she recognized the speaker.

"Sorry," the masculine voice said, moving closer to her. "I didn't mean to frighten you."

She turned her head and saw the faint flicker of light from the end of his cigar, smelled the fragrant aroma of the tobacco. "That's all right. It's just that I didn't know anyone else was out here."

He knew. Hidden in the shadows, content with the darkness that surrounded him, Beau had seen her emerge from the back doorway, backlit by the kitchen lamps, her footsteps soft on the planks.

A few steps more brought him inches from her. So close he could reach out his hand and touch one of the curls that hung below her shoulders. So close he could breathe in that gardenia scented perfume. So close he could imagine he heard her heart beat.

Damnation! He wanted badly to kiss her. Cover that mouth with his own until it yielded all its secrets to him. Slide his hands along the length of her neck and over the slope of her shoulders, down her arms and then up again to feather across the fabric that clung to her generous breasts.

He was achingly aroused just thinking about it. Could hell's fire be hotter than the blood coursing wildly through his veins right now?

Somehow, he doubted it.

He pitched the remains of his cigar into the night. "You shouldn't be out here by yourself, Mrs. Butler."

"But I'm not," she countered. "You're here." And was he ever. So close Abby could smell the distinctly masculine scent he used. So close she could put out her hand

and lay it upon his sleeve, feel the coiled muscles in his arm beneath the fabric of his frock coat. So close she could place her lips upon that delicate mole that rode high on his cheek, if she dared.

God, what fanciful notions had burrowed into her brain, twisting it into knots of sensually driven thoughts? Thoughts dark and deep, unfolding with a heat that flooded her body.

Dangerous.

That word aptly described him. Dangerous to her senses, to her sense of well being. Dangerous to her carefully constructed web of lies.

"You should go back inside, where it's safe."

Safe. Was she? Would she ever be completely safe?

"What makes you think that I'm not safe out here?"

"Do you *feel* safe?" he asked softly, his voice wrapping around her in the dark like a warm blanket.

"I think so."

"Do you, really?"

She imagined that she could clearly see the sharply focused look in his long-lashed eyes. "I don't frighten easily, Mr. McMasters."

"An admirable trait."

"I like to think so." Her mouth curved into a smile. "But, I am cautious."

"Prudent," he replied.

"If you like." Abby took a deep breath, satisfied. "I do think that I will call it a night now."

"Very wise."

"Would you make my excuses to Gussie? I can just as easily slip up the back stairs."

"Of course I will," he promised. "But, before you leave, may I have a last dance?"

She could hear the sounds of the music escaping from the open widows of the hotel, a soft, plaintive melody that she knew was about lost love and longing. "Here?"

"Yes." He slipped a hand around her waist, pulling her closer to his body.

Abby yielded, gliding slowly along the confined space with him.

As soon as the music ended, Beau released her. Then, he did something that stole her breath. He reached for her hand and brought it to his mouth again, but instead of brushing his lips across the back of her hand, he turned it over and kissed, if only fleetingly, the warm skin of her palm.

Abby trembled at the feel of his beard and mouth connecting so intimately with her flesh. Like a match, it struck sparks of fire in its wake.

"Good night, Mrs. Butler," he murmured, his voice low and achingly soft. "Thank you for our dance."

Abby curled her fingers around her palm unconsciously as if she could capture the magic of the moment. "I forgot . . ." she started to say.

"What?"

"I can't get into my room from the outside door. I locked it before I came downstairs."

"A very *prudent* move," he said with a slight smile. "Then go back in the way you came out."

"What about you?"

"I'll walk around to the front, so no one will get the wrong impression."

"And what impression is that?"

"Ah, that you and I . . ."

"What?"

"Had a rendezvous."

"A rendezvous?"

"Would you prefer a romantic interlude?"

"Who would think that?"

"Why, anyone who chanced upon us here, in the dark," he said, pausing for a moment to let the last word sink in, "alone."

Alone. Just the two of them. Surrounded by the night. An intimate encounter.

Yes, that's how it *could* look to someone else. "Thank you, Mr. McMasters."

"No thanks are required, ma'am," he stated gallantly. "A gentleman is always careful of a lady's reputation. And please, call me Beau."

"Is that short for Beauregard?"

"No," he replied in that silky voice. "Just Beau."

"And I'm Abby." The moment that she uttered the words, she almost wished that she could call them back, especially when she realized why she'd been so eager to relax her hold on formality: She wanted to hear him say her name. Wanted to know what it would sound like spoken with his accent.

"You'd better go in now before anyone comes looking for you."

"Good night, Beau," Abby said, her hand on the glass doorknob.

From the enveloping darkness she heard a rich, soft chuckle, then a whispered, "Until tomorrow . . . Abby."

Chapter Five

"We had reports that a young woman fitting your daughter's description was sighted in Dallas, Tucson, Vicksburg and Denver, so we're checking them all out to see if any are viable, sir," the Pinkerton agent reported.

The man seated behind the big desk in a well-appointed office several stories above the bustling New York City street clenched his hands into fists, his anger palpable. "My wife has a sister who married a man from Vicksburg before the war, but I thought your agency had looked into that possibility when I first reported my daughter missing."

The man checked his leather-bound notebook, clearing his throat discreetly. "We did, sir, and found no trace of her then, but maybe she's come back."

"If that bitch has helped in any way to keep me from my daughter, I'll . . ."

The Pinkerton man swallowed hard. He didn't need the other man to finish his sentence; he could very well guess what Harold Breckenridge had intended to say. Three years of dealing with this particular client had given him an insight into the older man's character. And what he saw scared him at times, but he wasn't getting paid to give a damn, just to produce results. "I'll get in touch by wire with our man there and tell him to pay close attention to your sister-in-law." He double-checked the name. "Hettie Butler Walsh, correct?"

"Yes," was the gruff reply as Breckenridge stood and walked a few steps to the small butler's table, pouring himself a large measure of brandy from the Waterford crystal decanter. He neglected to offer the agent any, taking a large swallow before he returned to his desk, snifter in hand.

"I'm getting awfully tired of this cat-and-mouse game, Dellings," Breckenridge remarked coldly. "When am I going to see any results?"

"We're doing our best, sir."

The man behind the desk glowered up at the agent. "You are?" he sneered, resuming his seat. "Well, you can't prove it by me. All I've got is a large ongoing bill for your company's services, and no daughter. You mean to stand here and tell me that a mere female can befuddle the entire goddamned Pinkerton agency?"

"It's a big country, sir, and your daughter is quite clever."

"Clever?" Breckenridge's cold blue eyes narrowed. "You think so?"

"Of course I do, since she's been able to elude us so successfully. Don't you?"

"What I think is that your organization is highly overrated."

Dellings took offense at the banker's words, but was careful not to show it. This man had the power to back up any threats he made, implied or otherwise. "We won't rest until we recover your daughter, sir. You have my word on that."

"It had better be soon. My patience is about to end."

"I'll report back to you when I have some news."

"Hire more operatives," Breckenridge snarled. "I told you, I don't care about the *eventual* cost so long as you produce results. All I want is Abigail back where she belongs." He waited until the Pinkerton agent closed the door behind him to drain the last drops of the aged brandy before he hurled the exquisite glass to the floor, shattering it.

That damnable bitch! Thinking that she could defy *him.* That she could continually outwit the men he'd hired to find her. Well, he'd have the last laugh when she was found, and found she would be. If he had to populate the country with Pinkertons, he'd do so. She wasn't going to get away with it. Never! She *belonged* to him as surely as anything else in his life. And what was his, stayed his. Until *he* was done with it.

Breckenridge's florid, once-handsome face flushed even more from the combination of drink and his vexation at having been defied. He should have beaten the independence out of her. Made her see the error of her ways with a whip or his fists. Then, given her to a man who'd keep her in line and be grateful to him for the gift.

She was the fruit of his loins and that fruit must be passed on, but only to a man of his choosing. One carefully selected, who'd know how to handle a reluctant wife.

He'd found such a man only to have the chit tell him boldly that she wouldn't marry the gentleman he'd picked out. It had been right here in his office that she had faced him and uttered those words.

"I won't be forced into marrying a man I don't love, Father."

"You'll marry whom I tell you and like it."

"No," she'd said in that defiant tone, "I won't. You can't make me."

"Oh, but I can," he'd told her.

"You wouldn't."

"Yes, I would."

"Why?"

"Because *I* know what's best for you."

"And," she'd retorted, "it's a man who doesn't love me? A man I don't love. That's what you think is best?"

He'd banged his hand hard on the desk, scattering papers. "What's this idiotic notion of love got to do with marriage? Nothing, I can assure you. Love is for fools and shopgirls. You're neither. It's a business alliance between his family and ours."

"But he's a drunk. And he's cruel."

"No one said that he had to be a saint, missy. You're too damned stubborn by half. Why, anyone would think I was wedding you to an ugly, deformed ape the way you protest. So he drinks? What man doesn't? And as for cruel, well, I've seen no signs of that."

"I have," she'd declared. "He beats his horse. Whips him unmercifully for no good reason. And he treats those who work for him no better. I've even seen him take a whip to one of his grooms, a boy scarcely older than a child."

"He treats them as inferiors, which they are. What bother is that to you?"

"Bother? Of course you would think that, wouldn't you? You're as selfish as he."

"And as rich, don't forget that. Your children will inherit our combined fortunes. Think how wonderful that will be."

"The thought of bearing Billy Cullen's child is too loathsome to contemplate."

"Well, loathsome or not, you'll do it. As many times as it takes to give me a dynasty. God knows your mother couldn't do it."

"That's all I've ever been to you, isn't it? A brood mare!"

"You're someone I've invested a lot of money in and it's about to pay off."

"No."

He could still hear the way she'd said that word. Openly defiant. Daring him to challenge her.

And he had. The back of his hand had connected with her face, knocking her to the floor. She lay there, stunned for a moment, blood dripping delicately from her swollen lip. She'd touched her fingertips to it, staring at the red substance until she turned her eyes on him. He believed, in that instant, that he'd seen hate there; felt it like a living, breathing thing in the room between them.

Well, if she'd felt that way, so what?

She'd refused his offer of a hand up, preferring to get to her feet herself. Then she said the words he wanted to hear. "You win."

She hadn't meant them, he later discovered. It had all been a ruse to gain her freedom. Weeks later she'd fled his house on the night of her engagement ball, leaving him to look the unsuspecting fool to everyone there, most especially to her intended's family and friends. A man who couldn't keep a woman in line was, Breckenridge knew, a joke, someone to snicker at. Pity even.

Well, no one dared snicker to his face or offer him pity.

Damn her to hell for that! No one had ever ignored or disobeyed him and gotten away with it.

And she wouldn't, either. One way or another, she would be back under his roof, wed to another man he selected. Her former fiancé had married someone else not three months after his daughter disappeared. An ugly British cow who happened to have a title of her own.

He'd be damned if he'd let that incident get the better of him. He'd found a fresh candidate for his daughter's hand. An older, more experienced man, who was eager to swap his name and lineage for a considerable sum of money. A man with an heir already and plenty of bastard brats, which meant he was capable of siring children. And, more importantly, he was willing to hand over any future male offspring to his father-in-law to raise.

He was three years behind schedule because of her. Three precious years he couldn't get back.

Of course, when he'd made the initial marriage offer to Cullen, he was sure of his daughter's virginity, her value as a prospective wife.

Now . . .

God help her if she was damaged goods. For if that were the case, it would cost him a pretty penny more to sweeten the marriage pot.

The old walnut clock in his office chimed six P.M.

Breckenridge rose from his desk and carefully stepped around the broken glass, knowing that it would be gone by the time he arrived in the morning. Menial details like that he left to the office staff.

What he needed now was a way to unwind from this miserable day and forget about the ungrateful child who'd caused him so much aggravation.

His mouth thinned into a smile. Dinner at home and an evening at his club could wait. A stop off at his mistress's house would satisfy at least one appetite. She was the best kind of whore—needy and grateful. Willing to go to any lengths to please him, denying him nothing. She, unlike his recalcitrant daughter, was a woman who knew her place—which was whatever he said it was. Simple, really. No questions asked. No answers given. All she had to do was spread her legs, or open her mouth.

Life would have been so much easier if only Abigail had understood that.

Chapter Six

Abby couldn't help thinking about and reliving the events of the night before when she woke up, so powerful was the impression that Beau McMasters had once again made on her. Of all the people who'd attended the welcome party, he was the one most vivid in her recollections. He stood out like a bright, shining star, or the visiting solo artist in a provincial orchestra.

His solitary presence on the back porch was a reminder to Abby of the many times she'd felt the need to escape her surroundings when she'd been forced by her parents to attend numerous society functions that held no interest for her. Alone in a crowd, the worst kind of lonely. Trapped among people she had come to despise.

Well, maybe not all of them. There were a few exceptions, a few who maintained their humanity in the midst of the crowded, stagnant fishbowl that was, to her, New York society.

One of them had been her childhood friend, Beth Van Dorht. Sweet, gentle Beth. All she'd ever wanted from her life was a good husband and children. Yet Beth's dream was crushed when her father lost his fortune in wild speculating and killed himself, thus ruining his wife and family with the scandal. The remaining Van Dorhts were eventually cut from important social gatherings, from any kind of contact with people who were supposed to be their friends. Abby tried to keep in touch, but when the Van Dorhts lost their mansion on Fifth Avenue, they were forced to move upstate with Beth's maternal grandparents.

At least that's what Abby had been told. No answer ever came to the numerous letters she'd sent Beth, so she eventually gave up writing, mourning the loss of Beth's friendship, which heightened Abby's sense of isolation.

Only by chance did she happen to see her friend again.

Because she couldn't get money from her trust fund since her father tightly controlled it, a few days before she was planning to leave New York, Abby visited a pawn shop she'd once read about in *The Times*, a place known for its discretion handling items from the impoverished gentry. She'd decided to sell some pieces from her jewelry collection, adding the token gifts from her erstwhile fiancé. She appreciated the irony of having him help to finance her journey. She'd purposely chosen this area of the city, where she was a stranger, so that few questions would be asked about the gems she was exchanging for cash.

As she was leaving the small shop, the pawnbroker having been more generous than she expected, Abby had thought she'd seen her father's carriage across the street. Unseen, afraid to move, she watched it, certain that he had discovered her plan and followed her. However, it turned at the next corner and continued down the tree-lined side street. The relief that he hadn't found her gave Abby the courage to follow the vehicle at a discreet distance so she could see where it was going. She should have fled in the other direction and gotten as far away from him as possible, but for some unknown reason, she didn't.

The vehicle came to a stop outside a cluster of modest townhouses. She watched as her father emerged from his coach, walked to the end dwelling, strode quickly up the wide stone steps, and knocked on the door.

A moment later, the door opened and Abby gasped. There, clad in a garish red satin wrapper, her face made up and her hair unbound, was Beth, greeting Harold Breckenridge with a smile and a welcoming kiss.

Abby gagged, swallowing the bile that rose in her throat. She knew then how truly alone she was, and that there was no turning back from her plans.

But last night, for the first time in quite a while, she hadn't felt totally alone. Gussie and the rest of the townsfolk had done their share to alleviate that feeling. And so had Beau McMasters.

Had she done the same for him? It was hard to tell. All Abby knew was that she recognized the loneliness, the isolation that surrounded him last night. He hadn't spoken of it; hadn't needed to. Somehow, some way, she'd understood. And accepted it, as he had hers.

She yawned, in no real hurry to get up. Today was Saturday and she had no important plans, except to move her belongings to her new house and get started settling in.

Her house.

Her property.

Her responsibility.

How good that sounded. The deed had been given to her last evening, presented by the mayor from a grateful community.

When she'd accepted it, she'd felt a bit like a fraud. It was she who owed them a debt, one that she hoped she would be able to repay.

Abby rolled over, wiggling her toes beneath the well-washed, fresh-smelling cotton sheet. A garden. She wanted a garden to cover the bare earth and grass. But what grew here in Montana? Wildflowers by the score;

she'd seen them as she'd come into town. Nothing else came readily to her mind.

Well, wildflowers would be it for now. She would find out later what else could grow here. She'd talk to her neighbors.

Neighbors. Saying the word aloud gave her a sense of rightness, of real joy.

A chuckle escaped her lips as she inched upwards against the headboard. She didn't know a thing about gardening. Or cooking for that matter. Leastwise cooking more than a boiled egg or making oatmeal. Her skills in that area were severely limited, rudimentary at best.

Maybe if she asked Carl to teach her, she could learn enough to get by. And gardening. She'd have to find someone who could show her how and what to plant, and when.

Another chuckle emerged. Digging in the dirt, getting one's hands dirty as a result, and cooking, weren't things considered necessary to learn in her father's house. That was why one hired servants, to see to the domestic chores, duties considered beneath a lady's regard. She was there to supervise, not actually to *do* any of the work.

But Abby wanted to, and far beyond that, *needed* to for her own burgeoning sense of worth. To prove to herself that she could.

And there was no better time than now. Today.

Less than a half-hour later, she was downstairs, the majority of the hotel's breakfast customers having long since eaten their meal and departed. She scanned the room, smiling at the few remaining inhabitants, looking for the masculine face she'd unknowingly counted on seeing.

Too late, she guessed, casting a glance at the tall clock that stood in the corner. After nine-thirty.

"If you're looking for Mr. McMasters, he was up early and gone."

Abby turned, greeting Gussie with a smile. "I wasn't, actually."

Gussie arched her thick brows. "If you say so."

"I do." Another lie, albeit a simple one. She didn't want Gussie to think her a lovesick puppy, desperate for a man's attention. She wasn't. It just would have been nice to have seen him this morning.

"Will you be wanting something to eat?" Gussie inquired.

"Do you think that Carl would mind if I watch him make my breakfast?"

"Can't say as I think he'll mind. Why?"

Abby sighed. "Because," she confessed, "I can't cook."

Gussie grinned broadly. "Shucks. That ain't nothing to fuss over. Anybody can learn to cook. I could throw a meal together if I had a mind to, but why bother when Carl is so much better than me? He's got a way with food that makes me proud and puts me plumb to shame." She paused, giving Abby a wink. " 'Sides, if you plan on havin' guests over when you get into your house, it'll be right nice to fix them something tempting that you made yourself. Many a man's been won over by a woman's skill in the kitchen."

"Then you don't think he'd mind giving me a few instructions?"

"Let's go," Gussie said, taking Abby by the arm and leading her towards the large kitchen at the back of the establishment.

Carl, wearing a homemade apron over a simple work shirt and Levis, was measuring out ingredients for a pie when the ladies walked in to join him; Clara was washing dishes in the sink.

"Abby would like you to give her some lessons in cooking, Carl."

"If you don't object," Abby put in. "I could really use the help."

Carl grinned, revealing one gold tooth in the front of his mouth. "Be happy to, Miss Abby. Just let me get this pie in the oven and I'll start off with a few easy things."

"Sit yourself down right here," Gussie said, pulling out a chair for Abby at the wide table, which was piled with used bowls and mixing cups that Clara whisked away to clean. "I've got work to do, but I'll look in on you directly and see how it's going."

Abby took a seat, gratefully taking the huge, steaming mug of coffee that Gussie offered before she left. "Thanks," she murmured, watching as Carl trimmed the excess pastry dough off the peach pie, reshaping it to layer in a lattice pattern on top.

After he set the pie into the oven to bake, he turned, wiped off his hands and said with a grin, "Let's start with something simple. Breakfast."

Beau had risen early, saddled his horse, and gone riding for a few hours. To clear his head, see more of the surrounding land, or so he told himself as he curried the Paint upon his return to town. A lot of good that had done when he still saw her face, or heard her voice at odd moments. Like when he was in bed last night in the dark, tossing and turning, unable to fall asleep, recalling the feel of Abby Butler in his arms when they danced.

Trouble was, he wanted her in his arms again, but this time, in his bed. Or hers. Didn't matter. Hell, it didn't even have to be a bed. Near a thick stand of pine trees, beside the flowing waters of the creek that bisected his property, or beneath the robin's-egg-blue sky that went on forever.

Was the widow woman ripe for dalliance? A discreet affair of the heart? Because that's all it could be. He wanted no entanglements, no promises, no tomorrows. It was the now that counted.

If not, there was always Trudy's. The banker had been quick to recommend the bawdy house just outside of town. Best whores this side of the Rockies, Davis bragged. A man couldn't do better than to get his itch scratched there.

Beau would certainly keep that option in mind. But right now, he had to keep his thoughts focused on the business that had brought him to this town. Making the ranch he'd won into *his* property; informing the patrons of the saloon that it was under new ownership and would be closing until he could reopen it outfitted the way *he* wanted it to look—like the best, most elegant gaming den in the West. The kind of place that drew customers from all over, eager to try their luck. A place that needed a special name, a unique identity.

Beau laughed softly. Yes, he was that ambitious. The need to make his mark was a hunger yet to be appeased. It had dwelt within him since he was a boy and hadn't abated. Maybe it never would.

But he wouldn't give up. Not until he was satisfied. In every way.

"I decided that rather than try to move in all at once, I'd take a few things over to the house today and do the rest tomorrow, if that's all right with you?"

"I told you before, stay as long as you like, or need to," Gussie insisted, picking up two brown paper-wrapped parcels from the counter while Abby hefted a large wicker basket loaded with extra foodstuffs for her kitchen. Along with a few other items for her house, she had made a totally frivolous purchase, a dime novel, *The Legend of Gambler Jake*.

"You're leaving?" asked a masculine voice.

The ladies hadn't paid close attention to the sound of boots on the floorboards behind them, indicating another customer had entered the general store.

At the sound of that voice, both women immediately turned to face the speaker.

"I'm not going far," Abby said, her eyes fixed upward on the man standing before her. Today he was in basic black, broken only by the stark whiteness of his shirt and the gleam of his teeth. "Just to my new house."

"Then allow me to escort you both and give you a hand carrying those heavy burdens."

"That's not necessary, Mr. McMasters. I'm sure you're a very busy man," Abby protested softly. She thought that it might perhaps be better to keep some distance between them, given her disturbing fascination with him. And she'd deliberately chosen to use the formal form of address in Gussie's presence, despite his insistence last night that she call him Beau.

He, however, had other ideas. "Never too busy, Mrs. Butler, to help a lady," Beau replied with a wicked grin, easily removing the basket from her arm. He hadn't missed Abby's use of "Mr." when addressing him. The dark of the night had proved intimate; the light of the day set things back into a more formal perspective. "Now, if you'll show me where to deliver these."

Abby realized that he wasn't going to give up, so she straightened her shoulders and walked out the open door, leaving the others to follow. "It's not far. Close by the school."

"Well, now that you've got a helper, I'll go back to the hotel," Gussie said with a broad smile.

Abby almost groaned. Gussie was so transparent in her attempt to leave the two of them alone together. "I'd really like it if you came along too, Gussie," Abby insisted. "I could fix some tea and christen my new place."

Gussie heard the plea in her new friend's voice, but chose to ignore it. "You two run along. 'Sides, it's too hot for tea today. Why don't you both come back to the hotel when you're done and we'll celebrate with a pitcher of lemonade instead?" Without waiting for an answer, she stepped off the sidewalk and crossed the street, leaving Abby and Beau standing there.

Gussie Travers wasn't the only one who recognized the plea in Abby's voice. Beau heard it also. And it puzzled him. Why the sudden shyness, the hesitation to be alone with him?

"Have I offended you in some way?" he asked.

"Of course not," she responded. He must think her rude, when that was the farthest thing from her mind. He was simply being the gentleman he was brought up to be, helping a lady, nothing more. Obviously it was she who was dwelling on last night, giving it more importance that it deserved. Realizing that they were attracting a few stares from passersby, Abby conceded defeat gracefully. "Follow me," she said.

About ten minutes later they arrived at the door to her new home, having been stopped only twice by someone wanting to say hello, or introduce themselves. Abby removed the key from her reticule, turning the lock and opening the door. Ushering her guest inside, she took another look around, smiling as she did so. The contrast of this place to where she'd grown up was remarkable. Her tiny house here in Heaven's Grace could fit comfortably into the ballroom of her family's Fifth Avenue mansion, but at this moment, she wouldn't trade it for the world. Even unlived in, this place was much warmer, much more to her liking, than the cold enclosure in which she'd been raised.

"Where would you like these things, Mrs. Butler?"

It was his deep, warm voice, a voice she realized she would recognize any time, any place, that snapped Abby back to reality.

"Please," she said, indicating the table, "put them there."

Beau did so, and watched as she unpacked the items in

the basket. He was tempted to offer to help, but thought better of it. This was something he understood, the need to be in charge of one's own life, to arrange it so that it fit you and what you wanted.

And, he enjoyed observing her as she moved around the room, the swing of her long, golden-red hair captured in a braid that ran the length of her back, brushing the waistband of her skirt. A thin navy blue grosgrain ribbon, which matched the color of her wide skirt, held the plait together. Her white blouse was tailored, with no fuss or frills. Just plain and maybe slightly prim. His eyes were drawn to the rise and fall of her breasts each time she moved or took a breath.

Damn! She looked young, and much too vulnerable.

Perhaps that was part of what pulled him toward her. The vulnerability in her eyes. It was something he hadn't seen in a woman's eyes in a long time. In others he'd observed resignation, the spirit within long since dead or dying; cold ambition, emotions ruled by greed or the hunger for power no matter what the cost; weakness, the trapped, wounded soul of a prisoner of fear and loathing; contempt, the superior glances of dismissal and disapproval that had been directed his way; anger, the heated snap of fire; calculation, the playing of odds; or lust, the undeniable craving for satisfaction; and even in some instances, kindness, the soft appeal of comfort.

But he also saw pride reflected deep in Abby Butler's blue eyes, and a will that wouldn't be broken. In that, he recognized a characteristic he'd seen, on occasion, in his mother's eyes, as well as his own.

God, she was intriguing. That was something he hadn't felt about a woman in a long time. His dormant curiosity was piqued, prodded in such a way as to be achingly alive.

Abby could feel his gaze on her as she made quick work of arranging her purchases, taking care to leave the novel in the basket, hidden from his view. It was a sign of her innate grace that she hadn't dropped anything in her haste to complete her task. She was aware of how he seemed to fill her kitchen, imbuing it with a masculine magnetism that was as real and elemental as the forces of nature.

She was trying to put away a sack of sugar on a high shelf, lifting herself on tiptoe to reach it when she felt the heat and solid strength of his body behind hers. His hand removed the article from hers and easily placed it where she wanted it to go.

They remained there, spooned against one another, for no more than an instant before she turned, lifting her head to look into his face. The glance they exchanged seemed to go on forever, though less than a minute had actually passed. It was the slow stroking of his index finger along her cheek and down her throat that made Abby's eyes drift shut.

Then, abruptly, the caress ended.

"I think we'd better be getting back to the hotel, or else Mrs. Travers will wonder what's become of us," Beau said softly, moving toward the doorway. God, how he wanted to linger, to continue, not to mention take it further, closer, by joining his mouth to hers, learning the taste and touch of her.

Abby's eyes snapped open. Better, she cautioned herself, to keep them that way, open and clear, as they'd always been.

"Yes, I think we'd better do just that," she echoed, unaware, as they walked out of her house, that someone was watching them.

He stood far enough away in the shadows of the pine that he wasn't noticed by the couple.

Whore of Babylon and the spawn of a defeated enemy, he thought, anger and bitterness welling up inside him.

They were up to no good, he could feel that in his bones. But now wasn't the time to strike. He must be patient and wait for a sign.

Then, God's will be done.

Chapter Seven

Since it was her first Sunday in town, Abby decided that she would make an effort to attend church that morning.

However, after that day's service, she doubted that she would be in a hurry to go back. A little of the Reverend Whitcomb went a long way. He was most definitely a "hellfire and damnation" preacher, one who saw sin and corruption in every part of life and who warned his flock about the inherent ruin they all faced. As she'd sat there, listening to the cold-eyed parson who called himself a man of God, she couldn't help comparing him to the Reverend Alden of St. Timothy's, the small, quietly elegant, well-supported Episcopal church she'd attended in New York. Alden's weekly sermons stressed God's love and forgiveness, the spirit of brotherhood, the need to open one's heart to the tender mercies found in following one's faith. Reverend Alden saw God as pure love and preached accordingly.

Whitcomb saw God as man's jailer and practiced accordingly.

No wonder less than half the town had come to the

church that morning. If this was what waited for them, they would do better to find their own path to the deity.

Like a sudden sweep of wind, a memory flashed into her mind. Even now, several years later, she could still recall the looks on the faces of the two people who'd come to St. Timothy's to be married one evening. She'd offered to be a witness, since neither the bride nor the groom had family close by. Watching the couple exchange their vows in front of no one but the reverend and herself, Abby was struck by the deep love clearly visible in their eyes.

Theirs was a real marriage, not a brokered deal for the aggrandizement of wealth and power. Jedidah Stone had been a soldier in the Union Army, wounded in Gettysburg. Sally Malone had been a maid in Abby's house, determined to marry the man she loved, no matter that he was missing his left leg, having left it in a heap along with the other amputated limbs of his fellow soldiers in a makeshift battlefield hospital.

She'd stood there, listened to them speak their vows, knew they'd meant them with all their hearts. That night she had beheld a shining example of what real love was—a true, lifelong commitment between a man and a woman who understood, respected, and accepted one another.

It was then, too, that Abby realized she couldn't settle for less than that for herself. Her wedding gift to them had been fifty dollars to help them start their new life. Their gift to her had been equally important—they'd opened her eyes to the possibility that someone could care for her in the same way and not just because she was Harold Breckenridge's daughter, heiress to his considerable fortune.

Noise in the street brought Abby back to reality. She dodged the buckboard coming in her direction and narrowly missed being ambushed by a group of children playing what looked like a rambunctious game of tag.

Smiling, Abby crossed to the hotel, in need of a strong cup of coffee.

As she entered the building, she was stopped by a woman seated at the table nearest the door, who reached out her hand to lightly grasp Abby's arm.

"Mrs. Butler?"

"Yes?" Abby responded.

The thin blonde woman dropped her hand and rose from her chair. "Can we talk to you?" She indicated the woman who shared the table with her, a robust black woman. "That is, if you don't mind being seen with us?"

Abby surveyed each of them quickly—they were dressed in respectable attire—and saw nothing to object to or question. "And why should I mind?" she inquired.

" 'Cause we work at Trudy's," the blonde replied. Seeing the blank look on Abby's face at the mention of her employer, the woman explained. "It's a sporting house ma'am."

"Oh," Abby said, a slight hint of color flushing her cheeks. "I see."

"So, Glory and me won't be offended if you refuse to talk to us like most of the ladies in this here town. We're kinda used to it. Only Gussie is nice to us, letting us take meals here when we've a hankering to."

"I'm sure that she feels your money is as good as anyone else's," Abby replied, silently adding, *no matter how it's earned.* Bartering, that's what she'd heard these women did. Exchanged their bodies for money.

In another time, another place, Abby realized that she might have been forced into the same situation, by her own father. *Judge not lest ye be judged.*

Abby addressed the blonde with a smile. "Do you mind if I sit down?"

Both women smiled in return. "No ma'am. Join us," the blonde said.

Abby took a seat at their table, stopping Clara to ask her to bring a cup of coffee.

"Coming right up, Miss Abby," the girl replied.

"Now," Abby said, concentrating on the blonde, who appeared to be the spokeswoman for the pair, "what do you want to discuss?"

The two women exchanged glances, then the blonde said, "Glory and me—I'm Cassie—we'd like to get us some book learning. You know, readin' and writin'."

"You want me to tutor you?"

"If that means teach us, yes, we do."

Abby's lips twitched with pleasure at the other woman's quick grasp. "It does."

"We can pay you, too," Cassie added proudly. "Whatever you want."

Abby thought the idea over for a minute. Teaching them would be a challenge of a different sort. "We can leave that until later if you'd like."

Cassie shook her head. "We don't want charity, Mrs. Butler. We get paid real well for our"—Cassie hesitated as she searched for the right word to describe her job— "experience."

Color again heated Abby's cheeks; she wet her lips. "I'm sure that you do."

"Then name your price."

Clara returned with her coffee and Abby took the opportunity to take a sip while she tried to decide what amount would be fair. It seemed that soiled doves had pride too—to refuse to charge would only offend them. Their lives came with a price tag, services—whatever they might be—rendered for money, and they clearly didn't want, or expect, favors from her.

Abby put down her cup and named what she thought was an adequate price. "How about a dollar a month?"

Cassie looked at her companion before she spoke. "Too low. We can pay more. After all," she said with a big smile, "we're Trudy's best girls. Five dollars would be better."

"All right," Abby replied, accepting the fee. "Now, when do you want to start?"

"How about next week?" Cassie asked hopefully.

"What's wrong with today?" Abby suggested, taking another sip of her steaming coffee. "Or are you . . . busy?" She wondered what it was exactly that they did for their male customers. Her knowledge of what happened between a man and a woman was sketchy at best. Her mother had never mentioned *it,* except to say that *it*—whatever *it* was—was "a woman's duty." The obedience she owed her husband and her lot in life to bear. Only men, her mother had stressed, got pleasure in the marriage bed, for women were above that sort of thing.

But, Abby wondered, were they? Here she was pretending to be a widow, a woman who'd lived with a man as his legal wife, with all that it implied. Abby was well and truly trapped by her own ignorance, for she couldn't admit her lie, that she was unwed and hadn't a clue what actually transpired between husband and wife. Was it as bad as her mother intimated? If so, then why did these girls look as if they liked being the "best"? And how did one judge the "best"?

She wished that she could have asked for an answer. Since coming out West, she'd seen some things, like animals mating. Was *it* anything like that?

"We don't have to work until after nine on Sunday nights. Trudy believes in keeping the day for rest and relaxing, 'cause Saturday night's our full-house night."

"Then Sunday it is," Abby said.

"You're not gonna back down, are you?" the blonde asked. " 'Cause we're real serious about this."

"No, I won't back down." Abby promised. She could see how important this was to them. "You have my word." She held out her hand.

The blonde hesitated for a moment, unused to a lady freely extending her hand to a whore. Tentatively, Cassie stretched out her own hand, as if expecting Abby to pull hers away at the very last minute. "Thank you, ma'am."

Glory added her thanks, too.

"Now, where and when?"

"That's up to you, Mrs. Butler. We know you can't come to a sporting house. That won't do for a proper lady."

"No, I don't think it would," Abby answered, silently acknowledging her position in the town. "What about my house?"

Cassie's big eyes grew even wider, clearly revealing her shock. "You'd invite us there, to your own home?"

Abby didn't hesitate in her response. "Yes."

"You really don't mind?"

"No," Abby answered truthfully. "That should be best for all concerned. I have a few things to do beforehand, so why don't we make it around three? Is that convenient for both of you?"

"That's fine, ma'am. Real fine."

"My house isn't far from here."

"Oh, we know where it is."

Abby's brows rose. "You do?"

Cassie smiled. "One of my most important and steady customers told me all about it. He was right proud that the town hired you."

Abby took another drink from her cup. How odd to discover that one's name was being bandied about in a house of ill repute.

A small smile curved her mouth. Her mother would have died of shame, and yet in the context explained, Abby found it oddly amusing.

"We'd best be going." Both women rose, leaving coins on the table in payment for their breakfast. "See you later then, Mrs. Butler."

Gussie crossed the room a minute later as Abby was finishing her coffee. "What was that all about?"

"They wanted to hire me—"

"For the *whorehouse?*"

Abby swallowed a laugh and shook her head.

"For what, then?" Gussie took one of the vacated seats.

"To teach them."

"Well, I'll be. What did you say?"

"That I would."

"Good for you. Their money's as good as anyone's. Better, considering how hard they gotta work to earn it. Ain't my idea of a life"—Gussie shrugged—"but that's just me." She leaned closer to Abby and whispered, "The thought of a parade of men as randy as goats waiting in line to rattle my bones doesn't sit well with me. Although," she added with a twinkle in her eyes, "there are a few exceptions I might make if I could do the pickin' and the choosin', and was a single lady. But, I ain't, 'sides, Carl's more than enough man for me."

Abby smiled in response, wishing that she knew what it was that Gussie was describing so that she could get the joke.

Sometimes, and this was one of those times, ignorance was a damnable nuisance.

The saloon was almost empty; obviously Sunday morning wasn't their busiest time.

The lingering smell of stale beer and ever staler bodies assaulted his nose once again as Beau walked in, a sure sign that cleanliness wasn't standard practice in this establishment. That would be one of the many things he would change.

It was also exceedingly dark; one window facing the street was crudely boarded up to cover the massive hole in the glass. Cigar and cigarette butts from overturned brass spittoons crunched under his boot heels. To the left, one lone cowboy seemed to be sleeping off a late night, the stench of vomit close by.

Beau fought a rising tide of anger and disgust at the condition of the place. This wasn't a saloon, it was a disaster.

But one that could, and would, be rectified, starting now.

He crossed the room, stood by the piano and tapped out a few notes. The damned thing needed to be tuned; the flat notes abraded his trained ear. He noticed stains left from glasses placed on the top of the upright, along with black burn marks from tobacco. Though not quite the elegant grand piano his mother had taught him to play on, it would do once it was retuned.

Beau looked around the room. The beefy bartender was snoring, mouth agape, sprawled out in a chair. The stupid bastard hadn't even bothered to lock the place up before he fell asleep. A robber could have bled this place dry.

Then again, Beau doubted that a would-be robber would get very much in the way of profit from this establishment in its current form.

He heard the stumbling, shuffling sounds of someone coming down the creaky wooden stairs and turned to look up, his hand on his revolver just in case.

It was another of the saloon's whores, looking very much the worse for wear. Her stringy, hennaed hair hung matted in uncombed rat's tales and her makeup was smudged, making her resemble a dirty dish crusted with leftovers. It was obvious that she hadn't seen a bathtub, or even a basin of fresh water, in some time. The ripe, pungent odor of unwashed flesh mixed with a very cheap perfume assailed his nostrils as she stepped near.

"Lookin' for a little early lovin', honey?" she said in a high-pitched voice when she saw him standing there.

His response was short, cold and emphatic. "No."

She rubbed at her sleep-encrusted eyes, pausing on the landing before proceeding down the last two steps. "Suit yourself, Mr. High-and-Mighty," she said as she walked past him. Her bare feet scuffed across the floor as she went behind the bar and reached for a bottle of whiskey. Pulling out the cork, she tipped her head back and drank heartily from it, wiping her hand across her mouth when she was done.

"Want a drink?" She offered Beau the bottle when he approached her. She leaned suggestively closer to him, her dirty wrapper falling open to reveal the skin beneath.

Hell, he thought, he could certainly use a good drink, but he wasn't about to sample the swill that was passed off here as prime liquor. Once was enough.

With a dazzling smile, he took the bottle from her hand, grasped it by the neck, and smashed it onto the bar, spilling the contents.

Rivulets ran across the top, marking the cheap wood.

"You crazy or what?" the whore asked, startled by the fancy man's sudden show of violence. "That stuff costs two bits a bottle."

The bartender woke up quickly. "What?" he asked sleepily. "What the hell is going on?"

Beau dropped what remained of the neck of the bottle to the floor. "You're fired," he said, addressing the bartender.

The man rose slowly from his chair, a mean look on his pockmarked face. "I'm what?"

"You heard me."

"Just who the hell do you think you are?" the bartender snapped, reaching for his gun.

Before the man could retrieve his weapon, Beau had his Remington unholstered and in his hand, aiming it in the bartender's direction. "The new owner."

The beefy man blinked, easing his hand away from his gun. "What?"

"I want you out of here. Take your gear and the rest of the trash"—Beau gave a nod of his head in the direction of the woman behind him—"with you."

"Hey now," the man protested, his voice going from sullen to pleading, "you can't do this."

Beau smiled. It was an engaging expression that had fooled many people who never bothered to look behind the charm to the underlying steel will. "Oh, but I can and I am."

"I'm owed money," the former bartender protested. "And I ain't leaving till I get what's coming to me."

"Have you ever heard the saying 'be careful what you wish for'?" Beau asked as he cocked the hammer of the gun, watching the man swallow nervously. "No, I thought not," he answered for the bartender. "I figure that you've been lining your pockets very well in the absence of the previous owner, so consider *that* your money due."

"You're making a big mistake. You need a man like me to run this place."

Beau's mouth curved into a smile again. "I think not."

"You can't mean me, too, honey?" the woman wailed, coming from around the bar and sidling close to Beau.

"Oh," he said in his most charming tone, his hand lifting the weapon until the long barrel of the gun coldly caressed her face from cheek to throat, "but I do, *chérie*."

"You damned Rebel bastard!" she snarled, making a gesture as if she meant to spit in his face.

In a soft, deadly voice, Beau warned, "I wouldn't if I were you."

She shrank back. The look in his eyes told her he wasn't kidding.

Beau pulled his gold pocket watch from his vest and checked the time. "If the two of you are not out of here in twenty minutes, I'll have you both thrown in jail for trespassing." He pointed the gun back towards the bartender while the woman took the opportunity to run back upstairs. "Unbuckle that belt and drop it. Kick it over here."

The other man complied.

"Good. Now take whatever's yours and get out of here." Beau bent and picked up the gun belt as the man moved in the direction of the stairs, tossing the shoddy leather rig over his shoulder. Then he went behind the bar and removed the sawed-off shotgun from its hiding place. He checked to see if it was loaded, removed the shells, and put it back. Next, he emptied the bartender's pistol as well, pushing it onto a shelf out of the way.

Satisfied, he walked a short distance from the bar, choosing a seat against the wall, where he could see the room. He sat, marveling at the cowboy who remained asleep, oblivious of what had transpired.

Beau reached into his coat and withdrew his cigar case, placed a slim cheroot into his mouth, then removing a match from the small silver case that held them, struck it across the table with a snap of his wrist, lighting his cigar.

In several weeks the furniture and equipment he'd ordered in San Francisco would be arriving, sent by train and then by wagon, along with a couple of girls he'd enticed away from the Golden Palace. Daisy and Flora would add a welcome touch of class and spice to the soon-to-be-refurbished surroundings. With them as hostesses, his club would be able to attract a better sort of customer, the kind that came back for more and brought friends.

He'd also placed orders with one of San Francisco's finest wine merchants and arranged for a continuous supply of the very best liquor, especially champagne and brandies. Cases of whiskey, including imported Irish and Scotch, along with Kentucky's excellent bourbon, would soon be on hand for his patrons' drinking pleasure. Rotgut moonshine on these premises was a thing of the past, starting immediately.

Beau hadn't forgotten that he needed some furnishings for his ranch house, either. A telegram to his great-aunt in New Orleans had taken care of that. She'd see to it that the pieces he wanted were removed from storage and shipped up the Mississippi, then overland. He'd waited a long time to claim what was part of his heritage, and little by little, he was taking possession. His dreams were becoming a reality. No one and nothing was going to stop him. Not now, not ever.

Beau glanced up at the seedy-looking buffalo head hanging over the back of the bar. One eye was missing, as was some of the beast's fur.

"You're next," he said, coolly taking aim.

The buffalo was now completely blind.

"Funny how quickly a body can get used to another person, ain't it, Mr. McMasters?" Gussie asked as she laid a plate filled with fresh pan-fried trout and mashed potatoes in front of him.

"I suppose so," Beau responded, slicing into the tender fish.

"Ain't no supposin' about it," she said. "I'm sure gonna miss havin' Abby Butler hereabouts."

Beau's fork halted halfway to his mouth. "She's gone?"

Gussie nodded.

"Where?"

"Finished moving into her own place today. I asked her to have dinner here tonight but she said that she wanted to get used to eating alone, the sooner the better."

She hadn't even said good-bye, he thought. Simply walked out of his life with not so much as a "by your leave" or a "fare-thee-well."

Who was he kidding? She owed him nothing.

But still . . .

"She plumb forgot to take the pie Carl baked for her as a welcoming gift. And I can't deliver it," Gussie said with a sigh. "Tonight's my ladies quilting circle."

He casually offered, "Why not let me?"

"You wouldn't mind?" she asked, unable to completely disguise the pleased tone in her voice.

Beau saw through Gussie's machinations and accepted them since they didn't conflict with his own plans. "I'd be most happy to take the pie, with your compliments."

"Not too much trouble?"

"Think nothing of it," he reassured her with a seductive smile. "My pleasure, entirely."

"That eases my mind considerably," she stated. "I would hate to see such a fine pie go to waste."

"I doubt that would have happened."

Gussie chuckled. "You're probably right, Mr. McMasters. Carl makes one fine pecan pie, if I do say so myself."

"Pecan?"

"You like that?"

"I've been known to eat a few slices on occasion." He thought of the wonderful recipe that his mother had made when he was a child, rich and sweet, thick with roasted pecans and a touch of bourbon.

Gussie gave him a searching glance. "Can't tell." She patted her own ample hips. "Wish I could say the same for me."

Beau grinned and stated gallantly, "I'm sure that Mr. Travers doesn't have a single complaint."

She returned his grin with one of her own. "Not a single one." She glanced at Beau's empty cup. "Clara, come here and give Mr. McMasters some coffee 'fore he decides to take his business somewhere else."

"Not a chance," he replied as Clara hurried over to refill his cup.

It had been a long day and Abby was tired. Her first session with Cassie and Glory had gone better than she'd expected. They were both eager to learn, and made good use of their time, promising to keep to a schedule of practicing their letters until the next lesson.

They were so unlike the image she'd had in her mind of women forced into prostitution. Neither one was a downtrodden victim begging for help. Each had her reasons for choosing their particular line of work; they'd been straightforward regarding it that afternoon. What surprised Abby was their honesty in telling her why they had chosen their profession, and the practical way they looked at what they did.

While Cassie was the more talkative of the two, Glory was not lacking in the wherewithal to express herself.

The first word Cassie wanted to learn to spell was "whore."

When Abby asked her why, the blonde replied, "Because that's what I am."

Abby had responded, "You're more than that."

"Not now, Miss Abby," Cassie stated, "but I aim to be."

Their frankness was another reminder to Abby of her own treasure chest of fabrications and half-truths.

Pushing that thought aside, she cleared away the remains of her supper, which had been very simple, consisting of a hearty sandwich and coffee. No need, she thought, to overtax her cooking skills, such as they were, the first night in her new home.

Abby glanced around the kitchen, her nostrils filled with the smell of coffee brewing as she made a fresh pot. It mingled with that of the lovely vanilla-scented beeswax candles she'd brought with her from Denver. Placed upon the table, they gave the room a sweet scent, so much better than the oil from a lamp. Candlelight was softer, gentler, more romantic, as her aunt Hettie used to say.

Romantic.

Abby was a spinster masquerading as a widow. What need or use had she for romance?

Her gaze fell on the dime novel that lay on the table where she'd left it. Not quite epic literature, yet it spoke to her, the author being, surprisingly, a female also. She felt somehow connected to the plight of the heroine, caught between her concern for the town's sheriff, her childhood friend, and the handsome, devil-may-care gambler who'd recently come to town. In the end, the heroine chose love over mild affection.

It was all so simple, easily wrapped up in the slim volume. If only her own problems could be so easily solved.

But they couldn't be. That was why she had to run, hiding from the whole truth. Her father would never willingly let her have control of her life. And she would never capitulate, having tasted freedom, having been willing to pay the price for leaving the gilded cage.

Too much had happened ever to go back and pretend otherwise.

A smile kicked up the corners of Abby's generous mouth. So what if the hero of the story had been big and blond, with the looks of a Germanic prince, and the sheriff slim and dark? When she read the novel, she saw them reversed.

The knock on her door startled her.

Grabbing the dime novel, she quickly thrust it behind a tin of coffee in the pantry.

Abby moved to answer the door, trying to wipe from her mind the picture of a dark-haired man with a slow, Southern drawl.

"Who is it?" she called out, her hand on the bolt, a frisson of fear sliding along her nerves as she realized that she was all alone.

"Open the door and find out," the masculine voice challenged.

The breath caught in her throat and without a second thought, she unlocked the door.

Chapter Eight

"I come bearing a gift," Beau declared as he stepped across her threshold, a tip of his dark hat in her direction.

"Isn't that what the Greeks said to the Trojans?" Abby asked, head tilted to one side, eyes sparkling. "Should I be suspicious?"

Beau laughed, and replied in mock horror. "Why, you wound me, ma'am. My intentions are strictly honorable." *At least for the present moment,* he added to himself. God, but she looked enticing, even so simply dressed. Tonight her long hair fell loose about her slim frame, held back from her face by two plain combs that anchored the waves. Pleasure, he was sure, could be had by reaching out his hand and stroking it, feeling the texture as it drifted through his fingers. Enhanced by candlelight, it glowed with an inner fire.

Once again, she thought, he seemed to overwhelm the room—or was it merely that he overwhelmed her?—when he stepped inside. "So," she asked, moving toward the stove and removing the coffeepot, "what is it that you've brought me?"

"Food of the gods."

Abby paused in the act of pouring two cups. It struck her then that she hadn't even asked him to stay and join her. She'd automatically lifted another cup from the shelf without thinking.

"And that would be?" Abby asked, resuming her task.

"Pecan pie, fresh from Carl's oven. Gussie said it was to be a housewarming gift. Since she couldn't bring it herself, as she had someplace else to be, I volunteered to see it to your door."

Her eyes momentarily feasted on his face before she forced herself to break the contact. "How very thoughtful of you, Mr. McMasters."

"Beau," he said softly, reminding her of their whispered words of the other night.

"How very thoughtful," she repeated as she placed the cups filled with fresh coffee on the table, "Beau."

He gifted her with a self-mocking smile as he placed the pie on her table. "Now, that wasn't so difficult, was it?"

"No." It might not be difficult, Abby decided, but it certainly was *intimate,* as was the situation she found herself in now, with him, alone, in her kitchen, getting ready to sit down and share coffee and dessert. She'd felt that smile all the way down to her toes. A tingling vibration of electricity that passed from him to her, like a charge of lightning skipping along her veins.

She brought out small, everyday china plates, along with her cutlery, and realized that this simple task was giving her more than a modicum of pleasure. Perhaps, she admitted honestly, it was also the company.

Oh yes, she decided, it was very much the company.

As she made to sit down, he said, "Allow me," and held out the chair for her.

"Thank you," Abby replied, taking a deep breath. She undid the ribbon that held the cloth together and unwrapped it, then removed the pie plate from inside. She could smell the fragrant aroma of pecans, molasses, and melted sugar. "Mmm," she said, inhaling deeply. "Heaven."

"Or at least close to it," he added, thinking that it was the receiver rather than the gift that deserved the appellation of divine.

"You will join me, won't you?" She didn't care right then what anyone would say about her entertaining a single gentleman in her house, or even how this would look. All that mattered was the moment. Her new situation demanded a certain standard of behavior, yet she couldn't dismiss him, couldn't insist that since he'd discharged his duty, he should leave.

What she *should* do, and what she *would* do, were two different things.

Beau removed his hat, placing it on the nearby wooden rack by the door. "I'd be most honored."

Manners smooth as silk and a tongue to match, she thought as she cut through the pie, giving him the first slice, then cutting another for herself. This made up for the guilt she'd felt this morning when she left the hotel without telling him good-bye. She'd wanted to. She didn't want to speculate why it had become so important, preferring to focus on the here and now.

And he was there, eating with her in easy familiarity as if they'd known each other all their lives instead of mere days. What was it about this stranger that made her feel more at ease with him than she had with her own flesh and blood?

"I'm sorry that I didn't have an opportunity to say my farewells when I left the hotel today," she said as her fork lifted for another bite of pie, "but you weren't to be found on the premises."

"You looked for me?" he asked, his eyes meeting and holding hers. "I had business to take care of that couldn't wait."

"On a Sunday?" Abby realized that her remark might sound a trifle derisive, which she hadn't meant, so she hastened to clarify. "Forgive me. I didn't mean that as a criticism." She lowered her lashes, concentrating on the taste of the pecans instead of staring into his long-lashed eyes.

"None taken," Beau hastened to add. "It's just another day of the week, more or less."

"Really?"

She sounded surprised, he thought. And why not? Obviously she'd been raised on her weekly dose of faith and salvation, same as he'd been. However, he had discovered that Sunday was no magic talisman against the demons. As a child he'd believed that. As an adult he knew better. He'd learned that lesson as a youth, watching, powerless to help, unable to break the bonds that held him, as his mother and father were driven from their home by a crowd bent on vengeance and retribution. That crowd had cared little that it was the Lord's day when they jeered, cursed and spat upon the couple, whipped into a frenzy, he'd later found out, by remarks attributed to his grandfather.

"Yes."

The one word he uttered carried a weight, a certainty that needed no other explanation, even if it did raise Abby's curiosity.

Beau looked into those blue eyes, now filled with questions, questions she was far too polite to ask. In someone else he might have been amused at reluctance to satisfy blatant inquisitiveness; in others he would have turned a blind eye on an attempt to delve into his affairs. With her, he found himself tendering an explanation of his business. "I closed the Bad Penny today."

"The saloon?" Gussie and Mayor Cooper had pointed the run-down establishment out on their walk through town.

Beau nodded.

"New broom sweeps clean?"

Beau lifted his fork and took another bite of the sumptuous pie. "You could say so."

"And what'll you do with it?"

"First, give it what you said: a thorough cleaning. The condition that place is in makes a pig pen look positively regal in comparison." He couldn't keep the disgust from his voice.

Abby laughed. "If it looked as bad inside as it did outside, I can see why you would need to do that."

"My dear, it looked even worse. However, it's nothing money, and a professional eye, can't fix." Beau took delight in telling her about the stuffed buffalo head that had hung over the bar until he paid someone to bury it on the outskirts of town.

"Why there? And why bury it?"

"Call it a peace offering, or simple justice."

Abby wondered what he meant, but declined to ask. "Are you going to reopen the saloon?"

"Yes and no." He gave her an enigmatic smile that she couldn't ignore.

"Meaning?" she demanded softly as she rose to get more coffee for both of them, returning a moment later with the pot in her hands.

He liked the fact that she asked questions; that she wasn't afraid to engage him in conversation, unlike some women who merely sat politely and let him do all the talking. That could be so boring, so predictable. She was neither.

"I do plan to reopen it, but not as a simple saloon."

"You, I think, would never do anything *simple*," she stated without hesitation. "I'd hazard a guess that it's not in your nature."

Observant, too. With a slight nod of his head, he responded. "Thank you for the compliment. I intend to have the finest gambling emporium in the West rebuilt on the premises. A bar unlike anything ever seen around here:

stocked with top quality liquor instead of the pigswill that was formerly served. And I mean to change the name, along with the image."

"To what?"

"What do you think of the Creole Lady?"

Abby thought about it for a moment. It sounded like something filled with old-world charm, evoking a lush sense of style and place. "Definitely distinctive, especially in this area."

"That's the idea."

"Then it works." She smiled. "Something tells me that there will be nothing else like it in all of Montana." It would be unique, just like him. Sophisticated. Elegant. A breed apart.

"Will you honor me by being my personal guest at the opening?" His voice was soft, enticing. "Although, I will understand if you feel that you cannot. I do realize it's a great favor I'm asking of you."

Favor? Couldn't he see that he was doing her one? That by offering to share his moment of glory, he was according her a measure of respect as an individual. Women weren't welcomed to gentlemen's clubs in New York, where gambling was a popular entertainment. Even friendly games in the homes of society's elite banned women. The brandy and cigars were for men, just like the games of chance. Their exclusive domain.

"Have I offended you?"

"No," she replied, "you most certainly have not. I'd be happy to come to your grand opening, whenever it is."

"If for any reason you change your mind, don't hesitate to tell me." Pressure could be brought to bear upon her, he realized, from those in the town who might frown upon the new school teacher consorting with the owner of a gaming establishment, even if he owned one of the largest ranches in the area, too.

"I won't," she promised. "And I never break my

word"—she paused, clarifying her statement—"especially to a friend."

Friend? Was that how she saw him? Damned if that was all he saw in her. Friend didn't begin to cover it.

"When will you begin teaching school?"

That was an abrupt switch of topics, Abby thought, watching as he helped himself to another slice of pie albeit a thin one. "Next week."

"And what are you doing tomorrow?"

"I was planning on going to the schoolhouse in the morning and sorting through the books and papers that are there to see what the previous teacher had done with the children. I'm afraid the texts I observed from my brief visit the other day seemed woefully old, the bindings frayed and torn. I may have to order some new books, which appear to be a rarity in this town. Maybe I can interest the town council in building a library. That's a good idea, don't you think?"

Abby thought of the hundreds of volumes lying dormant in her parents' house. Hundreds of books going to waste for want of readers. Only she had ever made use of the grand library, finding it a refuge from the reality of life outside its doors. The books could be put to much better use here, where they were scarce. What a gift she could bestow on her new home.

But, she acknowledged, that would remain forever out of her reach. Any claim she could have made on those books was gone.

He could read her face clearly when she talked. The idea of a library, of books themselves, brought out a light in her eyes, a hint of a smile on her wide mouth. "It's an excellent idea," he confirmed.

Beau imagined that the town might be lacking in the necessary means to fund a project such as a library. He had both, along with numerous leather-bound volumes in careful storage back in New Orleans. And more could be ordered. Enough to fill a building of some size, with more than enough for his personal use left over.

"I'll back you on that, whenever you want. Just say the word."

Abby regarded him over her coffee cup. "You will?" She was surprised and pleased. "Why?"

"Because ignorance is never really bliss, it's merely ignorance. Besides, if I plan to be part of this town for some time to come, then I should see that it's all it can be."

The urge to touch him, to reach out her hand and squeeze his in companionable agreement was almost overwhelming.

But she couldn't. What would he think if she did? Such an overture might be misconstrued, thus damaging the tenuous bonds of friendship they were forging. She wasn't a practiced flirt, able to charm a man while holding him at arm's length. Nor was she completely comfortable with the attraction she felt for Beau McMasters. It was much stronger, sharper, than anything she'd experienced before. And since it was all so new, it was somewhat frightening.

Beau also had the urge to touch Abby. To run his thumb along the contours of her mouth, stroke his knuckles across the curve of her cheek; skim his fingers down her throat.

But he wouldn't. Not yet. The time wasn't right.

Instead, he asked, "Will you come riding with me tomorrow?"

"I'd like that," she answered.

"Good. Leave it to me to arrange everything." Beau rose. "I'd best be leaving now."

Abby also got up. "Thank you again for bringing me dessert, and staying to share it with me."

"It was my pleasure, Abby." Beau reached for his hat and put it on. God, how he wanted to kiss her. Take those lips with his and feast on the honey they contained. He paused, reaching for her hand instead. He brought it to his lips, lingering briefly before saying in a darkly seductive whisper, "Your servant, ma'am."

Then he was gone.

Abby leaned against the closed door, holding out her hand. The skin still tingled where his bearded lips had touched. What, she wondered with a reckless abandon, would those lips have felt like against her own? Soft? Teasing? Or masterful? Her previous experience of kissing had left her unmoved, or worse yet, bored, as if something were missing.

Now, thinking about his lips, she grew warm, a flush of heat centered deep in her belly, but reaching out to all parts of her.

Intoxicated. That's how she felt. As if she'd indulged in too much champagne. Giddy with sensations and an unexplained longing. For what, she just wasn't sure.

But whatever it was, she suspected he held the key.

"You sure can pick 'em, Mr. McMasters," said Josh, the thin lad who worked at the livery stable mucking out stalls and feeding the horses. "She's a real beaut."

Beau ran his hand along the filly's neck, smiling with pleasure as the animal responded to his knowing, instinctive touch. "She is, isn't she?"

"Who's she for?"

"A lady."

"Sorta figured that. It weren't for no man, nor no whore, that's for sure. This here animal is quality."

Beau's dark brows rose. "What would you know about whores?"

The boy scuffed his booted foot against the straw. "My pa's gonna take me to Trudy's next month for my thirteenth birthday. Said time's come to be a man."

Beau listened to the gangly youth and thought about his own first time, so many years, and bodies, ago. It had been in the arms of an older woman, not conventionally beautiful, but with the warmth of character and charm needed to help a naïve boy experience his initial sexual pleasure. His teacher had been a twice-wed widow, Creole to her fingertips, with knowledge to spare. She was a friend of his mother and father, in whose home he'd been offered shelter when his world had been devastated by the senseless death of his parents.

He could still recall the sticky, jasmine-scented air of that night. A night filled with pain and loneliness that overwhelmed the boy he'd been. Tears he'd held at bay for his tragic loss spilled out in a hot, bitter runnel, soaking his cheeks.

She'd called his name softly, opening the door to his bedchamber.

Embarrassed, he'd tried to wipe away the damning evidence of his loss of control, but she would have none of that. Placing her branch of candles upon the marble-topped nightstand, she sat down upon his bed, stroking his brow. "Cry if you must, *chèr.* I do."

"I shouldn't."

"Nonsense," she scoffed. "You are only human. Not a stone, nor a plaster saint fit only for prayer and suffering. We are all creatures of feeling. How little or how much, depends on us. It is good that you mourn the loss of two such fine people, a man and woman who loved each other in spite of all the odds against them. You are their son, proof that they lived and loved. Never forget that." She drew him into her arms, pillowed his face on her breast.

Moments had passed, moments when comfort became something else. Her woman's body, the feel and smell of it, chased away his sadness, replacing it with a burgeoning stirring of youthful lust. Life hurt and his young flesh demanded pleasure to ease the pain, to affirm that there was something beyond the despair he felt oppressing him like a smothering blanket.

The scent of jasmine clung to her smooth skin. He could smell it in the valley between her breasts.

His hand lifted of its own accord and cupped one small, fabric-covered breast, feeling the nipple stiffen as he did so.

Then, realizing what he'd done, he felt shame, removing his hand until she brought it to her flesh of her own volition, holding it against her bosom with her own, trapping it there.

Beau lifted his face to hers and saw the gentle smile that curved her mouth. Slowly, carefully, she leaned over and placed her lips against his own.

Then, she released his hand and stood.

"Don't leave me," he'd pleaded.

"I have no intention of doing that, *chèr*," she said, untying her robe, letting it slide to the floor. Next, her lawn nightgown followed, until she stood there in the soft light of the candles, unashamedly naked.

He couldn't take his eyes from her and all the secrets that her female form held.

"Boys are crude, fast and selfish, *chèr*," she'd said as she joined him in the wide bed, taking the lead, "no matter how old they are. Men are strong and sure, sharing and giving pleasure." Now it was her turn to have her hands on him, caressing, searching, molding, discovering. "Any fool," she said as she rained heated kisses across his slender body, following the path her hands had blazed, "can take a woman—a real man makes love."

Beau had never forgotten her words, or her skills.

He repeated her advice for the stable boy.

"I thought women weren't supposed to like it?" Josh asked, his pale eyes wide, "Unless they was whores."

"Pleasure," Beau stated, "is an art, Josh. A gift. A man isn't truly a man unless he knows that for a fact." His smile was self-explanatory. "Women like loving when it's done properly."

"So's I'm not to poke her and get it over with?" the boy questioned.

"Poke! Mon Dieu." Beau sighed. "No. You must learn to relax and appreciate the beauty of the act as it can be."

Josh scuffed his booted toe again. "Maybe you'd be willing to pick out one of Trudy's girls for me, seein' as how you're more"—he hesitated for a moment—"experienced than my pa."

With a wry smile, Beau acknowledged the implied compliment. "I'll see what I can do."

"Gosh, thanks, Mr. McMasters. I'd be real obliged."

"Enough to see that my horses get extra care?"

The boy grinned. "You betcha. Whatever you want."

Beau reached into the pocket of his trousers and pulled out a coin, handing it to the boy. "See that you do."

Josh gasped in gratitude and shock. The gentleman had given him a gold eagle, worth five dollars. "Thanks a lot. I ain't ever had this much money before."

"Would you like more of the same?"

"Whatcha want me to do to earn it?"

Beau shrugged. "This and that."

"Nothing bad? My pa'd whip me good if I did something wrong."

Beau quickly reassured him, elaborating on what he wanted. "Be my eyes and ears in this town. Tell me what you hear, what you see." It couldn't hurt to have a reliable source of information reporting to him. "Before my new club opens, I might need your help in getting it ready. And you might also have to run errands for me."

"That sounds all right."

"Good. Then we have a deal?" Beau held out his hand.

Josh brushed his callused hand against the denim that covered his legs before accepting the older man's. "Reckon we do."

* * *

As before, when she was getting ready for the welcome-to-town dinner, Abby couldn't help herself—she was excited. Going through her limited wardrobe, she discovered she didn't have anything that could be used as a proper riding outfit. Her regular clothes wouldn't do.

Snapping shut the door to the pine clothespress, she silently acknowledged that she would have to dip into her dwindling funds to purchase something she could wear today. Fondly, she recalled the royal blue velvet riding habit she was sure still hung in her closet in the Fifth Avenue mansion, along with an exact duplicate, ordered on the off chance that a speck of dirt would dare cling to the fabric and mar its pristine appearance.

Such a grand ensemble would look terribly out of place in this frontier town. Here, she observed, women wore split skirts; a few audacious souls had even worn trousers, like a man.

Carefully counting out her paper and coin, Abby swiftly calculated what she had left and what she could afford to spend. This was another facet of her newfound freedom, learning to make do with a lot less money than she was used to. There was no more "send the bills to my father's attention." That had ceased the moment she left, and, she had to admit, it was for the best. She'd learned when someone else paid for the goods, he generally wanted to call the tune.

Abby smiled, remembering the "rainy day" funds she still had hidden aside—one hundred dollars stashed away for an emergency. While in Denver, she'd pawned the last of the jewelry she had brought with her. They'd been items she hadn't minded parting with. For her they held no sentimental value, as she'd been given them not in love, but to be a symbol of Harold Breckenridge's wealth. When she'd tried to object, when she'd asked for something simpler than the grand pieces he bought her, she was told her taste was far too plebeian, that she lacked the maturity to see how important it was to be jeweled in a fitting manner. Because she was an heiress, she had to look the part. Simple was not for those who could afford the best.

It was then that Abby understood the jewels were not really jewels; they were expensive manacles. She was nothing more than a walking, talking, breathing advertisement for her father's ambitions, and her opinions and wishes counted for nothing.

That her father had unknowingly provided her additional monetary means to finance her flight from his control proved amusingly ironic.

Abby added what she needed to her reticule, putting the remainder back in her locked box and sliding it into the drawer that held her underthings, her fingers brushing up against the stiff stays of her corset. Since coming to Heaven's Grace, she hadn't bothered much with it, preferring the more relaxed attitude of the women around here. Such things were for fancy wear, not for everyday, where they could only get in the way, restricting movement.

Closing the drawer, she placed her hands beneath her breasts, feeling only the cloth of her shirt and chemise beneath her fingertips.

Heresy. That's what her mother would have declared of her actions. A lady put her corset on in the morning; removed it at night, with no excuses in-between. "It separates us from the lower orders," her mother had droned on numerous occasions in answer to Abby's request to forgo it. "They're loose," she'd said, indicating her view of the servants and everyone not in what she considered *her* class, "accessible, as well they should be. We're most definitely not. Don't you forget that, my girl."

Abby could feel the rhythm of her own breathing under her hand. Each breath was drawn free and deep, unfettered by someone else's notions of what was right.

The sky was bright blue as she stepped outside her door, shutting it behind her.

She needed a new hat, too, she decided, blinking at the warmth of the sun. Not a fancy bonnet, but something of substance. Without it her fair skin would burn and blister. The occasional freckle the sun brought out on her cheeks she'd never minded. However, since coming west, she'd seen women with ivory skin like hers who didn't take care of it; the effects of that overexposure to the elements was devastating. Harsh, cracked, dry skin that was wrinkled like old shoe leather, making even a passably pretty woman look much older than her actual age. She didn't intend to let that happen to her.

Walking along the rutted dirt lane towards the main street, Abby wondered what sort of mount Mr.—Beau—would choose for her. She hoped it would not be a plodding creature whose docility would bore her to tears. She was counting on him to select an animal that would challenge her skill.

A smile kicked up the corners of her mouth. He hadn't a clue as to what type of rider she was, so perhaps thinking he would know what kind of mount to select was expecting a bit too much from him.

However, she couldn't help thinking that if anyone could read her mind when it came to horses, it would be Beau McMasters.

When the general store came in sight, she crossed her fingers that they would have what she needed in stock. She was acutely aware that Heaven's Grace wasn't New York, or any cosmopolitan city where garments could be obtained with ease as long as one had money.

Striding purposefully along the wide street, then stepping up on the planked sidewalk that led to the shop, Abby wasn't aware of a pair of masculine eyes that followed her progress from a short distance away.

Beau leaned up against the post that supported the roof

of the hotel. Mrs. Butler, he observed, was in a fair hurry.

He inhaled on his thin cigar, blowing the smoke lazily away. He couldn't wait to see her face when he presented the horse he'd picked out for her. Grace. Beauty. Spirit. A mount well matched—in his opinion—to its eventual rider.

He'd lain in bed last night, her face the only thing on his mind. She was in so many ways a puzzlement. An enigma he needed to unravel. A body he yearned to possess.

It was only a matter of time.

Chapter Nine

"I think that I have just what you're looking for right over here," Mrs. Cooper remarked, coming from behind the counter of the general store to help Abby. "Got it from a catalogue from St. Louis and I've sold several of them." She moved a few items around on the display shelf until she found what she was looking for, buried underneath a stack of gingham aprons.

"Ah, here they are. Only two left." Mrs. Cooper pulled out both of them and narrowed her eyes, giving Abby's form a thorough glance. "Think that this one will suit you better." She held up a split skirt made of buttery soft fabric that Abby recognized as deerhide.

She took the skirt from Mrs. Cooper's outstretched hand and held it to her waist; it looked too big by several inches.

"Oh dear," Mrs. Cooper said when she saw the extra inches, "guess that's not gonna do. Just when would you be needing this?" She grabbed a straight pin from a puffed red velvet pincushion on the counter and measured the difference.

"Today," Abby replied.

"Oh, that does present a problem, my dear."

"I know. It's just that the invitation to go riding came last night and I knew I was taking a chance that you might have something in stock that would fit me."

"If I'd had a day's notice, I coulda got someone to fix it up right for you so that it would fit like hide on a cow." Mrs. Cooper gave Abby another sharp glance, removing the skirt and placing it on top of a large wooden barrel marked SUGAR. "Though, if you still want to take that ride, I might have something else that could work for you. Mind, it's surely not what you're used to, but a few of the ladies around here have been known to make do."

Abby was determined to go on that ride with Beau, so she was open to any suggestions. "What is it?"

Mrs. Cooper stepped to the other side of her shop, past the potbellied iron stove, the two wooden chairs that flanked it, and the sleeping calico cat, stopping at the wide shelf that held several dozen pairs of dark blue denim pants. She picked up a few pairs, examining them carefully before she made her selection.

Walking back to Abby, she held up a pair to her customer's waist. "I think these will fit. Kinda hard to judge, though, since they're made for menfolk."

Abby glanced down at the fabric. Pants. Close fitting pants that were made to hug the wearer's shape.

"Well?"

"I don't know," Abby said.

Mrs. Cooper smiled. "There's many a day a body's gotta take what they can and make do, 'specially, you'll learn, in these parts. And, come to think on it, a vest might be just the thing to finish it off." She selected one that would also make a nice complement to the split-skirt, since it was of the same color and material, with a back of dark brown silk. "Slip this on, my dear."

Abby did as she was asked.

"Now, you go on home and try the Levi's and see how they look."

Abby sighed, remembering an expression she'd once heard: people late to the meal often had to make do with the remains.

Reluctantly, she nodded her head to Mrs. Cooper. "And what about a hat?"

"Got that too," the shopkeeper said, walking a few paces to the right and picking up a round hatbox from its resting place. "Don't get much call for fancy riding hats for ladies. I do better with sunbonnets hereabouts." She opened the flower-painted cedar box and unwrapped the tissue paper. "But this'll look quite nice, I'm thinking, on you, Miss Abby. Got it on a trip to San Antonio last year to see my sister. Saw it in the window of a ladies' dress shop and I couldn't resist, even if my husband thought me just the tiniest bit loco for buying it. Always figured that some day, some woman would come into my store and it would just be waiting for her. Reckon you could be that someone."

Abby's mouth fell open in delight when she saw the hat. It was dark brown felt, flat crowned, with a band of hammered silver around the brim. She couldn't resist trying it on right then and there.

"You look just fine, Miss Abby," Mrs. Cooper stated as she relieved Abby of the pants. "That hat fits like it was made for you. Nice to see that I was right after all." Her smile was self-congratulatory. "Wait till I tell Mr. Cooper. This is gonna cost him—dinner out tonight at the hotel, with all the trimmings." She placed a hand on her hip and nodded.

Abby walked to the long rectangular mirror that stood in a corner of the shop. She tilted her head from one side to another, admiring the design of the hat, which was unlike anything she'd ever worn. Smiling, she told Mrs. Cooper, "I love it."

"Will that be it, then?" the woman asked, folding the denim pants and wrapping them in brown paper. "Or do you need anything else?"

Abby spotted a pair of knee-high dark brown boots in another corner of the shop. They looked small enough to fit her, made, she judged, for a boy. "Let me see those boots."

"Moccasins would be much more comfortable," said the woman who'd just entered the shop, the bell tinkling behind her.

Both Abby and Mrs. Cooper turned in the direction of the speaker.

Abby recognized the young woman who stood there, a small woven shopping basket on her arm, a paper list in one hand. She'd been in attendance the night of the welcome party. It had been her father who'd had the not so pleasant run-in with Beau.

"What are they?" Abby asked, interested in both what the other woman had to say, and in the woman herself.

"Shoes worn by Indians," the girl replied. "Very soft shoes. They're made from deerhide for the most part, or when plentiful, buffalo. If it's a special pair, they're decorated with fancy beads or feathers." A wistful look came over the younger woman's face. "I had a pair like that that were given to me by the chief's wife."

"I'd love to see them," Abby said, taking note of the haunting, bittersweet regard in the girl's pale blue eyes, eyes that looked remarkably sad.

"Ain't got them no more. Pa burned them. Said they were fit only for savages, not for decent white folks."

Abby heard the thin thread of pain in the girl's voice. The shoes had obviously been special to her and she felt their loss deeply.

"That's too bad," Abby murmured, stepping closer to the girl, "for I would have really liked to have seen them. They sound beautiful."

125

"They were." A small smile curved the girl's lips. "Prettiest things I ever did own."

"Maybe some day you can get another pair."

The smile evaporated. "No. Pa will never let me."

Abby looked at the girl, at her thin, sallow face and downcast eyes. There but for the grace of God, she thought. Here was a young woman who looked as if she'd been trampled by fortune and circumstance, yet there appeared to be a spark of life left. A kernel that if properly cultivated, might grow stronger.

It wasn't her business, but Abby didn't let that matter. They had something in common, enough for a tentative gesture of friendship. "I'd like to hear some more about the moccasins sometime."

Surprise sounded in the girl's voice. "You would?"

"Yes. I'm new to this part of the country and I've got a lot to learn about all the people who live here. Anything you could tell me about Indians, I would love to hear." She held out her hand. "By the way, I'm Abby Butler."

The girl raised her head and stared into Abby's eyes, joining her hand with Abby's in the proffered handshake. "No fooling? You're really interested in learning about Indians?"

Abby smiled. "No fooling," she repeated. "Come by my house whenever you like."

The girl lowered her head again, regret in her tone. "I don't know if I can. Pa's got a lot of chores for me to do. He says that idle hands breed the devil's joy."

Abby exchanged a look with Mrs. Cooper. She bit back the acerbic comment that rose in her throat.

Instead, she took a deep breath and forced a smile to her face. "My offer still stands. If you ever want to come and talk or join me for a cup of coffee or tea, you're more than welcome."

"Thank you kindly, Miss Butler."

"No thanks are needed, and it's Mrs. Butler, though I'd like you to call me Abby."

"And I'm Sabina Baser."

"Like I said, Sabina, just feel free to come 'round when you can." Abby glanced at the clock on the wall behind the counter, then handed the hat back to the shopkeeper, who placed it in the box. "Let me see those boots, Mrs. Cooper. You can wait on Miss Baser while I try them on."

Abby took one of the empty chairs and unlaced her right shoe, slipping it off while Mrs. Cooper quickly filled the girl's order. Sabina didn't linger, she promptly left the store when her shopping was done. Abby wriggled her stocking-clad toes before putting her foot into the boot.

"How do they fit?"

"Just a trifle big," Abby answered.

"Here," Mrs. Cooper said, pulling a few wads of cotton from a nearby glass jar, "stuff this inside."

Abby did so to the next one and it fit perfectly. "Add these, too," she said, putting her shoes back on after tugging the boots off her feet. She mentally tallied the amount of her purchases; it was more than she wanted to spend, but if she planned on doing any serious riding, necessary.

Mrs. Cooper opened a ledger next to her cash register and recorded the items Abby wanted, along with their value. "It's on your account."

"Account?" Abby asked, coming to the counter to collect her purchases. "But I can pay for them now."

"No need," Mrs. Cooper informed her. "Your credit's good here."

"Then why did I see Miss Baser pay in cash?"

"That's because her pa's credit is worthless. Come time to pay up and Hank Baser'd have all the excuses known to man, and then some. All it really amounted to was that he liked to drink it away at the Bad Penny. Truth be told, he ain't ever been much of a farmer. Won't surprise me to hear that he's lost what's left of his farm."

"Then how does he make a living?"

"His daughter. Sabina's a wonder with a needle and thread. Folks need something repaired, altered, or just plain sewn, she's the one they go to." She paused. "Leastwise most do. There's some that don't, 'cause they figure that somehow she'll taint their goods, but they're few. Most reckon her work is what's most important."

"Taint?" Abby lingered over the word Mrs. Cooper had used. "Why ever would anyone think that?"

"My dear, don't you know?" Mrs. Cooper confided. "Oh, of course you don't, what with you being new here and all. She was once a captive of the Indians. Lived with them, one of the Sioux bands, for nigh onto a year. It's rumored that she was even married to one of them, though no one hereabouts knows the truth of that as she don't talk about it."

"Married?"

Mrs. Cooper shrugged. "Her pa tells a different story. Said she was"—she paused, lowering her voice, even though they were alone in the store—"raped."

Rape. Abby gave an involuntary shudder at the thought. She knew what the word meant; she'd seen the damage done at close range when one of the teachers at the girl's school in Denver was attacked last Christmas. She saw the torn clothes, the bruised body, the vacant eyes. Heard the tears and the recriminations. And then she, along with another of the staff, found the body of the victim hanging in her room a week later on New Year's Eve. Turned out the woman's soon-to-be husband had spurned her after hearing the news: the letter he'd sent her, breaking off their relationship, was still tucked in her apron pocket.

If Sabina Baser had been violated, that could account for the wan face and timid demeanor. At least the girl hadn't given up on life, Abby thought. She was still alive, despite her despair, despite any shame. For that, Abby respected her. When a lot of people figured you were better off dead, it took courage to stay alive.

"While you was trying on the boots, I asked her if she'd be able to alter the skirt so's it would fit you properly and she agreed. Took it with her."

Abby picked up her packages. "If you're sure then about the bill, I'd better be going."

Mrs. Cooper laughed. "Not like you're gonna be running out on us, is it now?"

Abby inhaled sharply. She hoped not. She was so tired of running, of always looking over her shoulder, afraid that any stranger could be working for her father, with orders to bring her back to New York by any means possible.

But she wasn't going back.

No, she would never go back, not willingly. Not *any* way. She was done with that life.

Besides, the only place she was going today was for a ride with Beau McMasters.

Beau. How aptly named he was, she decided. In French it meant handsome. And the good Lord knew he was most certainly that. More than an ordinary man had a right to be.

"You'd best be careful if you're going riding. What with you being a stranger to these parts, you're liable to get lost."

"Thanks for the advice, Mrs. Cooper, but I won't be alone."

The other woman nodded. "That's right. You said that you was asked. Who's your escort?"

"Mr. McMasters."

"Ah-ha," the older woman said with a smile. "There's them that finds the dark ones attractive. Me, I've always been partial to light-haired men myself. My Benjamin was blond in his younger days. Hair like wheat."

"Mr. McMasters is just being friendly, nothing more,"

Abby protested softly. She didn't want Mrs. Cooper to think there was something going on between them.

But, was that the whole truth? Abby wondered. Maybe yes; maybe no.

"He's certainly got the manners, you gotta give him that. Must be that Southern blood. Heard tell a lot of them are like that, real polite, loaded with charm enough to tempt a saint to stray. Even if we did whip their behinds in the war, it ain't like he's taking it personally, what with him coming this far north to settle. Shows that he's got him some spunk, not to mention," Mrs. Cooper added with a chuckle, "brains."

Beau McMasters didn't strike Abby as the kind of man who had ever been whipped or defeated by anything, nor the kind who ever would be. Life might have dealt him some bad hands—she had no real knowledge of that, just a supposition—however, he hadn't lost interest in the game. She could see that in his eyes.

A small, swift sigh escaped her lips. Those wonderfully expressive eyes. *Lodestar* eyes.

But, she wondered as she made her way swiftly back home, to what—or where—did they point the way?

"You fixin' to meet with someone special today?" Gussie asked as she refilled Beau's coffee cup.

"Now what makes you think that?" he queried, taking a sip of the fresh brew and giving his landlady a quizzical glance.

She put down the graniteware pot and promptly sat down at his table; only a few people lingered in the dining room. "You've got that look about you that says you can't wait to get out of here, but you ain't left yet. So I figure that you're waiting on someone. Am I right?"

Beau gave her the barest hint of a smile. "Caught," he admitted.

"Abby Butler, I reckon."

"Yes."

"Thought so."

"Oh, did you?" he asked, leaning back in his chair and fixing her with an arched brow.

"Who else?" she shot back.

"Any number of people could be my answer. My banker, my lawyer, even my ranch foreman," he argued.

"But they're not," she pointed out. While it was true that Gussie had observed him laying eyes upon many a female since he'd arrived in town, none seemed to hold his interest as much as the widow Butler. Whenever she was around, he was a man with a singular purpose, and that was to give in to his fascination. Like a man who'd found the mother lode and yet hasn't quite realized it.

Ah well, took some men longer than others to admit they was out and out smitten, she knew. You couldn't tell them flat out, they had to find it out for themselves. Of course that was half the fun of courtship. Discovering on your own how the other person felt and the strength of the attachment.

And Gussie reckoned it was powerful strong between those two. Any fool could see that and she was no fool. Not by a long shot. Other women flirted with him—she'd seen that right enough—and he was all charm right back at them. But he never looked at them like he looked at Abby.

It was the same way that gal looked at him. Almost like striking two flints against one another: Sooner than later you knew a fire was coming, brought on by sparks that couldn't be dampened, couldn't be ignored.

"You're right, Gussie. Mrs. Butler and I have an appointment to go riding."

"An appointment? Is that your fancy talk for a scheduled courtin' session?"

Beau laughed softly. " 'Fraid I'll have to disappoint you, Gussie, but it's simply a ride. Although I'll let you in on a little secret."

She chuckled. "I love secrets."

"I rather suspected you did," he said in a dry tone.

"Tell me," she insisted. "Did you find her a horse like yours?"

"Damn if you aren't a wonder, Gussie. Remind me never to play poker with you."

"Go on," she said.

"Yes, I did find Mrs. Butler a suitable animal. One I think she'll like."

If it comes from you, Gussie thought, she's sure to. "Don't keep me hangin' till Christmas! What's it look like?"

Beau gave her a description.

"My, my," she said, rising from her seat and picking up the now cool coffeepot. "What a fine pair you two are gonna make."

Abby felt incredibly strange when she pulled the denim pants over her lawn drawers. They were slightly stiff, yet they followed the lines of her limbs like a glove, outlining every curve. She glanced at the two scraps of eyelet that lay on her bed. She'd had to remove them from the underwear for fear they would bunch against her knees when she wore the pants. The waistband was a smidgen too big, so she took a white silk scarf from her wardrobe and threaded it through the belt loops, pulling it tight with a knot, the ends of which fell over her left thigh.

Abby stood in front of the cheval mirror, examining how she looked in these clothes. Yes, they were different, but for some reason, she felt freer. Altogether the outfit clothed a much-changed woman from the one who'd fled New York. It was like looking at another person in the mirror. Abigail Breckenridge was fading into the background; Abby Butler was emerging stronger and stronger with each passing day.

It was the latter whom Abby saw now. Who would Beau see?

She ran her palms along her thighs. A few washings would soften the durable material.

Suddenly a smile curved her lips. *Durable.* Made to last, come what may. Hidden strength. It was all there, reflected in the mirror's image.

She picked up the pieces of eyelet and tucked them into her pocket, along with a silk handkerchief that was identical to the scarf. Next she added the flat-crowned hat, adjusting the fit.

Satisfied, she stepped back, pleased with the outcome. She hoped that Beau would be, too.

He was more than pleased; he was amazed at the transformation. The woman who emerged from the small house was yet another facet of Abby Butler, one he wouldn't have suspected she had.

Beau could only stare at her for a few moments, taking in the clothes she wore, and the effect that they were having on him. Desire, raw and hot, slammed into his gut, almost stealing the breath from his body.

Pants and boots had never looked so good on any one body before. They appeared far from utilitarian when wrapped around her shapely hips and long legs. Every inch of her oh-so-feminine body was covered, yet it was the covering itself that fired the blood. Even the added touch of a scarf as a substitute belt, while rakish, was purely female, down to the embroidered red rose that he could see along the hem.

Abby flushed under his scrutiny. She watched as his eyes slowly ran down the length of her body and drifted slowly back up again. Had she made a serious mistake? Did he think she was foolish? Worse, was he going to change his mind about riding with her?

"Mrs. Butler, may I say, as always, you do possess a knack for"—he paused, long enough to let his gaze drop again, his golden eyes warm and assessing, before returning to her face—"surprises."

She wet her lips. "And you *like* that?" Her voice was soft, almost hesitant.

"My dear Mrs. Butler, I *adore* that."

Abby relaxed, satisfied.

"Now, I have a surprise for you." With his left hand he pulled the reins of a second mount forward. "What do you think?"

Abby was stunned. *What did she think?* She could hardly formulate a coherent thought at the moment, overwhelmed first by his reaction to her clothing, and now this. How could she have missed the extra horse Beau had brought?

Easy, she thought, for as she opened the door to her house when she heard him ride up, all that was on her mind was him. All else was temporarily obliterated, lost in a fog. Now she saw the animal.

"Do you like her? I most certainly hope so, since she's yours."

The impact of Beau's drawling words hit Abby hard. He hadn't rented the horse from the livery, or borrowed it from someone. It was a gift, from him to her.

It was a very personal offering, far too personal to accept. Yet she couldn't seem to voice the words that would reject his generous gesture. The horse was beautiful, and unique. White, covered with drops of black, like smudges of ink on snow.

"I can't." She finally made herself utter the words.

"Don't say that you can't accept her. I refuse to acknowledge that." Beau got down from his mount in one smooth movement, dropping the reins to his own horse.

"I shouldn't." Her protest sounded half-hearted.

He was only inches away, his voice low and audible only to her. "Of course you should."

You're a silver-tongued devil, Beau McMasters, Abby thought, watching as his lean fingers stroked the animal's muzzle. His hands glided back and forth as he leaned closer to the horse. Today—she assumed—because of the heat he had shed his coat, standing there in a white shirt with the sleeves rolled up, exposing his tanned forearms dusted with dark hair.

Abby was suddenly surrounded by warmth, both within and without.

When he unleashed one of his potent smiles upon her, she knew she would keep the animal; she couldn't resist the powerful appeal to her appreciation of beauty and her natural love of horses. Even if he wasn't aware of both, he'd succeeded in satisfying them anyway.

"How can I ever thank you for such a magnificent gift?"

Beau stepped closer to her. "Enjoy it," he whispered, handing her the filly's reins. "That's all I ask by way of thanks."

Abby approached the horse, trailing her own hand along the animal's neck and shoulders. The horse whickered in response and Abby grinned.

"You understand each other," Beau commented.

"I believe that we do," Abby said with a smile.

"Let me give you a hand up." Beau moved to her side as Abby put her foot in the stirrup.

"That's quite all right, I can manage," she said, swinging into the saddle. It too was new, and different in subtle ways from those she'd seen here in Heaven's Grace and elsewhere. Smaller, lighter, less cumbersome. This seemed much more comfortable than the heavy working model used by almost everyone out West.

As if Beau had read her mind, he said, "It's called a California saddle. Much better for just plain riding than the Texas version."

Beau stepped back, picking up the reins to his own mount. *Damn!* He wanted to touch her, even if it was only for an instant. Wanted to put his hands around her waist and lift her onto the horse's back. Wanted to let his fingers trail slowly down her denim-clad leg. Wanted to toss her hat onto the ground and fist his hand in her hair. Wanted to taste those lips.

Wanted to lose himself in the depths of her body, easing the hard ache that twisted his insides. Wanted to ride her hard and fast, then long and slow.

Was that too much to want?

Abby watched as Beau remounted, admiring the graceful way he moved, as if he and the big Paint horse were one. Instead of the hero of a dime novel, she pictured him as a cavalier of Old England; all he needed was a plumed hat and dripping lace. A man fighting for a cause he passionately believed in, riding one last time with his true love before he returned to the demands of his loyalty.

Sweet angels in heaven, her imagination had totally taken flight, weaving him into tales of the past when she should be concentrating on the present, and keeping her wits about her. For she had the strangest feeling that she would need them about her today more than ever.

Chapter Ten

They rode for almost an hour, over the broad expanse of grass and rolling hills, through meadows and across two creeks, past a herd of grazing elk, until they reached a spot overlooking a homestead.

Abby was grateful to stop. She hadn't ridden in so long that her lower muscles ached, unused to the strenuous pace her companion set. He was a superb rider, easy and graceful, one with his horse. Keeping up with him had been no simple task. Tonight she was sure her sore muscles would love a long soak in a hot tub.

The landscape was breathtaking. Stands of lodgepole pine trees dotted the area, along with other trees she couldn't name. A scattering of late summer wildflowers added spots of color to the lush grass. Abby saw a small herd of mixed breed cattle, perhaps thirty, grazing on the far right. A wooden fence encased some parts of the land, marking boundaries. Sitting nestled by the surrounding hills and several smaller buildings was a large house. From her vantage point, she could see several men engaged in various activities around the ranch, all looking extremely busy as they carried out their respective duties. A dog lazed in the sun, keeping a watchful eye on her puppies as they playfully chased each other.

Abby turned her head and fixed her glance on the man at her side. He, she discovered, was watching her, making no attempt to hide it. "This is yours, isn't it?"

Beau nodded.

She faced forward again, unable to let go of the vision before her: the pure, raw power of the land itself. Who cared if it was inherited by way of a card game instead of a deathbed? It was breathtaking in its splendor. As handsome a piece of property as could be imagined. Here mountains were not carved in brick, wood or steel; they were molded by God's hand in a fashion that outshone any grand design by man.

Abby took a deep breath of the pine-scented air, filling her lungs with all the scents around her. Some men carved empires and made their marks by subjugating everyone around them; others did it by manipulating currency, stock, property, or whatever they could; still a rare few simply happened upon their destiny and shaped it to suit their vision. Beau McMasters fell into the latter category, she suspected. He would mold what he was given, shaping it by the sheer force of his own indomitable will.

She twisted in the saddle. "May I see the house?"

"Not yet," Beau responded, hating to deny this lady anything right then, especially when she looked so lovely, her natural beauty far surpassing that of her surroundings. Her face glowed with happiness; her eyes sparkled with abundant joy.

Before Abby could ask, Beau carefully explained his position. "I don't want you to see it as it is now. I'd rather you see it when I'm done with it, which may not be for a few months." When he brought her to this house again, it would truly be *his* house. Today it wasn't. The main building was still a shell, an unformulated mix of wood and stone that held no heart, no trace of its new owner. Just bare bones lacking the inspired flesh of his design.

"When it's completed," he remarked, "I'd like to have you as my guest for dinner. Then you can fully appreciate what I've done to change it from what I found to what I want."

Abby's brows lifted in concern. "Do you think I'm a snob?"

Beau didn't miss the telltale hurt that flashed unexpectedly onto her features. Abby Butler a snob? Far from it, he thought. He'd had firsthand experience with snobbish females who saw what they were told to see and nothing else and who judged harshly, never caring about the consequences.

"I never believed you were," he insisted, watching as her face regained its previous expression. "It's just that when you see inside my house for the first time, I don't want your mind clouded or cluttered with remembered images of what used to be." God knows he had enough of his own past images to wipe clean, like the still-sharp memory of the magnificent plantation that should have been, by right of birth and blood, his. Now it was gone, reduced to ashes. Maybe if he'd seen it that way from the beginning, he could more easily sweep the past away. Still it lingered, mixed with memories from another lifetime. A lifetime best gone but unfortunately not quite forgotten.

"I understand," Abby replied. And remarkably, she did. Pride and dreams mattered to her, too. Funny, before coming to Heaven's Grace, she hadn't given much thought to dreams. Now she thought them possible, perhaps even within her grasp for the first time in her life.

At that moment, they both heard the approach of another rider. Pike, the foreman, came over the slope of the hill, reining in his big bay gelding and tipping his wide-brimmed Stetson hat in Abby's direction.

"How do, ma'am," he said, adding, "Mr. McMasters."

Beau made the introductions. "Pike, this is Mrs. Butler. Abby, this is Mr. Pike. He's in charge of running my ranch on a daily basis."

"Pleased to make your acquaintance, Mr. Pike," she said, extending her hand.

"Right happy to meet you too, ma'am," the foreman replied, moving his horse closer so that he could clasp her gloved hand. He grinned, nodding to Beau. "You were right. That horse and her fit together well."

Abby's mouth curved into a small smile. "Thank you, Mr. Pike."

The lanky cowboy's smile deepened in return. "Ain't nothing but the truth, ma'am."

And that ingenuous comment made Abby feel all that much better. Pike's words were genuine; he didn't have anything to gain—as others had in the past—by courting the favor of Harold Breckenridge's daughter and heir. Here, in this place, *she* counted, not her father. That knowledge brought a wide smile to her lips and a lightness to her soul.

"He's right, you know," Beau added, his eyes sweeping over her figure, lingering momentarily on her lush curves. "You and the filly are perfect together. Now you've got to name her."

"I hadn't thought of that yet."

"Well, while you're fixin' to think on it," Pike interjected, "why not come with me and let Cookie fix you up something to eat?" Pike removed his hat and raked a hand through his graying hair before settling the Stetson back in place. "Though you'd best not call him Cookie to his face. He gets mighty pis . . . steamed if you say that. Likes Rufus instead."

Beau liked any excuse to linger awhile longer with her, so he asked, "Would you like that?"

Abby was hungry, and, as if to illustrate, her stomach

made a gentle rumble. "Yes, I do believe that I would," she replied with a fresh smile.

Beau addressed Pike. "Is Rufus at the bunkhouse?"

"No, he's with a few of the men at the line camp a few miles north of here. Shouldn't take us that long to reach him. And there's a right pretty stream flowing by that's a nice spot to eat. Good for fishin', too."

"Then show us the way," Beau said.

Pike was right, Abby thought as they made their way to the line camp, climbing a little higher up. It was a beautiful spot, though he hadn't told them the half of it. They paused for a few minutes to enjoy the scenery while Pike rode on ahead.

Sunlight gleamed on the clear blue water, illuminating the rocks and stones below the surface. Every now and then she could glimpse a fish swimming swiftly by. She got down off her horse and bent, stripping off a glove so she could stick her hand in the current. It was cold, despite the warmth of the sun.

She contrasted this location with a late summer day in New York, teeming with people, the air hot and sticky. Even the wonderful Central Park hadn't provided so welcome and inviting an oasis.

Abby couldn't resist. She cupped her hand and scooped up some water, then drank, marveling at the chill.

Beau, who'd also dismounted, watched as she helped herself. When she stood up, water dribbled off her chin. "Allow me," he said, stepping closer to wipe her skin with his fingertips. Her flesh was warm and soft like the finest silk.

She looked at him, gazing upward.

If only they were alone. He wanted to touch her face, cup it between his hands and hold her still for his kiss. A long, slow, deep kiss.

But they weren't alone; Pike had ridden back.

Abby moved away from Beau, her flesh still tingling from the brief moment of contact with his.

Pike cleared his throat.

Both of them turned to face the foreman.

"Rufus has something waitin' for you at the chuck-wagon. He was just fixin' to clean up and go back to the ranch, but I caught him in time. 'Fraid it won't be what you're used to, but it's good, I can surely vouch for that."

They remounted and he led them to the wagon, where a man stood with his back to them, working on what was left of a large smoked ham, slicing off several pieces and putting the meat between two halves of buttermilk biscuits, served on blue graniteware plates.

"Rufus," Pike called out, "this here's Mr. McMasters and his . . ."

"Friend," Beau supplied with a smile as he escorted Abby closer to the food.

"His friend, Mrs. Butler," Pike finished.

The other man turned to face them, a wide, welcoming smile on his face, a plate in each hand. "Mighty happy to meet you," he said, his voice a low, raspy whisper of sound.

Beau stepped forward and removed the plates from the cook's hands, giving one to Abby. Rufus was a black man of middle age and height, whose white teeth gleamed against his ebony skin.

"So, you be the new boss man?" he asked Beau.

"That's a fact." Beau observed the cook's wiry body stiffen slightly. Sensing that his accent was the problem, he took a step closer to the older man and extended his right hand. "Pike's told us you're a valuable member of my outfit and one of the best cooks hereabouts."

Rufus took the younger man's hand, relaxing as he did so. "Learned when I was a boy at my mama's knee." His own cadence was slow, flavored with a distinctly Southern accent.

"You're not from Montana territory, are you?" Abby inquired, injecting herself into the conversation. She hadn't missed the looks the men had exchanged, nor the tense moment before Rufus accepted Beau's outstretched hand.

"No, ma'am, I'm surely not. I was born in Virginia," the cook replied. "On a tobacco plantation outside of Richmond. Most of what I fix best I learned there, so it's vittles with a history."

"Maybe you can learn to fix a dish with a dash more spice?" Beau asked.

"If you tell me how, I could surely give it a try," the cook promised. "What did you have in mind?"

"A few Creole dishes from New Orleans."

"That where you be from?"

Beau answered the cook with a nod.

"You be liking your food hot then," Rufus stated with a gleam in his dark brown eyes.

Abby sliced a glance at Beau as he responded, "The hotter the better."

She'd read about some of New Orleans's famed cuisine, food so spicy it stole your breath away, in one of her mother's many women's magazines. Exotic dishes with names like crawfish étouffé, jambalaya, gumbo. Tastes she'd longed to try; flavors she longed to experience. She'd once even broached the subject to her mother, telling her that she wanted to talk with the Breckenridge head cook about trying one of the recipes.

Her mother had said in a very starch-laden voice, accompanied by a delicate shudder, "You'll do no such thing. Why, the very idea is preposterous. Such food is for those unfortunate enough to live in that hot-blooded climate where seasonings influence behavior, and for the worse, I might add." Her mother had given another shudder, as if to underline the contempt she held for the torrid nature of the cuisine. "Temperate food is best," she'd opined in a condescending tone. "Settles the body and the mind, keeps both level, where they belong. As befits proper gentlefolk."

Change of any kind, Abby realized, terrified her mother. Variations in the normal routine were not to be tolerated under any circumstances.

"I'd love to sample it," Abby declared.

"You would?" Beau inquired softly, his vivid imagination conjuring up a discreet dinner party with only the two of them, as he initiated her to the distinct flavor of New Orleans food, to the strong chicory-laced coffee he'd learned to love at a young age. Hot as hell and black as night . . . or as white as the cream of her cheeks before a blush of color stained them.

"You be wanting something to drink with that?"

The cook's words broke into Beau's reverie, dashing cold water onto the image.

"I got a little coffee and some cold buttermilk."

"Coffee for me," Beau replied, swinging his head towards Abby.

"I'll have the buttermilk, please."

"Sure thing, ma'am."

"There's a small table in the line cabin over yonder if you want to eat in there," Pike offered.

"I'd rather eat out here in the open, maybe down by the water, if you don't mind," Abby responded, her eyes surveying the landscape once more. "It's far too lovely a day to waste indoors."

Beau asked her, "You don't mind that we'll have to make do?"

Abby shook her head, accepting the mug of buttermilk from the cook. "Of course not."

Remarkable, he thought, she adapted to events with the ease of a chameleon. "Then that's where we'll eat."

"I got an extra blanket that you can use if you'd like," offered Rufus, pulling out the colorful woven article from his wagon.

"It's lovely," Abby remarked, admiring the bold colors and intricate patterns. "May I ask where you got it from? I don't think I've ever seen its like before."

"From a trader passing through Heaven's Grace a year or so ago. Had him a variety of things, but I sure did like this one. Said it was made by an Indian tribe down Arizona way."

Beau tossed the blanket over his arm while Pike remounted his horse.

"You have a nice day, Mrs. Butler," Beau's foreman said, tipping his Stetson in her direction.

Abby smiled, tilting her head back so that she could see him. "You too, Mr. Pike."

"Boss." Pike nodded towards Beau, and pointed his horse in the direction of the ranch.

"I'll be heading back too," Rufus stated, closing up the back of the wagon. "When you're done, just put the dishes and the blanket in the line cabin and I'll get them another time." He grinned. "Awfully pretty day to be enjoying a meal in the open. Just watch out for bears and such."

Abby blinked. "Bears?"

"Or wolves," the cook said as he made sure all the latches were secure. "Don't have much truck with them most times, but every so often, you gets a mean 'un and you gotta be careful."

"Don't worry, Abby," Beau said in a soft, reassuring voice, "I won't let anything happen to you."

Abby believed him, realizing without hesitation that she did trust him to keep her safe. "I know."

"Then let's go find ourselves a spot, shall we?"

They found the perfect place not far from the line camp. Nestled by a small stand of lodgepole pines, carpeted with a bloom of flowers, it provided privacy and just the right place to put the blanket and enjoy a luncheon.

Abby removed her hat and Beau did likewise when they

settled themselves on the smooth wool. Because the blanket was not very large, they were forced to sit close. Abby couldn't help feeling a frisson of excitement course through her veins. She and Beau were all alone. If he were other than the true gentleman she knew him to be, she would never have considered either the invitation to ride or the prospect of a meal in so remote a location. But still, her heartbeat increased with the nearness of him. She had only to reach out her hand and she could touch him. Not, of course, that she was going to, but she could if she so desired.

Desire.

Was that the funny feeling she had in the pit of her stomach? Was that what caused the quick, unexpected catch of her breath? The rapid beat of her pulse? The flush of unexpected heat pooling in the deepest part of her female anatomy?

God, it was so unnerving. Especially as she had no one who could explain what was happening to her. Was this what every woman felt when close to an attractive man? Or was she some type of wanton? Did her father's licentious nature inhabit her as well? All she truly knew for sure was that she felt right being here with Beau. As to the other things, she would find a way of ascertaining the truth.

Beau watched as she carefully bit into the ham-and-biscuit combination. He took a sip of his coffee; it was cooling, he wasn't. Never before had any woman heated up his blood so fast, nor made him ache as deeply to join their bodies together. It went beyond hunger, beyond simple lust. It went to a place he'd never visited before: a place dark, yet also light; a place sweet and deliciously tart; a place filled both with tortuous restraint and wildly unleashed passions. A place uncharted, for which there was no map, no directions. Just strong instinct and need.

He'd felt that need since their first meeting. Stark and abiding. Hot and ready.

"Tell me about New Orleans."

Beau tossed the remains of his coffee aside, tilting his head to look at her. She was feeding a tiny piece of biscuit to a ground squirrel, which shyly approached Abby, grabbed his treat, and then sped off.

"What do you want to know?"

"What was it like there?"

"It's changed since I was a boy. The War did that."

She heard the unspoken sadness in his voice. "I'm sorry if the memories are too painful."

"Some are," he admitted with a shrug, "some aren't."

"Tell me about the happy ones, then."

Beau smiled, the action softening his features. "Going to the market with my mother. Watching her haggle with the merchants for the best price. She loved that. It was an ongoing game to her and them. Hearing her tell nonsense stories about the fruit, or the vegetables. Listening to her exchange gossip with a friend."

"You loved her very much, didn't you?"

"Yes. Not a day goes by that I don't wish she and my father were still here among the living."

She envied him that closeness. "And what about your father?"

"He adored my mother, same as she adored him, yet they still had room for me in their lives. He taught me how to ride, how to judge horseflesh, how to play cards. Most importantly though, he taught me to be a man and think for myself." Beau shifted so that he was facing Abby. "He was a good man. An honorable man; one who wouldn't back down when he believed in the cause that he was fighting for. A life without honor was no life worth having, he often said."

Honor. Did her father even know the meaning of the

word? Abby doubted it. He hadn't held her honor, her heart, to be of much value. They were mere abstractions, not worth a second of what he saw as his valuable time.

"Turnabout now," Beau insisted. "You're from back East, aren't you?"

She hesitated for a second. "Yes."

"Was your husband?" There, he'd brought up the ghost that stood between them.

"Yes." God, why did it hurt so to continue to lie to him? She should be used to it by now, having spun this tale out before. Rehearsed her part until it was letter perfect.

"How'd you end up here, in Montana?"

"My husband wanted to go out West after we were married. See the country. Escape what he saw as limited opportunities in the East. He thought it was too crowded, too confining there, and I agreed with him. Unfortunately, he didn't live to see his dream fulfilled."

"You didn't want to return to your home after he died?"

"I didn't have one to return to."

"No family?"

"None." That was almost the truth. As far as she was concerned, she was alone, an orphan in every way that counted save actuality. She had always been alone, really. For her there were no sweet remembrances of sharing, of loving in her childhood. There were only false expectations and admonishments, harsh rebukes and hidden agendas.

Unexpectedly, tears welled up in her eyes, and one single drop fell, wetting her cheek.

Beau saw it and moved closer, catching the droplet with his index finger. "Don't," he murmured, pulling her into his embrace. He felt her relax against him, accept the sanctuary he was offering. She sobbed for less than a minute, then gathered herself together. Crying, he thought, for her dead husband and the future they never had.

He touched his lips to the top of her head, to her warm, sun-kissed scalp covered with strands of reddish-gold. He slipped an index finger beneath her chin, raising Abby's head, moving his mouth to her brow, her cheek, the tip of her nose. Then, as her eyes locked with his, he took her mouth.

Sweet. Painfully sweet. Warm and soft, tender and inviting. He moved to deepen the kiss, releasing her chin and slipping one hand around her waist, while the other clasped her head, holding her close.

She clung to him, for fear of losing the sweeping feeling that assailed her, her fingertips sliding up his back until they grasped the satin of his vest. He was her anchor in a sea of sensation. No girlish fantasy could match the tempest-tossed magic of his mouth as it worked its wonderment on her. The odd feel of his beard as it rubbed against her skin added to the overall pleasure she was experiencing.

She thought she heard her name spoken softly in a hoarse, demanding voice when he broke contact for the briefest moment.

Beau cupped her face in his hands; observed the telltale flush of pleasure in her cheeks, the look of wonder in her blue eyes. He moved his thumb across her bottom lip, slowly and deliberately. Hers was a mouth made for endless kisses.

He groaned her name once again before resuming.

Abby found herself lying down on the blanket, with Beau's unfamiliar weight atop her, his lips pressed firmly and intoxicatingly upon hers, capturing and plundering at will.

It was all so intimate.

One of her hands shifted upwards to his hair, fingers threading through the longish dark waves, learning the texture.

She was in danger of losing her head completely, so

compelling and persuasive was the power he exerted over her awakening emotions.

When his lean-fingered hand curled around the firmness of her breast and gently squeezed, she bucked, suddenly afraid of where this was going. Too fast. Much too fast.

He pulled back immediately, forcing himself to take a deep breath and sit up. However, he couldn't resist looking at her soft, rose-hued lips, slightly swollen from his kisses. What he couldn't understand was the untutored response she'd given him. Almost as if she had never been kissed in her life. Certainly not in passion, nor with skill. And when his hand had grazed the wonderful weight of her breast, she stiffened as if in shock from the contact.

All sorts of questions were scrambling in his brain. For a widow, she had the damnedest knack of reacting like a well-brought-up virgin. Shy and hesitant, unsure of herself and what to do next.

Unlike himself. He knew what he wanted to do next—strip the clothes from her body and take her there, reveling in the scent and taste of her. Losing himself deep in her body. On such a warm day, scale her hills and valleys with a sliver of ice; watch as her skin reacted, watch as the ice melted when it came into contact with her heated flesh. Lick the beaded droplets off one at a time.

Abby sat up, color darkening her cheeks, one hand to her mouth, her eyes on his. Her breathing was finally returning to normal. She was flustered and unsure, her world tilted at a crazy angle. She was teetering on an unknown precipice, afraid that if she moved, she would tumble into an abyss.

She scrambled to her feet. "I think we'd better be getting back."

Beau got to his feet also, his eyes boring deeply into hers. "I won't ask your pardon because I wanted to do that. And, if you're honest with yourself, you will admit that you wanted it too." He gathered the blanket, plates and cups while she stood there.

Beau was right, Abby admitted to herself. She *had* wanted it.

And that was why she was apprehensive. She was out of her depth, fearful of being swallowed by the deep water of newly discovered appetites. She lowered her lashes. "Yes, you're right. I'm at fault, too."

Beau tossed the items aside and grasped Abby by her upper arms. "Fault?" he questioned, upset that she should think he was blaming her in any way. "I'm not talking about fault, Abby." He stepped closer, closing the distance so that only mere inches separated them. His next words were spoken softly, in that low, caressing baritone. "I'm talking about *wanting. Desiring. Needing. Making love.*"

Why, when he said each word, did it sound so intense, shaded with a nuance unique to him? With his voice, he'd forever altered the way she would hear those words, feel them, understand them.

"I can't," she whispered, raising her eyes to his, almost changing her mind when she saw the golden brown heat flaring there.

He smiled, top lip curled back slightly to reveal the white of his teeth. "If not now, then later. It's inevitable."

He seemed so confident, so sure of his ultimate success where she was concerned. Abby, however, wasn't. "You're that certain, are you?" she countered.

"I always play to win, *chérie*, remember that."

Beau escorted Abby to her door.

She noticed that their entrance back into town set some tongues wagging. Several of the people they had passed while riding down the wide main street didn't even bother waiting until they were out of earshot to make a comment. Abby didn't need to hear a word of what was spoken to know that she and Beau McMasters were the subjects of gossip—she merely needed to read the faces. In a town the size of Heaven's Grace, everyone heard news almost as soon as it happened.

She'd made up her mind on the way back that she should put some distance between herself and the far-too-handsome-for-her-peace-of-mind Mr. McMasters. Thank God she had her job to keep her busy for the present. She was there to teach and would concentrate on that. Time would allow her to sort out her feelings, put things in the proper perspective.

"When will I see you again?"

Abby hesitated, her hand on the doorknob. "I don't know," she replied, turning to face him. "With school starting, I'm not sure how free my time will be."

Beau put his hand over hers. "You're not afraid of me, are you, Abby?" he demanded in a voice as smooth as aged cognac. "You've got to know that I would never force you to do anything that you truly didn't want to do. Tell me you know that for a fact."

She quickly read the stark look of what seemed like anguish on his face, as if any doubts she might have had translated into physical pain for him.

Obeying an instinct, Abby put her other hand atop his to reassure him. "I know that." And she did. If he wanted to harm her, take more than a kiss from her, he could have easily done that today. There would have been no one to stop him.

"But?"

"I need time, Beau. This is all so new to me."

He found himself agreeing to give her that time. "As you wish. But it's not over." He inclined his head and walked away.

"No," she answered quietly as he remounted his horse, "it isn't over."

It had only just begun.

* * *

"Have they located her yet?"

While it was only late afternoon in Montana, it was already early evening in New York. Alma Breckenridge discreetly sipped at her sherry while her husband poured himself a whiskey. They had important guests coming to dinner, so he'd made an effort to be home early.

"Not yet." His bitter tone spoke volumes as to how he felt about that. Breckenridge downed the contents of the glass in one swallow and then refilled it. Damn that girl! He should have beat some sense into her, taught her early on not to get wild ideas. That was his fault. He'd been too lenient.

"Careful, Harold," Alma warned. "You don't want to get tipsy before the Gillyfoyles arrive. Wouldn't do to let them think you aren't in control."

"What's that supposed to mean?"

"Only that *you* somehow let our daughter slip through *your* fingers. I told you not to trust her. Warned you that she had a mind of her own, but you wouldn't listen."

He disliked being reminded of his failure. "I'll find her."

"Will you?"

"Don't ever doubt that. And when I do . . ."

"Do you promise me she'll be shown the error of her ways?" his wife asked.

"My dear Alma," he said, tossing down the second drink, "she'll be taught a lesson, all right. One she won't soon forget. I trust that meets with your approval?"

"Of course, Harold," she responded with a chilling smile, sorting through the social invitations that had arrived earlier that day. "You know best. I leave her well-deserved punishment in your capable hands. All I ask is that it fit the crime."

"It will, my dear. You can"—he smiled in a cold, hard way—"take that to the bank." When Harold Breckenridge broke a person, they stayed broken. His daughter would be no exception.

153

PART II

TILL THERE WAS YOU

Chapter Eleven

My dear Mrs. Butler:
I have the honor to acknowledge the receipt of
your most gracious note and do so look forward to
your charming presence at the formal opening of my
establishment, the Creole Lady, tomorrow evening.
I remain your most humble servant,
Beau McMasters

Abby stared at the bold, flowing script, imagined she
could actually hear the words being spoken as she read
the contents of the letter. Josh, who she knew was doing
odd jobs for Beau as well as working in the livery, had just
handed her the note as she was leaving school.

Unable to wait until she reached home, she opened it
right then, the words bringing a smile to her face. He
sounded so formal, so mannered. So unlike the passionate
man she knew he could be.

"Beau." She whispered his name. Then again. *"Beau."*

She had only seen him in passing these past six weeks.
So much had happened since that day they'd spent to-

gether. They'd each been so busy, caught up in the demands of their own new lives: he with his ranch and getting the formerly run-down saloon refurbished; she teaching her pupils and establishing a routine. They saw each other by chance on the street and in passing, at the mercantile, and occasionally at the hotel. Each time they were polite, exchanging friendly hellos, or making small talk about the weather. Yet underneath, heat simmered. She felt it and saw it reflected in his eyes.

As Abby entered her house, removed her coat and put on the kettle for hot water, she couldn't help recalling the special memory of his kisses. How the touch of his hands and mouth had wrought a change in her that day, the memory adding an undercurrent to each word, each glance they exchanged.

At odd times she would find the recollections fresh and unsettling, for she had no control over their occurrence, or the effect they had on her. Just thinking about the persuasive feel of his lips could send warmth shooting through her body. It was this particular unexpected heat that both thrilled and scared her. Having tasted the succulent fruit of sensual knowledge, Abby realized she wanted to repeat the process, including taking a heartier bite the next time. She yearned for it with an intense hunger heretofore unknown. The craving occasionally threatened her sleep, causing her to wake from dreams heavy with strange longings.

Yet what of him?

She poured boiling water into the china pot and let the tea steep while she fetched a cup and saucer, along with a small jug of milk and a bowl of sugar.

Did he think about her, she wondered, as often as she thought about him? Of their time together? Of what they'd shared?

Or had it meant so little to him that he was able to dismiss it as having no real consequence? No importance in his life whatsoever. Simply a pleasant diversion.

Had it been just another day, and she, just another woman?

Like the sharp prick of a needle, those questions occasionally jabbed at her. Abby wished she knew the answers.

She sighed. Was she being overly foolish? Turning the incident into something it was not? Did her face haunt him at odd moments as his sometimes haunted her?

In the middle of a geography lesson the other day, she'd suddenly lost her concentration, allowing a memory to interfere with her work. While grading papers at her kitchen table last week, she suddenly remembered the scent of the pines, the color of the sky at midday, the sound of rushing water, and she thought of him.

And whenever she saw Beau, it was all that much more vivid, stirring afresh the simmering sweetness. Somehow he'd passed beyond the bounds of the periphery of her world, moving toward the inner core, to a point no one else had ever breached. If she wasn't careful, she could get hurt. If she wasn't cautious, she could end up playing the fool.

This was all so very new to her, while he was a man, experienced in the ways of the flesh, of satisfying his desires. She didn't need a legal affidavit, nor a witness to attest to that fact. It was there, an intrinsic part of him, especially in his eyes. In the knowing way he looked at her that afternoon, and every other time since then. Eyes that spoke seductively and eloquently without a word. It was there in the tilt of his lips as he smiled. A warm, inviting gesture that bespoke a connection, an intimacy. A *bond*.

She could be wrong. Perhaps she was seeing what she wanted to see, believing what she wanted to believe.

Keeping all this inside her was making Abby almost crazy. She longed to share this information with Gussie, ask the older woman's advice.

But the lies that she'd told, however well-intentioned, held her back. Pretending to be a widow imposed certain restrictions on Abby, implied knowledge she didn't possess. Forced a false face of experience on her, one she couldn't shed without sacrificing the facade she had so carefully built up.

Maybe she could get around the truth, she thought as she poured herself a cup of tea, she could add details to her story, such as a husband too sick to fulfill his marital duties. That would give her the excuse to . . .

To what? Compound the lies even more?

No, that wouldn't work, she decided. All that would do would be to dig her deeper into the morass of mendacity. Enough was enough.

There had to be another way, another source to tap.

A soft knock sounded on the door, interrupting her reverie.

Abby rose, casting a swift glance at the small brass clock that rested on the sideboard. Her visitor was right on time.

"Come in, Sabina."

The other woman eagerly stepped inside the cheery room, a smile on her face. The clever little touches Abby had made turned a formerly bare shell into a welcoming place that invited guests to linger. Store-bought white lace curtains hung over the windows; a linen and lace tablecloth draped the pine table. Fall wildflowers spilled out of ordinary glass canning jars, adding a warm touch of color.

Sabina contrasted this to her father's cabin, which smelled of tobacco and dust. The spare rooms were dull and dingy, the way he liked them. Cleanliness was not important to him; he considered her "uppity" for even trying to keep the floors swept and the clothes clean. He'd often stated in a bitter tone that she was being bamboozled by that prissy schoolmarm's influence.

"Would you like a cup of tea?" Abby offered, her voice breaking into Sabina's thoughts.

"Much obliged, Miss Abby," Sabina responded, placing the loosely wrapped parcel she carried onto the table and removing her faded blue cotton duster, which had seen better days. "Weather took a cooler turn today."

"Yes, it did," Abby agreed, getting another cup and saucer while Sabina hung her threadbare coat next to Abby's heavier wool jacket. She hoped that Sabina would see to buying herself a new winter coat with the money she'd earned from transforming the bare bones material into a finished outfit for Abby.

"The skirt's hemmed and pressed just right," Sabina murmured as she took a seat, careful not to spill the tea as she added two spoonfuls of sugar and a splash of milk. "You'll be the most beautiful woman there."

Abby smiled over her own lifted cup. "I very much doubt that, Sabina."

"Why should you?" the other woman asked, helping herself to a small slice of pumpkin bread from the covered wicker basket. "It's the truth, plain and simple," she stated. "Wait until everyone in town sees you in your new dress. Why, no one hereabouts will even come close. You'll outshine them all without half trying. Men will be lining up to court you."

Abby wet her lips. "I'm not interested."

"People think you should be."

"People?" Abby asked, her eyes locked with those of her guest. "What people?"

"Why, some of the prominent ladies of Heaven's Grace, that's who," Sabina explained between bites of the hearty pumpkin spice bread. "I overheard Mary James and Mrs. Cooper talking about that just the other day when I was in the general store getting an extra spool of thread. They both said that you weren't born to be a widow; that sooner or later, the town's menfolk would wake up and see to it that you were once again a married lady."

Abby raised a brow. "That's for me to decide."

"That's what I told them."

"You did?"

"Yes. Told them that you should be left alone. When you're ready, you'll know it." Sabina dropped her gaze to the warm tea, staring into the cup as if it contained all the answers. "Some men take a long time to get over," she said, "if you ever can."

Abby caught the sad, wistful note in Sabina's voice and felt like a fraud when faced with her new friend's genuine loss. "You loved the man who took you away, didn't you?" She hadn't planned on asking the question; it just came pouring out after hearing the other woman's softly insistent words.

"He didn't carry me away in the way everyone hereabouts thinks, or says," Sabina responded with an honesty that touched Abby's heart, "like I was a victim to his *savage* lust. It was me," she confessed. "*I* begged him to take me away. *I* ran away, to him.

"And yes," Sabina admitted, "I loved him. With all my heart. He was a good man who deserved better than he got."

"What was his name?"

"Proud Bear," Sabina said, her voice soft and filled with love.

"Where did you two meet?"

"I was spending some time at my uncle's homestead near Helena when I first saw him. He was selling some of the ponies he'd caught and trained." She closed her eyes for a moment, picturing him at their initial meeting. "At first he scared me. I'd grown up listening to my pa talk about the 'heathen savages' and what they would do to whites, especially women, if they got the chance.

"Proud Bear seemed different. Gentle. And so very easy

to talk to. Besides, my uncle trusted him and that meant something to me.

"We began to meet whenever I could sneak away. Even if it was just for a few minutes, they were precious. Each time we met, it was harder and harder to leave him behind, but I knew that I had to come back home eventually. Back to Pa, who'd become filled with bile."

"He wouldn't let you stay with your uncle?"

"No. I had duties here. He made that clear when I asked to stay a little longer." *Chores,* he'd said in response to her letter begging him to let her spend more time with her uncle and his family. Chores she couldn't ignore any longer. Even though he'd had someone else write the note for him, his anger came through. She was inconveniencing him.

Sabina continued her story. "All we did was talk, honestly. Proud Bear told me stories about his people, about their ways, their customs. Names of things in his tongue. What it meant for him to live free, not on a reservation with rules and restrictions."

Abby watched as her friend's eyes glowed with warmth as she resumed her tale.

"He made me laugh, and I realized that I hadn't done that in a long time, since before my ma died."

Abby related to the story her friend was telling. There hadn't been much laughter in her house, either. This man from another culture must have seemed like an unexpected gift, sent to show Sabina that joy did exist in the world, if you left your heart open to it. How could anyone, especially a parent, find fault in that? Shouldn't your child's happiness be at least on par with your own?

"When I told Proud Bear that this was to be our last time together, he asked me to stay. I wanted to, so very much, but I was afraid. His life was so different from mine, as I was different from him. Stupidly, I told him so, much to my later regret.

"Then, when I returned home, Pa found out about my new friend and he accused me of doing some ugly things." Pain flared in Sabina's eyes. "I told him it wasn't true; Proud Bear respected me. Pa mocked me and said no Indian respects a white woman. All they want is to sully her, take her down to their level, which he thinks is below ours. He said I needed a lesson, and it was his duty to teach me."

Sabina lifted the cup to her lips and drank the remains of the cooling liquid. She would carry the marks of his whip for the rest of her life. "As soon as I was able, I ran away."

Abby reached out and gently gave the other woman's hand a quick squeeze. "Back to Proud Bear?"

"Yes."

"And he was waiting for you?"

Sabina smiled. "Yes. He said he knew I would come back. He'd seen it in a vision."

"You loved him that much?"

"And more. We were married the next day."

"Married?"

"Uh-huh. By a holy man of his tribe. I knew we wouldn't find a white preacher to marry us, and I didn't want to wait another day."

"That was incredibly brave." Abby thought of all this woman had risked for love, all she'd turned her back on, and all she'd gained. "Was he a good husband to you?"

Sabina, buoyed by her new friend's ready acceptance of what she'd done, the choices she'd made, nodded her head. "The best. I never knew a man could be so tender."

"I can tell you were happy," Abby observed.

"More than I thought I had a right to be."

"What do you mean by that?"

Color rose in Sabina's pale cheeks, cheeks that had filled out these past few weeks, a good sign that she was taking better care of herself. "Proud Bear was a loving husband, one who treated me special." She lowered her head and stared at the empty cup. "I'd bever been kissed by a man before, let alone been a wife to one," she admitted, her voice barely above a whisper. "Does that make me bad because I enjoyed it?"

Sabina had enjoyed all of it. The caring. The sharing. All the intimate aspects of being a married woman. Of living her life with a man who was genuinely concerned about her. Her wants. Her needs.

Abby didn't know what to say at first. Then, she remembered vividly the way being held in Beau's arms, his mouth on hers, insistent and demanding, made her feel. Excited. Alive in a fashion she hadn't dreamt of before. How could anything that made you feel so good, so alive, be bad?

"No," Abby replied. "Of course not."

"Pa and Reverend Whitcomb said that Proud Bear was a heathen, and that I was a whore for sharing his bed. Doubly so because I went willingly." Sabina raised her eyes to Abby.

The other woman's desperate need for approval touched Abby. "Of course you weren't a whore," she stated firmly in answer to the unspoken question. "Proud Bear was your husband, the man you'd given your heart to, trusted your life with. In the eyes of God, you were his wife. You didn't sell your body to him for favors, for jewels, or for some lofty position in society. It was *your* free choice, given in love. That can't be wrong."

"Your husband must have been a happy man, Abby."

A knot fixed itself in Abby's stomach. She wanted to repay honesty with honesty, yet she dared not for fear of upsetting the balance of her new life. "We shared something very special." My imagination, she added silently. Now, when she thought about her fictitious husband, the warm feelings she pretended to have were helped by another face, real instead of made up. A sardonic, bearded face that had somehow inched its way deeper into her heart and her life. Carved itself in her consciousness with all the skill of a master artist.

"It's getting dark out," Sabina announced. "I'd better be going back to fix Pa's dinner." She stood up, then glanced at the package on the table. "I'm sorry. I got to talking so much, we never had the chance to see if that skirt was the way you wanted it."

"I'm sure it is," Abby said, getting up also. "But, should it need a last-minute adjustment, can you come to the hotel tomorrow and help me with it?"

"You changing over there?"

Abby nodded. "Gussie offered me a room so that I could have the chance to take a bath after school before I put on my new dress. That's something I miss," she added with a wistful note, "a nice hot bath. Here I can heat water and wash off, but relaxing in a tub is so much better."

"Did you know that Mr. McMasters had one put in at his new club?"

"He did?" Abby lifted one hand and put it to her throat, her mind filling with a picture of him in the hotel's oversized tub. His long, lean limbs surrounded by warm soapy water. "How do you know?"

"Because I was there when they delivered it. Came all the way from San Francisco."

"What were you doing there?"

"He needed a bit of sewing work done and I was happy to help. Paid me real well for my time, too." Sabina slipped on her coat. "And can you imagine? He's got another one just like it, only slightly bigger, that's going in his ranch. Never heard of a man who liked to bathe so much. But then, he's a real gentleman. You can tell by his manners. Even treats the girls that came to work for him proper-like."

"What girls?" Abby tried to keep her voice even.

GET UP TO 4 FREE BOOKS!

You can have the best romance delivered to your door for less than what you'd pay in a bookstore or online. Sign up for one of our book clubs today, and we'll send you **FREE* BOOKS** just for trying it out...**with no obligation to buy, ever!**

HISTORICAL ROMANCE BOOK CLUB

Travel from the Scottish Highlands to the American West, the decadent ballrooms of Regency England to Viking ships. Your shipments will include authors such as CONNIE MASON, SANDRA HILL, CASSIE EDWARDS, JENNIFER ASHLEY, LEIGH GREENWOOD, and many, many more.

LOVE SPELL BOOK CLUB

Bring a little magic into your life with the romances of Love Spell—fun contemporaries, paranormals, time-travels, futuristics, and more. Your shipments will include authors such as LYNSAY SANDS, CJ BARRY, COLLEEN THOMPSON, NINA BANGS, MARJORIE LIU and more.

As a book club member you also receive the following special benefits:

- **30% OFF all orders through our website & telecenter!**
- **Exclusive access to special discounts!**
- **Convenient home delivery and 10 day examination period to return any books you don't want to keep.**

There is no minimum number of books to buy, and you may cancel membership at any time. See back to sign up!

*Please include $2.00 for shipping and handling.

YES! ☐

Sign me up for the **Historical Romance Book Club** and send my TWO FREE BOOKS! If I choose to stay in the club, I will pay only $8.50* each month, a savings of $5.48!

YES! ☐

Sign me up for the **Love Spell Book Club** and send my TWO FREE BOOKS! If I choose to stay in the club, I will pay only $8.50* each month, a savings of $5.48!

NAME: _____

ADDRESS: _____

_____

TELEPHONE: _____

E-MAIL: _____

☐ **I WANT TO PAY BY CREDIT CARD.**

☐ VISA   ☐ MasterCard.   ☐ DISCOVER

ACCOUNT #: _____

EXPIRATION DATE: _____

SIGNATURE: _____

Send this card along with $2.00 shipping & handling for each club you wish to join, to:

**Romance Book Clubs
20 Academy Street
Norwalk, CT 06850-4032**

Or fax (must include credit card information!) to: 610.995.9274.
You can also sign up online at www.dorchesterpub.com.

*Plus $2.00 for shipping. Offer open to residents of the U.S. and Canada only.
Canadian residents please call 1.800.481.9191 for pricing information.

If under 18, a parent or guardian must sign. Terms, prices and conditions subject to change. Subscription subject to acceptance. Dorchester Publishing reserves the right to reject any order or cancel any subscription.

JOIN NOW!

"From some fancy house in San Francisco. Real pretty, they are. Daisy and Flora."

"And they came all the way to Montana?"

Sabina nodded. "Seems like Mr. McMasters knew them from when he lived there."

Pretty, and with a history linking them to Beau. Just how friendly were they with him? And they were from San Francisco. A city that even back East was known for its glittering sophistication, coupled with its wild ways.

"I've got to go. After I get Pa's supper, I've still a bit more to do on Mrs. Cooper's dress." Sabina smiled. "Had to let it out a mite." She grinned. "Too many of Carl Travers's, pies I think. Thanks for the tea."

"My pleasure, as always," Abby assured her. "Will I see you tomorrow night?"

Sabina shook her head. "No. Mr. McMasters invited me personally, but I don't think I care to be there. Too many people."

"Well, if you change your mind, let me know. You're more than welcome to join me."

Abby shut the door and leaned back against it for a moment after Sabina left. A slow smile formed on her lips as she reached for the package, releasing the string that held it together. Her fingers smoothed over the material, enjoying the texture, admiring the color. Perfect, she told herself as she gathered it up in her arms. Simply perfect.

Everything was ready for the gala opening tomorrow night. Beau had seen to every last detail personally. Still, he couldn't help wishing it were taking place tonight because of one special guest, a guest he longed to see.

He strolled through the downstairs, running a hand over the roulette wheel, spinning it into life, watching the ball drop into a black slot. He picked up a deck of cards that one of his dealers had left on the table and shuffled through them with all the ease and skill of his professional status. He flicked one up on the table, then another. The king of spades. The ace of clubs. *Twenty-one*.

A smile lifted the corners of his mouth. Luck was on his side; everything was falling nicely into place. His dreams were taking shape faster and better than he could have ever hoped.

Almost all, he amended. There was still one remaining, one which might prove the hardest to secure. Having Abby Butler.

He flicked over another card—the queen of hearts.

"Seeking your fortune, *mi caballero?*" asked a soft, feminine voice.

Beau turned and smiled at the small, dark-haired woman, who held a cup of hot chocolate in her hands. "I've already found it."

She smiled, then took a sip of her steaming drink. "I think you have." She glanced down at the cards on the table. "Are you going to tell me her name?"

"Whose name?"

She laughed. "*Her* name. Your queen of hearts."

Beau raised a dark brow, his expression carefully controlled.

"Have it your own way, *querido,* but I'll find out soon enough."

Beau leaned down and dropped a quick kiss on the woman's smooth cheek. "Curiosity, *ma chère,* killed the cat."

"So?" she asked, licking the foam from the chocolate off her top lip. "What's one life when there are eight remaining?"

Beau chuckled. "Trust you to be the eternal optimist, Flora."

She gave him a rueful smile, then shrugged her slim shoulders. "You're evading the question."

"What makes you so sure that there's a woman in my life?"

"The fact that neither Daisy nor I have shared your bed since we arrived." She reached out her hand, stroking her long-nailed index finger along his cheek, then over the lean line of his close-cropped beard.

"I didn't hire you for that."

"Of course not," she said, her finger now trailing across the full expanse of his lower lip. "It would have been an added benefit of working for you, though," she said with a seductive smile. "A bonus, I believe it's called."

Beau gently removed her hand, lifted it to his lips for a perfunctory kiss. "I'm flattered."

Flora's black eyes fixed on him. "You should be," she said with a deepening smile before she added. "But you're not going to tell me, are you?"

Beau placed the deck on the table. "You'll meet her tomorrow."

"So, I was right."

He shrugged. "In a manner of speaking."

Flora laughed. "I was right, which is all that matters. You care that much for her?"

He thought for a moment before he answered her. "I've never met anyone like her," he stated. Abby Butler was like an unfinished portrait; there were still portions of the canvas that had been left bare, to be filled in later, gradually, one spot of color at a time.

"That's not what I asked."

"But that's all the answer you're going to get."

Flora backed off, wisely realizing that she couldn't push Beau any farther. She switched to a safer topic. "You've created something extraordinary here."

His eyes quickly surveyed the room. "You should have seen it when I first came to town. I was tempted to set a match to it and watch it burn to the ground."

"That bad?"

"Had you and Daisy seen it then, you might have thought I was mad even to think I could accomplish the task of transforming such a place."

Flora ran a hand through her long, loose hair, placing her empty cup on a nearby table. "Mad? No." She shook her head. "Determined? *Sí.*" She moved closer to the heat of the nearby iron stove, first warming her posterior, then her hands. Her eyes focused on the long oak bar, the highly polished brass foot railing, the wide flow of mirrors that flanked the centerpiece of the back bar: a large oil painting of a magnificent house nestled in a grove of live oaks. She only gave it a moment's glance before dismissing it, then moved to pick up a recently opened bottle of bourbon and poured them both a drink. "Much too soft for me," she said, commenting on the artist's use of color. "I much prefer something stronger, bolder. With colors that remind me of my home." She sipped the dark amber liquid. "I don't see you living there at all."

Beau laughed—a dark, ironic sound. "I never did. That's the point of owning it now."

Flora looked perplexed. "I don't understand."

"It doesn't matter."

"Does *she* understand?" she asked slyly, finishing the remainder of her drink, her dark eyes on her employer.

Beau's lips curved into a small, seductive smile.

"You're not going to tell, are you." It was a statement instead of a question. "So be it," she said with a shrug. "Some secrets are made to share; others are not." Flora leaned over and gave him a quick kiss. "Be happy."

Beau pondered the words as Flora climbed the stairs to her room and he poured himself another drink. He *was* happy, he discovered. Tomorrow night he would make a declaration: Beau McMasters is here, and here to stay. Finally.

And, tomorrow he would share his triumph with the one woman he wanted to include.

Ever since that afternoon on his ranch, the memory of her sweet kisses and lithe body had almost consumed him. The sound of her sighs. The smell of her hair. The feel of her skin. The taste of her mouth. The look in her eyes—blue eyes filled with wonderment and surprise. As if this were her first brush with passion, with heat so white hot that it threatened to explode, turning them to ashes in its wake.

Her eyes. Those same eyes that boldly met his before lowering. The becoming rush of color that stroked her cheeks like an artist's brush, soft and pure, whenever they chanced to meet.

He was a man used to kisses and all that came with them. Yet with Abby there was something more. Something he couldn't define. An added ingredient that changed the recipe. Improved the outcome. Damned if he knew what it was; damned if he cared.

What mattered was that come the following night, she would be there with him.

Where they went after that . . . ?

Good question.

He tossed back his drink, savoring the aged bourbon. Tomorrow there would be champagne. A shared drink from the finest bottle he had in his personal stock, in celebration of his triumph.

Champagne-flavored kisses. A mouth sweet and hungry as his own. A mouth waiting, eager for the adventure.

Damn! but he ached with the want—the need—of her. Hot and hard, it seethed through his body, sending pulses of scorching heat tearing into every last corner of his soul. Almost impossible to ignore. Almost impossible to deny.

He had only to mount the stairs and knock on one of the doors if all he wanted was quick relief. He would be welcomed, no questions asked, no answers sought. It would be so very easy.

Yet he couldn't bring himself to do it. Not when it was Abby's face, her body, her soul, he longed to possess.

And he would.

Come tomorrow . . .

Chapter Twelve

He stood in the shadows, watching, waiting, biding his time.

Dozens of people crowded into the newly reopened den of iniquity. He could hear the gay laughter, could see the Sunday-best clothes, could recognize the people entering, including prominent members of the community.

Their coming had put a stamp of approval on this new venture, this slap in the face of all that was holy. A temple of sin, a coven of debauchery. It was a travesty of all that was good. Bad enough that the last place had been permitted to exist, but this? This was wrong.

No, more than wrong—it was an abomination.

Couldn't they see? Didn't they know? Depravity dressed in a fancy getup was still depravity.

He sighed. Once again it was up to him to show them the way. The *true* way to salvation. Later they would thank him for it. Like children, they needed a strong and mighty hand to lead them down the righteous path. Without him they would never find it. They would be lost. He alone knew what was right, what was proper. Moral laxity couldn't be tolerated. It had to be plucked out and destroyed before it could infect every aspect of life.

The sound of a carriage forced him deeper into the shadows. No one must see him until he was ready.

It was the Great Whore, along with several of her daughters of Eve, arriving as if they had a perfect right to be here, dressed in their gaudy outfits of sin, flaunting their exposed flesh. They besmirched the town by their mere presence and insulted him. Their laughter and silly chatter disturbed him.

He recognized two of them in the dim light as the ones who went to the schoolmarm's house several times a week, thus confirming his low opinion of *that* woman. She consorted with whores, therefore she must be a whore herself. And a whore shouldn't be teaching the town's children. It was an affront, both to God and to him.

More voices came drifting through the night.

It was the mayor and his wife. Didn't they realize they should have ignored this summons? They were supposed to be a righteous example to the rest of the town. Instead, they, too, succumbed to Satan's inviting wiles when they should have been strong and resisted.

It was all the fault of the schoolmarm and the gambler. With them had come this invasion of impropriety.

Now it was up to him to rectify it. By any means necessary.

And he knew just how he could accomplish his task, and who would help him achieve his goals.

God was watching—and so was he.

It was crowded inside the newly renovated casino. Every possible inch of space was filled with people: some making use of the fancy gambling facilities; others enjoying the fine wines, including imported champagnes, offered at the bar, or the food attractively displayed on the long tables set with linens and fine china. For the men there were humidors of expensive cigars available for sampling; for the ladies, small china boxes filled with selections of dried fruit and chocolate.

A short black man played the piano in one corner of the room, the sound of Mozart and Chopin mixing with that of spirituals and popular tunes. Accompanying him were three other musicians, their stringed instruments adding a touch of harmony and grace to the proceedings.

Beau surveyed the room with pride. Most everyone he'd invited had shown up. By all accounts, this was a huge success. He'd been waylaid by several people who sang the praises of his new establishment, promising future patronage. Dealers were busy handling all the people who wanted to try their luck against the house. Even two drummers, who were in town for the night, promised to spread the word about the *Creole Lady* to the other towns they visited.

Yet still Beau wasn't satisfied. He wouldn't be until *she* arrived. When Abby Butler walked in his door, then he would feel the night was complete.

Smiling, Flora made her way through the throng to Beau's side. "She's not here yet, is she?" she whispered when she got close.

His reply was terse. "No."

"Don't fret. She will come."

Beau smiled raffishly; he could never remain cross with Flora. "I know that."   •

"You're sure?"

"No doubt in my mind."

Flora laughed. "None in mine, either," she said in a teasing tone. "What woman could resist you, *mi cabellero?*"

"Some have."

She took an inventory with her dark eyes, slowly contemplating the man standing next to her, up, down, and back up again. "Now you are being modest."

He shrugged his shoulders.

She squeezed his arm. "Then they were fools."

Beau favored her with a deep grin. "Spoken like a true friend."

"*Sì, mi amigo,* always." Her tone was affectionate, filled with the warmth of one who loved, and who would have done more if the gentleman still wanted. For them, it had only been a sharing of the flesh, not the true heart, though she knew that they cared about one another. That was Beau's gift. Making women feel special in his arms, as if in that moment, they were all that mattered. The hurried rush of coupling exclusively for his own gratification was not for him. The fast and furious need to find his release, leaving the woman unfulfilled. In bed he was more than generous, sharing everything in him but what was most important: his heart.

Ah, Flora thought, such was life. Perhaps there was a man for her in this town. Someone to laugh with, love with. Maybe this man coming toward her and Beau? Older. Settled. Perhaps one who would appreciate a lady of many skills.

"Who is that?" she whispered to Beau.

He flicked a glance in the direction she indicated with a tilt of her head. "Benjamin Reynolds. Owner and publisher of *The Heaven's Grace Weekly.*" Beau looked at his companion, adding, "A man of some substance, *chère.*"

"The best kind," she purred.

Beau chuckled, kissing her forehead. "Good hunting."

"Ah, Mr. McMasters, what a difference you've made here," Reynolds said when he reached them.

"How kind of you to say so," Beau replied affably. "May I have the pleasure of introducing you to a dear friend whose help in seeing my dream realized was invaluable, Señora Flora de Lopez y Speranza."

Flora bestowed on the newspaperman her best and brightest smile, the one guaranteed to reduce men to groveling supplicants.

Instead of falling at her feet, Reynolds extended his hand. "Mighty glad to make your acquaintance ma'am."

Ma'am? Flora narrowed her eyes. *"Señor,"* she said stiffly, her lips compressing tightly as she ignored the man's hand. "If you will excuse me, *querida,*" she murmured to Beau, "I must see to the other guests."

"Right pretty gal, ain't she?" Reynolds stated as he dug out a small notebook from his jacket pocket. "Exotic. Like an orchid planted in prairie grass." He pulled a stubby pencil from the same place. "Tonight, you have the town in your grasp—and in such a short time. Any comments?"

Before Beau could respond, he sensed the presence of the woman he was waiting for. Turning, he saw Abby as she entered through the open front doors, following Gussie and Carl Travers. She was, without a doubt in his mind, the proverbial belle of the ball. Her red hair was up-swept, with several ringlets cascading around her almost bare shoulders, teasing the curve of her neck. A neck that should have been dripping with precious gems. Sapphires, to match the deep silk taffeta of her gown. Though it was not the Worth original she would have been wearing if he'd been paying for her clothes, this creation did her justice, revealing her enticing neck and creamy bosom.

In a sea of homespun, gingham, cotton and wool, she was the beacon of elegance. She had style, grace, sophistication. Much more than any schoolteacher or governess he'd ever seen. No humble origins for her. Genteel poverty now, maybe, but she was to the manor born. Even if he was the only one in the room to recognize her sophistication, she had it. Carriage straight, head up, smile on, she sailed through the room like a duchess.

"Later," he said to Reynolds, walking away from the newsman.

Abby saw Beau coming towards her, striding confidently through the crowd like a feral wolf through a field of sheep. God, but he stole her breath away. When their eyes connected across the room, she could feel the heat, the pure simmering fire that began in her belly and worked its way upward, singeing her lungs.

"Here, honey, I think you need this," Gussie said as she handed Abby a glass of chilled champagne. "He's sure a handsome fella, now ain't he? There's no denying he's the man of the moment, sure enough setting this town on its ear."

Abby clutched the glass and brought it to her lips, savoring the tickle of the bubbles. Gussie would get no argument from her—Beau McMasters was a man dressed to dazzle. His lean frame was clothed in dark gray wool—merino, she guessed. His frock coat fit his broad shoulders, tailored specifically for him. So were the trousers, lovingly following the lines of his long legs and muscular thighs. A lighter gray satin vest covered a pristine white shirt. Even the engraved silver buckle of his holster caught the light of the many chandeliers and glowed brightly.

His dark hair was gleaming, with thick waves any woman would envy. Abby longed to dispense with her gloves and touch it, feel it run through her fingers. Unlike many of the men, his hair was clean, without dirt, grease, or pomade to mar its natural beauty.

"This is sure one fine place you got here, Beau," Gussie said. "Me and Carl think it's quite an improvement over what used to be here. And so does the town. This here's a real enough showplace. Something classy. Sure to bring more business to Heaven's Grace."

Beau leaned over and kissed the older woman on the cheek.

Gussie blushed.

"Please don't forget that you and Carl are among my special guests this evening," Beau stated. "Avail yourselves of the tables. Whatever you play, it's on me. My dealers know that."

"Why, thank you, Beau," added Carl Travers. "That's right nice of you."

Gussie set her empty glass of champagne on a nearby table and grabbed her husband's arm. "We'll leave you in good hands, Abby. Enjoy yourself."

"I'll see that she does," Beau promised.

A flutter of sensation flickered in Abby's belly when she heard his words. Plenty of people were there, yet for her, it was as if they were the only two. How did he manage to make her feel like that?

"You honor me and my establishment, Mrs. Butler."

She wet her lips with a quick flick of her tongue. "It looks as if I'm not the only one, Mr. . . . Beau."

"Free food and drink have a way of filling a room."

"That's true. But you have other attractions here as well." She glanced around the large renovated space. The opulence of the furnishings and the skillful blending of colors and patterns were the essence of sophistication. What she would expect of a business in a big city, not in the wilds of Montana territory. She recognized the high-quality crystal and china she saw, exclusive in design, and quite expensive. A Belter sofa was against one back wall, flanked by two equally beautiful chairs. Polished mahogany side tables gleamed with numerous coats of beeswax. Silver candelabras glowed in various spots. Numerous Aubusson rugs covered the heart-of-pine floors.

"Where did you find these wonderful furnishings?"

An enigmatic smile crossed his lips. "They were in storage."

"Storage?"

"Yes. They belonged to a piece of property I bought in New Orleans some years back."

"Whoever parted with them must have been saddened by the loss."

"He wasn't happy to part with them, no."

"I can well imagine. Such treasures should have passed to someone in the family."

They did, he wanted to say. "The man had no say in the matter. The house and its contents were sold to pay his debts."

"How sad."

"Don't waste your time mourning his loss," Beau added in a dismissive tone.

Abby tilted her head to stare at Beau. There was a certain hardness to his face, and in his eyes a coldness that chilled her.

This was the face of a man who could be a bitter enemy if crossed. It was there in the implacable look, the taught line of his mouth. Why? she wondered. What was it about this sale that merely talking about it wrought such a mercurial change in him?

"Still, he must have been comforted in the knowledge that his possessions were going to someone who could appreciate them," she offered.

Beau's face softened. "And you think that that's me?"

Abby answered without hesitation. "Of course, though why you wouldn't have wanted to save them for your own use surprises me."

"This *is* my own use."

She smiled. "You know what I mean. For your ranch."

"I am my own man, Abby," he said softly. "These pieces had no place in my home. They are where they belong." Like his grandfather's bed, used by generations of his family, which was now upstairs in his bedroom/office. He'd toyed with the idea of sending it to the ranch, but changed his mind. Other suites of furniture resided in the upstairs rooms; the rest had been sold in New Orleans. How fitting that some of his grandfather's favorite pieces were on public display in a gaming house. Where once the cream of New Orleans society had enjoyed the sight and feel of them, now the good citizens of Heaven's Grace did so as well.

"Whatever happened to the man who was forced to sell?"

"He died soon after." By his own hand, he could have added. Faced with the grandson he'd denied buying his house and all its contents, Jean-Marc Rivage had chosen to end his life.

"So, you finally got what you wanted all along, didn't you?" his grandfather had sneered as he put his name to the bills of sale.

"Not quite, Monsieur Rivage. I only wish that my parents could have been here to witness this."

"Humph," the old man said. "So they could gloat along with you?"

"Funny, I don't think either one of them would have done that. My mother, tender heart that she was, would have probably offered you shelter. And my father, as much as he loathed you for your treatment of his wife, would have acquiesced for her sake.

"I, however, have no compunction about turning you out on the streets, so that all the so-called friends you still possess can witness your abject humiliation. The bastard grandson you ignored and denied is now in full ownership of all that was yours. Think what your friends will say when they see every single item removed, the house gutted and razed."

"You would destroy my home?"

"Yes."

The old man straightened. *"Cochon."*

"So, I am a pig, am I? This from the man who whispered in the right ears and saw to it that his daughter and her husband were given to an angry mob, believing them to be spies? You have the gall to call me names?

"Once, I would have treasured this house. Cared carefully for its contents, as had *my*"—Beau took great delight in emphasizing that word—"family before me. Cherished it with a glad heart. You destroyed that possibility when you killed my parents. Now"—Beau looked around the grand salon—"it means less than nothing to me, as do you." To make his point more clear, Beau picked up a porcelain mantel clock, which he knew to have been a gift to his grandfather's father from Andrew Jackson for services during the battle for New Orleans. He held it up, admired the detailed work, the inscription in gold. Then, without hesitating, let it slip through his fingers, shattering on the hardwood floor.

"No!" the old man whispered in a strangled tone.

"Yes," his grandson replied. "This is how little I care for *your* traditions. May you think about that for however long you have to live."

It was then the old man smiled. "I see that you are a true Rivage after all. *Eh bien.*" He left the room without another word.

Some moments later, Beau, still in the salon glancing over the inventory his lawyers had prepared, heard the gunshot upstairs.

He was drawn back to the present moment when Abby touched his arm.

"Beau?"

"Forgive me, my dear," he stated, charm back in force, both in his voice and on his face. "How ungallant of me to let my thoughts drift when I'm in the company of the most beautiful woman here tonight."

Her low laughter sparkled. "My, how you do like to play the charmer."

"Play?" He gave her an exaggerated sigh. "You wound me, madam."

"Do I?" She wet her lips. "Somehow I doubt that. Flattery, my dear sir, is like a cut flower, nice while it lasts, but not to be taken for more than it is, a transient pleasure."

She recalled the endless empty words tossed her way by the many men who'd sought to woo her for her father's influence and fortune.

"Don't underestimate pleasure, Abby," Beau murmured in a low, soothing voice. "Transient or otherwise."

He'd skillfully turned the words around on her, bringing her into even more awareness of him as a man, one obviously very familiar with pleasure. She'd been flirted with before—had men swear undying love and desire, profess their devotion in many forms. It had all been part of the game, trying to capture her attention, and with that, her substantial trust fund.

But those attentions were nothing like this. This went beyond hollow boyish statements, beyond false declarations. This was real. For him, she was a woman. Not an heiress, nor a stepping stone to political influence or power.

Abby moved on to a safer topic, noticing the painting hanging over the back bar. The colors were soft, the house caught in the morning light. "What is that?" she asked, trying to divert his attention. "Your former home?"

He recognized her ploy and accepted it, for the moment. "No, not my home." He took her arm gently and led her closer to the painting. "At one point in my life it was the Holy Grail."

"How so?" He'd again aroused her curiosity.

"I thought owning it would give me all I wanted. Open up the world in ways I couldn't imagine."

Comprehension dawned on her. "It's the plantation you bought in New Orleans, isn't it?"

"Yes."

"It's beautiful."

"It was."

"Was?"

"It's gone now."

"What happened?"

"A fire consumed it."

"How terrible." She examined the painting as well as she could from the distance of the bar. "It looks quite old."

"It was built only a few years after the war for independence from England."

"A treasure lost."

"I look upon it as a perspective gained."

"How do you mean?"

He smiled, a smile, she noticed, tinged with sadness. "It was a false grail, not worthy of the effort or the sacrifice. A childhood dream that proved rotten with age."

"Then why do you keep the painting? Why not get rid of it?"

"To remind me that the past is just that—the past. Gone. It's what happens now that matters. Dwelling on the dream doesn't allow you to enjoy life as it is. Doesn't allow you to move on and forge a new destiny." He turned to face her, his look warmly sensuous and honest. "You know that too, don't you? It's why you came here, isn't it?"

A simple "Yes" was her answer. She did understand what he meant. Hadn't she fled New York and the trappings of her past to find a new life? A life lived on her own terms?

He handed her another glass of champagne, helping himself to one as well. "To the future."

Abby accepted the glass and brought it to clink against his.

"And to us," he said, his tone intimate.

"To the future, and us," she echoed, draining her drink, her eyes never leaving his. What she wanted at this moment was for him to kiss her, she thought. Kiss her as he had the day of the picnic, his mouth warm, searching, insistent.

Beau's thoughts went far beyond a mere kiss. God, he wanted to lead her up those stairs and find a bed as soon as possible. Did she know how utterly irresistible she was with that soft welcoming look in her eyes? He could imagine slowly stripping off the long gloves that she wore, kissing each inch of skin he exposed. Loosening the bodice of her dress, putting his hands on the soft flesh beneath, followed by his tongue. Sliding her stockings and pantalets along her legs, skimming his fingers around her knees and calves. Pushing up her skirts to slide between her creamy thighs, burying himself in her wet heat, sheathing himself as far as he could go, then making her his in the most primitive way possible.

Damn! That's what he wanted to do; what his body expected him to do. But he couldn't. Not here. Not now. Sleeping with the widow was one thing; destroying her reputation in this town was another.

"Mr. McMasters, Mrs. Butler, I have someone I'd like you to meet," said Mayor Cooper, interrupting the magic of the moment.

Beau set down his glass with a smile directed at Abby before he turned around.

He came face-to-face with a tall, well-built man in his late thirties, who topped Beau by at least three inches. The stranger wore a cream-colored Stetson pulled low over a head of thick curling brown hair. A mustache of the same color drooped low over his top lip.

"This here's our new sheriff, Adam Tyler."

Tyler removed his hat and held out his hand to Abby. "Mighty pleased to make your acquaintance, Mrs. Butler." He then shook hands with Beau. "You too, Mr. McMasters."

Beau sized up the potential rival quickly. "Sheriff."

"Ain't this great?" said Mayor Cooper. "More new blood coming to our town. Pretty soon we're gonna be double our size." He beamed, already seeing an increase in both his business and in revenue for the town. "Might have to build you a bigger schoolhouse, too, Mrs. Butler. Maybe get you an assistant, or even another teacher." He grinned. "Won't that be something?"

"Are you from around here, Mr. Tyler?" Abby asked.

"From just outside of Miles City, ma'am."

"Adam's daddy was a lawman, as are his two brothers," the mayor chimed in. "When the city council recently decided that we needed a permanent force of order in this town now that we're growing, I remembered the Tyler family. Adam was deputy to his brother Michah in Townson's Ridge. We're proud to have someone like him here."

"I'm sure that you'll come to love this town, Mr. Tyler, just as I have," Abby assured him.

He gave her a grin, deepening the dimples in his cheeks. "I certainly aim to try, ma'am."

"Then let me welcome you to Heaven's Grace and my establishment with a drink, sheriff. What do you favor?" Beau asked, signaling the bartender.

"Kentucky bourbon if you have it."

The barman quickly produced a bottle for the sheriff, pouring him a large jigger.

Tyler picked up the glass. "Your health, folks," he stated, downing the liquid. "Ah," he said with a sigh, "that is good. Very smooth."

"Would you care for another?"

"No thanks, Mr. McMasters. When I'm working, one's my limit."

"Ward," Beau called to the barman. "Mark this as the sheriff's personal bottle. On the house."

"Right nice of you," Tyler said.

Beau smiled. "Think nothing of it. Consider it a welcome to town present."

Tyler glanced around the room, taking note of the three burly men positioned at various spots. "Expecting trouble, Mr. McMasters?"

Beau smiled. "No, but it's smart to be prepared, just in case." His hand subtly caressed his Remington.

Tyler grinned, his big hand patting the ivory-handled Colt at his side. "I agree."

"Will your wife be joining you, Sheriff Tyler?" Abby asked, deciding that it was time to break up the not-so-subtle display of masculine tit-for-tat. Although it was amusing to watch the two men size each other up.

"Don't have one, ma'am. Ain't been lucky enough to find one that'll have a lawman. Too risky, they all think. Not that I blame them; it isn't a job that'll bring riches or fancy houses."

Abby quickly defended her sex. "Not every female thinks like that, I can assure you."

"Beg pardon, ma'am. I wasn't meaning no disrespect. Just calling it as I see it."

"In this town you'll find plenty of females looking for a good man, sheriff," Mayor Cooper added. "We'll just have to make sure that you meet them."

"Thanks. I'd appreciate that," Tyler said, a sparkle in his hazel eyes.

That gave Abby an idea. A small dinner party at her house, with Beau, Sabina, Gussie and Carl, and the new sheriff. Casual and cozy.

"Well, if you'll excuse us," the Mayor said as he moved off, "I've got a few more people to introduce the sheriff to."

"What's behind that cat-ate-the-cream look?" Beau asked Abby.

"I was just thinking that there's someone I'd like the sheriff to meet."

Beau chuckled. "You're going to play matchmaker?" His laugh covered his relief. For a moment, he'd thought Abby might have been interested in Adam Tyler for herself.

"Yes, in a manner of speaking."

"What other manner is there?"

"I have a friend that I think he might enjoy meeting."

"Who?"

"Sabina Baser."

"You're serious, aren't you?"

"And why not?"

Beau laughed softly. "She doesn't seem to be the type . . ."

Abby bristled slightly. "The type to what?"

"Interest our new sheriff."

"You'd be surprised."

"I would indeed," he stated. "She seems so quiet and contained."

"Perhaps," she ventured, "that's what he would like."

Beau raised a dark brow. "And you know this how? You just met him."

"Call it a hunch."

He shrugged.

"I'm going to invite him to my house for dinner, along with Sabina. And you, of course."

"Why thank you, ma'am. I'd be most honored."

"Gussie and Carl, too. That way it won't seem *so* over-whelming for either of them."

"Why, Mrs. Butler, I marvel at your perspicacity."

"As well you should," she teased. "Are you free this coming Sunday?"

He smiled. "I am your humble servant, ma'am."

"I doubt you were ever anyone's humble anything, Beau."

He laughed, but he didn't keep it up. At that moment, a lone figure crept into the room, standing by the door.

Abby followed Beau's gaze, catching the Reverend Mr. Whitcomb appraising the scene. His lips were pursed, his face sour.

"It looks as though I have an uninvited guest. Pardon me, my dear, while I see to having him removed."

Abby laid a hand on his arm. "Be careful, Beau."

He stopped and brought her gloved hand to his mouth, kissing the blue silk material lightly. "I cherish your concern for me. Don't worry, though."

Before Beau could reach him, one of Beau's men approached the reverend, intending to escort him out.

"Don't touch me, you heathen," Whitcomb snapped. He raised his voice, effectively drawing everyone's attention. "I beg you all to leave now before you destroy your souls. It may already be too late. This is a house of sin, run by a spawn of Satan, sent here to corrupt you and our town. See," he said, pointing to a group of women at the roulette table before he was subdued by Beau's man, "there's the Great Whore and her minions. Mixing with decent folk. Tainting the very air they breathe. They've already corrupted the schoolteacher."

"I'll thank you to keep your mouth shut, sir," Beau instructed Whitcomb in a cold, deadly voice. "No man insults a lady in my presence."

"Lady? She lets whores into her home. Only a fellow whore would do that."

"I think you've said about enough," Sheriff Tyler stated, reading the situation correctly and responding before it could escalate. He recognized the deadly gleam of anger in Beau's eyes.

"Whitcomb," Beau said, "if you ever mention Mrs. Butler's name again in that way, you will have me to deal with, and that you really don't want, not if you value your miserable life."

"He threatened me," Whitcomb shouted. "You all heard it. I'm a man of God, not of the gun."

"I doubt that God would claim you," Beau said, "at least not any God I know."

Tyler grabbed hold of Whitcomb's arm and walked him out the door, past the sidewalk and into the empty street. "I suggest that you do some thinking about what you said in there."

"You don't understand," Whitcomb protested. "I know the truth."

"Well, that's right nice for you, but I don't think those folks inside really care for your version. Now go on, get out of here before I take you in for disturbing the peace."

Whitcomb huffed. "You can't do that."

"Now that's where you're wrong," Tyler stated in a slow drawl. "I can and I will if you don't get out of my sight. I've seen your kind before, Reverend, and I don't like 'em."

"You'll be sorry."

"I'm sure I will for something I may do, but in this matter, I won't." Tyler turned and went back into the casino.

"Are you all right, Abby?" Beau asked when he reached her side.

"Yes, thank you."

"Take no notice of him."

"I don't. However, it's not fun being in the middle of this situation."

"He won't come near you, I promise."

"He doesn't have to, Beau. All he has to do is get people to believe what he says."

"Then I think it's time for him to leave town."

She grabbed his arm, this time afraid that he might act upon the cold hatred she'd seen in his eyes. "Leave it alone, Beau."

"Don't worry, *ma chère*. I think it can be accomplished by a few well-chosen words in a few influential ears. If not . . ." his voice trailed off. "Forget him. He's not worth your bothering about. Now"—he took her arm, leading her toward a heavy table laden with food—"let's have some of these tasty dishes and forget all about this incident."

"Will you?" she asked, watching as he quickly assembled a small plate piled high with a sampling of the food.

He smiled, handing her the plate.

"That's what I thought," she concluded.

Chapter Thirteen

Abby woke late, having tossed and turned in her bed the night before. She got up several times, checking her mantel clock, looking around as she thought she heard noises outside her house. It appeared to be only the wind, though after the incident at Beau's club, she was skittish.

And she knew it was more than Reverend Whitcomb's outlandish outburst that kept her awake, it was her growing connection to Beau himself. She'd felt the almost overwhelming attraction flare up as soon as she entered the Creole Lady and saw him there. He was a man naturally imbued with the mantle of authority. In any herd, he would be the leader, the one others looked to to set the standard. Not because he bullied, or cajoled, she'd observed, but because of the force of his personality. She'd witnessed this a few times before, in New York, and one or two other places in her travels. Some men, like her father, bought authority; others, like Beau, received it as their rightful due.

Abby smiled as she thought about it while she made her way around her kitchen, making coffee. Yawning, she reached for the iron skillet, added a thick pat of butter to it, and broke a couple of eggs, placing it over the heat.

Beau had seen her to her door late last night, having been unable to dissuade her from returning to her home. "What if Whitcomb comes looking for you?" he asked when they reached her little house. "I'd feel better if you stayed at the hotel."

"He won't come."

"How can you be so sure?" He stood close to her, eyes wary.

"Because of you," she said in a soft whisper, her right hand reaching up to lightly grab his shoulder before she stood on tiptoe to deliver a kiss to his bearded cheek. "Whitcomb wouldn't dare." Beau made her feel safe, protected, like a knight of old; her personal *chevalier* who would see that no harm came to her. "He'd have to go through you, my guardian angel, and he doesn't have the nerve."

Beau smiled, then drawled, "I'm no angel."

It was Abby's turn to smile. "To me you are." Unlike the paintings she'd seen of sweet, gentle, cherubic figures, surrounded with light and soft colors, he was dark, formidable, a warrior archangel with a flaming sword, all power and determination.

"Give me your key," he insisted, holding out his hand.

Abby withdrew it from her reticule, handing it over. Beau slipped it into the lock and proceeded into her kitchen, lighting her lamp, and then making his way through the rest of the house. Abby walked in, aware of the intimacy of having him in her house. She heard his boots as they crossed the floor, checking the interior.

"Everything appears just fine."

"I told you so."

"So you did." He placed her key on the table, then lifted her gloved hand to his mouth. *"Au'voir."*

Just as he was making his way through the doorway, Abby called out, "Beau."

He turned, a warm smile on his lips. "Was there something else?"

Abby looked at him, framed there, her eyes holding his for several moments. She exhaled deeply.

"I'd better go," he whispered.

"Yes, perhaps you should," she'd said. Go, before I ask you to stay, she'd added silently.

Later, when she heard the noises, she wished that she had asked him to remain.

And do what? Sit platonically in her kitchen all night long? Sleep on the floor of her bedroom, like a guard dog on watch? Or join her in her narrow bed, sharing the night with her?

In the few minutes she'd spent reminiscing, her eggs were scrambled, and the sliced bread she'd placed in the oven to toast was done.

Each day she was getting better at cooking on this wood-burning stove. Growing more confident in her abilities to survive here, or anywhere. Not only survive, she amended, but thrive.

And maybe reach out for love?

Why not?

Was this fascination with the gambling man the beginning of love, she wondered, or a lesser facsimile?

Abby wished that she knew. For whatever it was, it was certain that Beau McMasters had an effect on her. An intense one, judging by her reaction to him last night. Especially when all she wanted was to leave the opening night party behind and find some quiet place to be with him. Some place where no one could find them. Where they could enjoy each other's company without interruption, prying eyes, or wagging tongues.

A soft rap on her kitchen door broke into her thoughts.

193

She peered though the dimity curtains she'd hung there and relaxed when she saw her visitor. Opening the door, she greeted Sabina with a hug. The weather was colder today, and the last remnants of Indian summer were turning into a harbinger of the winter to come.

"I was just about to have breakfast, Sabina. Would you like some?"

"No thanks," the other woman replied. "I had breakfast a few hours ago, long about dawn."

"Well, then join me for some coffee while I eat mine."

"Now that I'd be happy to do." Sabina hung up her coat and got herself a cup of the piping hot brew. "I couldn't wait to hear all the details." Seeing the fresh toast, she decided to take a piece of it, spreading the thick slice liberally with peach preserves. "So what happened last night?"

Abby yawned over her coffee, smiling at the woman who sat across from her. "I had a very good time, for the most part."

"The most part? What does that mean?" Sabina asked, sipping from her own cup.

"There was an . . . incident that threatened to ruin the evening, but it was seen to quickly before it got out of hand. The Reverend Whitcomb decided to crash the event, and in doing so, delivered a rather venomous attack on several people who where there, myself included."

"Him." Sabina uttered the word with contempt.

"Yes," Abby agreed with her phrasing. "*Him*. Seems as though he wasn't happy with the opening of the gambling club, nor with Beau and his guests." She took a quick sip of coffee. "It appears we're in league with the devil, according to Whitcomb."

"No one took him seriously, did they?"

"No one there last night did, as far as I can tell. When he was evicted, there were sighs of relief. It's the people who weren't there, the people who believe what he preaches, that may cause a problem."

Sabina groaned. Her father was one of those who admired the reverend's positions; he certainly could quote portions of any sermon when he wanted validation for his own opinions.

"You don't have anything to worry about, Abby. The people in this town have come to care for you very much." Sabina's mouth kicked up in a smile. "I've heard some folks talking about what a difference you've made in the short amount of time you've been here. People hereabouts respect you."

"That's nice to know," Abby said, buttering another slice of toast. "I want to stay here." Every day this place was more her home, the first she'd ever truly had. She belonged here. And she *mattered.* What she did, what she thought, were of value. She was part of a community now. A larger family of sorts. Being a Breckenridge wasn't a factor in whether or not someone liked her. No one here knew her real last name. Butler was all they knew, or cared to know. The comfort that afforded her was beyond measure. She was tired of running. Tired of picking up and moving on like a vagabond or a criminal on the run. She'd done nothing wrong, yet she was hunted all the same.

"I'm glad." Sabina looked across the table, meeting Abby's eyes. "I can't tell you what your friendship has meant to me."

Abby reached across and grabbed her friend's hand, giving it a squeeze. "If it's meant half as much as yours has to me, then that's enough."

"I never had a chance to share my thoughts with anyone like this."

"Nor have I in a very long time." Abby thought of her former friend, now her father's mistress. That friendship had been lost to her, and she missed the confidences she and Beth had exchanged, the dreams they'd shared.

"Don't you ever long to return to the East?"

"No," Abby replied without hesitation. "That part of my life is over."

"You're sure?"

"Yes," Abby stated in a strong, determined voice. "Nothing"—and *no one,* she mentally added—"could ever make me return. I think that this is where I was meant to be."

"And Beau McMasters being here helps, doesn't it?"

Abby grinned. "It doesn't hurt."

Both women laughed at that remark.

"Do you think that he's the marrying kind?" Sabina asked.

Abby's face grew thoughtful. "I honestly don't know."

"You'd like him to be, wouldn't you?"

"I don't know."

Sabina laughed. "I'm not sure as I believe that."

"It's true."

"Because?"

"He's one of a kind." Abby thought of the man she had seen last night. Complex. Sophisticated, and yet dangerous when riled. A man of deep passions. Intensely male. Someone who brought out a side of herself she'd never suspected—the sensual woman lurking beneath her clothes. A woman who was discovering what it was to genuinely *want* a man.

"He's a maverick," Abby continued. "I'm not sure that he's looking for a wife."

"But if he were?"

Abby shrugged. "I can't speculate."

"So pretend that he is looking. Would you want to be a wife again?" Sabina queried.

Again. Here was an opening to tell Sabina the truth, or at least some of the truth. But Abby let it pass. Her long-employed caution held her back.

"What about you?" Abby asked, turning the question

back to her friend. "Are you interested in marrying again?"

Sabina gave a sad smile. "I honestly don't know. I think that I might, someday. I've always wanted a home of my own, children. Someone to care for, to grow old with. What I thought I was going to have with Proud Bear."

"Have you ever met anyone here in Heaven's Grace who fits your idea of a possible husband?"

"Not so far. That isn't to say that some men haven't approached me." Sabina lowered her eyes. "But what they want isn't what I'm prepared to give."

"And what's that?" Abby swallowed the last bite of egg.

"My body. I could have probably made a living at a place like Trudy's if I wanted to do that. Or I could have lived with a man without taking his name." She took a deep breath. "Someone asked me to do that. He flat out told me that I wasn't what he wanted in a wife, seeing how I'd lain with an Indian, but I was what he was looking for in a *poke*. That I should be grateful for that crumb and jump on his offer right quick seeing how no decent man would ever want to marry me."

Abby was stunned. How awful to be told in such a crude manner that that's all you were good for—being a whore. "Grateful?" she said sharply. "Of all the utter gall."

"I told him that my *husband* was ten times the man he was, and I wouldn't insult Proud Bear's memory by stooping so low as to lie with a sidewinder like him."

Abby chuckled. "Wonderful."

"I never told anyone that."

"I appreciate that you confided in me."

Sabina sighed. "It was Whitcomb who said it."

"Whitcomb?" Abby rolled her eyes. "Somehow that doesn't really surprise me. Why didn't you tell someone?"

"He said no one would believe me. That he was the respected one in this town, and that I was ruined, nothing more than a slut."

"He's a self-important ass," Abby hissed. "A little man of no real consequence. He proved that again last night. Forget about him. He's not worth your trouble."

Sabina nodded. "You're right," she said, "he's not. Now, tell me what you thought of Mr. McMasters's place?"

Thinking about that, and Beau, Abby's face lit up. "It was beautiful. I've never been in an establishment like his."

"It's one pretty place, all right. All them fancy things gathered in one building. Like something out of a story-book. And him the prince."

"Prince?" Abby wondered if Sabina was falling under Beau's spell, too.

"Yeah. In all the stories my ma used to tell me when I was little, there's always the handsome prince who lives in a fine castle. He saves the princess from the evildoers."

"And you see Beau McMasters as a prince?"

"In a way," the other woman said. "He's like no one I've ever met. Gets things done his way."

"That's for sure," Abby agreed. Beau McMasters was a force all his own. "You like him?"

"Yes. He's a gentleman, and he's never treated me with anything but respect."

"What about more?"

Sabina laughed. "Goodness no. Besides, he's got eyes only for you." She became serious. "He's not the man for me. Never was, nor will be."

"Why?"

"He's what you said. A maverick. Apt to go his own way. Like a wildfire. Burning hot, fast, and bright."

"So?" Abby kind of liked her friend's vivid description of Beau.

"I want a slow and steady fire. Warm and comforting. Always there."

Abby thought that the town's new sheriff fit that bill.

"I'd like you to come to dinner here next Sunday. Are you free?"

"I think so." Sabina paused. "Will there be anyone else?"

"Yes. I planned to invite Gussie and Carl, Mr. McMasters, and the new sheriff."

Sabina's eyes opened wider. "What new sheriff?"

"Mayor Cooper introduced him to us last night. It appears that the town is getting big enough for a regular lawman."

"What's he like?"

"Impressive," Abby said. "Very tall, with an easy smile. A *comforting* presence, I'd say. Not too young, nor too old. The right age."

"For what?"

For what I have in mind, Abby thought, but didn't say out loud. "For being a sheriff. Not too young to be thinking only of a reputation he can build, nor too old to do all that the position requires."

"You're sure you want me here?"

"Silly. Of course I do. I invited you, didn't I? Besides, I'm counting on you to help me. My cooking isn't up to Carl's, or yours, and while I can ask Carl to make one of his wonderful desserts, I'd like to be able to make the main meal. I'll need you to make sure that I don't forget something and ruin everything."

"You won't."

"I might. Preparing a dinner for six isn't like feeding oneself."

"Your ma never taught you?"

Abby almost laughed at that notion. Alma Breckenridge going down to the large kitchen in her Fifth Avenue mansion to prepare a meal? Heaven forbid. That was for servants to do. All her mother was interested in was seeing that the meal was what she ordered and served accordingly.

"No, I wasn't allowed in the kitchen." That was true

enough. Her mother forbade her to go there; not that it stopped her, until her mother fired the cook who let her daughter linger too long among the servants. Tossed the woman out without a reference, a sign of the ultimate in displeasure, ensuring that the woman wouldn't find work in any upper crust household in New York. Having learned her lesson, Abby never ventured to the kitchen again. Her "wild willfulness"—as Alma Breckenridge called it—wouldn't be the cause of someone else losing their livelihood.

"No matter, then," her friend assured her. "I'll be here to help you if you need it."

"Good," Abby said. "I have the feeling that this will be a special meal."

"I agree with Mr. McMasters," Mayor Cooper said, adding a splash of evaporated milk to his coffee. "It's more than time for Reverend Whitcomb to go."

"I think so, too," Gussie added, passing along a plate of warm biscuits topped with honey, fresh from her husband's oven.

"So, do we take a vote to see if we're all in accordance?" Beau asked, taking a sharp drag on his cheroot. He was tired, having closed the casino late the night before, after a better-than-expected opening. He was sleeping when the summons to this emergency meeting was called, and was somewhat surprised that he was included. If it had been up to him, Whitcomb would already be gone, helped out of town last night. Willingly or unwillingly, it mattered little to him either way.

Mayor Cooper nodded, asking for a show of hands.

All around the table in the private dining room of the hotel signaled their acceptance. "Good," said the mayor. "Though I feel it's something that has to be done, especially after last night's scene, still, it's a sad day. Whitcomb's been here for several years and filled a need. . . ."

"We can hire another preacher," Gussie put in. "Until then, there's nothing to stop us from meeting every Sunday in the church. Carl here can do the reading, and we'll take it as it comes. God will provide."

"It's settled, then," Mayor Cooper pronounced. "I'll go and see Whitcomb this morning and give him the news. Best break it to him as soon as possible."

"Do you want company?" Beau asked, sending a puff of smoke dancing into the air.

"No. I'd best handle it alone," Cooper responded. "Now, we've other business to discuss, so we'd better be getting to it."

"You've got good taste, *mi amigo,*" Flora said over her cup of hot chocolate. "But then you already know that, don't you?"

Beau gave her a lazy smile as he helped himself to coffee, along with a hearty portion of eggs and bacon from the silver chafing dishes on the mahogany sideboard.

"What prompted that comment?"

Now it was Flora's turn to smile. "Your choice in women."

He sat down, picked up the monogrammed linen napkin, laid it across his lap, then tucked into his late breakfast.

"You can ignore me all you want, *caballero,* but it was there to see."

"What was?"

"Your blatant *interest* in the schoolteacher. She is quite lovely, though that's to be expected if she caught your fancy."

"She's more than merely a pretty face."

"She would have to be for you to care," Flora commented. "Since I've known you, you've never been interested in the ordinary, or the empty-headed. She is neither."

Beau lifted the china cup to his lips, draining the contents. "You're right about that. Abby Butler is unique."

Flora rose from her seat, making sure the tie to her dark red silk wrapper was fastened securely, picked up a smaller silver pot and poured herself another cup of hot chocolate, liberally lacing it with a splash of cream. "She's not shared your bed yet, has she?"

Beau's fork halted halfway to his mouth, the thick slice of crisp bacon dangling from it momentarily before he placed the utensil back on his plate. "What?"

"Don't be coy, *amigo*," she teasingly scolded, tossing back a thick section of black hair.

"I don't wish to dis—"

Flora laughed lightly. "Ah, how prickly you've become."

"Prickly?"

"*Sì*. Like a shocked maiden aunt."

Beau laughed. "I doubt that."

"So, why hasn't this woman become your woman in every way?"

"What makes you so sure that she's *my* woman in any way?"

"You." Flora resumed her seat at his right hand. "Last night, I could see it in your eyes. Then, later, it was in the way you danced with her, the way you held her, talked to her. I'm not blind."

"But you've got quite a vivid imagination."

"Nonsense. I see what is clear."

"Or what you think you'd like to see."

"No. I see true. I always have, much to the chagrin of others." She placed a soft, well-cared-for hand on his arm. "Why do you wait? She is yours for the taking. I could see it in her eyes, too."

"It's complicated. Let's leave it at that."

"Does it have to be?"

"For now, yes." Beau wasn't inclined to explain the wide range of his feelings for Abby, feelings which escalated each passing day. And for once in his life, he wasn't ready to rush a joining. Savoring the outcome had become a pleasurable mental game to him. Wondering *when*. Imagining *how*. Weighing each scenario for the optimum effect. Like right now, thinking of her sitting at the opposite end of the table from him in this small, cozy room, prim and proper, until he introduced her to the delights that could be found in dining. Rosy-nippled plump breasts freed from the confines of a stiff corset, covered with a dollop of whipped cream. Fingers dipped in vintage port, then sucked dry. Champagne drizzled over an exposed rounded belly; following the path of the liquid with one's tongue as it trickled towards a feminine mound.

"Beau?"

He gave her a rueful smile as he snapped out of his enjoyable reverie.

"Love is always a complication," Flora pronounced, shrugging her shoulders. "Sometimes good, sometimes not. It all depends on fate." She rose, kissing his cheek. "Don't let your pride stand in the way. As I recall," she said fondly, "you can be most persuasive with women. If you both want this, then something can be arranged to your mutual benefit. Now, it's time for a long soak in that marvelous tub you brought from New Orleans. Ah, such a thing is a treasure. How I missed the luxury of warm water and bath salts when traveling here." With that she sailed out of the room, leaving Beau alone at the table.

If they both wanted it. Beau knew that he did. And he suspected that Abby did too. Yet how to persuade her, and how to protect her at the same time. She wasn't a whore to casually summon to his bed. No, she had a presence of her own, a stake here now, and a reputation to think about. God knows that vile toad Whitcomb had tried to sully her good name. That man knew nothing about honor, and even less of a lady's concern for her position.

A good thing that he was on his way out, for if he had remained in Heaven's Grace, then Beau would have had to take care of the situation personally.

The tall clock in the corner of the room chimed the hour.

Beau checked his pocket watch. Time to check the account books and go over the supplies before the doors of the Creole Lady were opened for the evening trade.

And what then, after his work was completed? It was far too lovely a day to stay inside, albeit colder than yesterday, with the first frost having arrived this morning.

A ride would do me good, he thought. Perhaps Mrs. Butler could be persuaded to accompany him. Not too far or too long as night was creeping closer to the afternoon now; more a chance to exercise the horses.

He laughed softly. Who was he kidding? Certainly not himself. A ride was an excuse to be with her. Alone. A chance to make up for time lost these past months. Because, if he didn't kiss her again, and soon, he was going to explode. Need was building, rising within him. Like a drunk bereft of the bottle, all he needed was one small sip. One tantalizing taste to quench the parched desert of his soul.

"They've decided I'm no longer needed here," Whitcomb snarled to the smaller man in the rectory as he packed his meager belongings.

"All the work of that fancy man and his whore, I s'pose?" the other man asked.

"Yes."

"They need to be taught a lesson. A hard lesson."

"And I need you to be my instrument," Whitcomb instructed. "God's instrument. You see the truth and know what must be done. These silly fools are blinded by the devil and his minions. They can't see what's happening. But you and I do. No one else has the courage to fight the demons."

The other man nodded in agreement. "What do you want me to do?"

Whitcomb smiled, a sick, twisted perversion of a real

smile. "Just as a rabid dog must be put down before its bite infects all who come in contact, so must these sinners. God commands it. I leave the time and the way to you."

The man's thin chest puffed up. "I won't fail you. Count on me."

Whitcomb took a deep breath. "I do."

Chapter Fourteen

"How about we stop and rest the horses?" Beau asked as they crested a small ridge. The afternoon ride had proved an adventure. As the cloud-smudged sky darkened, cold invaded the hills, sweeping down along the rolling fields of grass.

"Carl said that snow will be here soon," Abby said as she led her horse to the small stream that cut through the grass. She lifted her face to the wind, sniffing, a smile on her face. "He's right. It smells like snow."

"*Smells* like snow?" Beau queried, his gaze on her. "What's that supposed to mean?"

Abby laughed softly. "It's an expression my governess used to use. We'd walk along the streets in New York, and when the sky looked like it is now, she'd say you could smell the snow in the air. She was usually right."

"You had a governess?"

Abby stiffened; she hadn't meant to reveal something like that. It was a result of feeling too relaxed, too *comfortable* with this man.

"Sort of."

Beau smiled. "How do you *sort of* have a governess? You either do or you don't."

"She was a woman who took me under her wing since she lived in our building." Well, Abby reasoned, that was true. Her governess had lived in her parents' house, and had looked after Abby, until Alma decided that the woman was being far too "familiar," with her daughter. Servants should know their position, her mother opined, which wasn't being a surrogate older sibling to a Breckenridge.

"And what else did she teach you besides how to forecast snow?" he asked with a slight chuckle.

"That life was best experienced for oneself." Abby sighed. "Never let anyone live your life for you." A flash of defiance sparked in her eyes. "That, and a love for Shakespeare."

Beau recalled his own tutor instilling in him a love for the Bard. "We have that in common, then. Which play is your favorite?"

Abby thought for a moment. "*Much Ado About Nothing*. I love the battle of wits between Beatrice and Benedick."

"Ah," he responded wryly, "the lovers who believed in the parry and thrust of words instead of the blade."

"And what about you?" she queried, pulling her mare back from the water.

She watched as Beau slowly stroked the neck of his horse, running his hand along the Paint's long, uncut mane. It was a gesture that caused a hitch in Abby's breath, so unconsciously sensual that she could almost see his hand doing the same to her unbound hair.

"*Julius Caesar*," he replied, leaving his hat resting on the top of the saddle pommel as he moved closer to her. "Ambition, envy, politics, love, betrayal. What more could one want?"

"A happier ending?" she quipped.

"So speaks the optimist."

"So speaks the cynic," she retorted.

His eyes clouded slightly, shadows flitting across them momentarily. "Better to see life as it is, I've learned, instead of how I'd like it to be."

She watched as the wind ruffled his hair, as she wanted to do. "Do you think I'm foolish to feel more hopeful?"

"Not foolish, never that," Beau said as he slipped his hand around her waist, and tipped her chin up with the other. "I admire that you don't let the tragedy in your life taint your soul."

He *admired* her. He wouldn't, she thought, if he knew that she was as capable of mendacity as anyone else. More so than some. "I . . ."

"Ssh," he whispered, his mouth blotting out her words.

Abby willingly surrendered to his kiss. Her arms clung to Beau, pulling him tighter. Solid and strong, he was a rock.

No, not a rock, she corrected herself before she totally gave up control, reveling in the sensation of heat mixed with incredible joy; he was fire—white hot and scorching. Consuming with a pure flame.

It was then that a wild noise split the air.

"What's that?" Abby asked, breaking away from him slightly, looking about in the direction of the sound.

Beau focused and saw the animal on a rise north of them. "A bull elk from the sound of it," he said, watching as the animal bellowed again. "I've seen several on my property."

"What's he doing?"

"Calling for a mate."

Abby listened to the mournful, primal sound as the powerful creature lifted his head, which was surrounded by a wide set of antlers. Nature at its most basic, she thought. Unlike human society, filled with polite rules and regulations. This was true, real.

Like Beau's kiss.

She turned towards Beau, away from the sight and

sound of the animal, her eyes connecting with his. Removing her gloves, letting them drop to the grass, Abby lifted her hand, her fingers skimming across his cheek, feeling the soft scrape of his black beard along his jaw. Then her hand moved higher, to his thick waving hair. Slowly, her fingers threaded through it, then pulled his head closer to hers, her mouth seeking his.

God, had he ever held a woman as responsive as Abby Butler in his arms? Beau doubted it. She was one of a kind—like dry tinder waiting to combust.

He heard her soft cries, the low moans coming from her throat. Felt her nails digging into his back. Somehow, his frock coat was tumbled on the grass, along with her wool jacket as they met, shirt to shirt. Within minutes, he'd unbuttoned her soft chambray, exposing her chemise-covered skin to his hands. No stiff corset hindered his fingers as they skimmed across the thin lawn fabric, untying the ribbons, loosening several of the buttons so that he could slide his hand inside, capturing her flesh. Like the elk, he had called for his mate and she'd responded.

"Ah," she sighed as he momentarily lifted his mouth from hers. He glanced into her passion-glazed eyes, smiling at the reaction. Bending his head, he placed his lips on the crest of her breast, hearing her gasp.

The finest velvet wasn't as soft as her breast. His palm cupped the weight, his fingers stroking the stiffening nipple.

Abby's womb tightened, flooding her lower body with wet warmth. The ache between her legs deepened with each touch of his mouth or hand. Like a wanton, she reveled in the sensations he brought forth. Before her knees buckled totally, Beau scooped her up in his arms and laid her on the soft silk interior of his frock coat.

The man watching them from the outcrop of rocks not far away felt his groin tighten painfully as he observed Beau and Abby. He stood there, his eyes never leaving the couple and their shared private moment.

Whore. Coupling in the grass with a no-account gambler. Letting him put his hands and mouth on her milky white skin. Even from this distance, he could see the woman was clearly enjoying the attentions of the man, her movements enticing, her moans carried by the wind.

His grip tightened on the stock of his rifle, while his other hand loosened the buttons that held his trousers together. Freeing himself, he stroked his small, semi-hard penis, getting it to expunge his seed within seconds of his maneuvering.

Spent, he took a deep breath, angry when he noticed his flaccid member. He came too fast, as always, if he came at all. Lately, he'd only been able to do it if he was watching. He'd been careful that his daughter didn't find the peep hole he'd made in the wall of her bedroom. The tiny knot-hole in the wood was his salvation, enabling him to observe as she lathered herself with a cloth while taking her daily bath. Sabina's body was filling out. He could see the changes in it when she stripped off her plain clothes and drew the piece of flannel across her skin. Her hands on her small breasts excited him; the cloth sliding between her legs usually had him biting his lips to stifle the sounds of his arousal. Then it was over.

Like now.

He rebuttoned his pants, moving away from the tiny drops that dotted the one large rock he was hiding behind. Lifting his rifle, he took aim; he'd followed them to complete his mission, and now was the perfect opportunity, when they were both vulnerable to their animal lust.

A sound stopped him. It was a horse and rider, coming hard on this spot from about two miles away.

The elk heard it too and took off.

Shit! He'd have to try some other time. He scrambled for cover, glad that he'd hidden his stolen horse on the other side of this place in a thick copse of lodge pole pines.

It was the new sheriff. If he hurried, he could get away unseen.

However long it took, he would get them both. They were sinners of the worst sort, so it was his duty to follow the preacher's instructions. It was up to him to cleanse the town of its wickedness. Hadn't he proved that before when he struck down his daughter's Indian lover?

He smiled nastily as he mounted his horse. No one ever suspected him of that and no one ever would. He'd been too careful, too clever. He'd gotten away with murder once—there was nothing to stop him from getting away with it again.

Adam Tyler reined in his horse, certain that he'd spotted someone there among the rocks only a few minutes before. He eased out of the saddle, his gun drawn just in case.

Stepping carefully, he maneuvered his way along the rocky ledge, alert to the sounds of the area. Birds chirped; not far away the receding sound of the bull elk could be heard. Tyler edged closer to the ridge, then spied something wet on one of the rocks. Bending, he sniffed the air near the spot.

There had been someone here—recently. A man. No doubt about that from the evidence left behind. Unfortunately, the ground here was far too rocky to find a proper trail.

He stood, looking around. It was then Tyler spotted what the man most likely had been looking at—a couple, entwined in the low grass near the creek, horses standing at the ready.

Even from this distance, he recognized them. Looked as though the gambler and the schoolmarm certainly enjoyed each other's company, so much so that they were oblivious to anyone else.

Feeling like a peeping Tom, he turned away, then fired his Colt into the air.

Startled, Beau pushed Abby behind him as he drew his Remington, searching the area where the sound came from. He saw the sheriff waving his hat from the ridge. Beau relaxed, holstering his weapon. "Appears we've got company," he said. "Adam Tyler."

"Oh my God, do you think he saw us?" Abby asked, her face flushed with color as she hastily arranged her clothes.

"Yes."

"How can you be so calm?" Her fingers were shaking as she stood up, pushing her shirt back into her split suede skirt. Had she completely lost her mind? Coupling with Beau McMasters? Out in the open, where anyone could see them?

Abby grabbed her matching jacket and slipped her arms into it, brushing off the slivers of grass from her clothes.

She thought that she must look a sight—her hair was a tangled mess; her lips felt swollen; her breasts were tender, the material of her chemise and shirt rubbing against her nipples, still tight from the ministrations of Beau's hands and mouth. God, but she'd never imagined a man would put his mouth on her like that. And his fingers, strumming her like a master musician, easily finding sensitive places that burst into unexpected song. He'd skimmed them along her entire body, pausing at the apex of her thighs, stroking over the fabric, exerting gentle pressure until she thought she would explode from the sensations wracking her body.

Before she put on her deerskin gloves, Abby bent down and cupped her hands into the cold, clear water and drank, easing the dryness in her mouth, then splashed some onto her warm face and neck. It cooled her quickly, making her shiver. Just as Beau had made her shiver. Uncontrollably.

She sliced a glance in Beau's direction—he was standing there, watching her, his dark eyes intent. Slowly, she stood up, and as she did, his gaze wandered down her body and back up. Then he smiled. A deep, satisfying grin. Instead of feeling angry that he seemed to be taking what happened between them so cavalierly, she couldn't help returning the smile.

"No regrets?" he asked as he settled the black hat upon his head.

"Only that we were interrupted," she responded boldly. That was true. She had been on the verge of *something*. She wasn't sure of *what*, but it had been coming. Building. Coursing. And having an audience ruined the moment. Spoiled it. Postponed whatever strong currents his ministrations began. Made her long for the next level, the next sensation, the next effect. That this one man could make her ache with unfulfilled, unrepressed want amazed her.

Beau threw back his head and gave a hearty laugh. He'd been afraid that she would balk at her feelings. He searched her face for any sign of real shame, of lingering doubts. None appeared.

"The next time . . ." he paused.

"The next time what?" she asked.

Beau stepped closer. His voice was a husky whisper of raw sound. "The next time, I promise, will be better. Very private. And we'll finish what we start."

Any response Abby would have made was silenced by the arrival of the sheriff.

"Howdy, folks."

"Hello, Sheriff Tyler," Abby said as she faced the other man. Though she didn't regret what had happened between her and Beau, she did regret that Sheriff Tyler had found them in such a compromising position. She couldn't tell from his impassive face what he thought. A woman's good name was important—here it counted for something. As a teacher, she needed the respect her job afforded her.

"Afternoon, ma'am," he said as he tipped the brim of his Stetson in her direction. His tone was polite, with genuine warmth.

Abby relaxed. She couldn't detect any censure in his tone, or more importantly, in his face.

"What brings you this way?" Beau asked.

"What with the fracas last night, I thought it best to keep an eye on you two. When I came round the Creole Lady looking for you, I was told you'd gone out with Mrs. Butler. Figured that I'd take a ride around and see if I could find you. Good thing I did, too."

"Why's that?"

"'Cause I found someone was watching you two."

"What?" Abby gasped. Someone else had seen them, spying on her private moments with Beau?

Beau laid an arm across her shoulders, pulling her close. "You know who?"

Tyler shook his head. "Not yet."

"Maybe it was just someone passing through."

"I don't think so. From what I saw, he'd been there for a bit."

"You're sure that it was a man?" Beau asked.

"No doubt in my mind."

Beau thought there was more to Tyler's remarks, something the man wasn't saying.

"I'll be happy to ride along back to town with you both," Tyler announced. "Getting dark soon, and you never know what kind of varmints are lurking about."

"We'd be happy for the company, Sheriff," Abby said as she and Beau remounted their horses. Immediately, she was flanked by both men as they headed back in the direction of Heaven's Grace.

* * *

Beau was waiting for the knock on his office door. "Come in."

Adam Tyler sauntered into the room and closed the door behind him.

Beau lit a cigar and handed one to the sheriff. "Now, what didn't you tell me out there?"

Tyler struck a match and took a deep drag on the fragrant tobacco, then told Beau what he'd found.

Beau downed a quick drink of bourbon, slamming the glass back on the tray with a thud. It made him sick to think that someone had pleasured himself while watching him and Abby together. What had been for him a special moment was now tainted by this revelation. "Don't say anything to Mrs. Butler about this."

"Wasn't going to," Tyler drawled. "A lady don't need to hear about some worthless son of a bitch polishing his pistol."

"I'd love to know who it was."

"So would I."

"Do you think," Beau asked as he poured himself another drink and handed one to Tyler, "that it was Whitcomb?"

"No. I checked before I came here. Whitcomb was on the stage when it left town this afternoon. I've got witnesses to that fact. Could have just been a passing cowboy, or a kid, getting way too excited."

"But you don't think so, do you?"

Tyler shrugged his shoulders. "No. Something is nagging at me, and when I get that feeling, I pay attention."

"Me too."

"Then I suggest you be extra careful, and make sure that Mrs. Butler is too."

Beau looked Adam straight in the eye as one hand brushed the holster of his Remington. "No one's going to touch her, or they'll answer to me. You can bet your life on that, Sheriff."

Tyler smiled. "I kinda figured that out for myself."

"I have someone I trust who can look out for her when I'm not around."

"Who?"

"Boy that works for me doing odd jobs."

"Then set him at it as soon as possible."

"I already have."

"Seems that we're to have supper together."

Beau grinned. "I take it that Mrs. Butler extended her invitation?"

Tyler nodded. "That she did. And I accepted. Be right nice to have a home-cooked meal. She a good cook?"

"I don't know," Beau admitted.

"Hmmm . . ." the sheriff said, one eyebrow lifted.

"I do know that when Mrs. Butler puts her mind to something, it gets done. She's made an enormous change in the schoolhouse and the education of the town's children."

"Already figured she was one of your favorite citizens hereabouts."

Beau glanced at the other man, then lit another cheroot. "She's one of the smartest, most fascinating women I've ever met. Courageous too. Made a life for herself after being left a widow." He took a deep drag of smoke, exhaling slowly. "That kind of determination is something I admire. To rebuild a life in the face of defeat takes guts." He paused, getting up, walking toward the window, casting a glance out to the night sky. Lights abounded around the town. If he narrowed his eyes, he could see in the distance, just outside of the town proper, the house that Abby lived in. Curls of smoke lifted from the stone chimney. She was inside, safe and warm. Many nights he stood here like this, watching. Wishing that he was there, with her. Waiting. Wondering.

Today he was certain that she wanted him, too. Enough to come to him. Soon. It would be soon. It *had* to be soon.

Chapter Fifteen

"I think that went rather well, don't you?" Abby asked as she handed a dripping wet plate to Sabina.

The other woman smiled. "Everyone seemed to like the meal," she offered, drying the item and setting it into the open cupboard, "and each other."

"So, what do you think about the new sheriff?"

Sabina was thoughtful for a moment, as she took another plate and dried it. "He seems quite nice."

"Only *nice?*" Abby asked, tilting her head to one side so that she could see her friend's face.

Sabina flushed, then lowered her lashes. "He is dedicated to his work, I think."

"Very handsome too."

A wide smile crossed Sabina's mouth as she lifted her lashes. "Yes."

"I do believe that he liked you too."

"Really?" Sabina twisted the cloth in her hands.

"I do," Abby assured her. "He certainly enjoyed sitting next to you, from what I could tell. I noticed that he directed most of his conversation to you."

"He was being polite."

Abby clucked her tongue. "Nonsense. He was more than polite—he was genuinely interested. And why shouldn't he be? You're a lovely woman, Sabina."

"With a past."

"As if that matters," Abby opined.

"It does to some people in this town."

"Very few, I'm sure."

"Well," Sabina said, "probably a lot fewer since you've taken me under your wing."

Abby laughed lightly. "I think you give me too much credit."

"Not really. It's true."

"It's you who's changed, Sabina. In how you carry yourself. In your smile." Abby picked up the second granite-ware pan, filled with the rinse water, and dumped it into the bigger one, containing the soapy wash water. "Could you get the door for me?" she asked.

Sabina opened the kitchen door just as Beau and Tyler entered the kitchen.

Beau grabbed the heavy item and removed it from Abby's hands. "No need for you to do that." He stepped carefully so as not to spill the contents on her floor, or more importantly, on himself. He tossed the water onto the flower bed that flanked the back door. "There, all done," he said as he handed the empty pan back to Abby, who placed it in the deep well of the sink.

"Would you gentlemen care for a brandy?" Abby offered.

Beau shot a glance at Tyler with a raised brow. "I would, yes."

"None for me, Mrs. Butler. But I would like another slice of that pie and a glass of milk instead."

"Sabina, would you see to the sheriff's pie while I get a glass of brandy for Mr. McMasters?"

"Sure." She busied herself with removing a clean plate from the shelf and slicing Tyler a large piece of the crumbly apple pie. "You had cream on your other slice, didn't you, Mr. Tyler?"

"Nice of you to recall," he said, moving closer to her.

Sabina added a splash from the jug on the table, handing him the plate. "Now, let me get the milk for you."

"Thank you, Miss Sabina."

He watched as she moved efficiently about her task, taking note that they were alone. Abby and Beau had left them for the parlor. He liked the plain white blouse she wore, tucked into a dark brown wool skirt that flattered her slim figure. He even enjoyed the hint of a white, lace-edged petticoat that peeked out from under her skirt when she turned around.

"May I presume on our short acquaintance and ask you to help me out?"

Sabina handed him the glass. "With what, Sheriff?"

"I need someone to show me the town, give me some background on who's who around here."

Sabina grinned. "That shouldn't take much time. Heaven's Grace isn't as big a place as some that you're used to."

"Which is why I need someone who's familiar with it. If I hope to do my job and establish myself here, I need to get a good idea of the lay of the land."

She looked at him, tilting her head slightly to look into his warm eyes. "Then I'd be happy to offer what help I can, Sheriff."

"Adam, or Tyler if you'd like."

"Adam," she said softly, trying out the familiarity of the sound on her tongue. "That's a lovely name. The first man God created."

"Who ended up getting kicked out of paradise. Wouldn't like to repeat that," he added dryly.

"I didn't mean . . ."

Tyler smiled, a wide grin. "Never thought you were hinting that the townsfolk were about to do the same to me, ma'am. I expect that I'm here to stay, for as long as they'll have me."

"And why wouldn't they?" Sabina asked. "We've needed a regular lawman here for some time. Folks hereabouts feel better now that you've come." She settled herself into one of the kitchen chairs. "Safer."

Tyler followed her example, easing his tall frame into the seat opposite her. "And do you feel safer, Miss Sabina?"

"Of course. A town without law isn't much of a town."

"Depends on the kind of law dispensed."

"*Kind of law?*" Sabina repeated. "What other kind of law can there be but the right kind?"

"The wrong kind," he responded. "I've seen some towns run by corrupt men, eager to take what they could, placing a yoke upon the very people they swore to protect." Tyler took a large swallow of milk, draining half the glass. "They don't usually give up that power easily."

"You've had some experience with removing them then?"

He sighed. "A few."

She leaned forward in her seat. "Wasn't that dangerous?"

Tyler shrugged his wide shoulders. "It needed to be done."

Brave, as well as handsome, Sabina thought, liking him even more. In that instant, he reminded her of her late husband.

"So," he asked, "will you be my guide tomorrow? That is, if you don't have something else to do?"

"I can make some time after luncheon, if you'd like. My morning is spoken for, what with finishing off a dress for Mrs. James's daughter's birthday party."

Tyler smiled. "That'd be just fine, Miss Sabina." He took a bite of the pie, then drank some more milk. "You do the outfit you're wearing?"

"I did. Along with Mrs. Butler's."

"You're right talented, ma'am."

"No," she replied modestly, "just handy with a needle and thread."

"Now, don't you go disparaging yourself, Miss Sabina. Takes a heap of know-how to do something that pretty." He reached out his hand and lightly touched the collar of her blouse. "Fine amount of detail here in that stitching," he said, making reference to the delicate embroidery that edged the pointed collar. "Looks like a tiny bear."

"It is."

"Something special to you?"

Sabina lowered her eyes and looked at the table for a brief moment before lifting her head and gazing into Tyler's face. "Yes," was all she said.

"Lovely work," he replied. "Always had a hankering for something like that, on a handkerchief maybe. My initials, all done up in fancy script. Something for church, or special occasions."

Sabina watched as he resumed eating his pie, mentally sketching out a pattern with his initials, combined with a star, done in gold thread. She had a few scraps left from the fine lawn that she'd used for the new petticoat she had made herself last week. Hemmed, with the design and initials, the handkerchiefs would make a fine gift. Maybe for Christmas.

Gosh, she wondered, was that too familiar? After all, she'd only just met the man.

And yet, sitting across from him at the table, she had the distinct feeling that she'd known him for a very long time. Comfortable. That's what he made her feel—*comfortable*.

"What do you think is keeping them?" Abby asked as she poured some of the aged brandy that Beau had brought with him to the dinner party. For the gentlemen after the meal, he'd said when he arrived, though Carl had left with Gussie after dinner, pleading things to do back at the hotel, and it looked as though Sheriff Tyler wasn't interested at the present.

He took the glass from her, lingering over the touch of their hands, watching as she poured one for herself.

"I didn't know you enjoyed brandy."

She put the glass to her lips, sipping gently. "I must admit that I acquired a taste for it some years back."

"My dear Mrs. Butler, you do continue to amaze me," he said with a husky chuckle. Just when he thought he had her figured out, she turned another page, revealing something else. Damn, but he liked that about her. Her unpredictability when he thought he knew all there was to know. "I shall make sure that you're never wanting for it then."

Abby sighed at the taste of the smooth, aged flavor, taking another sip, all the while keeping her eyes on Beau. He stood mere inches from her, and her mind was filled with memories of their time together. She watched as he finished his drink, caught up in the swirl of feelings that jumbled about in her blood, in her brain.

Beau put down his glass upon the small side table and gave in to what he'd wanted to do all through dinner.

His lips met hers with a fierce passion, his mouth moving in to claim his prize.

Abby never noticed that she dropped the glass onto the hooked rug beneath her feet, the remains of her brandy splashing lightly about her hem.

Her hands were busy sliding around Beau's firm middle, under his frock coat, over his vest, working their way to his back, pulling him closer as the kiss deepened. Thoughts of her dinner companions fled as trembling sensations fluttered through her body. All she knew was him. He wooed her with persuasive gestures, with knowing hands and a more-than-capable mouth. She returned each kiss with another, sharing the moment, engaging in reckless abandon.

Beau lifted his head, taking in a deep breath of air as he watched the play of emotions over her face. Pupils huge and dark, skin tinged with color, breathing ragged. A woman eager to be bedded. Ripe with promise.

Damnation! He couldn't collect on that promise now. Again, it wasn't a good time, what with Tyler and Sabina in the next room.

"Abby," he said softly.

She burrowed into his chest, taking solace in the warmth she found there as she struggled to get her breathing under control. God, she was frustrated. What was it about this man that reduced her to a willing supplicant?

His charm? Considerable.

His voice? Warm and tempting as the brandy.

His hands? Capable of inducing a pleasure so hot.

His mouth? An instrument of pure seduction, tempting beyond measure.

She heard the quick beat of his heart, indicating that he was as moved as she was. Beneath the hand resting against his chest, she could feel the deep breaths he took, the movement of taut muscles. Suddenly, the barrier of his shirt and vest were almost too much to bear. She was torn by a desire to just rip them open, exposing that golden flesh to her eyes, to her hands, to her lips, to her mouth.

Wanton. Slut. Whore. She could hear the echo of these words thrumming in her head, the voices mixed. One instant they were her mother's, her cold voice despairing of her offspring; the next it was Whitcomb's, righteous indignation punctuating each word.

Ladies didn't contemplate ripping at a man's clothes like a starving animal in search of a meal. They were contained. Quiet. Calling upon inner reserves of dignity. In control.

Maybe.

Abby knew that right now that wasn't her. It would, she knew, never be her with this man. He brought out a wildness in her, a yearning for more than tepid affection.

223

Beau slipped a finger beneath her chin and lifted it up, giving her a quick kiss. "What are you thinking?"

"Something I probably shouldn't," she replied.

"Like what?" he asked. He knew what *he* was thinking—that he wanted to scoop her up and find the nearest bed. Failing that, floor or wall, it didn't matter, as long as he could have her. He fought the urge to toss up her blue wool skirt, slip through her pantalets and let his fingers glide into the depths of her nether curls, searching for the heated moisture that pooled there.

"Nothing," she replied, moving away from him to the small rough-hewn mirror she'd hung on the wall. She took a quick glance in it and saw someone with slumberous eyes, a well-kissed mouth, and a deep smile that was laced with burgeoning power.

"Looking for this?" Beau asked as he came up behind her, dangling a velvet ribbon in his hand.

Abby inhaled sharply as he gathered her hair to one side, bent his head, inhaled the fragrance on her neck. "Roses," he murmured through a deep sigh. His lips scorched her nape; his tongue laved the area until he let the thick skein of hair fall back into place. "Such a pity, really."

"What?"

"To keep it bound."

Their eyes met in the mirror. Abby's drifted shut as Beau stroked her hair from her crown to the small of her back.

Carefully, he placed the ribbon under and around, tying it tightly. "There now. All right and proper."

Her eyes opened and she glanced back into the mirror again, looking at the two of them reflected there. Abby doubted that the word *proper* applied to her now, if it ever really had.

Somehow, she didn't care. Better to be alive and aware of who she was, instead of a well-dressed, hollow, life-sized doll, lacking warmth or emotion.

"Excuse me," piped up a voice from the other side of the doorway. "I'm going to be on my way now."

"Sabina," Abby murmured, wondering if her friend could guess what had transpired between her and Beau. Of course she could, Abby realized. Her friend had eyes; she could read the truth. It was written there on her face, plain, without trim or geegaws to disguise it.

She was a woman enthralled by a man.

Abby, followed by Beau, walked into the kitchen. "Thank you both for coming tonight. We will have to do this again."

Beau offered, "What about at my ranch?"

Abby turned to face Beau. "Your house?"

"Why not? It's just been refurbished to my specifications. A Thanksgiving dinner is, I think, the right time to christen it." He smiled, white teeth gleaming against his black beard. "Don't we all have something to be thankful for this year?"

Abby cocked her head, looked at the sheriff and Sabina.

"I'd like that," Sabina said.

"So would I," replied Tyler. "Kinda like the idea of the four of us making a celebration of the holiday. What with no family hereabouts, it'll be nice to be with new friends."

Beau smiled. "Then it's settled."

Tyler helped Sabina into her coat, then put on his own, a thick shearling.

Beau lifted his long leather duster from the coat rack and slipped it on. "I'll walk out with you both," he said. He turned to Abby and lifted one of her hands to his mouth. "As always, Mrs. Butler, an evening spent in your company is time to be cherished." His lips lingered for just a moment on her flesh as his eyes gazed deeply into hers.

Her skin sizzled where he touched, and Abby could almost willingly lose herself in the golden brown depths of his eyes. As Lady Caroline Lamb had said about Byron— he was mad, bad, and dangerous to know. Except that

Beau wasn't mad. But he was bad—bad for her preformed plans. He opened up so many different doors when she'd thought she'd already made her choices. And as for dangerous—well, he certainly was that to her senses.

Sabina interrupted her friend's wayward thoughts when she leaned over and placed a kiss on Abby's flushed cheek. "I'll talk to you soon."

Abby hugged the other woman, then extended her hand to the sheriff.

"Thanks, Mrs. Butler. I enjoyed myself," he said, pausing as he released Abby's hand and glanced in Sabina's direction, "very much."

"You're very welcome, Sheriff Tyler."

Sabina and Tyler headed out first, followed by Beau. Abby stood in the doorway, a wide smile curving her mouth, watching them mount their horses. Both Beau and the sheriff tipped their hats to her before they left, Beau nodding to the heavy, older man who stood in the shadows of the house, rifle at the ready. He'd stationed men outside her house each night, as well as Josh, who watched her during the daylight hours. He wasn't taking a chance with her safety.

Abby wasn't sure she needed this protection, but she went along with Beau's suggestion because she thought he would continue to do it anyway, whether or not she approved.

And it did make her feel secure. As if she were someone he treasured enough to see protected. Not because he wanted to control her as her father had, but because he cared.

Closing the door, she secured the latch, turning the key. She picked up the branch of candles on the table to light her way to her bedroom, contrasting the simple gesture to the gaslight sconces and lamps in her former home.

House, she corrected. Never a home in any sense of the word.

As Abby undressed and readied herself for bed, Beau filled her thoughts. Each day he became more important to her, more an integral part of her life.

Was this love?

As she slid under the heavy, down-filled quilt, she acknowledged that it very well could be.

Shit! There were too many people around her now, Baser thought as he faded into the lingering shadows, gripped by anger. Every blasted night the fancy man had a guard set on the house. In the morning some snot-nosed kid was there to escort her to the schoolhouse.

He just couldn't get a break. And now she was inside, making herself cozy with a gaggle of whores while the kid waited outside, a mean-looking dog at his side. Damned cur just about caught him the other day. Barked up a storm until the kid called him back. Sure, he could have killed the dog, but he risked discovery that way. He couldn't take that chance. If he were caught, he wouldn't get an opportunity to fulfill his mission. This was important work—it needed completion. Only he could mete out the punishment the sinners deserved.

He'd have to pray for a sign. Ask God to show him the way.

"We heard you had a nice dinner party here the other night," Cassie remarked as she added two spoonfuls of sugar to her hot tea. A splash of milk followed.

Abby paused in the act of removing a still-warm thick-crusted apple pie from the length of fabric that protected it. Cassie and Glory had brought it with them when they came for their weekly reading lesson.

"Appears news travels fast," Abby stated, cutting slices and then placing them on plates.

Glory, who had a full-bodied laugh, chuckled. "You could say that not much happens in this town that we don't know about. When people come to Trudy's they relax and talk."

Abby laughed. "More than talk, I'd say."

It was Cassie's turn to chuckle. "One of Mr. McMasters's dealers was in the other night. Seems he pays them very well and they can afford the best." She smiled, indicating herself and Glory. "He wanted us both, and he was most happy to talk before, during and after."

Abby placed the plates before each of them. "He wanted you both at the same time?" she asked, her eyes wide.

"Some men like ebony and ivory, and he sure is one of them."

"But *both* of you in the same room?"

Cassie laughed. "Honey, not just in the same room, in the same *bed*."

Abby sat down as Sabina entered the room. She had arrived just moments before, having brought the items that the doves had requested she make for them. She heard the last few remarks. "He made love to you both?"

Glory nodded. "Not that I'd call it *making love*," the robust black woman said. "It was more like the best *poking* to be had in these parts."

"I can't imagine. . . ."

Cassie spoke up, a knowing twinkle in her eyes. "I don't guess that you could, Miss Abby."

"Do you like it?" Abby asked, curiosity getting the better of her.

"Don't matter none if I do or not, Miss Abby, long as the customer does."

"We're both pretty good at faking it when we have to," Glory supplied.

"Faking what?"

Both doves looked at Abby. "Pleasure. Enjoyment. Making the customer think that he has us screaming in heat. Each man who comes to us has to believe that he's the only one who can make us come."

"Come where?" Abby queried.

Glory and Cassie erupted in laughter. "You never heard that expression before?"

"No," Abby replied.

Sabina added, "Neither have I."

"Oh my," Cassie said, taking a deep breath. "It's a crude way of saying that you experienced wild pleasure. That he was man enough to take you to that place and have you shaking with joy."

Sabina nodded. "I understand."

"Your man took you there, right?" Glory asked.

"I once bit his shoulder to hide my cries," Sabina confessed, "for fear of waking up his sister, who slept nearby."

"You fake this feeling for your customers?" Abby asked.

Both women nodded. "Most times, yeah."

"They don't notice?"

"No," Cassie said with a cynical tone. "Most are too busy making sure that they get themselves happy to care about anything else. You do, however, have the rare customer who likes you to go there before him. Who makes sure that you're satisfied before he comes."

"Did your man give you pleasure, Miss Abby?" Glory asked.

Abby swallowed. "It was most pleasant, yes."

Sabina caught the look in her friend's eyes—why was there a hint of something missing there? As if Abby was play-acting.

"Now I'll just bet that Mr. McMasters is one fine stud," Cassie said with a chuckle in her voice. "He's got to be hotter than a whore on nickel night. Something about his eyes that tells me he knows how to pleasure a woman so she don't have to fake it any time." She took a large swallow of her cooling tea. "Now, where are those garments I ordered?"

Sabina opened up a large carpetbag that held the items

the doves had requested. Fine lawn robes, pantalets, camisoles of silk and petticoats.

"You are an artist, Miss Sabina," Glory crowed, fingering the delicate garments. "Wait till the other girls see us in these. They'll be so jealous."

"Ain't nobody ripping this off me," Glory declared. "If they try, I'll cut it off and toss it out the window."

Abby decided not to ask Glory to clarify what "it" was. "Do some men who visit with you try to mistreat you?"

Cassie smiled. "Not anymore. I had one once who tried. Had a knife on him and too much liquor. Wanted to carve me up some, but he never got the chance. One slice and I screamed my head off. Bashed him on the head with the chamber pot. Miss Trudy had him tossed out, but not before one of the guards at the house fixed it so he'd never do that again. There's some things I'll do for money, and others I won't."

"You have a choice, then?"

"Sure. Wouldn't stick it out there if I didn't. Some girls have specialties, things that others in the house won't do, so the men know beforehand what they are. Trudy's got a menu, with prices listed. The callers know what, and who, they're getting before we go upstairs."

"Yeah," Glory said, "some of the girls have their regulars, and some don't. They like variety so they don't have to feel like they're married, doing it with the same man night after night. Me, I like virgins."

"Virgins?" Abby asked.

Glory smiled. "Yep. I like to get a boy that knows nothing and make him see what it means to be a man. Ain't nothing like seeing a boy change before your eyes. Kinda sweet and shy, then when he gets some tutoring, you feel that you've kinda helped out whatever woman he later takes to wife. It's important that the first time be something special, be it man or woman. I take extra time with them." Her dark eyes clouded over. "My first time was bad."

Abby spoke softly. "What happened?"

"I was raped by a drunken cowboy," Glory admitted, her voice matter-of-fact. "My ma was feeling poorly and my dad was away on a cattle drive. We had a small farm in Texas, and Daddy made extra money helping on long drives. My two older brothers went with him, so I was the only one home with Ma when she got sick. I had to ride into town and fetch her some medicine. On the way back, my horse pulled up lame. I was fixin' to walk back when he came upon me.

"I'd stopped to get my breath—it was kinda hot that day. I asked the man to give me a ride home so that I could get this medicine to my ma.

"He said yes. Helped me up on his horse, then he rode in the opposite direction.

"I tried to get down. He slapped me. Knocked me off his horse. He was on me before I could stop him. Fought, but it weren't no use. He was bigger than me and didn't take him long to pull out his part and rip up my dress. He poked me so hard I thought I was gonna die right there. All I could do was cry and beg him to stop.

" 'Course he didn't until he was through. Said that I was broke in all nice now; that I should thank him for taking the time to show me the ropes. He mounted his horse and rode off, left me there to make my way back home as best I could."

Glory paused. "I was ten years old."

"Oh my God," Abby exclaimed, tears forming in her eyes.

"No man ever did that to me again without first paying for it," Glory added.

"And yet you want to make it special for others?" Sabina asked. She couldn't imagine the horror of that experience.

"I have to, you see. Maybe they'll recall how good it was for them and make sure that they give it back to someone. My first time was stolen from me; this way I get to control someone else's."

Glory directed a question to Abby. "Your man make it special for you?"

Abby sighed, shrugged her shoulders, then changed the topic. After Glory's honest accounting of her life, Abby didn't have the stomach to pollute the conversation with another lie.

Sabina lingered after the other two women left, their lessons for the day completed, their purchases happily tucked away in their elegant buggy.

"Would you like another cup?" Abby asked as she lingered over her third.

"No. I've got to get going. I only stayed behind to ask you something."

Abby wet her lips. "What?"

"When Glory asked you about your husband, and what it was like for you, why did you hesitate? I noticed something in your eyes at that moment, and also before when Cassie made her comments about pleasure. Something like fear." Sabina paused, not sure how hard to press for her answer. "You never really speak about him. Why? I shared my feelings about Proud Bear with you."

Abby spoke softly. "There is no *him*."

"What did you say?"

"There is no him." Abby took a deep breath and looked her friend squarely in the eye. "There never was."

Chapter Sixteen

"What do you mean, no *him?*" Sabina asked, dumbfounded by her friend's comment.

"Just what I said," Abby responded. "My husband doesn't exist. He never did."

Sabina's eyes widened. "But . . ."

"I lied."

Sabina looked at her friend, seeing the truth in Abby's eyes. "Why?"

"Because it was so much easier that way."

"Easier for what?"

Abby took a deep breath. "For me to make myself disappear."

"Why would you want to do that?"

Abby explained, leaving nothing out. The burden of keeping so many secrets, juggling the lies, had finally worn her down. Unburdening herself was like removing a tight-fitting garment that threatened to constrict her until there was no life left in her body.

"You poor thing," Sabina murmured, putting her arms

around her friend. "How awful that must have been for you."

Abby smiled slightly at the words "poor thing." She doubted that anyone would have ever used that term to describe the Breckenridge heiress she'd once been.

"It just sort of got away from me," Abby confessed, moving to the kitchen chair. "I needed the new identity to survive, to outwit the people looking for me, but I never counted on using it forever. Or that it would be so painful to continually keep up the pretense. Especially since I came here. Just about everyone"—she gave Sabina a skewered smile—"has been so wonderful to me, accepting me at face value, that it's been hard to keep up the false front." Abby licked her lips. "Then, when Trudy's girls were talking about their experiences, especially Glory, I started to feel sick that I was keeping the truth from the people here."

"You don't have anything to worry about, Abby," Sabina assured her. "No one here in Heaven's Grace wants to see you unhappy, or so worried that you have to be looking over your shoulder all the time. What your last name is or isn't doesn't matter. Not to me, not to the others who care about you. All I need to know is that you're someone who brings joy to others. A friend I can trust."

Moisture glistened in Abby's blue eyes. "Thank you."

"No thanks are needed between friends." Sabina fixed Abby with a direct glance. "So, you've never been with a man then, have you?"

Abby shook her head in the negative.

"No one in New York you even considered having as a husband?"

"No one," Abby answered.

"That's kind of sad," Sabina noted. "What with how big I've heard New York is, you'd think that there would have been someone you might fancy."

"The men that I met weren't interested in *me*. Marrying

me would have gotten them my father's influence and money, not my heart. The very idea of imagining some of them with me in my bed was enough to make my skin crawl."

Sabina smiled in agreement. "I know what you mean. Before Proud Bear I wondered what it would be like to be courted by someone from around here."

"And were you?" Abby asked. "Courted, that is?"

Sabina shrugged. "Pa didn't take a liking to anyone hereabouts. And truth be told, neither did I." Sabina paused; her face had a faraway look, as if she were recalling something pleasant. "When I was fourteen I had a dream. At first it made no sense. Then, later, after I met Proud Bear, I knew it was a sign."

"What kind of sign?"

"Indians call them visions. They go on spirit quests to seek the future. I saw mine clearly in a dream, one that haunted me for years since I kept having the same one.

"I was in a meadow, up in the high country, asleep under a tree. When I woke, I saw a big brown bear near the water's edge. He kept staring at me. Funny thing was that I wasn't scared of him. I got up and walked over to him, stroked his thick brown fur and wound my arms about his neck."

"And?"

"Nothing. I would always wake up then. What about you? Any dreams like that?"

Abby laughed. "Not about bears." Then, she recalled the one dream, or piece of a dream, that she'd had as a young girl. "There was one that recurred several times. I was in the grand ballroom of my parents' house. There was a small chamber orchestra playing, and it was my first grown-up event. But instead of wearing a traditional white gown, I was in blue."

"Is that important?" Sabina asked.

"It is in New York. Girls make their debuts in white.

Only white. The guests were all standing with their backs to me, and I was looking for my partner, the young man I was supposed to have the first dance with. I ran across the ballroom floor, searching for him without knowing who it was that I was looking for."

"Did you find him?"

"No. I never did. Later, I used to get close enough to see someone standing in the shadows, just out of my reach. Before I could get to him, the dream vanished and I woke up."

Sabina smiled. "Maybe you weren't meant to find him in New York."

"Or maybe I wasn't supposed to have a *him*, real or otherwise."

"You don't really believe that, do you?" Sabina inquired. "Not after meeting Mr. McMasters."

Abby sighed. "I just don't know."

Sabina reached across the table to take her friend's hand. "I think you do," she offered.

"What I do know," Abby acknowledged, "is that for me, he's different."

Sabina stated simply, "You love him."

Abby smiled, happy to admit the simple fact she'd come to realize. "Yes, I believe I do," she stated. "I miss him when he's not around. I miss not being able to share things with him, like my day at school—which children are progressing better than I thought; who needs extra attention; which pupils I'm earmarking for special projects."

Standing up, Abby walked to the cupboard, stepped up on the small stool, and pulled out a wicker basket from the top shelf filled with fragrant pinecones gathered by her students. She touched the plaid cloth and ribbons, donated by Mary James, which lined the basket. "I want to show him what I plan to use to decorate my home for the holidays. Ask him if he has any further suggestions, anything he'd like to add. It's important to me that he feels comfortable here." She replaced the item and then resumed her seat.

"I want to find out how his business is doing. Is he satisfied with the results of his changes? Has the Creole Lady brought him what he sought?" She absently fondled the ribbon holding her braid in place. "I want to know what he thinks about certain things—books we've both read, music, art."

Did he appreciate the same kind of music that she did? Did it move him in the same ways? What about art? Would the paintings that fascinated her fascinate him? "So many things."

"And you want to lie with him," Sabina added with raw honesty.

"I do," Abby admitted. "At least I think I do. However, it's not that easy."

"Because you don't know if he wants to marry you?"

"Because I don't know if he *loves* me. He wants me, that I know." Abby licked her lips. "I know if we were to be together, it wouldn't be his first time."

"But it would be his first time with you," Sabina stated with a soft smile. "Each time you lie with a man, it's different. Sometimes it's quick; other times it's gentle."

"Were you afraid your first time?"

"Yes," Sabina acknowledged. "What with me not knowing anything of the real way it was between a man and his woman, it seemed kinda scary when I was faced with it. I mean I'd seen some animals around the farm. But nothing prepared me for my wedding night."

"Ah, the wedding night," Abby said quietly. "My mother told me about that." She took a deep breath. "She made it sound horrible and sordid. She said it was something to be endured; to be put up with as the price one paid for being a wife. According to her, no decent woman *wanted* her husband that way. It was a duty, not a desire."

"She was wrong," Sabina offered without hesitation.

"Wanting to be with your man when you love him is right. No doubt in my mind about that." A soft smile tugged at her mouth; her eyes warmed with memories. "Proud Bear made my first time special. He was patient, gentle, and showed me how a man cares for a woman he loves."

Abby recalled the words of Cassie and Glory. "He gives her pleasure."

Sabina smiled. "Exactly."

Abby stood up, wrapping her arms about herself. "Do you think Beau is that kind of man?"

"I believe so, yes." Sabina paused for a moment before she continued. "You'd like him to be, wouldn't you?"

Abby nodded. "Yet, to be honest, I don't know if I could be with him without marriage." Abby laughed. "You know, in a way that's kind of funny."

"How so?"

"Because I left New York because I didn't want to get married without love. I didn't want what I saw as a life-long partnership with someone I had little liking or respect for. Now here I am, boldly considering the prospect of being with someone who's not my wedded husband."

"He cares for you, Abby," Sabina observed. "I truly do believe that. Whether or not that's enough for you, only you can decide."

Abby asked her friend, "Would it have been enough for you? If you weren't able to have married Proud Bear, would you have given yourself to him all the same?"

"Yes, because he was the man meant for me. My heart knew it, as did my body. Had I not been with him, my life would have been that much poorer; my soul that much lonelier. Knowing him, loving him, even for so short a time, was worth the risk."

Everything was set. The invitations were written and dispatched.

Beau relaxed in front of the fire blazing in the massive

stone fireplace. The polished wood floors gleamed warmly in the light of the flames. The large tufted leather sofa in a deep shade of brown matched the wing chairs that flanked the fireplace. Two colorful Indian blankets, bartered for beef at the general store, were tossed over the couch to add color. The matching rug had been thrown in for free.

He sipped some very expensive brandy and took a long drag on his cheroot, enjoying the smell of the woodsmoke that filtered through the warm room. Comforting.

All that was missing was a woman to share it with.

Beau smiled. Not just any woman would do. It was Abby Butler, or no one.

In his mind's eye he could envision a portrait of her hanging over the large stone mantle. She'd be dressed in blue. Candles would surround her, giving her skin a warm glow, and adding highlights to her burnished red hair. A soft smile would grace her generous mouth and light up her eyes. Ah, her eyes, Beau thought. They would shine brighter than the sapphires she would wear about her throat.

He turned his head to the side, glancing at the long dining table that he'd had made special for this house. Carved by a local man, it was a one-of-a-kind piece. He could see her presiding there at his holiday dinner, charming their guests. The perfect hostess. Gracious. Elegant. More than a match for any New Orleans or New York matron.

And then later, after everyone had gone home, she would still be there. Sharing a brandy before bed. Clad in a long velvet robe of the darkest blue, lightly trailing the floor as she swept along the wood in her bare feet. Her hair unbound, cascading around her curving hips.

Real hunger rose within Beau at his imaginary picture.

God, had he ever hungered in so many ways for a woman as he had for her?

The answer came easily: *No*.

Abby Butler was unique, a once-in-a-lifetime woman.

He rose from the couch and paced around the room, finally stopping in front of the new bank of windows he'd had installed so that this room was flooded with light during the day. Outside, the sky was carpeted with stars, bright with moonlight.

"Darling." In his mind he heard her speak. "Is something troubling you?"

He'd pull her into his arms and kiss her deeply, reveling in her soft mouth and her excited responses. His hands would loosen the robe, sneaking inside to cup a breast, to skim along a hipbone. Boldly he'd stroke his fingers through her nether curls, enjoying her gasps of delight, her damp, welcoming flesh.

She'd reach for him, just as eager as he was to make love. Unbuttoning his trousers, she would free him. Then, bending, she'd kneel and love him with her skilled tongue and more-than-capable hands. "Only for you," she'd whisper. In his fantasy he was the man who'd taught her that, not her late husband. That shadow figure was a sickly man, lacking in spirit or strength to teach her true pleasure.

God, his vision was so potent he could swear that he could feel her hair as his hand rested on his own thigh.

"Sir, is there anything else?"

Beau took in a deep breath, his fantasy shattered by the male voice.

He turned and faced the speaker. "No, that's all, Dooley."

"Then Lacey and I will be turning in, if you're sure."

"I'm sure." He started to turn aside again but stopped. "One thing. Everything is ready for the Thanksgiving meal?"

The other man smiled. "Most definitely, sir. Got a turkey fattening up just fine. The smokehouse has several nice hams hanging there, and the root cellar is stocked with enough vegetables to feed the entire town. Springhouse is filled with extra butter and milk. Your guests and the hands won't go hungry, no sir."

"Good. This dinner is most important."

Dooley gave his employer an easy, knowing grin. "Thought as much. Me and Lacey will do you proud, sir."

"Thank you."

"Night, then."

"Good night to you too," Beau said, walking to the fireplace. He stood there for a moment, gazing into the flames.

Years began to disappear—all of a sudden he was in a different house, contemplating linking his life to another woman's. All around him he could hear music and laughter. And why not? It was his engagement that was being celebrated. Barely twenty-one, and in love as only a young man can be, he felt indestructible. His fiancée was sweet, and though slightly spoilt by her rich papa, she was kindness itself, a balm to his wounded soul.

Or so he'd thought up until the moment she broke their engagement.

Looking back, Beau hardly recognized the youth he'd been then or what he'd been feeling. The only thing that still remained real was the feeling of betrayal.

Telling her that he needed to talk to her in private, Beau had maneuvered his way into his future father-in-law's study while he waited, impatiently, for the woman he'd asked to marry him just a week before. Despite the words of love they'd spoken, they'd spent precious little time alone. Now they must so that he could tell her all about himself. He wanted to share, to tell her about so many things that had gone into making him who he was.

Alas, he never got the chance. Her father did that for him. He'd hired someone to check into Beau's past, and it was all detailed, in black and white, for her to read.

And read she had. Creeping into the room, holding the papers tightly in her hand, she'd asked, "Is it true?"

"Is what true?" Beau had responded, bewildered by her sudden change from sunshine to storm cloud.

"*This?*" she gasped, handing him the papers, careful not to touch his hand as she did so.

He scanned the neatly handwritten sheets. "Everything here is correct, yes," he admitted.

"And you didn't think I should know?"

"I hoped that it wouldn't matter. I was planning on telling you tonight."

"You say that now," she snapped.

"My word is my honor, Lillibeth."

"Honor? I don't care about *your* precious honor, sir. It's mine that worries me if this farce is allowed to take place."

"You consider love a farce?"

"Yours, yes, when you kept such a secret." She yanked at the small ruby on her finger, pulling it off and placing it on her father's desk. "There. Take it back. I have no more use for it." She shuddered. "And to think I let you kiss me."

"Take a shot of whiskey, my dear," he drawled in a cold tone. "It might just help you wash the taste of me from your mouth. But I doubt it. Once you've had a sample of spice, and liked it, it's hard to do without."

He'd walked out of her house that night a wiser, harder man. At the time he'd thought his pride had been shattered. Now he could see that it had been merely bruised. Easily repaired. He'd foolishly fallen for a pretty face without substance. Yet, he'd learned a valuable lesson. One he'd never forgotten.

Now the risk of revealing secrets would be greater. The stakes were higher; the consequences more intense.

But she had to know.

Soon, he thought. *Soon.*

"Seems that she was spotted in Denver. This time the information is quite reliable."

"Denver?" Alma Breckenridge repeated in a questioning tone. "What's she doing there?"

"From what the Pinkerton informant said, she was teaching at some common girl's school," her husband answered as the butler poured him another glass of whiskey.

"Is she still there? Have they caught her?"

"No," grumbled Breckenridge, tossing back his drink. "The damned fools have lost her again, though they say they believe they know where she's going."

"My God, that girl amazes me," Alma replied, sipping at her glass of champagne. "She skips from place to place, never seeming to linger long enough for the detectives to grab her. I declare, she's like a ghost."

"Well, soon enough she'll be wearing earthly chains," Alma's husband promised, stabbing his fork into a thin slice of pheasant.

Alma glanced down the table at her husband. "You really think so?"

"I *know* so." He snapped his fingers and the butler refilled his glass again. "If they don't find her, they know there'll be hell to pay. I told them that I want her home in time for Christmas."

Alma studied her husband's florid face. "You have another husband picked out for her?"

Breckenridge gave his wife a snide smile. "Exactly."

"Whom do you have in mind?" She hoped that it was someone who could keep the minx in line, no matter what method he had to use. God knew it would be bad enough if their friends actually discovered that Abigail had left them like some common drudge, without a by-your-leave. She'd done some fancy maneuvering to stop anyone from finding out. Her daughter, she explained to friends, was high-strung. Nervous. So, they'd been forced to send her to a sanitarium for her nerves, somewhere quiet where she could recoup. Reflect. Come to terms with what being a wife actually meant. If Alma could stand it, then so could her daughter. After all, marriage had its compensations.

Alma examined the new bracelet that surrounded her wrist, four strands of matched pearls and diamonds. It was an early holiday gift from her husband. Bought, no doubt, to appease his conscience. For that she cared little. Let Harold have his whores. The more time he spent with them, the less time he sought in her bed, which was how she preferred it. Lying there while her husband rutted like a pig was hardly a position she enjoyed. She *endured* the humiliation because she understood it was part of the bargain that was marriage.

She'd tried to teach her daughter that such was the stuff from which powerful alliances were made. Not drivel-laden poetry. Not spring cotillions and autumn harvest balls. It was putting up with the pain and the sorrow of having your body invaded by some sweaty, hairy beast whenever he felt like it because it was his *right*, his expected *bonus* when he took a wife.

Her closets were filled with expensive clothes from the finest shops in New York and London, tailored just for her; her hand-painted china jewelry boxes were laden with gifts worth fortunes. And she'd earned them. Each and every single item.

Damn that ungrateful bitch for running away. There was no excuse. The Breckenridge name demanded sacrifices, as did the life they all lived.

Harold finished eating before he answered his wife. He observed the bracelet he'd given her before dinner gleaming on her small wrist. He had known she'd like it. It was hard and cold, much like her. Damned if he didn't examine his privates after lying with her to make sure he didn't suffer frostbite. Slipping between those thighs was like screwing a block of ice. He got no real satisfaction from it; he did it merely to remind her who was in charge. Who controlled her body.

Breckenridge gave a little smile of satisfaction. The trifle he'd bought her was the price for being caught the other day with one of their numerous housemaids. He'd thought he'd locked the door to the library. Too late he'd discovered his mistake when Alma entered and caught him bending over the girl as she lay face down across his desk, her black wool skirt rucked up to her waist, his stiff cock rammed into the girl's luscious white ass.

"Give me a few minutes, would you, my dear?" he requested as he took in his wife's tight face, then proceeded to finish his business, thrusting away for a few more moments before spilling himself into the tight channel. Alma had left before he was done; he'd heard the soft click of the door.

Tears streaked the girl's face as she rearranged her clothes. Harold reached out his hand and squeezed her plump breast, hard. "I suggest that you find a different place to work, my dear. Your *usefulness* is at an end here."

"But sir," the girl said, wiping away the salty tracks of moisture that clung to her cheeks, "I got nowhere else to go. I need this job, I do, and the extra money you promised me for doing what you asked."

"That, my good girl, is not my problem. Seeing as how my wife saw us, she won't want you around here to remind her. Get your things and get out before I have you tossed into the street. And as for extra money, I don't recall having mentioned that at any time."

"But you did, sir," she protested, trembling in pain. "I wouldn't have let you do those things to me if not for the money. You know I need it for my family."

"You wanted it, my dear. Let's not dress it up as anything other than what it was," Breckenridge insisted as he buttoned his trousers. He pulled out some coins from his pocket and dropped them into her hand. They totaled less than a dollar.

She dropped them onto the carpet. "You can keep your

change, sir," she said and left the room with her head held high.

The girl did as she was told, making her exit from the Breckenridge mansion that night, and all it cost him was a bauble.

He licked his lips in remembrance. Damn, that little Irish coal miner's spawn had been a fine piece of ass. A virgin both front and back; tight and hot as he liked it.

Oh well, he rationalized, it wasn't as if he'd run out of maids. A steady supply had come and gone, and would continue to do so. Didn't the little fool realize how lucky she'd been? She'd had a *gentleman*. Been broken in by *quality*.

"Harold? Did you hear me?"

"Oh yes, Alma, you wanted to know whom I'd picked out for Abigail. Desmond Carruthers."

"Lady Timond's grandson?"

"The very same. Seems he's in want of a wife, and a bit of pocket change. Both of which I can provide."

"Then it's settled?"

"I had the contracts drawn up this morning. Carruthers is a dullard and a fool, but he'll suit." And if he didn't, then it would be too bad for him. Accidents sometimes happened, even to very careful people.

"Then all we need do is produce her."

"That, my dear, is what I hired the Pinkertons for. This is their last chance. Either they find her soon, or they'll forfeit the remainder of the fee. I mean to have this settled before the year is out, one way or the other."

"What if they fail?"

"Failure had better not be part of their vocabulary, Alma. I made that clear. That chit has cost me dearly and I want to collect." He banged his fist on the table, causing the china to rattle. "There's no one who can stop me from getting what I want. No one."

Chapter Seventeen

When Abby woke up on Thanksgiving morning, a blanket of snow carpeted the ground. Frosty swirls of ice made an interesting lace-like pattern on her window as she moved aside the curtains.

Shivering, she made her way quickly to the kitchen and added more wood to her stove. Next, she fixed a pot of coffee, putting it on to boil as she cut a thick slice of the dark bread she'd bought yesterday from the new German baker who'd recently come to town. Stomach grumbling, she spread it liberally with fresh-churned butter from an earthenware crock and wolfed it down, licking a dab of butter from her finger.

She smothered a laugh. If New York society could only see her now. Instead of the formerly pampered banking heiress, she was a self-sufficient woman who could actually make her own coffee, and ate standing up in her own kitchen, with nary a servant in site.

Admittedly, she did occasionally miss having access to unlimited funds, but never enough to give up the life she had now to return to the former.

A pleasing smell filled the air as the coffee perked.

Huddled in her warm, thick robe, Abby turned the lock and peeked out the kitchen door, spying one of her ever present protectors. Smiling, she called out, "Good morning. Would you like a cup of coffee?"

"Why yes, ma'am, I would," the cowboy replied, as he hefted himself out of a sturdy wooden chair.

Abby handed him a steaming mug.

He touched the brim of his hat. "Thank you kindly, Mrs. Butler."

"You're welcome, Woodrow," she said, watching as the long-haired man took two big swallows.

"You make a da—mighty fine cup of coffee, ma'am," he said as he handed the empty granitewear mug back to her.

"Would you like another?"

He grinned. "If it's not too much bother."

"No trouble at all," Abby assured him, stepping back inside her house to get him another cup and pouring one for herself. Though she liked the idea of some form of protection until things got sorted out, she hated putting anyone into harm's way for her sake, or making anyone stand post for her in the cold. Even though he was warmly dressed for the weather in flannel and wool topped by a long leather duster, she still felt a pang of guilt that he had to endure miserable conditions for her sake.

"Can I get you something else?" she offered when he took the second cup from her.

"No, ma'am. This'll do for now. I had me a nice hot breakfast back at the ranch early this morning, and I'm good till dinnertime."

"Are you riding back there with us?" she asked, her breath coming in small puffs on the cold air.

"Yes, ma'am. Mr. McMasters wants to make sure that nothing happens to you and your friends on the way to his place."

Abby smiled at the mention of Beau's name. "He's very thoughtful."

"Yes, ma'am, that he is. More so," Woodrow said as he took a smaller sip this time, "than the last man we called boss. Mr. McMasters made sure that we have a right good meal today, too. Turkey and ham are on the menu. So's all the fixin's. Me and the rest of the crew are right grateful for that."

She was curious about his obvious delight. "Is that something special?"

"Begging your pardon, ma'am, but the last man who owned the spread was a tight-fisted bas—fella, when it came to his crew. Nothing opened up his purse strings, 'cepting if it was for himself. Now you take the new boss, he pays us regular-like; made sure the bunkhouse was repaired when the main house was; bought more supplies for the winter, and gave us all some extra money on account at the general store for our own use. He—heck, he even tossed in some new blankets. Not those thin, piss-poor ones that you'd find in any old camp, but clean new ones from Pendelton. Thick and warm. And real pillows. Gosh, haven't had me one of those since I was a boy living in Texas."

"What did you use before?"

"Some horsehair stuffed inside a piece of mattress ticking, ma'am."

"Horsehair?"

"Yes, ma'am. Not the easiest thing to sleep on, but once you've used a saddle, it ain't so bad. Now you'd best go back inside 'fore you freeze out here." He smiled deeply. "It sure wouldn't please Mr. McMasters none if that was to happen." He handed her the cup. "Right nice of you, ma'am."

"I appreciate your willingness to stand duty here," she said. "I know it's not what you're used to doing."

"Happy to do so, ma'am," he replied with a smile. "Makes a change from my regular day. And a lady like you shouldn't have to worry about some no-account threatening you. And 'specially not on a day like today, one made for being joyful, for counting life's blessings."

Abby turned and stepped back across her threshold. She had a lot, she acknowledged to herself, to be thankful for: a new home, a new life.

Finally, she was done running. This town and the people here had convinced her of that. The Pinkertons be damned. If they found her, then so what? They couldn't force her back to New York, back to the clutches of her father. She'd committed no crime. Here, in Heaven's Grace, she had friends to help her. Here she had a chance for a life lived on her own terms. Here she had possibilities, a worthwhile position, the opportunity for real happiness. The kind that lasted through thick and thin. Solid. True. She wasn't ever going to give that up, not without a fight.

Breakfast done, Abby was on her way to her room to get washed when she heard voices outside.

A hard knock sounded on her kitchen door, along with Woodrow's booming voice. "You got visitors, Mrs. Butler."

Abby reopened the door to see Cassie and Glory standing there. "Hello," she said, confused. Had she made an extra appointment with them and simply forgotten? She asked them that as she indicated that they should come in.

"Why, no, Miss Abby," Cassie said in a bright voice as she pulled off her gloves, casually dumping them on the kitchen table. "We're here to give you something. A token of our thanks for all the lessons you've been giving us."

"You didn't have to . . ."

"We know that," Glory insisted warmly. "It's something we wanted to do." She handed Abby a wooden box tied with a colorful ribbon. "Go on, open it."

Cassie chuckled. "Something for a special occasion."

Abby untied the bright scarlet ribbon and lifted the lid on the elegant cedar box. Inside was a lace-edged creamy white table runner, folded over. Lifting the edges aside, Abby gasped at what it contained. Two fine ivory silk chemises were nestled there, along with two pairs of lace-edged silk drawers, each with her initials in navy blue thread. Her fingers skimmed the material, feeling the luxury of the silk, touching the tiny mother-of-pearl buttons on the chemise.

"Do you like them?" Cassie asked.

"They're exquisite," Abby responded. She picked up one of the drawers and held it up. So fine was the material that light passed through it easily. The same could be said of the chemises. While they would cover her flesh, they would also reveal every detail of her skin. The kind of garments, she realized, made to please a man. "I don't know what to say."

"Just tell us that you like them," Glory said.

Cassie added, "And that you aren't offended."

"Goodness, why would I be offended?" Abby demanded, carefully placing the garments back in the box and replacing the lid. It was then that she saw the carved initials set on the top of the box: AB

"Because we wear the same things, though in bolder colors."

"For your customers?"

Cassie chuckled. "Not likely. I wear them for myself. Makes me feel good, like quality."

"Besides," Glory chimed in, "these pretty things wouldn't last too long with some of our patrons. Better they should paw or tear the plain old cotton working clothes than our fancy gear."

"I'm thinking that you won't be a widow lady for long," Cassie stated, a merry light in her blue eyes. "Save these for your new husband. If they don't get him stirred for the wedding night, nothing will."

Glory rolled her eyes and groaned, "Cassie."

"What?" the other woman asked. "I'm telling it true. Men like seeing pretty things. And they like seeing them with the lights on." She gave Abby a sly smile. "If more women in this town remembered that, we might not be so busy some nights.

"Course," she added, "if more men put some effort into what they did, it might make a difference, too. A man unbuttoning his drawers and just shoving his tool inside isn't likely to get a woman in a welcoming mood."

Glory grabbed her friend's arm. "Come along. We gotta go."

"You're not *working* today, are you?" Abby asked.

"No. Miss Trudy wouldn't allow that," Cassie said as she slipped her hands back into her rabbit-fur–lined leather gloves. "It's a holiday for us too. An extra day of rest is something to be really thankful for, what with this town growing so much. Lordy, it's gotten so busy, Miss Trudy had to hire some more girls to help with the overflow. Why, we even got us some Chinese ladies from California to add to our mix." Cassie grinned. "Me, I'm gonna crawl back into bed and finish that book you lent me. I want to see what else happens to those March sisters. Personally, I would have slapped that little Amy silly if she'd tossed my hard work into the fireplace like she did Jo's."

Abby smiled: *Little Women* was one of her favorites. She was so proud of Cassie's progress when it came to reading; the woman had graduated from dime novels to actual books in such a short amount of time. "Take your time. Miss Alcott's book should be savored, like a fine meal."

Cassie chuckled, getting in the last word. "Or a good lover."

A short time later, Abby considered Cassie's words after she dried off from her lukewarm wash. Her fine lawn chemise rested on the bed, ready to be put on, along with the rest of her undergarments. Still, the cedar box beckoned from its resting place on her dresser. She opened it again, letting the towel slide from her body to the floor. Carefully, she buttoned up the chemise, feeling the cool slide of the silk on her skin. She stepped into the drawers, adjusting the ribbon ties at her waist. Turning, she caught sight of herself in her mirror and gasped. The garments gave her skin a pearly glow, revealing the buds of her nipples, the dark red thatch between her legs.

Slowly, Abby ran her hand along the chemise, imagining that it was another hand. A recognizable masculine hand. Instantly her nipple puckered. Her breath came in a slow gasp as she continued, skimming her fingertips down along belly, her thighs.

Heat flooded her skin, mixing with the cool air that circulated in the room.

Lord, what was she thinking?

Decidedly wicked thoughts, she acknowledged as she pulled on a pair of stockings, adjusting the garters that held them up. *Deliciously* wicked, she amended with a smile on her lips as she slipped the heavy cotton petticoat over her head and pulled the ribbon secure about her waist in the back. She flounced the hem, a wide band of cream eyelet, for effect. Once she could never have imagined standing in front of her mirror, pretending she was preening for a man. Dressing to please him, even if he never saw what was beneath her clothes. Today, however, it occupied a keen place in her mind.

As did Beau.

Had it been fate, or merely luck that had brought them both here?

She shrugged her shoulders. What did it matter? What really counted was that they *were* here, together. That something wonderful had led them both to this place, to this new life.

Destiny. Her mother had harped on that word incessantly. It was Abby's destiny, Alma had said over and over, to be born a Breckenridge, to marry the right sort of man, to have the right sort of life, to do what her parents thought best.

Abby laughed. She'd challenged that destiny and won, outwitting them both. For a moment, she wished they could see her now. Happy. Content. All without the things they thought mattered. But, she knew, even if they could see her, they would never understand. Never recognize the woman she'd become. All they would ever see was the asset they could use, never the person. Never *her*.

She wiped away a stray tear as she fastened her skirt. Never again would she have to endure a Thanksgiving meal in a household that never understood the meaning of the holiday. Tonight she was off to make a new tradition.

"Where you fixin' to go dressed like that?" Hank Baser demanded of his daughter.

"I told you before, Pa, I was invited to have holiday dinner at Mr. McMasters's ranch, along with Mrs. Butler and the new sheriff."

"And didn't I tell you that that man's home isn't a fittin' place for my daughter?"

"I don't agree," Sabina stated calmly. It felt really good to stand up for herself, for her friends. No longer cowed or controlled by her father, she was making her own decisions again and liking them. Finally, good, bad or indifferent, they were hers alone.

"Well, who cares if you agree or not!" he shouted. "I said you're not going."

Her answer was soft and resolute. "I am."

"Getting a mite uppity all of a sudden, aren't you?" he sneered. "Think that just because you got some new clothes and new friends that you're as good as them? Or"—he stepped closer to his daughter—"that you're better than me? Well think again. You're a whore. You dirtied yourself with some goddamned Indian, pretending that you were his wife." He gave a sharp bark of laughter. "*Wife*. More like a squaw, servicing a filthy heathen. Think anyone will want you now after you spread those legs of yours for a redskin? I tried to protect you, telling everyone that he kidnapped you, forced you to be his whore. You should be grateful to me, instead of flaunting yourself like some nickel slut."

Sabina took a deep breath, her father having just made her latest decision much easier. She went back to her room and when she returned, she was carrying a large carpetbag.

"What's that?"

"My things. I won't be coming back here tonight, or any other night."

A nasty look crept into Baser's eyes. "What do you mean?"

"That I'm tired of living in this hovel," Sabina explained, "of trying to keep it clean and watching you treat it, and me, as some kind of whipping boy." She took a deep breath and expelled a sigh. "I'm sorry that life didn't treat you as fair as you thought it should, Pa, but that's not my fault."

"It's your duty to care for me, missy."

"I tried, Pa," Sabina stated. "But it's no use. You don't care about me, except as someone who's there only to serve you. Well, that's not good enough for me anymore. I'm better than that."

"The hell you are! Who put those stupid notions in your head?" he demanded. "That highfalutin strumpet who poses as a teacher? That fancy gamblin' man with his smooth tongue?" He paused, narrowing his eyes. "Or is it the new lawman? I saw the way he looks at you. Won't be long before he's sniffin' at your skirts, missy, looking for some of what you gave that Indian."

"You're disgusting," Sabina said coldly.

"No, digustin' is lying with a dirty redskin and calling it love when it weren't no such thing. It was lust, vile filthy lust that should have been beat out of you, along with any false pride, 'cause you got nothing to be proud of."

"That's where you're wrong, Pa. I have a lot to be proud of, starting with myself. I let you bully me into thinking this town wouldn't accept me for who I was, and what I did. Well, you're wrong. People have proved that to me over and over these past few months. I don't have to walk around with some imaginary scarlet letter on my chest anymore."

"What are you talking about?"

"It's from a book, Pa. A *book*. Something you have no use for. Well, I do. Ma used to read to me, tell me stories. Abby helped me rediscover that. She showed me the beautiful world I could find again if I looked."

"Claptrap."

"No, Pa, it's magic. It was when I was a child and still is. Just because you don't care for it doesn't make it so."

"And this *new* world," he sneered, "how you gonna survive in it? On your back?"

"You would think that, wouldn't you?" Sabina asked as she pulled on her coat. "Always believe the worst and expect the same was your creed." She adjusted her new hat on her head, then pulled on her gloves.

"Well, you're wrong, Pa. I'm making an honest, profitable living with my sewing. Because of that, I've got a chance to open my own shop in town and I'm taking it."

"How you gonna afford this shop?"

"It's not your concern," she stated. "Just know that I'm gonna make it a success."

"You'll come crawling back here when it fails."

"No," Sabina insisted, her voice filled with steel, "I won't. When I walk out this door, I'm never coming back, no matter what."

"Then get out!" he shouted.

Baser watched her do just that; she closed the door softly behind her.

Anger boiled to the surface. He stomped around the small room, railing at this turn of events. How dare she leave him? He glanced towards the area that served as his kitchen. No dinner waited for him there. He slammed his hand down upon the rickety table. He yanked open the oven door—nothing inside the cold, dark interior.

The *bitch!* Didn't she know she was forsaking her duty to her father?

It was all their fault—the snooty schoolmarm and the fancy-man gambler. They'd done this to him. Filled his girl's head with ideas; tempted her with lies and promises that would never come true.

Sinners all. And that being the case, they had to be punished. Tonight. He'd been derelict in his duty. Because he was, God was showing him clearly that it must be tonight. He'd make her see the light of truth, and then the others . . .

Well, they would reap the whirlwind of their actions. They must be made to suffer as he was suffering. Hurried on their way to Hell. Damnation awaited them, and with it, his salvation.

The young woman was cold. Freezing. Huddled in her threadbare cotton coat, she walked quickly down the snow-covered street, eyes alert, looking for a place to stop and get warm.

"How much you askin', missy?" demanded one man as she moved to go past him. He grabbed hold of her arm, his fetid breath hot on her face.

"Let go of me, you filthy toad," she snarled, yanking her arm from his grasp.

"Well, if it ain't a whore with an air. Who you calling names, missy? I could call you some, too, if I was of a mind."

"Bugger off, you drunken sod." She stepped hard on his shoe and watched him yelp in pain, releasing her. Served him right, she thought as she continued on her way, hearing the curses he threw her way fade as she strode across the street. Filthy bastard thought she was his for the asking. Or the taking. Well, never again.

She kept walking, for nigh onto a mile, trudging through the cold sweep of the wind as it channeled down the wide streets of New York. Not many others were about this night, only those for whom the night meant business to be done.

Finally, a few feet ahead, she saw a brightly lit establishment. Several customers spilled out of the public house, laughter on their tongues. She came closer, stood near the door, yet far enough away from the street lamp so that she couldn't be seen. Hearty smells wafted out whenever a customer entered or exited. Ham. Beer. Potatoes. Bread. Irish cooking, to be sure.

Her stomach growled in anticipation. It had been days since she'd had a proper meal. Days since she'd had a chance to be in a warm place. She'd been reduced to hiding in alleys, seeking scraps. Too proud to beg for charity, she wandered, hoping for a place to rest, to find shelter. Turned out of her job without a reference, she would find no respectable house in New York to take her in. And she couldn't stay and be a burden to her mum if she was bringing in no money, for her mum had enough mouths to feed, what with her older brother being sent to prison for stealing food, and her da shot dead for the same back home in Ireland. No, Mum and the boys needed someone else to help them fend. Someone who didn't bring shame upon their door, what with her being branded a slut for all to hear. Wasn't long before the other tenants of their building made it known she wasn't welcome among good and decent people.

She licked her lips, hunger forcing her hand. There was

no other way. She had to do what she must to survive so that she could make things right. Restore, if even only in her own mind, some portion of the honor she'd lost.

A short, heavyset man in a thick tweed coat and a bowler hat approached the tavern from the other direction.

She took a deep breath and stepped into the light. "Excuse me, sir, but could you be sparing a wee bit of pocket change so that I could get something to eat?"

"Aye, that I could, my dear, if I was of a mind to," he said, his eyes bright and blue. "The question is, why would I?"

Ah, a tough customer, one who wanted value for his charity. "I'd be willing to make it worth your trouble."

"You would, would ya?" he asked, letting his eyes wander up and down her slender frame.

She stepped closer, reaching her hand up and letting her chapped fingers skim across his coat. "Indeed," she said, forcing herself to smile, to play the coquette, even as her stomach roiled at the thought of what must be done to secure a decent meal. Days without food had finally worn down what little scraps of pride she had left. "You'd not be regretting it, I can assure you."

"Then let's off and have that meal, my darlin'," he said as he opened the door and escorted her inside.

The bar was crowded with patrons. Male and female alike, each jostling for space. The air inside was thick with various scents, from cooked food to that of overly perfumed skin, to unwashed clothes and flesh.

"I think I can arrange a private room," the man said, steering her along with him as he approached the bartender.

"Colin, I'd have a word with you, if you please," he said.

She watched as he left her there to talk with the skinny man behind the bar. Sure she could feel many eyes on her, already knowing what she was about. Already wondering if she was his exclusively, or willing to negotiate with others.

"Come along, then," the man said. "There's a room upstairs that we can use."

"I'd be wanting to eat first," she stated.

"And so you shall, my dear," he said. "Tom Collins doesn't expect something for nothing. I've arranged for some dinner to be sent up."

He took her arm and led her through the bar, towards a small staircase in the back. "Go on up."

"What about you?"

"I'll join you in a little bit. I'll be having a pint, and when I'm done, I'll be meeting you there."

"You trust that I'll still be there?"

"I trust that you'll keep your word." He reached out a hard, work-roughened hand, lifting her chin. "You will, won't you?"

She looked at him, saw a flash of kindness in his eyes. With that, she smiled, then turned her back and calmly walked up the stairs.

Inside the room at the top a barmaid was leaving, an empty tray in her hands. "This be the place you be lookin' for, my dear."

She nodded. "Thank you."

The barmaid gave her a thorough glance. "Tom likes 'em young, he does. And pretty."

"Does he now?" she asked.

"Oh, he does indeed, love. Make no mistake, he's a powerful man to have on your side, so don't be forgettin' it. Relax. Eat your food, 'cause you look as if you could do with some fattenin' up. It'll be over afore you know it."

She walked into the warm room, happy to see the small fireplace was lit. She stood in front of it as she removed her coat and tossed it onto the nearby chaise. A small table and chair were set up, with a tall glass of dark beer and a plate piled high with slices of ham and chunks of cheddar cheese. Ignoring her dirty hands, she went after the food as any starving person might, washing it down intermittently with swallows of the strong brew.

Several minutes later, she heard the creak of the stairs.

"So, you're still here," Collins said, coming inside and removing his hat and coat. They joined hers on the chaise.

She stood up, wiped her hands upon the only thing she had, her dress. God, if her mother could see her now, she'd get a blistering lecturing about cleanliness.

With that image, she burst into laughter. Her mum would do more than lecture her if she was to know what she was really doing here.

"What's so funny?" he asked as he began unbuttoning his wool trousers.

"A private joke," she responded, wondering how he wanted to do it.

He took the seat she had vacated in front of the fire. Slowly, moving his legs wide, he removed his flaccid member from his pants.

Ah, she thought, he wants that, does he? The *other* had liked that as well, teaching her how to give him satisfaction in this manner.

She took a deep breath, squaring her shoulders. The time had come to pay the bill for her food.

She kneeled before him, her head in his lap.

When her task was done, she stood up, finished the remaining beer in her glass, trying to erase the taste of him from her throat, and said, "I need one other thing, Mr. Collins."

He refastened his clothes, a satisfied flush on his face. "And what would that be?"

"A gun," she said quietly.

"And what would a girl like you be wanting a gun for?"

"I can't be saying."

He stood. "You don't mean to be harmin' yourself, do ya?"

"No," she reassured him. "I'm not looking to be taking my own life."

"For protection, then?"

"Of a sort."

"Well," he said, "I'll see what I can do. When do you need it?"

"As soon as possible, Mr. Collins."

"Stay right here," he instructed. "I'll be back."

She waited while he went back downstairs, finishing off the bits of cheese that were left.

In a matter of minutes, he'd returned. He pulled a small gun from the inside of his frock coat. "Would this be useful?"

She took the item from his hand. "Is it loaded?"

He nodded.

She walked over to the chaise, bent and picked up her coat, slipping the weapon into one of the pockets. Smiling, she turned. He was watching her carefully, as if unsure whether she'd meant what she said before.

"You've been most agreeable, Mr. Collins," she said as she approached him, leaning over to place a chaste kiss on his cheek. "I won't be forgetting your kindness to me."

She turned to exit the room and he gently took hold of her arm. "If ever you need me, I'm a good friend to have," he said. "That's no bragging, either. Ask anyone hereabouts. Find me here most nights, too, should you decide to come back."

"You never know," she responded, her hand caressing the gun in her pocket. "My mum says that God never closes a door that he doesn't open a window."

With that, she made her way down the stairs and through the still crowded bar. Her mind clear, her thoughts focused, she emerged into the cold, stinging air, her direction set.

Chapter Eighteen

"Welcome to my home."

Those words, delivered in the smooth, deep voice that Beau McMasters possessed, sent a chill down Abby's arms, even though they were covered in a heavy wool coat. Standing there, he looked every inch the handsome host: from the tip of his polished boots to the striking midnight-blue wool frock coat, which covered a vest of the same color, only in silk. A snow-white shirt completed the look. And, she noted, it was the first time since she'd known him that he wasn't wearing his ever-present Remington pistol.

Stepping down from the hired carriage that Beau had sent for his guests, Abby placed her gloved hand in his.

He raised it to his lips, smiling seductively. "You do me a great honor, Mrs. Butler."

With that, she sank into a deep curtsy, her coat and skirt trailing in the snow. "It is I who am honored, sir," she replied, meeting his eyes with her own.

A discreet cough sounded behind her.

"Ah, Miss Baser, and Sheriff Tyler," Beau stated, slipping Abby's arm in his, "forgive my bad manners in ignoring you. It was not intentional, I can assure you."

"I reckon I can understand it, Mr. McMasters," the sheriff drawled. "Beauty, in the form of these two lovely ladies, is almost more than a body can bear."

Beau laughed. "My sentiments, exactly." With his free hand he took Sabina's and raised it to his lips as well, bringing a spot of color to her already cold-flushed cheeks. "Now, please come inside."

They all stepped up to the wide planked entrance and walked through the refurbished doorway into the newly formed space. From several tiny, dark rooms, Beau had formed a large, single space that welcomed his guests with warmth. A fire was blazing in the large stone hearth; the wooden floor had been scrubbed and repaired so that it gleamed with a soft, polished sheen. Scattered heavy rugs brought in more muted colors.

A black man of medium height appeared through the doorway that led to the back of the ranch house, where the kitchen was located. "Good evening," he said as he approached, a hint of a smile on his face. "May I see to your coats?"

Beau helped Abby with hers while Adam Tyler helped Sabina; then both men handed the garments to the waiting man.

"I'll be right back with some refreshments," he said as he made his way back through the same door.

"That's Dooley," Beau explained. "He and his wife Lacey have been a very big help in getting this place the way I want it. I don't think I could have completed this refurbishment without them."

"Well, it sure looks mighty fine," Sabina offered.

Beau chuckled. "You should have seen it before I moved in. Fit more for keeping cattle than people. I don't think the previous occupant had ever actually cleaned it. Dust and soot were all over. Windows. Walls. All closed off with very tiny dark rooms." He gave a quick glance around the room, his face proud. "Now it's mine."

Like the saloon before, Abby thought, Beau had put his stamp on the building, molding it to his vision. Turned something that was a loss into a profit. He had a gift—seeing what could be within what was. "It's beautiful." Admiration was in her tone and on her face.

"You like it?" he asked, coming closer as Sabina and the sheriff moved towards the expanse of windows.

"Yes," Abby replied, her heart beating faster. "I feel very comfortable here."

"I hoped that you would."

She sliced him a glance. "You did?" she murmured.

"Of course."

"Why?" He was so close she could inhale the fragrant scent of his soap. Would his bed smell the same?

"Why do you think?"

Abby wet her lips with her tongue. "I don't know."

"Don't you?" he asked provocatively, whispering the words in her ear.

"I want you to tell me," she countered.

"Later." That word held a deep well of promise. "Ah, Dooley has brought us some champagne."

Dooley held an exquisite silver tray, upon which rested four fluted glasses. He served the women first, then the men.

Before Beau could speak, Abby stepped in. "With your permission, may I make the first toast?"

Beau nodded his head and smiled. "Of course you may."

She raised her glass. "To our host: For taking a raw dream and molding it into a gracious reality. May this home be all that you wish."

Abby's eyes never left Beau's face, so she didn't see the exchange of knowing glances between Adam and Sabina while they lifted their glasses in toast.

"Now, my turn," Beau said, lifting his glass so that the

crystal flashed with prismatic color in the light of the overhead chandelier. "In my travels I've learned of a wonderful expression that the Spanish use to welcome their guests: *Mi casa es su casa*." He paused, fixing his glance on the other couple before returning to Abby. "My house is yours. Please, take that literally. Each of you is welcome to my ranch at any time, without an invitation." Beau touched his glass to all the others and drank deep, then added, "May this be the first of many happy gatherings here for us."

"I'll gladly drink to that thought," Abby replied, smiling her acceptance of Beau's wish. "And may I add, to new beginnings."

"To new beginnings," the others repeated.

"I can't recall when I've enjoyed a holiday meal more," Abby said as she dabbed her creamy-white linen napkin to her lips. This was no mere polite toss-away for Abby—she truly meant it. Instead of long, boring dinners surrounded by her parents' so-called friends, or solitary meals while on the run, this was a night to treasure. She was relaxed, content, happy.

Happy. A word she hadn't had much knowledge of, or use for, before she came to Heaven's Grace. Before she met Beau McMasters.

She glanced down the length of the table and her eyes met his. A jolt of pleasure so intense it was almost painful flooded her body. Even across the distance that separated them, his presence was still potent, still consuming. His look was frank, raw, and seemingly hot. His nostrils flared slightly, as if he was scenting her. Not for him the gentle, adoring glance of a pretended swain. This was Antony claiming Cleopatra; Henry Fitzempress his Duchess Eleanor; Darcy his Elizabeth. Proud men in pursuit of their destined lovers.

And was she his?

Breaking contact, Abby lowered her eyes to the table setting, needing to put some distance between them. This was all so new; all so confusing. To be wanted for herself, and to find that she wanted, too. Wanted hard and deep. Wanted fierce and hot. He was like spice, that added dash of pepper, cinnamon, or cloves that took life's flavor from plain to scrumptious.

Lord, but she was being overly fanciful, and hardly holding up her end of the conversation. She'd noticed earlier the fine initialed design on the napkins: a bold McM, set off by a trail of vines; it was one of the loveliest things she'd ever beheld. The workmanship was sheer perfection. "I've been meaning to ask, whose talented hand did these?"

Beau smiled. "My mother."

Abby's fingertips lingered on the smooth stitches. "She had a rare gift."

"She did indeed," Beau acknowledged. He could still see her, working close to her branch of candles, catching all the light that she could on many evenings in New Orleans. His father would sit in the opposite wing chair, reading his paper. As a child, he couldn't read the glances that passed between them; as an adult looking backwards, he knew now they had been full of love. Deep and abiding love that stirred the air, that quenched the soul. It had always been that way, even to the last night of their lives, before the howling mob came.

"She was considered one of the best needleworkers in New Orleans. Many patronized her small, select establishment." His eyes glowed with added warmth. "That's how she met my father. He wanted a gift for his parent's wedding anniversary. Upon seeing something similar in a business acquaintance's home, he demanded to know who had done such work. The man took him to her and my father promptly ordered two sets: one was for his mother and father's table, the other for his own."

"How soon after did he call upon your mother?" Abby asked.

"That evening. He told her that he hadn't ever been a patient man. Unless he acted, he was sure someone else would."

A singular man, Abby decided, much like his son. "And what did your mother have to say?"

"That many already had offered." He recalled his mother telling him one afternoon that, indeed, many men had made offers to her, and for her. Protection and prosperity. All she had to do was agree to be there, for them, whenever they wished. One or two even hinted at marriage, perhaps. "I chose love, *mon petit*," she had said. "I never regretted that. Never could I have bartered to another man what I gladly give your papa. One day you will understand what I speak of now. You will know that love can never be *bought* or *sold*. It is a gift. Unique, and so very precious. Those who believe otherwise have never truly loved."

"They were married a week later."

Abby smiled. "They knew what they wanted."

"Oh, without a doubt," Beau agreed, looking intently at her. "In that respect, I am very much their son."

Abby wet her lips. "You go after what you want."

"I always have."

"And you get it."

"Yes," he drawled, his eyes warm and inviting, "I usually do."

"I admire that about you, Mr. McMasters," Sabina said, almost hesitant to offer an opinion. So tangible was the connection between him and Abby that she feared breaking it. She'd once had that connection with her own husband, and recognized it now with them.

Beau tilted his head in the direction of his other female guest. "Why thank you, Miss Sabina. I greatly appreciate your kind words."

"I mean them," she insisted, lest he think her a false flatterer. "I can't imagine how different this town would be without you and Abby. The change you've both wrought in so short a time has been more than overwhelming. The town is growing, fed by your investment in making it a place to stop, instead of one merely to pass through. More businesses are opening,"—she paused, thinking of her own endeavor—"or expanding."

Sabina trained her glance in Abby's direction. "More children are attending school now. They're learning new things. You're influencing how people think hereabouts whether you know it or not." Like a ripple in a pond, the effects spreading outward from the source. "We're even getting a new preacher. All the way from back east— Philadelphia."

"I'd have to agree with what Miss Sabina just said," the sheriff added. "Since I've been here, granted only a short while, I've seen plenty of changes too. Makes me happy I decided to come here." Adam looked across the table and smiled deeply at Sabina. "Mighty happy, I might say. This is the kind of place a man can see calling home. Maybe even raising a family with the right woman."

"Ah yes," Beau drawled, "the right woman." His glance focused on Abby. "So much depends on that."

"Or the right *man*," Abby countered.

"*Touché*," Beau stated, lifting his glass in her direction before he consumed another swallow. More and more, he was becoming certain that *she* was the right woman for him. She possessed intelligence, beauty, and courage.

But was he the right man for her? Slowly, surely, he had moved beyond wanting to become merely her sometime lover. Once that would have been enough to satisfy. Not now. Now he wanted more. Wanted the surety of possession—deep and complete. No turning back. No regrets.

Later he would ascertain if she felt the same.

Beau addressed his guests. "Would you all care for coffee and brandy?"

Adam nodded.

Sabina answered, "Coffee only for me, please."

"Both will do me fine," Abby responded.

Beau called for Dooley and requested that they be served their drinks in front of the fire.

The sheriff escorted Sabina from the table, as Beau offered his hand to Abby.

"Gussie tells me that I have something else to be thankful for—you donated quite a number of books to the town's new library."

He shrugged.

Her hand tightened on his arm. "Modest too?" This was said with a deep smile. Each day, in so many ways, he was deepening his imprint on her heart. "She also said that you didn't want any credit."

"For what?" he asked. "To brag? To get a notice in Mr. Reynolds's paper?" He took her in the direction of the windows.

"You're not a braggart, Beau. No one who knows you could ever think that."

"As ever, I am humbled by your kind thoughts."

"Nonsense," she chimed in. "I doubt anyone or anything could ever humble you."

"Oh, I might be able to think of a thing or two," he responded with a twinkle in his eyes and a husky tone to his voice. "Besides, the books weren't being used."

"So, you didn't buy them just for this then, did you?"

"No."

"They're yours?"

"In a fashion. Part of an estate I acquired." He remembered one of the poems in a volume he had kept for himself. *She walks in beauty, like the night.* Yes, that could have been written for Abby. For the woman who stood in his house, who had eaten at his table. Mysterious, like the night. Compelling, like the night. Filled with eternal beauty, like the night. And perhaps, like the night, she would be the bringer of peace, of respite from daily cares.

"The man who formerly owned them never had much use for them from what I was told; he had them only for show. Better that they should be put to use here than left to gather dust as they had been."

"He didn't read?" she commented. "How very sad. And utterly wasteful."

"Let us just say that he had no real love for what was contained in the volumes he amassed."

"Like you do?"

Beau smiled as he guided her closer to the window. "My parents instilled that in me. Over many days and nights . . ."

Suddenly the glass they were standing in front of shattered.

Beau's eyes opened wide; he inhaled deeply. He pushed Abby out of the way, then fell to the floor.

"Beau!" she screamed, seeing the blood seep through his white shirt. "Oh my God," she said, "he's been shot!"

Abby knew she would never forget that sight—Beau lying on the floor, blood pouring from the wound in his side—for as long as she lived. One moment he was there—vital, healthy. The next, crumpled in pain and barely conscious.

Now he lay in his large bed, his clothes hastily removed, his breathing labored.

"Perhaps you'd like to wait outside, ma'am," Dooley suggested. "We've got to cut out the bullet and it's not going to be pretty, not a sight for a lady to witness."

"I'm not leaving," Abby insisted, stepping closer to the bed. "Do what you have to do, but I'm staying put."

"As you wish then," he said. Dooley lifted the white sheet and checked the thickly wadded cotton that he'd used to stop the bleeding.

271

Abby gasped. It was red and sodden with Beau's blood. "Is he going to live?"

"I don't really know, ma'am. Depends on where the bullet is lodged inside. If we can get it out and if the wound doesn't fester . . ."

She wrapped her arms about her middle. God, she prayed, don't let him die. Please.

She took a deep breath. "What can I do?" she asked.

"The sheriff sent to town for the doc, but there ain't no certainty that he can get here, what with this weather. Since you all came, it's been snowing fit to swallow up grazing stock whole. I'm thinking we can't wait much longer to get this thing out of him, lest he get worse."

"Have you ever done this before?"

He shook his head. "No, but I've seen it done."

"I can do it," spoke a deep voice from the doorway.

"Sheriff," Abby said as she turned to the sound. His boots, she noted, were soaked, his face red from the raw wind. "You had no luck finding the person who did this?"

"No, ma'am. Me and some of the hands here sure gave it a good try, but the snow wouldn't let us track him. Blew drifts over any tracks the bastard might have made."

"Much as I would have liked you to catch him, I guess it's better that you're here to dig out the bullet."

"Just let me take off these wet boots, ma'am."

"Don't bother," she insisted. "It matters little if the floors are wet or the carpet gets dirty. What matters most is that Mr. McMasters not be allowed to die."

He stepped inside the well-appointed room, approaching the bed. Adam looked down. "He say anything?"

"No," murmured the other man.

"That's for the best. You got water boiling?" Adam undid his cuffs and rolled up his sleeves, having shucked his frock coat on a nearby chair.

"I'm going down to get more. I've done cleaned up the wound as best I can. It's still bleeding." Dooley peeled back the new cotton wad he'd placed against the angry wound so that the sheriff could get a proper look. "It's not as bad as before, though."

"We got some whiskey?"

Abby grabbed at the bottle on the marble-topped night table. "Right here."

"Splash some on the wound itself," Adam commanded.

Abby did as she was told, hearing the low moan from the man on the bed. "He felt that."

Adam nodded. "Bring in some more lamps. I'm gonna need a lot of light. He's not totally unconscious, so he may wake up while we're doing this." He stood up and faced Abby. "You can handle this, can't you?"

She looked up. "Yes," she answered.

"Then I reckon I'll have to take your word for that. I want you to hold his hand, keep him still as you can. Sabina can get the other side."

Lacey came in, a large kettle filled with hot water in her hand. She filled up the porcelain wash basin. A fire had been laid in the stone hearth, so that warmth filtered across the room.

Sabina followed her into the room, a pungent poultice in her hands. She set it down temporarily and went to the sheriff, her hand on his arm, squeezing gently before she continued on to the other side of the bed.

"He's got to remain as still as possible," Adam stated. "Can't have him thrashing about when I've got my knife in him." With that he pulled out a sharp-bladed Bowie knife and proceeded to the fireplace. Sticking the blade to the flames, he heated up the tip, then poured a drop of whiskey over it for good measure.

Abby licked her lips, her hand reaching out for Beau's. She took it in hers, adding her other hand to form a tight bond with him. Leaning down, she brushed her lips across his, whispering, "Don't you dare die on me, Beau. You hold on, you hear me?"

She thought her hand was being crushed, so tight was his grip. Beau might not seem to be all there, but a good deal of him was, judging by the strength he still retained. He squeezed hard when the blade sliced deep into his skin. Bile threatened to erupt in her throat, but Abby forced it back when she glanced down. His beautiful warm golden skin was torn, with blood seeping down his side and into the thick towel that had been placed there. Adam's fingers were covered in blood as he searched for the object that had done so much damage.

At that moment, Abby knew without a doubt that she could kill. The person who had done this to Beau evoked a rage within her the likes of which she had never known. Anger, fear, and frustration warred within her. Even if Adam removed the bullet, he might still die. The coward who'd done this might never be found.

No! she silently screamed. She wouldn't allow that to happen. Not when she had something very important to tell Beau.

God, she felt a lot like a Breckenridge at that moment. Ordering fate to obey her command. Wanting to move heaven and earth to her bidding.

She heard Beau moan again, then go still.

"Got it," Adam proclaimed, holding up a bullet in his bloody hand. "Now, we need a splash more whiskey poured into the wound again and I need to get this sewn up."

Sabina let go of Beau's hand and moved from the other side of the bed. "Let me."

"Can you do it?" Adam asked.

"Watch me," she added, picking up the small needle and putting it against Beau's skin.

Abby was drained. Every ounce of strength she possessed had been willed into Beau. He slept now, deeply and comfortably. Several hours had passed since the removal of the bullet. A sandwich lay half-eaten on the bedside table.

A cup of coffee stood cooling beside it. Forcing herself to eat and drink, she could only take a few bites before the roast turkey tasted like hay. As for the coffee—it could have been ambrosia or mud as far as she could taste. All that mattered was that Beau recover. That he come back to her.

She leaned over, picked up the cloth that lay in the small washbasin of cool water. Ringing it out, she placed it upon his brow, hoping to cool any potential fever.

That task completed, she stood, easing her cramped back muscles from the chair she'd been in for a little over three hours. Moving about the room, she noticed things she hadn't before. A group of silver-framed daguerreotypes on the opposite wall, resting on a table that matched the nightstands. She picked each one up, gazing at what she assumed were his family. A handsome man and a lovely woman—his parents. They looked happy; more than that, they looked in love. A secret smile curved each mouth, as if they shared a secret not known to many.

The next was of a solitary woman. She was clearly a relation to Beau's mother, so close was her resemblance to the other woman. She was seated in a walled garden, a marble fountain behind her, and a well-fed cat on her lap. Pearls appeared to be her favorite jewel, as they decorated her throat, ears, and wrist.

It was then that Abby saw the painted portrait hanging on the wall over the table.

Moving closer, Abby examined the rich colors used to capture the female figure. She was seated in a garden similar to the one in the dagguerreotype. Moss-draped trees and magnolias dotted the background. Roses surrounded her head. Abby swore she could almost smell the fragrance, feel the heat of a sun-drenched day.

The woman was Beau's mother. She had no doubt. Beautiful beyond words. Her hair wasn't her son's deep sable shade; it was more brown, shot with golden lights.

Her eyes were a pale green, alive with feeling. And her skin . . .

It was then that Abby noticed the color that the artist had used. *Café au lait.* Creamy with a hint of dark golden warmth beneath.

"I wish that I could have found who did this," Adam said as Sabina joined him on the tufted leather sofa.

She reached out her hand, placed it on his. "I think I know who it is."

"What?" He turned in his seat.

"My father."

"What makes you think so?" He listened while she gave her reasons, holding her hand in his.

"Then as soon as I can, I'll be paying him a visit."

"Just don't go alone," she begged. "He's liable to do anything, what with the state he's in. Mean. Cornered. Maybe if I go with you, he might relent."

"You're not going," Adam stated firmly. "Do you think I'd let you within a foot of a man like that?"

"You may not have a choice."

"Oh, but I do. You're not going. No way. No how."

"You can't stop me, you know."

He lifted a hand to her face. His fingers tilted her chin. "That's where you're wrong. I can, and I *will.*"

"But you won't," she insisted.

He smiled. "No, you will."

She looked at him.

"You can't leave Miss Abby alone here. You and I both know that. She needs you."

Sabina sighed. She couldn't deny what he said was true. Abby did need her. And if the unthinkable happened, if Beau died, Abby should have a friend near to help her through the crisis. If only there had been someone for her after Proud Bear was shot . . .

Shot.

"Oh my God."

"Sabina, what's wrong?"

She hadn't realized that she'd spoken aloud. "My husband was killed by a gunshot. A rifle." Tears welled in her eyes. "I never knew who did it."

Adam drew her into his embrace, where she relaxed, enjoying his solid strength. "Now," she whispered, her voice ragged with tears, "I think I know."

Chapter Nineteen

It was a little after midnight in New York City. Gas lamps flickered softly along the street, casting eerie shadows on the brick path in the garden.

The Breckenridges had been home just over an hour, their carriage safely tucked away in the thick stone carriage house. The driver and groom had retired for the night, along with the other servants who lived in the rear of the mansion. She'd made sure of that. Some she'd seen leaving earlier, those lucky enough to get the night off since the Breckenridges were not at home.

She smiled deeply. How wonderful to find their comings and goings chronicled in the newspapers. And why not? They were among the leaders of New York society—the high-and-mighty, the better-than-you-and-me.

Well, not so much better come tomorrow, she thought with a smirk.

She'd even waited long enough for their maid and valet to help them prepare for bed. By now they should both be ready for their appointment with destiny.

It was getting colder, and she shivered in her new coat

as a sharp blast of wind hit her. Well, the coat was not really new, but it was to her. Generously provided, the owner of the charity shop had confided, by another upper crust lady, who no longer needed it. A few meager coins and it was hers. She savored the warmth it provided, along with the lined leather gloves. Like a real lady, she felt, good as any of them.

No, she amended, she felt better than they right now. She was going to get her rightful vengeance on those who had treated her, and others like her, as inferiors. Her brand of justice would be served, meted out to those who held themselves above ordinary rules. Above an ordinary reckoning. Like the landlords in Ireland, they could buy their way clear of any punishment. Too many people looked the other way—pretended that bad things didn't happen, would never happen, in such a house.

And it would always be his word against hers, against any of the girls who had wanted to tell, but never did.

So it was up to her to get the justice they deserved. For her there was no turning back. There hadn't been since that last humiliating night.

A cunning smile touched her mouth. This was planned out, she even had an alibi, an irrefutable one.

Ah, she wished she could be telling someone the irony of that. Granting as a favor to one man the act she had been forced to perform for another. It was a fine joke.

Restless, she gripped the heavy key in her hand. Before she'd been dismissed, she'd filched the one hidden in the master's study. Never knew when something like that would come in handy, like now.

Sure that it was time, she crept out of her hiding place in the shadows. Stealthily, she made her way across the lawn and fitted the key in the back door. Carefully, she urged it open, stepping softly across the familiar stone kitchen floor.

It was dark inside the room, the fire in the hearth long

since extinguished. She dared not light a candle, or flick on the gas jet wall sconce for fear of waking someone, namely the cook, whose room was close by. Fortunately, she knew the way, and was in no special hurry.

She took her time going up the stairs that led to the family rooms. Closer and closer she came to her quarry. Excitement danced in her veins. Not much longer now.

"Are they certain that it's her?"

"Not a doubt. Says right here that they've finally gotten an eyewitness." Harold Breckenridge held up the telegraph that had been waiting for him on his return from a boring dinner at his wife's cousin's house. The only salvation of the evening was the news his host had shared with him—the opening of a discreet new bordello less than an hour from New York. It was fully stocked: size, color, age, or sex—it mattered not. Whatever a "gentleman" wanted was his to order. For *members* only. Members who could afford the price of their pleasures.

He glanced at his wife. Now there was a word that could never be associated with her. She sat primly in her chaise longue, her legs covered by a thick, glossy robe of sable. Beneath that she wore a thick, well-buttoned gown of white flannel. Some women could make what she wore inviting, radiating intense sexual heat; his wife wasn't one of them.

He read the message: "Found her! Montana territory. Eyewitness. Dispatching man to apprehend."

"Perhaps," Alma suggested pointedly, "it might be better to send several men." With that, she went back to her book, adding, "We wouldn't want her to slip through our trap again, now would we?"

"I've already thought of that. I've drafted a wire to send telling him that very thing." He paced towards the fireplace, where there was a blaze in the hearth. He crushed the telegram in his fist. "Soon she'll be back here, right where she belongs."

"And aye, 'tis a fine pity you won't be here to see it," came a soft, lilting voice from the doorway.

Alma looked up; Harold spun around. Both wore shocked expressions on their faces.

"Who are you, and how dare you enter my bedroom?" Alma demanded. "Get out this instant before I have you thrown out."

"Now, I'm sure I've already had that happen, so no thank you."

"What *are* you talking about?"

The woman stepped further into the room so that both the Breckenridges could see her face clearly.

"You," they both said, though not in unison.

"Aye, come back for a wee visit."

"You insolent slut," Alma raged. "Get your disgusting self out of my house."

"I aim to do that right soon, ma'am," the younger woman said, "as soon as I finish the business I've come here to do."

"And what business is that?" Harold asked. "Come to try and fleece some money out of me?"

"No. You had your chance to pay me as you'd promised, but the word of a Breckenridge meant nothing in the end."

"What is she talking about?" Alma demanded.

"Why, fancy her not knowin' that you've got a lyin' tongue," the woman said with scorn in her voice.

Harold stepped closer, giving the young woman a sharp look. "Get out of my house, whore. You don't belong here."

"And who was it after makin' me a whore?" she asked in a cold tone. "I came to this house a virgin, just looking for some honest work to help feed my family. Wasn't long before you were sniffin' around my skirts, like a dog in heat. Finding excuses to be where I was. Putting your ugly hands on me."

"And you," she accused, pointing to Alma. "All the while pretending that you know nothing of your husband's doings."

Alma ignored the other woman, instead telling her husband, "Get your Irish strumpet out of my sight."

Harold made a move to step closer until he saw the gun now leveled at him, heard the click of the hammer.

"I'll be thanking you not to take another step until I tell you to."

"What?"

"Don't pretend to be hard of hearin' now, Mr. Breckenridge."

"You little cunt."

"Ah, and is that supposed to make me tremble in anger? Cry in shame? I think not." Now it was she who stepped closer. "Your words have no meaning for me anymore. The only thing I want to hear is you begging for my forgiveness. That's the only way to satisfy my honor."

He snorted. "You'd have a better chance of marrying the pope, you backstreet Irish slut."

She laughed. "Good. I was afraid you were going to make this too easy."

"What are you talking about?" Alma demanded.

"Why, retribution, ma'am," the younger woman announced. "The Day of Judgment has come."

"You're mad," Alma stated.

"Oh, I've gone beyond that, ma'am," the woman said, deliberately misinterpreting the older woman's words.

Alma's face tightened. God damn her husband and all his whores to hell. How dare this piece of trash sully her sanctuary with her immigrant tongue and her sluttish looks? Defying her. Mocking her. "Will this do to silence your precious *honor*?" Alma removed her diamond ring and tossed it in the girl's direction. "You can sell that and live well enough. Take it and get out." And then I will send the police after you quicker than you can say whore, Alma decided. You'll spend the rest of your miserable life in jail, where you belong.

The young woman bent down and retrieved the ring from where it lay at her feet, careful not to let either of them out of her sight. She put the ring in her pocket and smiled.

Alma waved her hand in dismissal. "You can leave now."

"Oh no, ma'am. Not before I get what I came for."

"You want more?" Harold asked, annoyance rising in his throat.

"I want what I came for. What I'm entitled to."

"I've had enough of this farce," Harold said. He made a move, but the girl was faster. The gun rose until it was pointed at his face.

"I won't hesitate, you know," she said.

"To what? Rob us blind?" he demanded.

"To kill you."

"You're joking," he said.

"Am I?"

Harold stepped back. He had to get the gun before she made good on her threat. But how? A shot fired this close could hurt him if she pulled the trigger. He had no thought that she would actually kill him. Still, better to play along for the moment. He sure as hell had no wish to put himself in a bullet's path.

"Undress."

"What?"

"I'm only going to say this one more time. Undress. *Both* of you."

Harold shot a look at his wife. She shot him an even darker one. He removed his shirt, pocketing the solid gold cuff links and shirt studs; Alma tossed back her lap robe.

The young woman moved her hand, the one holding the gun. "All of it."

"What for?" Alma questioned.

"Because I said so," the other woman replied.

Alma huffed as she unbuttoned the neck of her gown. "Must I?"

"Yes," she said in a cold and final tone.

I'll make sure that the prison you go to will be the last place you ever see, Alma thought, stripping off her gown and holding it to her thin body.

Harold stood in his silk long johns; Alma clutched at her flannel, still wearing her pantalets.

"Finish."

Harold unbuttoned the garment and let it fall to the ground. He stepped out of it, hating the woman for the humiliation she was putting him through. He'd make her pay. He'd see to it that this bitch suffered as she'd never suffered before.

"Now, both of you, move to the bed."

Alma still held the gown in front of herself. As she passed by, the girl whispered, "Drop it, now!"

Alma did so, her eyes going even colder.

Both of them were standing by Alma's bed. The young woman let her eyes travel over their bodies, much as an assayer did a piece of ore. She laughed. "Not much without them fancy clothes, now are you? A skinny, dried up hag who all the fine clothes in the world can't disguise. And you—" she looked pointedly at Harold. "Not so high and mighty now, are we?"

Her glance skimmed over his flabby belly and small, stubby, limp penis. God, she wanted to shoot off that offending member. Destroy it.

She took a deep breath. Ah, all in time.

"Face the bed, Mrs. Breckenridge."

Alma did so.

"Now, bend over."

"Are you mad?" Alma raged.

"Do it!"

284

Alma did so, her pale, wrinkled skin showing whiter against the dark blue of the rich brocaded bedspread.

"Now, do to her," the younger woman instructed, "as you did to me."

Harold stepped closer to Alma. His gaze went to the backside of the woman he'd called wife for longer than he could remember. No desire stirred. Nothing.

"What's the matter? Does it only happen for you if you have someone you can control? Someone whose life you hold in your hands?" Anger raged in her voice and she fought to rein it in. "Or would you do better if you thought it was me? Someone younger, someone prettier?"

Those words stirred something in Harold. His mind quickly provided a picture, a picture of the Irish slut bending over his desk, his flesh slapping into hers, pounding away. God, it was working. He could feel the rise in his flesh. He shoved into his wife's unwilling body, feeling her tense, hearing her scream of agony. He pushed her head into the bed, keeping up the rhythm his body set.

When I'm done fucking this bitch, I'll take the other, he promised himself. And when I'm done with her, she'll. . . .

It was the last thought Harold Breckenridge ever had.

Alma, her head still in the bedspread, heard the sound of the gun; felt the weight of her husband's body as it jerked and then fell off her. She lifted her head, dragging in air and then nothing. . . .

The young woman stepped back, satisfied.

The sound of a scream brought some of the staff running up the stairs.

Tandy, the new upstairs maid, stood there, her body heaving up her breakfast upon the fine oriental runner in the hall.

"What's come over you, girl?" the housekeeper demanded. "You've made an ugly mess here."

The girl was still shaking, her features blanched and

drawn, her eyes wide with fright. "In there, Mrs. Bradford," she managed to say before she heaved again.

Mrs. Bradford, followed by the butler, stepped over the broken shards of Wedgwood china that lay scattered on the floor. Hot tea seeped into the blue and white Chinese wool carpet.

"Oh my *God*!" Mrs. Bradford said, turning her head from the horrible sight.

The butler swallowed the bile that rose in his throat, putting his handkerchief to his lips.

There, upon the bed, lay his employers. Their naked, blood-soaked bodies in a tangle. A pistol was clutched in the lifeless hand of Alma Breckenridge.

He turned and quietly shut the door. "Best fetch the police." He signaled to another of the upper housemaids who was lingering in the hall. "Send Dashom for the authorities. Tell him to hurry. We have a tragedy here."

"You think that she killed him, then herself, Inspector?"

The other man nodded, jotting some things down in his notebook. "Ah, that I do. Sad, very sad." He glanced around the drawing room, his eyes taking in all the riches on display. The fine furniture. The lovely paintings. The costly sculptures. "And we'll never know the why of it." He shut his well-worn leather book. "Good of you to tell me what you saw before you covered the bodies."

"I couldn't leave them there for all the world to see."

"I understand. Sad business." He stood up. "Hear that there's a daughter?"

"Yes, Miss Abigail."

"And where's she?"

"I don't honestly know, sir."

The inspector shot him a sharp glance beneath the brim of his bowler.

"It's the honest truth, sir." The butler looked around the room. "Guess it won't hurt no one to admit the truth now.

She disappeared several years ago, though no one's supposed to know. They put out the story that she was at some rest home, taking a cure for melancholia. All the while they've been trying to find her, to bring her back home where she belongs. Why, Mr. Breckenridge even has had the Pinkertons looking for her. That's how much they wanted her returned to them."

"Well," the inspector opined, "that's one very rich lady now, isn't it?"

"Yes, sir. Miss Abigail is the sole heir to both of her parents."

"No leads as to her whereabouts?"

"Not so's I know of, sir."

"Maybe that caused her mother to become melancholic. The thought of her young daughter all alone somewhere, far from home. Bound to affect a mother's mind. Women are ever the fairer, gentler sex. They can only handle so much."

"So, what news?"

"Death by misadventure."

"Misadventure?"

"They suspect murder and suicide, but they won't let a word of that leak to the papers. It was an accident, that's what will be printed in tomorrow's papers. A very tragic accident that robbed New York of two of its finest citizens."

The young woman gave a hearty laugh. "You were right."

"I invariably am, my dear."

"Aye, and modest, too."

He pulled out a small pouch from his jacket pocket. He tossed it to her.

"What's this?"

"Look inside."

She jingled the velvet, but heard no sound. Hastily she opened the pouch. Money folded neatly and held with a silver money clip met her gaze.

"How much?"

"Near unto five hundred, my dear. All that I could get for the ring."

"That was for you, for helping me."

"I did that because I wanted to."

"I know, but you didn't have to."

"Ah, but you see, I did. When I was a wee lad, my elder sister was a servant in a fancy lord's house in Dublin. She was raped after being there only a month. One of the lord's drunken friends thought it a good idea to have a taste of real Irish flesh, or so he said. I tried to avenge her but was beaten for my troubles and sent into exile."

"And what happened to your sister?"

"She hanged herself. So you see, my dear, in a way, you were helping me, too." He took the pouch from her hand and closed the drawstring, returning it to her hand. "How's about taking me to dinner tonight, lass?"

"My pleasure, Mr. Collins," she said with a smile, linking her arm through his. "I'd be right proud to do just that."

Chapter Twenty

"Is she here?" Gussie asked of Dooley as she stepped across the doorway of McMasters's ranch house.

"Miss Abigail has hardly left Mr. Beau's side these past several weeks except to go back to town and get some fresh clothes," he informed her.

"I kinda figured that." Gussie smiled as she handed her thick beaver-pelt coat to Dooley, along with her deer-hide riding gloves. "Would have been here sooner but for the weather and all. That was some storm that hit right after Thanksgiving. About snowed the whole town under for two weeks."

"Yes, ma'am," Dooley agreed as he hung her coat upon the new oak and brass coat rack. "It was pretty bad out here too. Miss Sabina kept Miss Abby company, and the sheriff was here most of the time too, when he wasn't off looking for who shot Mr. Beau."

Gussie leveled a glance at Dooley. "Heard that they think it was Hank Baser?"

He nodded his head. "That'd be the name I've heard mentioned."

Lowering her voice in a conspiratorial tone, she asked, "How's Mr. McMasters doing?"

Dooley grinned. "Take more than some white-trash coward to keep that man down. He was up and about sooner than the doctor expected. 'Course, he was put in his place by Miss Abby, who insisted he stay in bed and rest. She's up reading to him now. If you'd wait here," he said, indicating the wide leather couch in front of the banked fire, "I will go and fetch her."

"No need to do that," Gussie insisted, gazing at the wide set of polished steps that led to the second floor. "I can tromp these old bones up the stairs and see them both."

"Just take another sip, Beau," Abby coaxed, holding the elegant silver spoon to his lips.

"I'm not a sickly child, Abby," he reminded her in a somewhat bored voice, "I can do it for myself."

She smiled. "I know you can." She handed him the spoon, brimming with the thick beef stew that Lacey had made. "Trouble is, will you eat it all?"

"I promise," he said with a dazzling smile, his mood making a quicksilver change as he devoured the tasty concoction.

"See that you do."

"Nag," he teased.

"Call me whatever you like, I'm just so exceedingly glad that you're here at all." With that she lifted her hand and softly brushed back the black waving curls on his forehead.

Beau turned his head, bringing his lips to the palm of her hand. "Abby . . . I—"

"Why, I thought to see a sick, injured man when I entered this room," Gussie crowed as she strode into Beau's bedchamber, a wide grin on her face. "One who was barely hanging back from death's door." A deep grin split her face. "Looks to me like you're pretty near fit to get back to business." She cast her eyes upon the couple, taking in the intimate scene. Beau lay propped up upon a heap of fluffy linen and lace-covered pillows, his upper body clad in an open white shirt, which exposed the dark covering of hair on his wide chest. A thick coverlet of cream matelassé, topped by a deep wine red quilt, sheltered his lower limbs.

At his bedside sat Abby. Her long red hair was tied back simply with a white ribbon; her clothes were simple, too: a plain blouse of cream cotton tucked into a dark blue wool skirt, with a hint of lace from her petticoat peeking below the hem.

"I hope to be back to the Creole Lady next week," Beau stated, wiping his mouth with the lace-edged linen napkin at hand.

"We'll see what the doctor says about that," Abby informed him. "After all, Beau, it wasn't too long ago that we weren't sure you were going to live."

"Darlin'," he murmured softly, looking directly at Abby, "there was never any doubt in my mind." He shifted his attention back to Gussie. "Have you had luncheon yet, Mrs. Travers?" He lifted another spoonful of his stew from the bowl that lay upon a hastily assembled bed tray. "My cook certainly knows how to produce a masterpiece from simple items. And the biscuits," he lifted a half of one, spread thickly with butter, "are a little bit of heaven," he added as he gobbled the whole slice.

"I already had me some food before I left the hotel, Mr. McMasters, so I'm mighty fine, though I don't think I'd turn away a cup of coffee or something stronger," she said. "It's right cold out there."

"You didn't come alone, Mrs. Travers, did you?" Beau asked, concern on his face.

"Sure did. Weren't nothing to it now that the snow has melted a bit and you can see the road. Got me a shotgun along, so I'm not worried. Would have been out here sooner except that we had a lot of guests at the hotel who couldn't leave town, what with all the snow stopping the stages from getting through. No time to think, let alone get out and about to visit."

"I'm happy that you came," Beau said, taking a small sip of the red wine in his glass. "But don't let me hear of you going back to town alone. I've got plenty of men, one of whom can ride escort to see that no one bothers you."

"Well, that's right nice of you, and maybe I will do just that."

"No *maybe* about it," Beau stated.

Gussie cocked her head to one side. "My, aren't you the ornery one?"

"Ornery?" Beau repeated, puzzled. "Where I come from a gentleman never leaves a lady to fend for herself."

Gussie laughed. "Well," she politely pointed out, "this ain't where you *came* from, it's where you're *at* and *this* lady can manage all by herself. Though," she said as she grabbed one of the biscuits off the tray for a sample tasting, "I'll ease your mind and let you play master this once."

Abby's gaze quickly flew to Beau's face, wondering how he'd react to Gussie's innocent remark.

She needn't have worried. Beau took it for what it was, a gentle rejoinder.

Gussie munched on her biscuit and watched Abby's face as Beau finished off the meal. There was a woman in love—no doubt about it. It was plain for all the world to see. There'd be a wedding soon if she didn't miss her guess. Yes, injury or no, this was a couple bound for the sheets without a doubt. *Legally* bound, that was. Especially if she had any say in it. Hmmm, maybe a wedding on New Year's Eve. Something to see the new year in proper.

Abby rose from her chair and picked up Beau's tray as

he adjusted the pillows. "I'll check on you later," she admonished her patient.

He smiled a rather wicked grin. "Yes, ma'am."

Abby returned that smile, hers full of promise. She then turned to her friend. "How about something hot to drink, Gussie?"

"That'd be real nice," Gussie answered as she closed the door to Beau's room and followed Abby back down the stairs, where Dooley waited for them.

"I'll take that, Miss Abby."

She handed the tray to Dooley. "Thank you. If it wouldn't be too much trouble, could we have some hot chocolate?"

"No trouble at all, ma'am. Lacey has already fixed a pot, and added just a touch of something smooth to keep away the chills; Mr. Beau's fine old brandy."

Abby led the way to the leather couch. A low pine table had been placed close enough to support the tray that Dooley brought in. On it were two large ironstone mugs and a dainty chocolate pot, filled to the brim with the hot beverage. A small matching pitcher held fresh cream. "I hope you don't mind the bigger mug instead of the cup that matches the service," Abby asked as she handed her friend the drink.

"Lordy, no, that's fine by me."

"Good. The tiny cups just weren't enough for me. I adore hot chocolate, and drinking just a small amount when I want a lot more seems a waste of time and effort." She smiled to herself—her mother would have been appalled at what she would have considered boorish behavior, admitting that she loved something more than the *polite* amount. Abby proceeded to take a long, healthy swallow of the beverage, sighing when she was done. "Excellent."

"Makes mine seem a might less tasty, that's for sure. I'll have to steal the recipe."

Abby laughed.

"Haven't done much of that lately, have you?" Gussie asked.

"No, not really."

"Then I'm right glad that I could bring it about."

Abby leaned over and kissed the older woman on the cheek. "I did so miss you, Gussie."

"Honey, I doubt that you'd really miss anyone around here exceptin' that big handsome man upstairs. My, he's one nice lookin' fellow, with or without clothes."

Abby chuckled. "I certainly agree with you on that—he's one handsome man, but I must beg to differ that I wouldn't miss you, or some others around here. This place has truly become my home. And you—" Abby paused, searching for the right words. "You've been like a mother to me, and you can't begin to know how much that means to me."

"And I think of you as the child I never had," Gussie conceded, beaming at the younger woman. She took another long swallow of her drink as she hurried to get her emotions under control. "Probably didn't really get to miss anyone, as I've heard that you've had plenty of visitors out here."

"Ah," Abby said, "you know about all the company that's come calling since the shooting? I never would have imagined that so many people would make the effort to come out here."

"Heard tell from Mary James that about half the townsfolk and most of the people hereabouts have been out to see what's what. Even heard tell that some of Trudy's girls were here."

Abby recalled with a smile the shocked look on Dooley's face when he answered the door and saw the two doves standing outside, demanding to be let in. "That's right. Glory and Cassie came as soon as they heard what had happened. They stayed and helped nurse Beau when

Sabina and I needed a break. Mrs. James brought over some soup, along with some of her clothes to tide us over until I could get back into town. I'm sorry that I didn't call on you, but I didn't want to waste a minute of the time I was away from him."

"Child, I can see that you love him, and I know how you must have been hurting, waiting to see if your man was gonna die or not. Ain't no need to worry about anything else."

Abby put down her mug, rose from her seat, then moved towards the wide bank of windows. She lifted her hand and touched the recently replaced pane, gazing across the open landscape. Sunlight glistened on the vast expanse of snow that covered the ground. In the distance she could see a small herd of deer stepping sure-footedly through the thick white powder as they made their way across the land. So peaceful and beautiful now, as if violence had never touched it, or them.

"I was never so scared in my life," Abby admitted, wrapping her arms about her waist. "There were times when I thought Beau was going to die, and that I'd never have a chance to tell him how I really feel."

"And did you?"

"No, not yet."

"What in blue blazes are you waiting for?" Gussie prodded. "Another shot?"

Abby turned and faced her friend. "No. It's just that we haven't had any real time for talk. Someone's always around. Or it just isn't the right moment."

"Make your own moment," Gussie suggested. "Don't wait for a good time. Tell him. Easy enough to see that he loves you. That you love him. Not everything runs by a timetable, 'specially out here. A man's measure is quickly taken. You got to be able to sum up a body right fast, 'cause sometimes it means the difference between life and death. That man upstairs passed my test a long time ago."

She paused, sharpening her glance. "What you got standing in your way?"

What indeed, Abby thought as she checked the enameled clock by her bedside. It was almost midnight. Everyone was asleep. Or should be.

All she could think about as she tossed and turned beneath the covers were Gussie's words. They had haunted her all through the evening. In the midst of dinner, with Beau downstairs—the doctor having declared him ready to resume some activities—she was distracted.

Gussie was right. It was more than time to talk to Beau, to tell him what he truly meant to her. To face the truth about the past—both of their pasts. She desperately wanted a future with him, a future unshackled by half-lies and unspoken realities.

She reached for her robe, belting the tie about her waist, briefly imagining what her life would have been like had she never left New York; had Beau never left New Orleans.

Years of emptiness for her. Endless hours of frustration compounded by bitterness.

But, she reasoned happily, they *had* both left, each searching for a new start. A fresh chance at happiness. It served no purpose to wonder "what if" now. Now demanded action on her part.

Silently, hoping to wake no one else, she opened her door and padded barefoot the few steps across the hallway to Beau's door. Without giving herself time to think, she turned the doorknob and walked in.

Beau was sitting at his desk, poring over some papers, adding a column of figures in his head. He heard the noise of the handle turning and reached for the Remington, cocking the hammer back slowly.

She was bathed both in the soft glow of the candle she held and in the light from his lamp. Her thick red hair was becomingly loose, so that it floated around her body as she moved.

Warmth bathed his loins, heating his blood. It was all he could do to remain seated, remain calm.

"I don't think you'll have need of that," she said, pointing to the lethal weapon he held. "I come unarmed."

Beau smiled as he released the hammer, then placed the gun back upon the desk. "Nonsense, my dear," he said, his eyes taking in the sight of her. A dream come achingly to life, standing there before him. "You are always armed: with intelligence, beauty, and most of all, your innate class. Such are the weapons of a true lady. All she needs to disarm any gentleman."

He waited for her comeback—and nothing happened. Instead, she lowered her eyes momentarily. His tone was low, intimate: "What is it, Abby? You've been dancing around something these past few weeks. What's on your mind? And why now?"

"You," she said, moving closer to him. "Us."

"What about us?" he demanded softly, forcing his hands to stay still when all he wanted was to reach out and draw her body next to his, capture that sweet mouth.

"There never seemed to be a right time to talk." She took a step and then changed her mind, walking instead to the low wing chair that flanked the stone fireplace. Sitting down, she snuffed out her candle and took a deep breath. A low fire stirred, its flames dying slowly.

"There are a few things I think you have a right to know about me."

"I know all I need to know about you," he stated.

"No, you don't," Abby insisted, meeting his gaze. "You know what I've wanted you to know. That isn't the same thing."

"Everyone has secrets, Abby." He knew that better than most.

"Maybe," she said, her eyes never leaving his, "but I

don't want there to be any between us. Not anymore. Not ever again."

Beau sighed. He had plenty of his own. And, he suspected, she was aware of some of them. Ever since the night of the shooting, when he was caught in a world between the dead and the living, neither he nor she had spoken about the family pictures she must have seen in this room. Common sense told him that she was more informed than she'd let on—she probably had interpreted correctly what they meant.

"Say what you will, then," he said gently.

She wet her lips. "My last name isn't Butler. It's Breckenridge. Butler is my middle name." She waited for the recognition. When it wasn't forthcoming, she continued. "Abigail Butler Breckenridge."

When he still didn't respond, she rolled her eyes. "You don't know the name?"

"Should I?" He relaxed a bit in his desk chair. "Is Breckenridge your late husband's last name? Or isn't he really dead?"

"I have no husband." It felt as if a weight the size of a blacksmith's anvil had been lifted off her shoulders.

"What?" He straightened up.

"No husband. I made him up so that no one would question me too closely. So that I could do what I wanted without arousing suspicion."

"And why would anyone question you?"

"To collect the reward my father offered for my return."

"Reward?" She wasn't a widow. Wasn't a wife—never had been. So many questions were answered by her confession. But more questions waited to be asked. If not a wife, then what?

"My father was bound and determined to get me back, so he set the Pinkertons to the task. Money talks, even this far away from New York and his influence." She paused, watching the play of expressions across his face. "Have you ever heard of the Breckenridge Bank?"

Awareness dawned on his features. "You're *that* Breckenridge?"

She nodded.

"I heard my father talk about that bank once. If I recall, his family did their business there."

"His and half of New York City."

"So what's a banking heiress doing way out here in the wilds of Montana?"

"May I trouble you for a glass of water?" she said, side-stepping his query for the moment.

"I only have this glass," he said, holding up the one he'd drunk from.

"That's fine."

Nodding, he poured water, then brought it to her, taking a seat in the opposite wing chair. He watched as she drank most of what was in the glass. He liked that about her—the way she never merely pretended to be thirsty.

"Thank you."

"You're most welcome," he responded, wondering if she would remember his question.

"I ran away from home. Or to put it more bluntly, away from my parents' house, where I lived. It was never a home to me," she stated baldly. "More like a prison. A place of utter loneliness and fear. Had I stayed, I would have been forced into marriage with one of my father's cronies, or worse. I couldn't let that happen."

"So you fled."

"I had no other choice."

"Yes," he said, smiling. "You did. You could have stayed and submitted to your father's plans. Many girls would have done just that and thought nothing of it. You, however, made the choice that was right for you."

Beau understood. She heard it in the way he said his

words, with pride and admiration. Like healing herbs, they soothed her soul. "I couldn't live that life. I couldn't be treated like property, as if I had no say in the matter."

"Unlike some of my ancestors, who had no choice whatsoever in the matter," he said quietly. "You know, don't you?"

"About your mama, yes, I do. I knew when I looked at the painting of her. She's so beautiful, Beau. Why don't you have that portrait hanging downstairs?"

"Because, my dear, not everyone has your acceptance of my lineage. And you're right. She was beautiful. In every way. One of the loveliest quadroons in New Orleans, with men flocking to be her protector. She chose my father, because she loved him and because he wanted to marry her, knowing everything." Beau rose and paced a few steps, turning to face Abby. "She was a quarter Negress, you understand?"

She nodded.

"That means that I'm what those in New Orleans who keep track of such things like to call an octoroon."

"So?"

"In some sections of the country, that's as damning as being a Negro pure."

"I don't care."

He gave her a cynical smile. "There's lots that do. Who always will."

"That makes no difference to me," she announced. "I saw your blood, Beau. It was all over me that terrible night. Red. Just like mine. I don't care about anything, or any*one*, else. All I know is that I love you," she stated, the admission springing clearly and calmly from her lips. "I love *you*, Beau McMasters. The man you are here and now. That's all that matters. That, and your telling me that you love me too. Do you?"

She was on her feet and in his arms, their mouths as entwined as their bodies. When that first kiss ended, both were breathing hard.

"God, that's all I've wanted to hear for the longest time," he murmured as his mouth sought her throat, lightly feathering kisses across her neck. "Love you?" he asked, his lean-fingered hands cupping her face. "God, woman, I'm beyond the word love as others define it. I *want* you," he whispered darkly. "I *yearn* for you." He took her hand, placed it against his flat stomach, then lower, to the part of him that stirred proudly to life. "Deep and hot, like the blade of a knife, searing into my flesh and beyond. That's what love is for me—the kind of love that I never thought I'd find—nor really cared about for the longest time. Until," he admitted, "I met *you.*"

He put his mouth to hers again; this time it was soft, fleeting, like the touch of a feather gliding across flesh. "And then I discovered," he continued, "that love was even more than that. It could also be gentle, like a soft, warm rain that falls on a late afternoon in New Orleans. Lazy." He loosened the tie that held the robe closed at her waist, pushing it off her shoulders, letting it puddle to the floor. He reached out his right hand to cup her breast, testing its weight. "Seductive," he breathed, as he bent his head and put his open mouth to her flesh, his tongue making wet circles on the fabric of her night rail.

He smiled at her low gasp of sound. "Do you like that?"

"Yes," she responded, her voice catching as he did the same to her other breast. Some odd sensation fluttered in her belly, deep inside, like a building pressure. Her breath was coming faster, in hurried little pants as sensation washed over her.

God, his hand went lower there—pressing lightly against the material that separated her skin from his. Close, but not close enough. Throbbing. She could feel the throbbing getting stronger. Making her want—what?

Him? Oh yes. And whatever he could do to ease the aching tension between her legs.

The next thing she knew, the air was cold against her skin. Her naked skin. Her night rail was lying across the recently vacated wing chair.

Instinctively her hands went to cover herself, and then she forced them back to her sides. Shame wasn't a part of this, and what was to come. Shame didn't belong here. Nor did false modesty. She wanted him to look. She wanted him to touch. She wanted him to like what he saw. Needed that in some primeval way she didn't fully understand.

"Magnificent. Like an old master painting come to life."

His gently spoken words only stirred the flames higher.

Again his mouth met hers; their lips mated as his fingers slipped into her warm flesh and probed, skillfully finding his target.

If he hadn't been holding her, she would have collapsed sobbing to the floor, so strong was the release that came from the mere touch of his fingers in her body. Her cries were captured by his mouth. She spun out of herself, her vision momentarily shattered.

Suddenly she was lifted into his arms, carried to the big bed. The covers were turned back, rumpled from his time there earlier. The sheets felt so cool against her skin, adding another layer of sensation to that which was threatening to overwhelm her again. His scent lingered on the linen, wrapping her in his maleness.

She lay there, waiting, watching.

Slowly, he unbelted his own robe, letting the smooth, expensive material fall away from his flesh. Inch by inch, it lowered until he kicked it away, little caring about the garment.

Abby fixed her eyes on him—all of him. If she were a painting, then he was a sculpture. Pure marble finely molded and carved, revealing all the sinewy strength of his being. From the wide shoulders to the hair-dusted chest, down to the slim hips and long legs. And back upward to the essence of him. Strong. Hard. Bold.

She bit back a giggle, the thought crossing her mind just then that Glory was right—comparing him to a stallion was justified.

He saw her faint smile, her welcoming look.

It was all the invitation he needed. Climbing into the bed beside her, he couldn't wait to kiss her again. Her arms wound about him, her skin melded to his. She was a partner in the game; a lover to be cherished. She was holding nothing back.

Making love had never been like this. It had never been this clear in his mind that this was what it was like to be completely in love, completely in trust. Adept at pleasuring women, he took all his skill, all his acquired knowledge and put it to good use, making the first time for them the best it could be. His mouth induced; his hands caressed; his body moved.

Hot. Tight. Wet.

He could feel her small nails digging into his back, marking him as surely as he would mark her. He eased into her until he felt her maidenhead give way, capturing her small cry of pain with his mouth. "Shush," he said, his voice ragged, forcing himself through sheer will to slow down his movements. His muscles tightened with the effort until he heard her raw, husky voice.

"Don't stop. Please. I want to know."

He saw it in her eyes; heard it in her words. She was his, ready for their union. As eager as he. Driven by the same passion. Captive of the same desire. Hostage to the same overwhelming feeling.

It was all the encouragement he needed.

Beau McMasters came home. . . .

Chapter Twenty-one

Abby snuggled closer to the warmth, burrowing deeper into the blankets. The air was cool—the sun had risen several hours ago. She couldn't recall the last time she'd slept so late.

Ah, maybe that was because I spent the better part of last night otherwise occupied, she thought, her mouth curving into a broad smile.

Bliss. She understood that word intimately now. Understood and reveled in the meaning, the feeling it evoked. Pleasure beyond expectation. Desire fulfilled. Knowledge enhanced. Her life had changed yet once again. Changed in such a way that there would never be any turning back. Never any need to. All she wanted was here, sleeping beside her.

The pillow upon which her head rested stirred.

Beau.

Her arm curled around his waist; the heat of his skin made her smile. Flesh to flesh. Man to woman. Strength to strength.

"Mornin', darlin'," he said, following up his words with

a kiss to her hair. His arms gently encircled her, pulling her closer.

He held her tenderly; one of his hands moved to her bare back, soothing and stroking softly. Abby felt safe. Cherished, for the first time in her life. This was the final part of her rebirth. This was the place she was meant to be—the haven of her soul. In this man's arms she was truly home—all the home she wanted—all the home she would ever need from now on.

"Happy?"

"Yes," she responded, kissing one dark nipple, "more than you can ever know."

"I'm not so sure about that, darlin'," he murmured, adjusting his position so that he was further up against the pillows, moving her with him. "I'm pretty damned happy myself."

Abby trailed her fingers across his chest, feathering small kisses in their wake. "Then we're both beyond a mere trifling word such as happy. We must search for something new. Something that truly describes this feeling."

"I don't know if you'll ever find it," Beau said, his mouth creeping closer to her ear. He certainly wouldn't. This woman had brought him something he couldn't have known he needed: peace. A respite from years of blowing from place to place like a tumbleweed tossed by the vagaries of the wind. For her he would risk anything—dare anything. Pay any price that fate demanded. All he wanted was to be with her, love her.

When had it all changed for him? When had she quietly stolen into his very blood so that to be without her was to be without life itself? Maybe, without knowing, the very first day that they met.

He'd thought himself a lucky man before, the cards more often than not in his favor. He hadn't known the half of it. *She* was his luck. Meeting her had changed his life—irrevocably. All the capricious whims of fortune were mere bagatelles until now. Until her. His own special Queen of Hearts.

"Marry me."

Abby raised her head. It took all of her will not to scream "Yes!" at the top of her lungs. Instead, she paused, took a deep breath and asked, "Are you sure it's what you want?"

"Never doubt it," Beau stated, warmth infusing his tone. "I want you to be my wife."

"When?"

"As soon as we can." He lifted her face for his kiss. "And as soon as you say yes."

"Yes," Abby whispered, seeking his lips with her own. "Yes!"

Beau took her willing mouth in a hard, possessive kiss, his tongue mating with hers as he pulled her atop him. "Let me show you another way," he murmured, adjusting her legs so that she straddled him. "Now, let yourself feel the rhythm." He moved under her, letting her feel the sway of his body until she fell into the pace, moving slightly faster as she began the ride. His hands stroked her hair, her back, urging her on. Her breasts bobbed to the music her body made, increasing the movements of their unique dance.

Abby liked this. Felt in control and powerful as she saw the look that came over Beau's face. Heard the moans that began low in both their throats. Upward and upward the pleasure spiraled in her, taking her faster and faster. Urging her, pushing her toward the light. Undaunted, she couldn't hold back the soft cry of release as it poured through her.

Seconds later her lover joined her, his last final push into her sending her gasping again as she welcomed his release, his seed flooding warmly into her womb.

She lay exhausted against him, their bodies still entwined. He could feel the beat of her heart, hear her contented sighs. He loved pleasure—the joy in experiencing the mating of bodies. Before Abby, that's all it had been. Fleeting pleasure. He took; they took. It was a game in which the players shared only fragments of themselves. One in which both participants soon became jaded.

Now that was all changed. In an instant, he was the teacher, using all that he'd ever learned, ever practiced, to show her the path. And she the willing pupil.

Now they had a bond—one that no one could ever break. Stronger than steel; harder than stone. Forged from love, it would forever bind them together. Now he truly understood the words his father had repeated to him from the marriage vows he'd exchanged with Beau's mother: "Those whom God has joined together, let no man put asunder."

When he'd awoken after the shooting and seen her sitting next to his bed, his blood on her clothes, her hand holding tightly to his, his first thought had been: Thank God it wasn't Abby who was shot. Life without her didn't bear thinking about.

"Is this coming week too soon for you?"

"For the wedding?"

"Yes."

"I have to get a dress."

He chuckled.

"Don't laugh, I want you to be proud of me."

"Darlin', you could wear bear grease and an antelope skin and I'd still be proud of you. Well"—he paused—"maybe not bear grease."

Abby gave him a playful shove. "I want to look my best."

"That was never in doubt. And you do—in whatever you wear. Hell, if it were up to me, I'd marry you here and now, except that I don't want to share this vision of you with anyone. Speaking of which, as much as I'd love to have you remain here all day, you'd best be going back to

307

your room before someone sees you coming out of mine in less than your most fashionable day attire." Beau tossed back the blankets and the cool air hit Abby's skin. "One more kiss before you go."

"Damnation, Beau. You could have had the kiss while I was covered. It's cold." She grabbed her robe, pulling it on, then gathering up her nightgown as well. You need to stoke the fire in here."

"Darlin'," he murmured, "when you're nearby, my fire is always stoked."

She laughed out loud. She realized then that she could never stay mad at this man for very long. His sleepy-eyed look, like a cat who'd lapped up the cream, made her want to toss the robe back off and rejoin him. God, how quickly she'd made the transition to wanton in his arms. It was as if she had been wandering in the desert for years, searching for water, only to suddenly find it here. Clear, sweet and pure, no other water would ever do for her. This was her wellspring—her forever fountain, quenching her soul.

Abby hiked up her leg and leaned over the bed, bending down to give him a swift kiss.

Beau had other ideas, slipping his hand into the loose folds of her robe, stroking her flesh.

She gasped in pleasure, sighing her delight.

It was at that precise moment, with her half on and half off the bed, her bare legs exposed, her hair in wild tumbles down her back, that the door to Beau's bedroom suddenly opened, and Sabina walked in, carrying a tray.

"I knocked," she said, her voice rising slightly, a blush staining her cheeks. Not difficult to realize just what she'd interrupted. "I guess you didn't hear me."

Abby took in the look on her friend's face—not an "oh-my-God-what-are-you-doing?" look; rather it was an "I'm so sorry to have intruded on a private moment" look. Sabina hadn't judged. Would never judge.

Abby smiled as she slid off the bed and belted her robe tighter, the nightgown trailing across her arm. "Now you'll have to marry me, sir. I believe I'm what you might call *compromised*." The last word was followed by a resounding chuckle.

"Why, my dear Mrs. Butler, I do believe you're right," Beau said with a wide smile. "I am most humble in asking for your hand in marriage yet again—with Miss Sabina here as a witness."

"Then once again, I do accept," Abby stated. She lifted the coffee cup that rested on the tray in Sabina's hands and took a sip. "Ah, I must have some of my own." She handed the cup to Beau, who immediately placed his lips where hers had been and drank. "Sabina, when you're done here, would you please meet me downstairs? I have, it seems, a wedding dress to discuss with you." With that, Abby walked proudly out of the room.

"I'm so happy for you both."

Beau smiled and handed the empty cup back to Sabina. "Thank you, my dear. Your good wishes mean the world to Abby and me."

Sabina set down the tray, then busied herself lighting the fire that had gone to embers. "I've been meaning to speak to you about something."

"Then why not let me get out of this bed and we can talk?"

Sabina kept her back turned so that Beau could leave the bed.

"All right, my dear, I'm decent." He laughed, belting his own silk robe tight around his waist. "Of course, decent depending with whom you talk."

Sabina laughed too, glad that he was making light of the situation.

"I want Abby to have the best wedding dress, and I think she'd like to have you make it for her. Is there material around here suitable, or shall we have to send for it on the next stage to Miles City?"

Finished with her task, she turned to face Beau. "There's a wonderful bolt of ivory satin that Mrs. Cooper just got in a few weeks ago. It should make a beautiful wedding dress. Or if Abby doesn't like that, there's something in blue."

"Send the bill for whatever you ladies choose to me. And Sabina, choose something for yourself while you're at it."

"I couldn't do that, Mr. McMasters."

"Why not? I can well afford it, my dear. You won't be making a hole in my pocket, I can assure you."

"It's not that." Bitterness edged her tone. "It's because of my father."

Beau arched a brow. "What has he to do with this?"

"I think he's the one who shot you."

"Baser?"

"He's so filled with hate that I wouldn't put it past him," she said. "When I left his house he was eaten by bitterness and rage. I didn't think he'd ever go through with his threats, but I have to believe now that he did. He's dangerous and must be stopped." She shuddered. "God, to think that I have his blood."

"Don't let that upset you, my dear. We're more than our blood, or some of us would be in dire straits." He stepped closer to her, lifting her right hand to his lips. "You're a lovely young woman who's overcome many obstacles in her life, a woman filled with light, so don't let him cast clouds on your future. You've been a wonderful friend to me, and especially to my Abby. More than that I cannot ask."

* * *

"I can see why you love him."

Abby smiled across the dining room table at her friend's remark. "He's everything I want. Everything I need."

Sabina decided to broach the subject of what she'd walked in on. "Did he make you happy last night? Was being with him all you'd hoped?"

Abby sipped at her second cup of café au lait. "More than I realized," she confided. "The small amount of pain that transpired when we first joined was worth it. Now I truly understand all the poets who wrote about this feeling, this *rapture*. And it was that, and so much more." She took another bite of her breakfast steak, devouring several pieces before she spoke again. "Sorry. I'm so hungry. Do you suppose it's because of last night?" Abby couldn't repress the smile that crossed her face. "Did it happen that way for you too?"

"Making love always made me hungry," Sabina confessed with a shy smile.

Abby touched her napkin to her lips. "How could anyone condemn this feeling?"

"There are many who do. Believe me, I know from first-hand experience."

"Jealousy. That's all it was," Abby assured her friend. "Those who condemn have never experienced it. Lord, when I think of all the lectures I received from my mother about how disgusting and horrible the marriage bed is . . . She said I should simply close my mind and focus on something pretty, like the jewels I should demand for putting up with my husband's 'rutting,' as she called it." Abby's blue eyes took on a sad cast. "What bitter grapes she tried to harvest."

"Feel sorry for her then," Sabina countered. "She will never have what you have had."

"You're right." Abby reached across and took her friend's hand. "It's we who are the lucky ones." She

311

drained her cup, refilling it one more time. "Now, let's discuss my ideas for the dress."

Damn! McMasters had survived. Even lost in this dump of a copper mining hellhole, he'd heard the news. The wily, no-good son of a bitch had managed to live. If only McMasters had stood still instead of turning at the same time as he'd fired his rifle, his shot wouldn't have been spoiled.

Baser slapped down two bits for another drink of cheap whiskey. It stung his throat, heating his already sizzling temper to white hot. Time to go back and finish the job. He couldn't leave it undone. But this time, he'd have to get rid of them all. Scourge the earth of all the sinners. Make them pay the price for their crimes. Even his own daughter. Slut, contaminating all the good men she touched. Choosing to side with scum rather than decent folk. Refusing to see the error of her ways. Ignoring the commands of the faithful. Wallowing in lustful filth.

It was his mission to see them all punished.

His duty to do what must be done.

For that he needed strength. Another jolt of the whiskey flooded through him as he scanned the dingy interior of the dirty tent, scratching his balls. Been way too long since he'd had himself a piece of ass. Didn't he deserve that? Wasn't it his due for the service he must render? A poke would set him right.

Not much of a selection. Several old cows who did nothing for him. Besides, looked like they was all taken, what with the miners hanging on them like flies on shit.

Then he saw her. Sitting back in the corner, with another woman who looked to be her ma.

He moved closer. His eyes narrowed as he feasted on the young girl's opened blouse, her soft, unwashed features. "How much you askin'?"

The older woman eyed him sharply. "How much you offerin'? This here's my daughter and practically a virgin."

"What's practically mean?"

"That she's new to this. Only had less than ten men bed her."

"Lyin' bitch," Baser muttered.

"Okay," the woman conceded, "maybe a few more." She pulled the girl's stained blouse lower, exposing the tops of her breasts. "But you won't be seeing this anywhere else. Make me an offer."

Baser dug out the money he'd been saving for a hot meal. He needed this more than food right now. He tossed the coin to the woman, who grabbed it quickly.

"That buys you ten minutes." She yanked on the girl's arm. "Go with him, sweetpea, and show him a good time." She pointed to the back of the tent.

The girl reminded him of Sabina. The way Sabina had been before the she-bitch had come to town. Meek. Biddable. He tugged on the girl's arm as he flipped back the tent's opening. "We got some lovin' to do."

"Still no word on Baser's whereabouts?" Beau questioned the sheriff.

"Nothing. I've got some wanted posters that I sent to some of the neighboring towns and Miles City, but looks like he's vanished."

"He'll come back."

"How can you be sure?" Adam asked, sipping at the brandy that Beau offered.

"Because he hates me. I've seen it in his eyes. You don't let go of hate like that and move on. He'll be back to try and finish. And because he must know that I'll never let him go—I'll make it my mission to see that he's found, dead or alive. Matters little to me."

The cold finality of Beau's words resounded through Adam's mind. He understood his friend's apprehension. Shared it, as a matter of fact. Baser wasn't a man who could be allowed to roam free anymore. He deserved to be caged like the wild animal he was. The danger he posed went beyond just McMasters. Now Sabina and Miss Abby were also caught in the sights of this man. He could feel that in his bones.

"So what do you want to do?"

"I'm going to make it easier for him to find me. I'm moving back to the Creole Lady."

"*What*?"

"You heard me."

"Are you crazy? You've got protection here at the ranch."

"And little good that did me the last time."

"That was a fluke."

Beau drained his snifter and refilled it. "No. Baser's a hunter. He made sure of his target and went after it. His problem was he didn't succeed. He'll have to try again. And this time, I want to be ready."

"By making yourself a sitting duck?"

"By bringing the game to my table. With my rules."

"Beau, this isn't a game. I think Baser is mad."

"Could be." He sipped again. "Probably. But that doesn't make him a match for me. I'm setting a trap and he won't refuse the bait."

"What if someone else gets caught? Have you thought about that?"

"Yes." Beau looked at the drawn drapes over the large window. The addition was Abby's idea. His magnificent view was obstructed by the wall of heavy velvet she'd ordered placed there. "I can't sit back and wait for him to strike again. This time it could be Abby. Or someone else who happens to be here. I can't take that chance."

"Have you talked to Mrs. Butler about this? Does she agree?"

"No, I haven't talked to her since she left for town earlier today with Sabina. She's got plenty on her mind as it is."

"She's not gonna like it."

Beau laughed softly. "I know she won't. That's because she loves me. As I love her, which means that this has to be done. Before anyone else gets hurt."

"Well, since I sure as hell can't seem to change your mind, I'd best hear your plans so that we can get everything into place."

"That's what I thought."

"Married? In a week?" Gussie threw her arms about Abby and hugged her tight at the happy news. "It's about time if you ask me. Plain to see that you two were made for each other."

"How'd you feel about holding the reception here at your hotel?"

"I'd be right happy to do that," the older woman stated, hugging Abby again. "Lordy, I feel like it's my own daughter that's getting hitched."

"And I think of you now as my mother," Abby responded. "In the short time I've known you, you've come to mean more to me than the woman who bore me. That being so, there are a few things that I must talk to you about. Things that need to be explained."

Abby sat in Gussie's private parlor off the main room of the hotel. She glanced at the worn, comfortable furniture, the odd splashes of color that Gussie had added to brighten up the dark room. A basket of knitting sat next to Gussie's feet, a pair of mittens half completed. A cheery fire blazed in the small hearth. A big ginger cat, a recent addition to the hotel, was curled up on the rag rug.

"Honey, you don't need to be makin' any explanations to me for nothing."

"I'm not who you think I am," Abby blurted out.

Gussie studied her for a moment. She looked at the younger woman, scrutinizing her intently. "You're not a teacher?"

315

"Not formally trained." As Abby started to elaborate, Gussie interrupted.

"Are you a thief?"

"No," Abby answered.

"A murderer?"

"No, but . . ."

"Then what you got to tell me about?"

Abby quickly gave her a shortened version of her story.

Gussie laughed. "Is that it? You're on the run from your daddy and his plans?" She shrugged. "Makes no matter to me, Abby. You're who you are, not who they want you to be. When you've lived as long as I have, you get to understand it's not where you were born, or how much money you got. It's how you are with people that matters. You treat them with respect, it comes back to you tenfold.

"And," Gussie wagged her finger, "if your daddy or his hirelings ever come here and try to take you back, they're gonna have a fight. No doubt about that. What with your man and your friends, he's gonna find that his money and power don't mean all that much here in Heaven's Grace.

"Now, let's talk about what you'll be wantin' Carl to serve during this reception."

"Welcome back, boss."

Amid shouts and cheers, Beau walked into the Creole Lady. His staff and customers came up and greeted him warmly. Flora sped across the room and gave him a hearty smack on the mouth to the delight of the crowd.

"How are you?"

"Fine, Flora, really."

"Then let's get you settled upstairs before this gathering gets out of hand." She linked her arm through his, guiding him up the wide staircase.

When they reached his room she let go, walked to the small table, and poured him a drink from the cold bottle of champagne she'd had put on ice when she'd heard he was coming back to the club. After pouring one for herself, too, Flora lifted the fluted crystal glass. "It's good to see you up and about. You had us all so worried." She sipped at the sparkly beverage as she took a seat next to him on the settee. "Though it seems you were in pretty good hands." She smiled broadly.

"Abby made sure I had the best of care."

Flora chuckled. "She was like a mama cougar protecting her cub when I visited." Her look was sly. "I don't think I'd want to go up against her."

"Wise woman," Beau said.

"Of course I am." She drained her glass, giving him a tender glance. "I think she is good for you. Very good."

Beau smiled. "She is. I'm going to marry her."

Flora laughed. "Ah, *mi cabellero*, I lived to see the woman who could capture your heart. When will you wed her? Soon, I think?"

"Yes, but we will talk of that later. Now I must ask your help in something else."

"Whatever you want, Beau. Any time. For any reason."

He picked up her hand and brought it to his lips. "Good. I knew that I could count on you. Now here's what I need you to do."

Chapter Twenty-two

The band of gold gleamed on her finger, bringing a small smile to Abby's lips. She was a married woman, as of two hours past. True to his word, Beau had arranged it all, bringing the wedding off without a hitch.

The hotel's main area, where the reception was being held, was decked in trailing white ribbons and dried flowers; the smell of cinnamon and cloves wafted through the air as thick, scented candles glowed brightly. Drinks flowed freely; a case of Beau's champagne lay nestled in a galvanized tin laundry bucket surrounded by chunks of ice. Several bottles had already been poured, along with a substantial quantity of French wine.

Food was aplenty, too. One long table held an amount sure to feed the entire town for days. In the midst of the assortment of meats and cheeses, breads and pies, was the wedding cake. A carved wooden figure of a bride and groom stood atop the two vanilla frosted layers.

Abby grinned at the crude likeness of her and Beau. Made for them by Josh, it was a wonderful gift. She'd made sure to thank him, bringing a blush to the boy's face when she kissed his ruddy cheek.

"Be time for you to cut that thing soon," Gussie said.

"I was thinking that too. Have you seen my husband?" Abby looked around the room, searching for Beau. He had left her side to talk to the sheriff when Flora came to offer her personal congratulations. Abby suspected that the hostess of the Creole Lady had been more than a friend to Beau in the past, but decided that that mattered little now. The woman's words were genuine. And, as she spotted the dark-haired woman sharing a plate with the owner and publisher of the town's newspaper, she knew Flora was no threat.

"He was here a minute ago. So many people crowded about that it's tough to see." Gussie smiled indulgently. "Missing him already, eh?"

"Yes," Abby responded with a smile. How funny to think that she could miss someone that less than a year ago she hadn't known existed.

"Well, he's got enough protection scattered around here. No one's gonna get in 'cept them that have an invite."

Abby nodded. Beau's men were everywhere, armed and with instructions to see that the reception ran smoothly. She longed for the time when they would be superfluous. Yet as much as she craved that, she also understood that at this moment they were necessary. As was the small derringer that lay nestled in the deep pocket of her wedding skirt. Since the shooting, she was never without it. Another precaution. As was staying at the hotel tonight instead of her nearby house, or returning to the ranch.

"Mrs. McMasters," boomed the new pastor, joining them, "I just wanted to say you made a lovely bride. My wife and I were so happy to have your wedding be the first of what I hope will be many happy events here in our new parish."

Abby shook both their outstretched hands. "Thank you very much, Reverend Warlow."

"It's always lovely to start off a new position with a joyous occasion rather than a sad one."

"I would imagine so."

"Yet you can't pick and choose, much as we'd like. Why, one of my best friends, who was recently assigned to a large, well-funded parish in New York City, had as his first task upon joining the congregation, the charge of presiding over a small, private funeral ceremony for a suspected murder-suicide.

"Though," he added in a hushed tone, "I understand that the papers did try to hide that fact since the man was a rather wealthy and influential banker." The Reverend Warlow paused, considering. "If I understand correctly, you come from back East, don't you?"

Abby nodded. "Yes, I do." There was no reason to hide that fact anymore. Her days of running were over.

"Then perhaps you may have heard of them. Name was Breckenridge."

Abby blanched. "What?"

"So, the name does sound familiar?"

"Yes," was all she could say.

Gussie moved closer to Abby, her arm about the younger woman's waist. Abby was glad of the support, fearing she might start shaking. *It couldn't be.*

"The news of their deaths even made headlines in the Philadelphia papers. They were quite important in the New York social arena, I was led to believe. Seems that there's a search on for their missing daughter. No other immediate family left but her to inherit the vast fortune."

Abby had to tell Beau. She forced a smile on her face as she thanked the Reverend again for the ceremony. "Now, if you will excuse me," she said as calmly as she could manage, "I must find my husband so that we can cut the cake."

"Of course, my dear."

Gussie pulled her into a corner, lowering her voice so that only Abby heard her. "Are you okay? Do you need something to drink?"

"No," Abby murmured. "It's just a shock, that's all. I still can't believe that it's my parents he was talking about. Dead . . ."

Gussie walked away for a moment, then came back with a small shot glass of whiskey. "Here." She pushed it into Abby's palm. "You might be needin' this."

Abby closed her hand over Gussie's, refusing the drink. "Actually, I don't think so," she said. "What I feel right now is numbness. Like something died a long time ago and I'm only just realizing it." She took a deep breath. "I should be crying, but I find that I can't."

Gussie snorted. "After what you've told me, I would be surprised if you could summon that much emotion for them." She drank the amber liquid herself, tossing back the drink with aplomb.

"I can't believe that they're gone." Relief flooded through Abby's body. And a sad emptiness for what might have been; for how she might have felt had they all been different people. Any natural love for them had long been eradicated, washed away like sands beneath the rough waves of their oppression and coldness. To pretend otherwise would have been an exercise in delusion.

Abby slipped her arms around Gussie's sturdy middle, hugging the other woman tightly. "I thank God for you, Gussie. You've taught me so much; given me so much."

"Lordy, it weren't nothin', my dear."

"To me it was." Abby's words were heartfelt.

Gussie wiped away a tear with her hand. "Now you go find your man. I'd best be seein' to the rest of the guests."

Abby moved through the crowd, searching for Beau in earnest now. No one seemed to know where he was. She caught the gaze of Sabina, who was sitting in a quiet corner with the sheriff, their heads close together, each having eyes only for the other.

"Sorry to interrupt, but have either of you seen Beau?"

"No, come to think upon it, I haven't," Sabina answered.

Abby looked directly into Adam's eyes. "And you?"

"I think he went to get something from his saloon. Said he'd be right back."

"How long ago was that?"

Adam shrugged his shoulders. "Might have been a few minutes ago."

"*Might have been?*" Abby stepped closer, keeping her voice pitched low. "I've got to talk to him now. It's very important."

"He'll be back soon."

"It can't wait."

Adam abruptly stood up. "What's wrong? Have you seen Baser?"

"No." Abby flinched. "Have you?"

Abby looked at her friend and saw Sabina's face cloud. "Tell me."

"It's nothing," the sheriff said.

"Tell her," Sabina insisted.

"Hush."

"I won't hush, Adam. She's got a right to know."

"Know what?"

"That someone spotted him, or so they thought, in Miles City a few days ago."

"Does Beau know this?"

"Yes."

"He never told me."

"No need to worry you," Adam assured her.

"I'm his wife."

"That's a certain fact after today," Adam said. "But still, he didn't want to worry you none."

Damn the man, Abby thought. Didn't he realize she

could handle the truth? About anything? Hadn't she proven it?

Her hand automatically went to the derringer, closing her fingers around it, feeling the solid weight of the tiny gun.

Then, quick as a flash, she realized Beau wasn't afraid she couldn't handle the knowledge that Baser might return—he wanted to protect her from going after Baser herself.

She sighed. He did know her. Knew that she would never let anyone harm him. As he would never let anyone harm her. Far from being afraid, she would have marched into hell itself to save him, never counting the cost to herself. That's how much she loved him. And she knew from all the little things he'd said and done this past week that it was how he loved her too. Without limits, reservations, or fear.

Abby released the firm grip she had on the weapon, removing her hand from her pocket.

Sabina watched the quick play of emotions on her friend's face. Gone was the dawning anger she'd just seen there—replaced by a calm determination. She actually pitied her father should he run into this woman.

Yet she saw something else in her friend's eyes. "Abby? What's wrong?"

"Just something I have to tell Beau."

Sabina turned to Adam, put her hand on his arm, and said softly, "Please, find Beau and bring him back here."

The sheriff nodded, plunked his hat back on his head and left the building.

"Now, tell me what else is going on," Sabina instructed, as she patted the vacant seat.

He watched from the shadows, careful to keep hidden from the heavily-armed cowboys who were on the gambler's payroll.

323

Seemed that most of the townsfolk were crammed into the hotel, with the lights ablaze inside. Some men stood outside, despite the chilly temperatures, catching a smoke or enjoying a drink.

How the hell was he gonna do what he had to do?

Damn town was about deserted. Streets dark and dim; storefronts locked up tight. All save for the flicker of light in the new saloon.

Then he saw him. Coming out of the doorway and onto the sidewalk, locking the heavy wooden doors of his place.

The rifle felt heavy in his hand.

He needed more light. And wouldn't you know, McMasters was surrounded by his men, who formed a human shield around the bastard. At this point he couldn't risk the shot—what if he failed? He could lose his own life.

He watched and waited—and then he heard the words that brought a smile to his face.

"I want to go back to the church for a moment. Something I need to take care of there."

How fitting, Baser thought. It's as if it's a sign. Do him there. His kind weren't fit to be in a church. First him, then his whore.

Baser sighed in relief. Soon . . .

He waited as the group moved up the hill to the church, which was still welcoming with a soft glow of light in the stained glass windows. He watched as McMasters went inside the building, while his men loitered outside, some talking among themselves while others rolled cigarettes and smoked.

He could sneak in the front entrance since they'd left that unguarded. The fools had moved to the side of the church.

His lips curled in a feral smile. Now was the time. . . .

Slowly he crept along the sidewalk, then across the dirt-packed streets, careful not to make any noise and thus alert McMasters's men.

He was so close now he could smell the smoke, hear some of the bawdy comments about the forthcoming wedding night.

Wedding night. Bah! He was here to make sure there would never be a consummation of this marriage.

Just then, several of the men moved away, walking back toward the hotel, promising that they would be back as soon as they got some whiskey to help ward off the cold night air. Only two men were left behind, Pike, the ranch foreman, and an older man.

The door gave way easily to Baser's hand as he snuck in. He spied McMasters in the front row, head bowed. He'd recognize that hat and that frock coat anywhere. Nothing plain about that peacock.

Well, fancy man, Baser mused, blood is sure gonna wreck that fine suit.

He stepped closer, laying the rifle down softly and reaching for his pistol. He had to be able to get away fast—the rifle would only slow him down. Besides, he wanted to get close enough this time to make sure he killed his target.

The cold feel of metal against his temple stopped him.

From the safety of the shadows at the back of the hall, Beau watched the little weasel sneak into the room. Smiled as Baser laid down his rifle, then watched him bring out the old Colt from his shop-worn holster.

His own Remington was secure in his hand, a trusted friend, as he moved up behind Baser.

"Don't move, or I'll blow your head clean off. And don't think I wouldn't enjoy it."

Baser trembled. "How?" was all he said, dropping his gun to the floor in a clatter.

"Trickery. Sure didn't take much to fool you." Beau ran the tip of his pistol along the other man's temple, clicking back the hammer. "My hat and coat on a dummy filled with straw. Horsehair pinned on to resemble hair." Beau laughed, low and cold. "Far too easy."

He leaned toward the other man. "You don't know how much I want to kill you," he said, almost crooning the words. "It would be so easy. Pull the trigger, and *wham!* All my troubles gone."

Beau could smell the other man's fear, then a sharper smell replaced it. He glanced down and saw the burgeoning pool spreading on the wooden floor, soaking Baser's trouser leg and boots.

"Yes," Beau said in a silky tone, "I could kill you and no one would blame me." He lowered his gun.

Baser dropped to his knees like a stone, his hands grabbing for Beau's polished black boots. "Please don't kill me. Please," he begged in a whimpering voice, tears streaming down his face. "I don't want to die."

Beau looked down upon the man and took a deep breath. "You should have thought of that before you tried to kill me." He raised his pistol and took aim . . .

Chapter Twenty-three

"Baser's been caught."

Abby breathed a deep sigh of relief, then turned to watch the sad play of emotions on her friend's face.

Sabina spoke softly. "Is he dead?"

"No ma'am," Pike said, "he's at the jail now, with the sheriff and Mr. McMasters. They're gonna be a while, so I was sent here to tell you not to worry none."

"My husband, he's all right?"

"Fine and dandy, ma'am. Got that sneaky bas—fellow. His plan worked. Mr. McMasters sure knew what he was doing. Sniveling little coward was all crying and such as we drug him out. Some of us wanted to just take care of him there, but the boss wasn't having none of that. Decided he was gonna let the sheriff handle Baser."

Pike tipped his hat to Sabina. "Think that was because you and his wife are such good friends. Likely as not he would have seen to the man's punishment himself if you hadn't been involved. Leastwise that's how I see it." Pike smiled. "Said I was to tell you, Mrs. McMasters, to go ahead and do what you had to do here and he'd be with you as soon as he could."

Abby touched the foreman's arm, giving it a fond squeeze. "Thank you for letting me know my husband is all right. I appreciate it."

"Weren't no problem, ma'am." He gave a fond glance sideways at the still full table of food. "Guess me and the boys will take some samples of the grub now that we don't have to be on guard."

"Feel free, please," Abby insisted. She didn't care if they gobbled up everything and then some—as long as Beau was safe.

Pike walked away, leaving the two women alone.

"I'm sorry, Abby."

She responded quickly. "For what? It's not your fault that your father is who he is. I've said that before. Please," she said, embracing her friend, "don't let this upset you."

"Still. . . ."

"Still nothing," Abby reassured her. "Don't worry about him anymore. He'll soon be out of our lives. Speaking of which, isn't it time you and Adam were getting a bit more serious about courting?"

Sabina blushed, recognizing Abby's adroit change of topic. "I think we're moving in that direction."

"I'm glad. From what I can see, he seems a good man."

"He is."

"Then I look forward to standing up for you at your own ceremony."

Sabina's eyes were thoughtful. "I don't know about that."

"Listen to me, don't let anything, or anyone, stand in your way once you've decided. I can see that he cares about you, as you seem to care for him.

"Now," Abby said, forcing a smile to her lips, "I seem to recall that this is a wedding reception. Let's put aside any sad thoughts and go on with the party."

* * *

"I can keep him here till the circuit judge comes through."

"Good. I don't want him getting out for any reason."

"Not a chance," Adam replied. He locked the door to the jail cells behind him, pocketing the key. The sheriff gave his newfound friend a keen look. "Though I have to admit that I'm surprised he's not dead."

Beau smiled wryly. "So am I." He placed a hip on Adam's wide desk, facing him. "It wouldn't have taken much for me to pull the trigger. When I think of all that man's done. . . ."

"What stopped you then?"

"Abby," Beau replied. "Remembering how lovely she looked when she entered the church. Watching her walk down the aisle toward me. Those memories kept coming back to me when I had Baser in my sights." He paused, stroking a hand across his beard. "Found that I couldn't defile that place with the scum's blood, much as I would have liked."

"No doubt it was him that shot you?"

Beau shook his head. "None. He confessed it all to me before you got there. Even to killing Sabina's husband."

"She kinda suspected he might have done it."

"No suspecting now. Kept rambling how it was the Lord's work. It was then that I'd heard enough and brought the pistol down on his head."

"Well, it's over now."

Beau stood up.

Adam chuckled. "Don't you have a reception to get back to?"

Beau smiled. "That I do."

"Damn, I almost forgot, what with all the excitement. Abby was looking for you, too. Said she had something to tell you."

"Guess I'll find out soon enough." Beau moved toward the door. "If you need any extra men, let me know. A few of mine can keep an eye on him."

"I'll let you know." Adam rose. "Now, you'd best be leaving before your bride comes calling."

His bride.

Beau smiled as he made his way up the stairs to where she was waiting for him. In his mind's eye he could easily see her as she'd walked down the aisle—breathtaking in her creamy satin dress, her veil floating about her face and over her shoulders. Since it was winter, and no fresh flowers were in bloom, she carried none. Nor did she need any to embellish the presence she created by merely entering the room. Later, when the weather changed, he'd gift her with all the flowers she wanted.

Replacing the worn, weathered, cheap band she'd been wearing as her pretend ring with something much more fitting made him smile. The look on her face as he slipped the thick, hammered gold band onto her finger was love itself. Her eyes had filled with tears, and their kiss was the promise of the future.

He had another gift for her in his vest pocket. Something special and filled with meaning. From the earth of his ranch, found and fashioned just for her. Another symbol of their new life. He'd ordered it with the idea of giving it to her on her next birthday, but decided, why wait?

She needed it. Especially after the news she'd received earlier. When he arrived at the reception, she'd run to him, hugging him close. After they did the required duties of a newly married couple, she drew him aside and explained the details of what the Reverend Warlow told her. Calmly, she related the news about her folks, and what it meant to her.

Now they were truly two of a kind. Orphans by fate. Gamblers both who'd risked all for a fresh chance.

What was it a Chinese brothel girl had once told him? Yin and yang? Male and female. Two strong forces brought together by fate. Destiny. Forever linked in harmony.

He recalled scoffing at that notion then, even though he'd had a grand example in his parents. Too many years spent traveling across the country had hardened him; seeing far too many empty marriages, bad affairs, and foolish choices had soured him on the idea of love. Lasting love.

Or so he thought. Until her.

Until Abby walked into his life.

He knocked softly on the door to the room they would share tonight. The same hotel room she'd been given when she first arrived.

This time he wasn't forced to watch through the glass. This time the precious contents of the sweet shop were all his.

"Come in, the door is unlocked."

He did so, standing just inside as the reality of his wife hit him square in the chest.

God, he'd thought her beautiful earlier. He hadn't known the half of it.

Like a Renaissance painting, she glowed with color. Candles surrounded her, emitting a sweet fragrance, and a delightful glow. No harsh lamps burned. A new fire had been laid in the small potbellied stove. The burning logs gave off a warm light. Her long, thick hair, the curls cascading about her body, was a burnished cloak against the long, floating cream nightdress. Lace abounded at the hem, the neck and sleeves.

This was no shy, trembling girl, but rather a woman, warm and welcoming. It was there in her blue eyes; in the way her lips curled in sweet promise.

He doffed his frock coat and vest, eager to join with her. Quickly, he bent and tugged off the high black boots and socks he wore.

When his hands moved to his shirt, she approached him. "Let me," was all she said.

Slowly, button by button, she undid each one, taking her time until she had them all undone. Her hands slipped

331

inside, feathering over the warm golden skin. Inhaling deeply, she bent her head and kissed the hair that dusted his chest, then the still-healing scar—evidence of his recent wound. Her tongue made forays, in and out, lightly skimming the planes and hollows of his body.

No practiced whore could have roused him as quickly as she did. His body throbbed and tightened, hardening eagerly in anticipation. His breath caught in tight gasps.

Gently, he brought her hands to his trousers, letting her feel her power over him.

Her smile deepened as she released the buttons that held the trousers together. Slowly, carefully, she eased them down the length of his legs, along with the short silk drawers he wore beneath.

The garments remained at his feet as he stepped out of them.

"Now you," he whispered.

She feasted her eyes on him, on the tall, lean length of him. From his tousled black waving curls, to the breadth of his chest, to his flat stomach, his long legs, and the part of him that rose in rapid response to her gaze.

He was all hers—from this day forward to the end of their lives.

"I love you, Beau McMasters."

"I know," he replied with a devil-may-care grin.

Slowly, as he watched, she undid the ribbon that held the top of her nightgown closed. It fell to her waist as she pushed the sleeves down her arms, letting the garment drop the rest of the way to the floor by itself.

His eyes darkened. His nostrils flared, catching her scent.

All his. He raked his gaze from the crown of her head to the soles of her feet, enjoying the perusal of all her features. Taut, high breasts, a soft belly, flaring hips.

He held out his hand. "Come here."

She never hesitated.

Sweeping her up in his arms, he carried her to the already turned down bed, putting her down gently, following her body with his own.

Their lips met hungrily. Their hands grabbed greedily.

Beau worked his way along her body, from her neck to her navel, lavishing kisses and caresses, until he reached her nether curls. He paused, savoring the soft sounds of her passion, then stroked his hand across her. Softly, deftly, he edged a finger into the soft red triangle. He watched with a wide smile as her legs fell open, as her breathing quickened. Deeper he went, bringing her higher and higher.

Then his mouth was there as his tongue introduced her to another kind of loving.

Abby gasped, her breath coming in small pants, then faster, higher as she began to soar, spiraling out of herself. "Beau," she cried as she fell back to earth.

"Darlin'," he promised, "this is only the beginning." Then he kept his word, joining their bodies together in one powerful thrust.

As her body took him deeper and deeper, Abby matched him in intensity, hardly believing it was possible so soon after the last climax. She clutched his body close, her nails digging into his back, riding the storm for all it was worth until she opened her mouth and bit down on his shoulder to stifle her screams.

Beau ignored the sharp sting of her teeth as he let the tidal wave of passion consume him as well, emptying his seed into her womb before collapsing.

Moments passed before the couple stirred.

Abby glanced at the mark she'd made on Beau's flesh. "I'm so sorry," she began.

His fingers to her mouth stopped her. "Sshh," he said, kissing her softly. "It's nothing, darlin'."

"But . . ." God, where had this come from? It was as if she had no control over her emotions, reacting like an animal in heat. All she cared about was the pleasure she was feeling; the pleasure he was offering.

"Never apologize for being truthful, Abby. It's who you are." Beau gathered her into his arms, loving the feel of her dewy skin next to his. He inhaled the fragrance of their loving with approval. "It's who I want in my bed." He brought her hand to his mouth.

Damn, he'd almost forgotten the gift he'd brought, so enraptured was he with his bride

"I've got something for you," he explained as he shifted her body and eased himself out of the bed. He walked to his haphazard pile of clothes and rummaged through his vest, retrieving the box.

"What's that?" she asked, pulling the bright blue woven blanket close to her chest. Without Beau beside her, the bed felt empty and cold.

"A token."

"For what?" She pushed her tangled hair off her face.

"The occasion of our wedding. It was meant to be a birthday gift, but I couldn't wait."

He joined her on the bed. "Open it."

Abby did, gasping as she gazed at the ring inside. "It's exquisite."

He slid it onto her finger, satisfied with her reaction.

"Where did you get this?" She held up her hand, watching the deep blue of the stone glimmer in the candle glow. A wonderful sapphire, nestled in an entwined branch pattern of gold.

"I found it in one of the streambeds on my property. Since I didn't have time to get you a proper engagement ring, I thought this might do."

"Might *do*?" she exclaimed. "I should think so." She leaned over and kissed him. "I love it.

"Now," she said, smiling mysteriously, "I have something for you. Not quite as beautiful, but I hope that you will love it just the same."

"What is it?" her husband asked.

"Close your eyes and hold out your hand."

Beau complied, wondering what his wife had in mind. For him, nothing could compare to the gift of her heart.

Abby located the small paring knife she'd brought up with her earlier. Taking a breath, she took the knife and cut a small line across her palm.

Boldly, she looked at Beau's wide palm, at the crisscrossed lines intersected there. In a moment their blood would intersect too, linking them together in a purely elemental way.

Beau felt the quick cut of the knife and jerked open his eyes.

His wife had placed her own palm against his bigger one, holding tight.

"Now we share the same blood. I am what you are," she said softly, tossing the blade aside, "as you are what I am." She unclasped their hands so that he could see the traces of blood on each of their palms.

Beau brought Abby's hand to his mouth and licked away the thin line of blood. She in turn did the same for him, then slid her other hand around his neck, pulling him closer to her lips.

And for the rest of what was left of the night, they reveled in their luck of the draw.

Epilogue
The Promise of Home

Six months later

"So you see, you are quite a wealthy woman, Miss Breckenridge."

"It's *Mrs.* McMasters, if you please, Mr. Haden," Abby corrected him.

"Of course," he responded, coughing slightly to cover his slip of the tongue, then looking down at the stack of legal papers that covered the desk at which he was sitting.

Her father's desk. Or it had been. Now everything in the opulent mansion was hers.

"Do you intend to live here again?" the lawyer asked.

Abby glanced around the room, at the valuable artwork that hung on the walls, at the expensive furnishings. Nothing here was to her taste. She couldn't imagine the Rembrandt hanging in the ranch house in Montana. Nor to have the marble bust of Caesar in her bedroom, nor the heavy dark drapes that smothered the room and held far too many secrets.

"No."

Mr. Haden seemed taken aback at her cold pronouncement. "I suppose you want to do some redecorating?" he asked.

"Not at the moment."

"Then what are you going to do? Sell it?" He cast a glance at the man sitting silently beside her. He wondered if the lady's husband was the reason she didn't want to live here? And if so, why? This was a wonderful piece of real estate. The envy of many New Yorkers.

Ah, that had to be it. The husband probably wanted to sell it and pocket the profits. After all, he would gain control of her fortune. Smart man, Haden theorized.

"I won't be selling it, either. I have other plans."

"If you don't mind my asking, what are they?"

Abby rose, walked to the window, and then pulled back the curtains, letting in sunlight. "I intend it to be a school for young ladies."

"A finishing school?" the lawyer probed.

"Nothing that ordinary," Abby stated with a smile. "It's to be a proper school for girls. A place where they can learn something more than to be decorous."

"What?" his voice went one octave higher.

"You heard me, sir. This is to be a place of purpose, a place where any girl who meets the criteria can get an education, no matter what her birth."

"That's rather radical, don't you think?" He turned his attention to Beau, who was blowing a smoke ring into the air. "And you sir? Do you support this folly?"

"Of course I do," Beau drawled as he took another drag on his cheroot. "My wife is free to spend, or dispose, of her inheritance in any way she sees fit."

"You're both mad."

Beau blew another smoke ring, this time in the lawyer's direction. "We very well could be, but it's not your money, nor your property, now is it?"

The lawyer recognized the tone of steel in the other

man's voice. "Sorry, Mrs. McMasters, I seem to have over-stepped my bounds."

"Yes," Abby agreed, coming back to her seat, "you did. However, that's not a problem as long as you do what I want."

"I'll see to whatever you wish."

"Very good."

Abby spent the next hour going over her plans, making sure that the man who represented her understood her conviction and determination.

"God, what a bore," Abby said as she moved to sit on her husband's lap as soon as the man left them alone.

Beau laughed. "He was certainly that." His hand caressed the swell of her stomach under the Worth day dress. He much preferred the more casual clothes she wore back in Montana. Much easier to feel her curves; less to remove. "Can you trust him?"

"Surprisingly, yes," she allowed. "He has a fine reputation for business and protecting his clients. Now that I hold the purse strings to the Breckenridge fortune, he will do as I ask." She placed a deep, hot kiss on her husband's mouth. "Or risk losing a rather sizable retainer. Privately, he can scoff all he wishes. Providing he follows my instructions, I care not." She stroked her gloved hand along his bearded jaw. "As long as you believe in what I'm doing, I couldn't give a damn about anyone else."

"Ah, such language in a lady. Must be all that easy-going Western influence." His eyes were dark with mirth.

"Why sir, I do believe that you're right about that." She rose from her very comfortable human seat and tugged at his hand.

"Come with me."

She took him down the dark hallway, out the large front door to the wide marble steps that led to the massive stone gate and the street beyond. Life teemed around them, from the smell of the horses that pulled the carriages, to the sound of voices coming in all directions. The afternoon was bursting with sunshine. As she linked her arm through his, Abby said, "Take me home, Beau."

"Darlin'," he responded, a quick kiss to her lips, "it'll be my pleasure."

Kissing
in the Dark
WENDY LINDSTROM

Her first lie is that she is a widow, but Faith Wilkins sees little choice in telling it. She moved to Fredonia to escape a deadly past, and safety depends upon maintaining the charade: She is a simple healer who moved to town to erect a greenhouse. She has to fool everyone, including Sheriff Duke Grayson, and she'll do whatever it takes to do so.

But Duke is persistent and clever, and Faith knows it won't be long before the handsome lawman uncovers all he wishes. And he wishes for Faith as his bride. But the sheriff is a protector of truth and justice. What will he do when he discovers her lies? It is one thing to kiss in the dark, but in the end, love has to withstand the light of day.

For the first time, Faith believes it is possible.

TEXAS TR★UMPH

ELAINE BARBIERI

Buck Star was a handsome cad with a love-'em-and-leave-'em attitude that had broken more than one heart. But when he lost his head over a conniving beauty young enough to be his own daughter, he jeopardized all he valued, even the lives of his own children.

Ever since leaving his father's Texas Star ranch, the daring Pinkerton agent and his lovely partner Vida Malone made it their business to ferret out the truth. But the twisted secrets he begins to uncover after a mysterious message calls him home might be more than anyone could untangle. Saving his father will require all his cunning and courage, as well as the aid of the most exasperating and enticing woman ever to go undercover or drive a man to distraction.